CW01667798

DRAKE'S BATTLE

Gideon Saint

ARCUS

ARCUS Editions

Copyright © 2024 by Gideon Saint

All rights reserved.

No portion of this book may be reproduced in any form without written permission from the publisher or author, except as permitted by U.S. copyright law.

DRAKE'S BATTLE

You don't have to read the Drake's War series in order.
(But it helps.)

DRAKE'S WAR

DRAKE'S BATTLE

DRAKE'S ENEMY*
coming soon...

WESTERN EUROPE MAY 1940

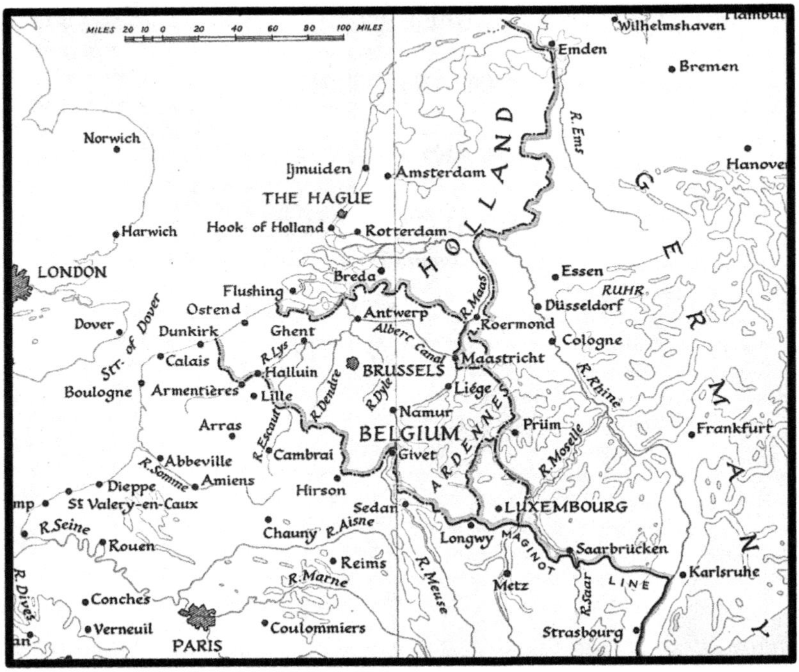

PART I

ARRAS

MONDAY 20 MAY 1940

Prologue

RUE SAINTE-BARBE, ARRAS, FRANCE - 00.15HRS

A MAN IN A civilian suit sat in darkness, at the desk in the small sitting room of Apartment 7, on the attic floor of a house on Rue Sainte-Barbe. His fist worked a Morse key swiftly, expertly, the tiny *di-di-dah* of the transmitter only audible through his headset as he dashed out the memorised code. He signed off with his usual, encrypted flourish: *Mit deutschem Gruß* – With German Greetings – *Viper*.

When the message was finished, he waited thirty seconds then repeated it, again and again, until he heard the faint, beeping response as it was finally acknowledged. He pulled off the headset and listened intently in the darkness. With the headphones off, the night air seemed strangely expansive. It was quiet, almost silent outside. Most of the civilians had been evacuated from Arras, those who had not already fled along the roads. The man picked up his hat from the desk and placed it on his head. He pulled a Browning FN Model automatic pistol from his trenchcoat pocket and slipped the safety catch off. He held it loosely in his right hand.

He stood still and listened a little longer. A cat miaowed on the attic roof outside the blacked-out window at the rear of the building. Then nothing.

He waited.

The street was eerily quiet.

He glanced towards the blackout curtains. Almost imperceptibly, he could hear the distinctive, rhythmic pulse of distant, far-off aero engines. *Heinkels.* Then there was a crashing din and a blaze of torchlight as the apartment door splintered open. The man was turning before he even heard them shouting '*Gendarmes!*' and in his hand the pistol crashed once, twice, three times, and brilliant, deafening flashes lit the room as he shot three rounds through the swinging apartment door.

The man leapt across the room in two great strides. He flung open the window at the back, oblivious to the crack of the glass and the groans of the wounded men behind him. In two seconds he was out onto the starlit Mansard roof, and into the warm, night air. He quickly turned to his left and took three shuffled steps. Easing his weight over the low parapet, his hands reached around to grasp the smooth paint of the iron drainpipe that he knew was there. He slid down almost silently, just the scrape of his shoes against the brickwork. His hands grew hot as he went faster and faster, then the shock and slap of leather as his shoes hit the paving. He jolted to a stop in a pool of darkness in the back yard.

The man felt a moment of surprise as the cool, blunt muzzle of a pistol stabbed into his cheek, cutting his flesh against the side of his teeth. A fist slammed into his kidney, sending a red flare of pain up through his insides.

'*Bougez-pas*,' came a gravelly voice in his ear. 'Don't move.' He could smell wine and garlic on the policeman's breath, and he offered no resistance as the Browning was levered from his hand.

'You're under arrest, you sack of shit,' the policeman said as he thrust him, handcuffed, through the darkness of the street and into the rear seat of a black Renault police car. The detective climbed into the back next to him, holding the pistol harshly to his ribs. 'I should shoot you now, you son-of-a-bitch. It would save me a lot of trouble.'

At first, the prisoner said nothing. He turned slightly to look at the detective, studying his face. Then he laughed. 'The war will be over in seven days, *mon ami,* and then it will be you in jail, and not I.'

'*Putain,*' the detective growled, and he shoved his pistol to the man's temple. His finger tightened on the trigger. After a moment, he let it fall away. '*Bah!* You're not worth losing my pension over.'

Moments later the car tore away down the adjacent Rue des Capucins, headlights dimmed to a strip of yellow, bell clanging, engine whining as the driver ripped it through the gears.

For a moment there was quiet on the Rue Sainte-Barbe, just the silent footfall of a black cat moving through the shadows. Then a tall shaft of light flicked up through the sky above the street. It was followed by another, then another. Columns of searchlights reached upwards, illuminating towers of smoke and wisps of cloud, against a moonless, star-littered sky. Over the next few minutes, the drone of aero engines grew and grew until it became an urgent throbbing, an all-consuming, pulsing sound wave, reverberating through the night air and rattling windows in the narrow city streets.

The skyline of the city of Arras flickered as Bofors guns opened fire. The air thudded with their brutal din, a repeating *pom-pom-pom-pom-pom*. Clattering Lewis guns sent up glowing orange and white ladders of anti-aircraft fire into the night, and hideous shapes of Heinkels and Junkers flitted through the search beams high above. The streets flashed and spasmed in a series of shuddering, cracking, detonations. And a hard, dark rain of bombs began to fall.

Chapter 1

BATTALION HQ, SOUTH DEVONSHIRE REGIMENT, MONCHECOURT, NEAR ARRAS, FRANCE – 02.45HRS

LIEUTENANT COLONEL CECIL HAWKER, commanding officer of the First Battalion, South Devonshire Regiment, slammed his cane down onto the desk with a crack that rang out like a gunshot.

'The war started ten days ago, Drake! Where the bloody hell have you been?'

Second Lieutenant Tennyson Drake held himself rigidly to attention, staring directly ahead. He was lit by the oily gleam of a hurricane lamp that stood on the corner of the colonel's desk, casting shadows across the olive drab canvas of the field tent.

'Sir! I have to see Lord Gort at once,' he said.

Hawker's clipped moustache twitched on his upper lip before he spoke. 'Gort, eh?'

'Yes sir.'

Hawker shook his head, as if to clear it. Lord Gort was the commander-in-chief of the British Expeditionary Force. 'Who on Earth do you think you are, Drake? Why would Gort want to see the likes of you?'

Drake kept staring straight ahead, not quite meeting the colonel's gaze. 'I have information, sir.'

The Colonel stepped back and glared through the darkness. His round, steel-rimmed glasses glinted in the light from the paraffin lamp as he studied the man before him. Drake's unusually dark red hair was filthy and matted. A purple welt from a healing wound ran down across his forehead. His face was battered, and freckled brown from the sun. His khaki serge battledress was torn, filthy, and his kit was mostly missing. He had no shirt, no tie. No helmet. No weapon, no belt, no entrenching tool. Instead of the regulation gleaming white, his singlet vest was black with dirt. He stank of stale sweat, and worse. His eyes were bloodshot, his face unshaven with five days' growth of beard, and his feet were bleeding into his boots.

'What – ruddy – information?' Hawker said, pausing momentarily between each word.

Drake licked his lips. 'The Germans are coming.'

The colonel snorted out a humourless laugh and turned away. He leaned on his desk. The war seemed suddenly very tedious. He adjusted his service cap and slapped his cane against the sides of his knee-high brown leather riding boots, which were bulled to a mirror-like shine. His pale jodhpurs were neatly pressed and his service jacket immaculate. Most field officers had adopted the more modern battledress, but not Hawker. Colonel Hawker was a stickler for tradition.

He glanced towards the tent flap at the large, tough-looking provost sergeant who had brought Drake in. The provost stepped forward into the circle of light, and hurriedly brought his right arm up to the salute. His third finger touched the steel rim of his green Brodie helmet, which had a red band running around the dome and was stencilled with the letters *MP*.

'We caught him sneaking back over them bridges on the river Escaut. Him and some Highlander, sir.' The redcap sergeant had a strong Birmingham accent. The Corps of Military Police ensured that they never used men from the same recruiting stations as those they were policing. He wore a revolver on his belt, and the weapon was attached to his shoulder epaulette with a green lanyard. There was a black brassard on his arm. His anklets and Sam Browne belt were a gleaming, polished white. He coughed before continuing. 'This one claimed he was an officer of yours, sir. So I brought him directly to you.'

Hawker nodded. 'Quite right, too.'

He pointed with his cane to the mapstand next to his desk. In the lamplight, the map showed the Allied and German positions clearly on the Franco-Belgian frontier and along the great river Meuse. Hawker shook his head once more. The war had only just started, and up in the north, the Dutch had already thrown in the towel. The BEF – the British Expeditionary Force – alongside their French and Belgian allies, were fighting hard in the north of Belgium, a hundred and fifty miles away, where the German army had pushed across the borders. But down here, in France, not far from British Rear GHQ at Arras, aside from the occasional menace of Luftwaffe raids, things had been pretty quiet.

The colonel glowered through the lenses of his glasses. 'The Belgians and the BEF are holding the line in the north, and the entire French

Ninth Army is screening us to the east. We're a hundred miles behind the ruddy front lines, Drake. Do you see?'

Drake ignored the map. He fixed his gaze directly ahead. 'The French Ninth Army no longer exists, sir.'

'Nonsense,' Hawker scoffed. He moved closer and sniffed the air. 'Are you very drunk, Drake, or just a little?'

'No, sir.' Drake stiffened. 'We were on a reconnaissance mission when the invasion started. We got cut off.'

Hawker stared, incredulous. His eyes seemed bigger, leering, magnified by the large, steel-framed lenses of his glasses. 'Reconnaissance mission, is it now? Under whose orders? By God, not mine!'

'I—' Drake hesitated. 'I couldn't say, sir.'

'Of course you can't, because it's balderdash. Well there you have it, Drake.' Hawker sighed, and rubbed at his face. 'I should have known better. You've let me – you've let the entire *regiment* – down.'

'I was with Captain Philips, sir. We were -'

'Philips!' Hawker snapped. 'And where the hell is Philips?'

'Captain Philips is dead sir.'

'Dead?' The colonel shook his head, peered at Drake through his thick, round glasses. 'You're raving, Drake. Admit it. You were drunk in the *estaminets* again.'

Drake said nothing. The colonel walked back behind his desk. He put away the movement orders and the fire plans he had been working on. His arm snapped suddenly upwards, and he pointed his cane out through the tent flap towards the darkness. 'Did you ever stop to think of the impression you've made on the men out there? I will not have a British officer deserting in wartime. You're worse than the bloody French!'

Drake fixed his gaze straight ahead. 'The entire BEF is in grave danger, sir, and I must see Lord Gort at once.'

Hawker sat down behind his desk with an air of resignation. He turned to the provost. 'Sergeant, would you excuse us for a moment?'

'Yessir,' the provost nodded. He turned on his heel and marched briskly out of the tent.

Colonel Hawker splayed his fingers out on his desk. 'You are to sober up and resume your duties with immediate effect. And for God's sake, make yourself presentable, Drake. You are an officer with the King's Commission – I expect you to act like one. For the sake of the *regiment*, and the *regiment* alone, my report will indicate that you were on leave when the invasion started, and you were injured in the bombing.'

Drake blinked his eyes shut for a moment. He opened them again before he spoke. 'I'm not drunk, I'm not raving, and I wasn't on leave, sir.'

Hawker spoke in an angry, staccato burst. 'Then tell me the ruddy truth!'

Drake took a breath before he replied. 'We were in Belgium when the invasion started, on secret orders. Captain Philips was trying to catch a German spy.'

Hawker sighed. 'And I suppose you'd like to see me the laughingstock of the BEF?'

A stony silence filled the tent.

'Your refusal to cooperate leaves me no choice, Drake,' Hawker eventually said. He called out, 'Sergeant!'

The provost sergeant marched smartly back in.

The colonel took off his glasses and rubbed at his eyes, then began to make notes on a pad of paper. 'I shall assemble a Field Court Martial at dawn. Until then Mr Drake shall remain in the custody of the provosts on a charge of desertion.' He looked up. 'As I'm sure you know, Drake, in time of war, a Field Court may try a soldier of any rank on any offence, and may impose any penalty. Sergeant, take him away.'

The redcap sergeant stepped up behind Drake. 'Yes, sir.'

Drake tried again. 'I really must speak to Lord Gort at once, sir.'

Hawker slammed his cane down across the top of his desk once more, making the provost jump. 'Enough, Drake! Save it for the Court Martial!'

The MP sergeant took Drake's arm. 'Will you come with me please, sir?'

Drake shrugged the man's grip off.

'Right!' The sergeant moved in front of him and pulled the handcuffs from his belt. 'I'm placing you under close arrest.'

Drake felt a sudden, sinking sense of despair. He was tired. So very, very tired. Why did everything have to be so difficult? He held out his hands and watched as the provost took out his keys.

As the sergeant reached forward to cuff him, Drake hesitated for a fraction of a second, then dipped his left hand down and neatly snatched the revolver from the man's leather holster. It was a .38 Enfield, fastened to his shoulder by a lanyard. Drake tugged the lanyard, hard. It pulled the provost off balance before it ripped free. Drake swung the pistol up and knocked him smartly behind the ear.

The provost sergeant crumpled to the ground with a groan.

Drake aimed the pistol at Colonel Hawker and slowly cocked back the hammer. 'Sit down.'

Hawker sank slowly into his chair. 'What the hell are you playing at, Drake? You must be out of your mind!'

Switching the revolver to his right hand, Drake bent down and took a bunch of keys from the provost's belt with his left. He stood up again. 'You can bring a Court Martial against me at your leisure, Colonel, but first I need to see Lord Gort.' He leant over and handcuffed Hawker's hands to the leg of his desk. 'Forgive me, sir, but the information in my report is far more important than my career.'

Hawker glared up at him for a moment. 'Career?' he snorted. 'You haven't got a bloody career. And don't fool yourself that I'll forgive you. You'll live to regret this, Drake, I promise you. You think the rules don't apply to you. Well, you're in for a nasty surprise. Lord Gort has brought back the death penalty for desertion, did you know that? I'll damned well break you, Drake! You're finished! Over! Done!'

Drake leant forward and removed Hawker's handkerchief from his breast pocket, and, keeping the pistol pointed at the colonel, stuffed the material into the man's mouth. He tied the provost's lanyard around Hawker's head to keep the gag tightly in. Hawker stared at Drake from behind the desk, through his large, round, wire-framed glasses. He spluttered and roared mutely into the cloth, and his face turned a violent shade of puce.

Drake ignored him. Catastrophe was hours, not days, away, and the BEF was woefully unprepared. Hawker's reaction had told him everything he needed to know. Drake had to find a way to see Lord Gort. Every other thought was blotted from his mind.

Chapter 2

BRITISH REAR GHQ, THE CITADEL, ARRAS, FRANCE – 09:35HRS

COMMANDER-IN-CHIEF OF THE BRITISH Expeditionary Force, General John Standish Surtees Prendergast Vereker, 6th Viscount Gort, VC, KCB, CBE, DSO & Two Bars, MC, stood staring at a map of France. Gort's forward GHQ was in transit, and in chaos, but here at his temporary Rear GHQ, in the deep, thick-walled cellars of the seventeenth-century citadel of Arras, at least the telephone lines were still working. Lord Gort turned slowly around from the mapstand as a tall young man in the white Sam Browne belt, white anklets and black brassard of the Military Police marched into the room.

Gort studied the uniform. 'Well? What is it, Sergeant?'

The MP crashed his boots on the flagstones as he came smartly to attention and saluted. 'I have information, sir.'

Gort frowned. He spoke with the lemony drawl of a Guards officer. 'What ruddy information?'

Drake stood rigid, staring straight ahead. His face, although bearing the marks of old bruises, was freshly shaved. The MP's uniform was a little tight around the shoulders. He could feel Gort's eyes boring into him. He paused for a moment before he spoke. 'I was gathering intelligence for somebody called The Chief.'

The room was silent for a full twenty seconds.

Lord Gort was a large, capable-looking man, with a round head, and brilliantined iron-grey hair. There was something hard in him, something that belied his rank and station. Something that made you think that if you ever disobeyed his orders he might strangle you with his own bare hands.

Gort eventually spoke again. 'Well, what breathtaking stupidity made you think it was a good idea to come barging in here?' He gave Drake a thunderous look. 'There are bloody protocols, man!'

Drake said nothing. Every man in the British Army knew Lord Gort by reputation. In 1917, during the Great War, as a young officer, Gort had been wounded at the battle of St Quentin. Despite his terrible injuries, he'd had his men carry him forward so he could lead them into battle. Bleeding heavily and barely conscious, he directed the attack from a stretcher. For that action he had been awarded the Victoria Cross, for valour, Britain's highest military honour. But that was twenty-three years ago, and Gort was now a peer of the realm, and a thickset, middle-aged man.

'For heaven's sake, let him speak, John,' said a quiet voice from the far corner of the dimly-lit room.

Drake glanced over in surprise. Lord Gort's bulk had dominated his attention to such an extent that he hadn't even noticed the slightly-built officer who was leaning against the far wall.

Gort looked across 'What? One of yours, is he?'

The officer shrugged. He had thin, receding brown hair and a greying moustache. But despite his age, his face seemed somehow boyish. 'We ought to hear him out, at the very least.' He spoke in a clipped, Empire tone.

Gort spun back around to look at Drake once more.

'Very well. Speak! There's only one reason I haven't had you removed already, and that is that I have no ruddy information!' The general crashed his baton against the mapstand. 'We're getting no sense from the French at all. That dithering fool of a commander-in-chief General Gamelin's been sacked, and his replacement, Weygand, is a madman. French deserters are swarming across the fields from God knows where, blocking every road. The RAF go out to take aerial photographs and they don't come back.' He struck at the great map board again with his baton. 'How in God's name am I expected to fight a war like this? We're getting reports of German panzers where they simply cannot be. It doesn't make any damned sense! For that reason, and that reason alone, I am willing to listen to crackpots and madmen.'

Gort pointedly looked at the other officer. A major, Drake noticed.

The major finally stirred himself away from the wall, and removed his hands from his pockets.

'Crackpots and madmen!' Lord Gort continued, 'If only they could give me some information. I need hard military intelligence – not phantoms, rumours, and downright lies. Weygand has told me to turn my troops to face back to front, and I don't even know why. I'm fighting this war completely bloody blind!'

Drake kept his eyes level, gazing straight ahead. 'Yes, sir.'

The general took a breath to compose himself. 'So, for your sake as well as that of the BEF, I hope that you have something useful to say.'

Drake observed the general and felt a sudden twinge of pity. The great man was like a bull, tormented by *piques*, unable to respond except by slow, blind charges at an enemy that kept skipping out of sight.

'They haven't told you, have they, sir?'

Gort slammed his fist down onto the table. He glared at Drake as though the force of his will alone were enough to squeeze the information out. 'Who hasn't told me? God damn it!'

'The French, sir. The French generals.'

Lord Gort spoke very slowly through gritted teeth. 'The French generals haven't told me exactly what?' Pent-up frustration was bursting at the seams.

Drake licked at his lips. His throat felt suddenly dry. 'They haven't told you about Sedan.'

Chapter 3

Drake realised that in the British Army, as in life generally, those who wielded the greatest power were often the furthest away from the truth. They had to make far-reaching decisions with very little direct grasp of reality. Reality, then, was going to come as something of a shock for Lord Gort.

'The panzers broke out from Sedan six days ago, sir.'

Gort's eyes burned. 'Six days! How many?'

Drake, still at attention, kept his arms by his sides. He pressed his fingers into the palms of his hands. 'All of them.'

'*All of them?* What the hell do you mean, *all of them*?'

Drake said nothing.

Gort stared, as if seeing past him into empty space. Eventually he spoke again. 'All of them. Good God,' and his face turned a ghastly pale. 'What of the French Ninth army?'

Drake dug his nails into the skin of his palms. 'Obliterated. Smashed.'

Gort examined at the map in silence. 'Six days?' he said. 'If this is even half-true—' His hand came up slowly to his face. He looked intently at the map boards and shook his head. 'Obliterated? How?'

Drake found it almost incredible that even now, GHQ still didn't know what was really happening. But somehow they didn't. It was a catastrophic failure of intelligence. He glanced over at the balding officer on the other side of the room, then back to the heavy figure of Lord Gort.

'You do know, sir, that the attack on Holland was just a feint?'

'A feint.' For a moment, the air seemed to drain from the room. Lord Gort appeared to be struggling to breathe.

The rage had passed. It was replaced now by limpness. And somehow the limpness was worse.

In the gloom of the bomb-proof cellars of the citadel, Drake felt uneasy tendrils tightening inside him, encircling his throat. *Claus-*

tro-bloody-phobia. He'd always had it, always hated it. He tried to kick the strange, anxious thoughts away to the back of his mind. He focused on the problem in hand. The British Expeditionary Force comprised around three hundred and fifty thousand men, but was dwarfed by the French army, which numbered in the millions. And Lord Gort officially came under French command.

Drake took a slow breath and tried to fit what he had to say into as few words as possible. It was just like giving a talk to the recruits in the lecture theatre. Just eight months previously, until the declaration of war back in September, Drake had been a schoolie – an army barracks schoolmaster – training would-be officers and NCOs in Arithmetic, French and German, and physical education: rugby, fencing, boxing, gymnastics, and cricket. He closed his eyes for a split second, tried to get it all straight in his mind. And then he could begin.

'Hitler has played us for fools, sir. All that noise in the north, Holland, northern Belgium, it was designed to draw our armies northwards. And it succeeded.' Drake pointed to the map. 'But the real attack was here. The *Schwerpunkt* – the point of maximum effort. Somehow they kept it secret. Seven panzer divisions, supported by forty other crack motorised divisions, through the point of least resistance. More than a thousand tanks. A hundred and thirty thousand men. And they are pouring unopposed towards the BEF's undefended eastern flank.'

Gort's eyes studied the map as he stepped towards it. He rapped his forefinger against the board.

'Sedan,' he said. 'Again. Of course.' He gave Drake a piercing look. 'And how do you know all this?'

Drake met his eyes. 'I was there. The French Army of the Meuse was shattered. The Ninth Army has disintegrated. That's why the roads are full of French deserters, sir. With the greatest respect, you have hours, not days. Rear GHQ is in grave danger of being overrun.'

Gort's face, now grey, gazed at the map board. He clenched the baton tightly in his hand, then absently rubbed at his cheek. Drake saw that everything was starting to make a horrible kind of sense to the old general. The nagging scraps of information that didn't seem to fit the big picture. The springtime rumours of build-ups to the south that Allied C-in-C Gamelin had ignored because it didn't fit their plans. The overwhelming sensation that somehow the war was slipping from his grasp. Gamelin's sudden departure and the new, shocking silence from the French *Grand Quartier Général*, which sat hundreds of miles away, in a chateau on the outskirts of Paris – a chateau that, in the interest of security, didn't have wireless. It didn't even have a direct phone line. And a motorcycle courier there and back would take at least 48 hours.

Gort looked up. His eyes had a hollow, bleak look to them. 'So the rumours of panzers at Abbeville might actually be true?'

Drake stopped short. 'Abbeville?' He stared at the map. Abbeville was on the estuary of the river Somme, near the channel coast. So the panzers were already more than forty miles *west* of them. The sheer audacity of it was almost overwhelming. 'Why Abbeville?'

The slim major spoke quietly from the back of the room. 'Isn't it obvious? There can be only one objective for an army that reports to Herr Hitler. Total victory.' His face twitched into a humourless smile. 'And if they're already at Abbeville, total victory is already within their grasp.' He turned to Drake. 'It seems that your information may have come too late.'

It was warm in the deep cellar of the old citadel. The air was stifling. But an icy rivulet of sweat trickled down Drake's spine.

Chapter 4

Colonels, brigadiers and major generals crowded into the basement room until it was full of yards of red stripe and gleaming brass.

'Gentlemen!' Gort barked out, and the hubbub fell silent. 'This young fellow has just brought me some rather startling intelligence.'

Senior officers of the general staff gawped at Drake in unabashed curiosity.

Gort moved to the map board, taking up a chinagraph pencil. Drake watched as the general, the old bloodhound, the Great War hero, began to pick up the scent.

'You may have heard disturbing rumours of panzers at Abbeville. It appears that the German objective is the channel coast. This is not – I repeat *not* – the rerun of the Great War Schlieffen Plan that we were given to expect.'

Six or seven voices all started at once, but were silenced by a single look from Lord Gort. The big general drew a thin arrow right through the centre of the Allied position, across Belgium and northern France. Drake saw now that he understood the terrible urgency of the situation. On the general's lips was the barest ghost of a grim, tight smile.

'If this intelligence is correct, it appears that there's a German spearhead that's using the river Somme to guard its left flank.' Gort ran his finger along the narrow corridor of the German advance, a gap cracked open between the BEF and the southern Allied reserves. 'They intend to cut our lines of communication. Slice us in two. And they may have already succeeded.'

He drew two sweeping arrows towards the BEF's position, one coming down from the north, the other circling up below them from Sedan. 'Down from Holland, and up from the Somme. It's a pincer movement. Classic Von Clausewitz. They're going to squeeze us. And there's not much we can do about it. We're going to feel the pinch.'

There was silence in the room. It appeared that many of the officers had been expecting a repeat of the 1914-18 war. Weeks, months, years of slow build-ups and stodgy offensives. Railhead supply dumps and time to build the lines all the way to the front. But it seemed they'd all forgotten that in 1914, nothing had begun like that. It had started with a sudden, lightning attack, and the German Empire had very nearly succeeded in taking Paris with the first roll of the dice. The Allies had only just stopped them in time, that fateful day on the Marne.

Drake watched Gort's face. Despite the dreadful news, the old general was rallying now.

'King Leopold of the Belgians has been going out personally to stiffen the morale of our allies in the north, and they are fighting tenaciously. The Belgian premier, Pierlot, has sworn to fight to the bitter end. With the north held, we must punch south, and fast. Link up with the French reserves behind the river Somme.'

Drake saw there was now a glint in the old general's eye, and he held the staff officers rapt. He was like an ageing prizefighter who'd been taking a beating, but at last had seen how to land a killer blow. 'With this mad dash for the coast, it seems that Jerry has left his northern flank horribly exposed. I think you will recognise the sentiment of Marshal Foch: *My centre is giving way, my right is retreating. Situation excellent, I shall attack.*'

They were interrupted then, as a harassed-looking adjutant threw open the door. 'Urgent message from CIGS sir. Tiny's on the phone.' The man looked around at the gathered staff officers, realising his mistake. 'General Ironside, that is.'

General Tiny Ironside, Chief of the Imperial General Staff, held the highest rank in the British Empire, and he was a great bear of a man.

'We've just found out that you're supposed to be meeting General Weygand and King Leopold today,' the adjutant continued. 'At Ypres.'

Gort snapped his fingers. 'Get a Lysander onto the runway.'

'For the summit, sir?'

'No. The ruddy conference can wait. I'm going up myself to take a look. If what this young fellow says is true, we shall have to act fast, gentlemen. Damned fast. We shan't any of us be getting any sleep tonight.'

The adjutant raised his eyebrows. 'When would you like the aircraft for, sir? I can ring and book it in.'

'Now, man! Now!'

The adjutant's mouth opened.

'Run!' Gort bellowed.

The officer turned and sprinted out through the doorway. A hubbub of urgent discussion filled the room.

Lord Gort nodded to the lean, balding major with the boyish face, who was still lurking in the shadows. 'Well, if all this has even a shred of truth to it, then the BEF owes your organisation a great debt of gratitude. You might have pulled us from the fire in the nick of time.'

The major gave a half-smile, then shot a look at Drake.

Drake immediately saw how it was. He did all the work, put his life and his career on the line, and a total stranger would get the credit. But that didn't matter. What mattered was that he was right.

The hubbub of the room dropped away as Lord Gort pulled himself up to his full height. On the map, he drew a thick arrow raking downwards towards the River Somme. 'We must counterattack south with everything we have. Punch through and link up with the French reserves. Do to the Wehrmacht what they are trying to do to us. Sever their lines of communication. Cut off the head of the snake.' He paused. Looked at the faces around the room. 'Gentlemen, I don't need to spell it out for you. The attack *must* succeed.'

'If it fails—'

The room fell into a stony silence. Just a distant thumping of bombs falling on the city, a sound that seemed to emanate from the earth beneath their feet. All the faces turned to stare at Drake, and he realised that he had spoken his thoughts aloud.

Lord Gort snorted. On the map board he drew an ever-tightening spiral around the BEF, closing in and in until there was nothing left.

'If it fails, we're facing annihilation. The destruction of the best part of the British Army. France will fall, taking Britain down with her. Hitler will overrun Europe.' He turned to the general staff. 'If the attack fails, Gentlemen, you can re-draw the map of the world.'

Chapter 5

DRAKE STEPPED PAST THE sentries of the Welsh Guards and out through the gates of the citadel of Arras. He was glad to be in the fresh air and sunshine after the gloomy cellars of Gort's HQ. He pulled the MP brassard off his arm as he walked. Removed the white Sam Browne belt. Took off the MP's helmet and threw it to the ground. Now he appeared like any nondescript British soldier in plain battledress.

He dragged his fingers through his hair. Unfamiliar emotions surged around inside him. Relief that Gort had taken him seriously enough to listen, but a slow, sick feeling of dismay now that he'd been dismissed from Gort's presence. The anti-climax of becoming a mortal again after walking for a moment with the gods. He was just a nobody once more, a forgotten pawn in the hideous game of war.

A low throbbing groan drew his gaze upwards towards the late morning sky. Little white clouds of Ack-Ack burst into being as if from nowhere, followed seconds later by the *pom-pom-pom-pom-pom* of distant Bofors guns. A squadron of high-level Luftwaffe bombers made black crosses against the blue of the morning sky. Deep, thudding, distant detonations trembled through the warm air. The bombs were dropping over the centre of Arras, a mile or so away. Smoke clouds rose above far-off rooftops. Somebody was on the receiving end of hell.

Drake thought briefly of Axelle, the Belgian woman he'd met on the day of the invasion. He'd never really told her how he'd felt. And then his stomach twisted up in a pang of guilt – he hadn't told her because he had somebody back home. *Hazel*, to be precise, in Devon. *Christ.* What a mess.

'Ah, there you are, sir,' growled a familiar Highland burr. 'Am I to presume we're in it up to our arseholes in it now?'

Drake looked over at his sergeant, who had been waiting in the shade of the avenue's trees, and now fell briskly into step beside him. Sergeant

Finlay MacTaggart was short of stature, but was a lean, tough-looking old soldier, and he never walked – he marched. He had his shirtsleeves rolled up. His sunburned forearms were wiry and muscular, scarred and inked blue with a lifetime of military tattoos. He wore the kilt of the Cameron Highlanders, dark blues and greens with red and yellow thatching, above long green socks that were pulled up over the thick lumps of his calf muscles. His traditional highland *sgian-dubh* dagger was firmly sheathed inside his right sock. His face was creased and burnt from decades in the sun, bashing up and down parade grounds at the four corners of the British Empire. Beneath the sergeant's olive-coloured tam o'shanter, his close-cropped hair was short, thick and wiry iron-grey.

'Armpit deep in the shit, Sergeant, would just about sum it up,' Drake said. 'We're being returned to unit. I've no doubt that Colonel Hawker will be only too glad to welcome us back into the fold.'

MacTaggart grunted. As they passed a group of tall, broad-shouldered Welsh Guards, the Scotsman's kilt drew good-humoured catcalls and wolf whistles. He cast a scathing eye in their direction and chose to ignore them. The old Scots sergeant had been steadfastly at Drake's side since the start of the invasion and had followed him all the way to Arras.

'Chin up, sir!' he said, adjusting his posture to ramrod straight, and gaining an inch of height. 'We're still breathing, are we not?' The Scotsman gestured along the road, towards the city, where a distant monument stood at a turning on the tree-lined boulevard. 'I'd like to pay my respects, sir, if I may.'

The structure ahead of them had red brick and pale limestone walls, and was topped by a zinc roof, which dully reflected the sun. Drake knew it had been designed by Sir Edward Lutyens, architect of Empire Memorials, and had been completed only eight years previously. A curved outer wall enclosed a large, open space. Doric columns supported wide, open gateways that seemed to draw the eye inwards. The Arras Memorial had an austere kind of beauty to it. Drake walked towards the entrance and read the engraving, carved high up on the great stone slabs of the wall.

1914-18
HERE ARE RECORDED
THE NAMES OF
35942 OFFICERS
AND MEN OF
THE FORCES OF

THE BRITISH EMPIRE
WHO FELL IN THE
BATTLES OF ARRAS
OR IN AIR OPERATIONS
ABOVE THE
WESTERN FRONT
AND WHO HAVE
NO KNOWN GRAVE.

Drake followed MacTaggart up the stone steps and into the open-roofed memorial. On a wide slab of an altar set beneath the open sky, were carved the words:

THEIR NAME LIVETH
FOR EVERMORE

A grassy, rectangular cemetery stood in front of them, where line after line of pale headstones stretched, regimental, across the lawn. Trees and bushes grew up in amongst the thousands of gravestones. Thousands of graves, for those lucky enough to be found and named and known.

To the sides, a twenty-foot-high wall, joined by grand arches, ran into the distance, supported by lines of columns in pale stone. The tall, stone-flagged walls of the memorial stretched away to Drake's right for close to a hundred yards, and on the stone walls were engraved thirty-five thousand, nine hundred and forty-two names in letters two-inches high – the names of those men who'd died and whose bodies had never been recovered. It was hard to grasp. The sheer scale of it was simply unimaginable.

Drake walked along the wall of the missing. The names were listed in vertical columns, reaching down from the top of the great walls, fourteen feet above Drake's head, to knee-height, where a stone bench ran along the base. The names were listed by regiment. Officers, NCOs and the massed other ranks below.

Drake's eyes scanned the letters, each one carved in Roman capitals: surname, then initials. Thirty-five thousand, nine hundred and forty-two men with mothers, fathers, children of their own. All dead. All lost. Their bodies swallowed by the unforgiving ground.

He stopped for a moment and watched as MacTaggart marched slowly out onto the open grass, staring at the rows of headstones. He realised with a jolt that the old sergeant must have known some of these men. Fought with them, side by side, as they died around him. He wondered what it did to a man inside. He shook his head, and walked on beneath the towering wall.

Eventually he found what he was looking for at the far end, close to the northern gate. He arched his neck, shaded his eyes and looked up. His own regiment had fought here, at Arras, in 1917. Twenty-three years ago. Just twenty-three years. His gaze followed the carved lettering in the stone slabs, fourteen feet above the ground.

SOUTH DEVONSHIRE REGIMENT

The officers were listed first.

CAPTAIN
MALTON, A.S. MC
SMYTH, T.
TWYFORD, P.J.

Beneath the captains came the lieutenants. Ten of them.

ABBOTT, M.J.
DONELLAN, P.
DRAYCOTT, F.
FOX, J.C.

The names ran on.

Then second lieutenants, a longer list – two dozen. Second lieutenants, back then, always leading from the front, had made easy targets for German snipers. *Thin knees*, the Germans had called them, on account of them wearing flared jodhpurs that narrowed into knee high boots. Per capita, they were far more likely to die than their men. Drake's eyes lingered over the carved letters as he read through the names.

CRACKNELL, R.
CROWTHER, C.
DIXON, S.M.
DODSON, J.

It was the first time Drake had seen his regiment's memorial here, and he hadn't expected to feel anything in particular. He gazed at the ground for a moment, gathering his thoughts. He'd been a small child, no more than three years old when the great battles around Arras had raged. And now, through sheer bloody folly, they were fighting the same war all over again.

He took a breath and stepped up onto the stone bench that ran along the base of the wall. And, standing on the bench, he stretched his hand upwards. He touched the warm, hard stone, then reached up higher. His outstretched fingertips ran across the rough texture of the stone-carved letters –

DRAKE, W.L.

William Leonard.

'Your father,' came a voice from behind, startling him. 'Now there's an interesting story.'

Drake spun around. A slightly-built officer in service dress was standing below him on the grass. It took a moment for Drake to place the man, seeing him now in bright sunshine, with his service cap on. It was the quiet major who'd been lurking in the dark corners of Lord Gort's chamber.

Drake bristled. 'What has my father got to do with anything?'

'I looked you up,' the major said. He held up a sheet of paper. 'The IO at GHQ passed me your report. That extraordinarily tall tale of yours about a German spy.'

Chapter 6

DRAKE JUMPED DOWN FROM the bench. 'It's not a tall tale, sir.'

He'd handed in a quickly typed-up statement to the intelligence officer at GHQ, telling how, in the opening days of the invasion, after the death of his Captain, Jack Philips, he and MacTaggart had chased down a German agent.

The major raised his eyebrows. 'I telephoned around a bit. You were promoted from the ranks. A Sergeant Instructor before the war. Schoolmaster – a barracks *schoolie*.' He said it as though it were something to be ashamed of. 'Came up the hard way. Never an easy transition, I am led to understand, Mr Drake.'

The major left the innuendo hanging. Drake had joined the army as a private at the age of fifteen after he'd run from home, and he'd dragged himself up by his fists and his wits, about as far as a lowly foot soldier could go: to warrant officer, second class – a glorified NCO. But with the outbreak of hostilities he had been quickly bumped to a real officer with the King's commission: *Second Lieutenant Ted Drake.*

An officer, but not a gentleman.

'That's right. Regular army. What of it?' he said.

'Well I dug up some rather *irregular* matters relating to your record. Your commanding officer described you with some rather choice words. *Unorthodox. Insubordinate. A danger to himself and the battalion.* You're to be charged with desertion and mutiny. A court martial awaits. Your colonel also states that you are a communist. And that's not to mention that stunt you pulled with the provosts. You're in rather a lot of bother, Mr Drake.'

Drake said nothing. He gazed dully at the major's uniform. A tailored cut, in the most expensive barathea weave. He knew the type. 'I'm not a bloody communist, sir.'

The major took off his peaked service cap, and rubbed at his hairline. A red line ran around his forehead – the imprint of the cap's rim. His dark brown hair was thinning from the front, but his face still looked somehow boyish; impish, even, in the warm morning sun. He had a broad moustache, streaked with grey, which lost its fine shape as he rubbed it with the edge of his hand.

'It seems you have little respect for authority. No regard for the established way of doing things. And this is not the first time you've been in trouble, is it?'

Drake glared at him. 'I was acquitted. I cleared my name.'

The major simply shook his head. 'Well it does seem that you're not cut out to be a regular army officer, wouldn't you say?'

This was it then. Drake knew what was coming. Demotion, at best. Thrown back into the ranks in disgrace. Or worse – the glasshouse beckoned. How did you spend the war, Grandad? *In jail.*

'I suppose you'll be sitting at the court martial?'

The major pocketed Drake's report and made a non-committal gesture. Drake frowned. There had been something bugging him, and now he knew what it was. There were no insignia on the major's kit. No regimental markings. He was a major – but a major of what?

The man considered Drake for a moment. Seemed to come to a decision at last. 'Here's the thing, Drake. I happen to believe your report.'

He suddenly had Drake's full attention. 'You do?'

The major reached into his breast pocket and pulled out a packet of Pall Malls. He glanced from Drake to Sergeant MacTaggart, who was still some distance off, in amongst the gravestones.

'Who the hell d'you think sent Jack Philips out there in the first place? *We* did. We'd been on that one for a while. And you figured it out from a standing start.'

Drake chewed the inside of his lip for a moment.

The major offered him a cigarette.

Drake shook his head. 'I gave up. Bad for the health.'

The major nodded, picked one out and twirled it between his fingers. 'However you did it, it was bloody well done.' He tapped the cigarette onto the packet, thoughtfully. 'What you said back there. To Lord Gort. It was foolhardy, naïve, and for a regular army officer, career suicide. But it was actually rather impressive.' His eyes came to rest on Drake's, disconcertingly holding his gaze. 'What I'm trying to say in a round-about way is we could use a man with a bit of spark. A man, I'd say, like you.'

Drake suddenly realised he was being interviewed. High up, droning Dorniers and Heinkels were leaving fine contrails of white vapour across the thin blue sky. The *pom-pom-pom-pom* of Bofors guns began once again in the distant city centre. The sky dotted with puffs of smoke. Seconds later, the ominous *thump-thump-thump* of falling bombs.

'Look around you, Drake,' the major said. 'There are two wars going on. The war you see, and the war you don't. The war you don't see is the war of information. We're currently losing both.' He held out his hand. 'Major Lyle-Smith.'

Drake looked at the hand for a moment then shook it. 'Second Lieutenant Tennyson Drake, First Battalion, South Devonshire Regiment, 56531182.'

'I know who you are, Drake.' Lyle-Smith gestured towards MacTaggart, who was still standing among the graves, staring at the headstones. 'Of course, you'll have to get rid of your sergeant.'

Drake looked towards MacTaggart, who was now on the other side of the cemetery. He studied the sergeant's Cameron kilt. Grey hair, and a face flushed by the continental sun. The blue-inked military tattoos that told a story of their own.

'Mons, 1914. The Coldstream,' Drake said.

The major looked startled. 'I beg your pardon?'

'Sergeant MacTaggart's service record makes for interesting reading, Major,' Drake said. 'The Marne. Ypres. The Battle of Loos, wounded. Delville Wood, wounded again. Military Medal. The Scarpe, then Passchendaele, wounded, then Cambrai, then he fought here, right here at Arras, in 1917. He's fighting again in 1940, Major. I don't think he's going to change sides now. Do you?'

The major gave Drake a humourless smile. 'Point taken, Drake. Point taken. How's your German?'

Drake shrugged. '*Leidlich*. Tolerable.'

'And your French?'

'Rather better. I've been in France since September, practising on the natives. I'm told I have acquired the accent of the *Pas-de-Calais*.'

'And what do you know of French politics?'

Drake hesitated. 'I'm a little hazy.'

'Something's rotten in the Third Republic,' the major said, 'and we think it goes all the way to the top.' He put his unlit cigarette to his lips, then put his hand on Drake's shoulder. 'Shall we take a stroll?'

Chapter 7

THEY WALKED AROUND THE memorial grounds. The major toyed with his cigarette. 'The French police have caught a traitor. A German agent.' He watched Drake for a reaction. 'You don't seem surprised.'

Drake shrugged. He wasn't. Fifth-columnists seemed to be everywhere. He didn't know which were more dangerous, the real or the imagined ones. He kept his mouth shut and waited. That was always the best way of getting information from those higher up the ranks. Authority abhorred a vacuum.

The major rubbed at his moustache again. 'Y Service picked up the signal. Couldn't break the code, but more or less located the transmissions. They made the mistake of tipping off the *Sûreté*.'

'Mistake, sir?'

Lyle-Smith snorted. 'The French police made a muck of it, of course. Half of them have communist sympathies, the other half are *capitulards* – defeatists – and would prefer a fascist regime to what they have now.'

Drake nodded. He knew that the French government had been disrupted by thirty-three changes of prime minister in the twenty-three years since the last Great War. Socialists, republicans, capitalists and communists had all been vying for power. The Armistice of 1918 had, for France, been a Pyrrhic victory. Socially and democratically, the Third Republic of France was a broken state.

'This agent – he's a nasty piece of work,' the major continued. 'Killed three men before they took him. I'm told that when the detective in charge threatened him with execution, he laughed in their faces. He said the war would be over in seven days, and the police would be the ones who were in jail.'

Drake stopped and turned, now facing the major. 'He might not be wrong, sir. The campaign's going badly.'

The major looked quizzically at him. 'Doesn't anything about that strike you as odd?'

Drake replayed what he had heard in his mind. It took him a moment. '*Seven days.*'

The major smiled. 'Good, Drake. Very good. Not a week, not a fortnight. Not ten days or eight or five. He didn't say the war will be over soon. He said the war will be over in seven days.'

'You think he was bragging.'

The major nodded. 'I do.'

'Then he made a mistake.' Drake rubbed at his face. 'Which tells us he knows something we don't.'

'Correct. And we need to know what it is. We may be on French soil, but Arras is our patch and as far as I'm concerned, this is very much a military matter. But it's a thorny issue, Drake. It's political. Our Gallic friends are jumpy as cats, and of course the French police don't like us treading on their toes. But there's something about this business that I don't like. Call it professional instinct. At all costs, I need to get hold of this agent before he falls into the hands of the *Deuxième Bureau*.'

Drake had had a brush with the French military intelligence agency before. 'I'm familiar with their methods, sir.'

Lyle-Smith narrowed his eyes and gave Drake a long, appraising look. 'My man can get you in for thirty minutes when their shift changes in the early hours. I'd like you to take a look at him. You speak the lingo. Perhaps you can loosen his tongue.'

Drake looked across at the major. 'I haven't had any interrogation training, sir.'

The major watched Drake for a moment, then his lip twitched. 'They tell me you used to box.'

There was a silence between them.

Drake heard distant gunfire, thumping somewhere near the horizon.

'I gave it up. Bad for the health. And I don't much like the idea of beating up a man who can't fight back. It all sounds a bit cold-blooded to me.'

Lyle-Smith regarded Drake with a kind of unsettling stillness. There was something unnerving about the major, something sinister beneath the boyish looks. Drake's skin began to crawl.

After a while, the major said, 'The preferred term, Drake, is *sang-froid*.' He spoke in an almost languorous manner, but there was a quality of dreadfulness to it that Drake couldn't quite put his finger on.

Lyle-Smith spun the unlit cigarette slowly in his hand. 'Hundreds of our men are dying every day. Innocent civilians are getting bombed in their beds. So don't tell me you're squeamish about handing out a bit of rough treatment.'

Drake said nothing. He gazed across the cemetery and caught the eye of Sergeant MacTaggart, who was watching them from a discreet distance.

'Before we go one inch further, I need a commitment,' Lyle-Smith said quietly.

'You make it sound as though I have a choice in the matter.'

The major narrowed his eyes. 'Listen, Drake. We're on the back foot here. All my best assets were in Brussels and other towns and cities now occupied by the Wehrmacht. Every day, another one goes off the air. Lord Gort is screaming for hard intelligence, and I've nothing to give him. All this–' and he gestured towards the city, where smoke was billowing in grey clouds above the rooftops. '—all this will happen soon to London – to Plymouth. Dark days are ahead. I'm sure you see where your duty lies.'

Plymouth. So the major really had done his homework. The shadows of another wave of Luftwaffe bombers flashed over the cemetery, and the Bofors guns started up once again in the city. Bombs began to fall in the distance, a heavy *crump-crump-crump-crump-crump.*

Drake's little half-brother, Alfie, was at school in Plymouth.

'No,' Drake said.

The major narrowed his eyes. 'I beg your pardon?'

'There's something that separates us from the enemy,' Drake said. 'Common decency. So I won't do it, sir. Find somebody else to do your dirty work. It's just not my style.'

Lyle-Smith calmly considered him, But Drake could feel the anger hidden below the surface. 'Are you seriously refusing me, Drake?'

Drake nodded. 'I am.'

'Then do not expect me, or anybody else, to smooth things over with your colonel.'

Drake felt his stomach twist. 'Then I'll just have to take my medicine, sir. Before he died, Jack Philips told me he reported to somebody called the Chief. You're not the Chief. Who is?'

'Jack told you that? *Tut-tut.*' The major brushed away the question. He consulted his wristwatch. 'Time is pressing. Report back to your unit.' He glanced towards MacTaggart, who was watching them from a distance. 'This meeting never happened, Drake. Do you understand?'

Drake nodded. Major Lyle-Smith turned and began to walk away.

After a few steps, he stopped, as though just remembering something. He began walking backwards as he spoke. 'Oh, and old Gort had something to say about you, Drake.'

Drake snorted. He wouldn't have been surprised if Gort had demanded that he be tied to the wheel, or flogged. He'd broken every rule in the book, and quite a number of rules that were so obvious they were not even written down.

'*Impetuous firebrand* was, I believe, the exact phrase he employed.'

Drake winced.

Lyle-Smith broke into a deep, throaty laugh, surprising in a man so slight. 'Oh, that's as close to a compliment as you'll get from John. He said you reminded him of himself when *he* was a damned fool young man.'

The major spun briskly around and began to walk away. 'Return to your unit. Await my orders. I'll be in touch,' he called out as he departed.

Drake frowned. 'I said I wouldn't do it, sir!'

Lyle-Smith waved a dismissive hand, and spoke again without turning. 'Oh, you'll come around, Drake, I can guarantee that. I like a man with a spine of his own. Consider yourself on temporary parole.'

Chapter 8

COMMISSARIAT DE POLICE, QUARTIER BAUDIMONT, ARRAS – 22:15HRS

A SHORT, ROTUND PRIEST in black robes and a biretta cap pushed open the door of the police station and walked nervously into the foyer.

A middle-aged *gardien* stood behind the reception desk. '*Bonsoir, Mon Père*,' he said. 'What brings you here, Father?'

'Inspector Lagrange telephoned me, an hour ago. I believe you have arrested a fifth-columnist. I am to hear his confession.'

The policeman frowned. 'At this time of night?'

The grey-haired priest opened his hands wide in a gallic gesture that somehow spoke of a man's impotence against the edicts of destiny. 'I am told he is to face the firing squad in the morning.' He leaned in closer, and spoke in an undertone. 'And I am to report anything of political importance that he may choose to confess.' He winked.

'Your name?'

'Monsignor Gillaud.'

The Policeman wrote the name down, and then looked down at the little priest with a newfound respect. He noted the golden gleam of the ecclesiastical ring on his finger.

'The corridor on the left, Monsignor. I will let *Sergent* Patou know to expect you.'

The monsignor thanked the policeman and made his way as indicated.

'*Faites attention, Monsignor*,' the policeman said. 'Be careful. He is a violent man.'

The priest smiled gently. 'Even the most hardened of criminals fear for their eternal souls.'

'As you say, Monsignor,' the policeman nodded.

As the priest went through the door to the left, the policeman pressed a button on his desk. 'Patou? The suspect has a visitor. A priest.'

He chuckled at Patou's indistinct reply, then sat down behind his desk on his stool. He heard the distant popping sound of anti-aircraft fire from the outskirts of the city and he wondered if the war would ever end.

Six minutes later, he jumped to his feet as the door was shoved open and Detective Lagrange came in, talking earnestly with a colleague. Both men looked exhausted.

'The priest you sent is here, Monsieur,' the policeman said with a knowing look.

Lagrange stopped. 'What priest?'

The policeman pointed to the door on the left. 'To hear the traitor's confession, sir.'

Lagrange stared at him for a moment. They heard the first shot then, thumping hard from deep inside the building. Two more shots followed.

'You bloody fool!' Lagrange snarled, as he drew his pistol and started running towards the cells.

PART II

THE ATTACK

TUESDAY 21 MAY 1940

Chapter 9

BRIGADE HQ, NEUVILLE-SAINT-VAAST, NEAR ARRAS, FRANCE - 04:30HRS

THE OFFICERS FELL SILENT as General Harold Franklyn stepped up in front of the map board. Franklyn's grey hair was balding and his moustache was almost pure white, but he seemed imbued with boundless energy.

'It's going to be a damned big show. We shall be supported by two infantry divisions of the French First Army. Two French tank battalions. Umbrella air cover from the Advanced Air Striking Force – that's the RAF to you and me. We attack due south. The Belgians are coming under heavy pressure in the north, but here—'

He pointed to the chart which showed the French forces on the river Somme, south of the German spearhead.

'--here, the French reserves will strike northwards. We're to break through southwards and link up with them. North and south. Pinch off Jerry's supply train. Hit him where it hurts. We're going to turn this ruddy show around. Any questions? All clear?'

Drake looked around the briefing area, which was just a canvas awning, under which were crowded several dozen officers of the brigade orders group. They were up with the first pre-dawn light. He glanced at his watch. It was just after four thirty a.m.

Across the ranks of seated officers, on the far side of the tent, Colonel Hawker was pouring over plans and muttering in a low voice to the thin-faced Captain Esmonde of the Devonshire's A Company. The colonel nodded in Drake's direction. It made him feel uneasy. By the chinless look of them both, Drake reckoned they were probably related. Colonel Hawker had been oddly pleased to see Drake on his return.

Drake had to assume that Lyle-Smith had pulled strings after all, and the whole incident with the provosts had been swept under the carpet. Or perhaps Hawker had realised it was in his best interests not to drag his own name through the muck, to avoid becoming a laughingstock among his men.

Drake turned his attention back to General Franklyn, who was fielding questions in front of the giant map. So this was it. The counterattack. Old Gort had really pulled the rabbit out of the hat. Got the French and British working together. That made a ruddy change.

Two French infantry divisions. Twenty-five thousand men. Two battalions of French armour – hundreds of tanks. And more coming up from the south. Just as well, because the British could only muster a couple of battalions, two thousand men at most from the South Devonshires and Durham Light Infantry. Drake wondered if they could really pull it off. The crowd of officers was buzzing with whispered conversation. If the counterattack worked, it could turn the course of the war in a single day.

General Franklyn spoke again, and the mutterings of the officers fell to silence. 'We believe that small elements of Jerry's seventh armoured division are somewhere in the vicinity. The Lancers ran into them yesterday, and came back bloody. There's no point hiding from you that it will be a tough match. But they won't be expecting us. There'll be no noise from the Royal Artillery to announce our arrival. We're hoping to achieve complete operational surprise.'

Franklyn shook his head and surveyed the rest of his gathered officers. 'We're to be called Frankforce, gentlemen. Gort's idea, not mine. Better than Frankenstein, I suppose.'

There was a laugh. The general quietened them with a gesture. 'Alright, settle down. That's enough levity. Today's attack will be no joke. Those of us who were in long trousers at the time will recall that fateful day in 1914 on the Marne.'

A hushed silence fell over the entire gathering. Franklyn held their attention. 'The German Imperial Army was racing south, sweeping all before them. It looked almost certain we were beaten and the Hun were bound to take Paris. Our men were exhausted, but they gathered themselves for a final stand. It was bloody, but we hung on by our fingernails. And then, shoulder to shoulder with our French allies, we punched back, hard. I don't need to tell you that we turned that show around. Well that's what we're going to do today, chaps. And Jerry liked it so much last time out that now he's come back for some more.'

There was another laugh. The tension among the officers was easing.

'Gentlemen, this is the counteroffensive we have all been waiting for. I know every single one of your men will fight like lions, so I shan't make a great song and dance of it. We've all been straining at the leash to show Herr Hitler what the British Army is made of. Well here's our chance.'

The officers cheered, and gave the general an ovation. Drake reluctantly clapped with them. He stared around and shook his head. They wouldn't be whistling if they'd seen what he'd seen. They obviously had no idea.

Outside the awning, a sour grey dawn light was creeping over the land. He'd heard nothing from Major Lyle-Smith. There was something about what the major had said that nagged at him, but he couldn't quite put his finger on why.

He jumped as a hand clapped him on the shoulder.

'Hello Ted. Back with us then?'

It was Bill Lucas, a fellow officer from the South Devonshires' first battalion. Bill had been one of the few friendly faces in the mess before the fighting broke out. In better times they had downed a drink or two and blown their wages in the bars of Arras and Lille.

'Hello Bill.'

Bill Lucas was younger than Drake was, had far less experience, but of course was already a captain. Winchester College. Exeter University. Sandhurst. Bill was a gentleman officer. Drake found it riled him, no matter how hard he tried to forget it. He'd had spent almost twelve years in the army, ever since he'd run from home – and the long arm of the law – at the age of fifteen.

'You must have really done something to get up the colonel's nose,' Bill continued. 'I'd love to hear all about it.' He clapped Drake on the back again. 'Hope to see you when the party's over, old boy.' Then he turned serious for a moment. He grabbed Drake's hand and shook it. 'Damned soldierly, Drake. Damned soldierly. Rather you than me, though, eh? Good man.'

Drake watched Bill's face, then turned away and gazed grimly out from under the canvas awning at the distant dawn horizon. So that explained why Hawker was so damned pleased to see him. He found his jawbone clamping tightly shut of its own accord.

The captain caught Drake's thunderous glare. 'Oh, buggeration, I've put my foot in it, haven't I?'

'I don't know,' said Drake through gritted teeth. 'Have you?'

Bill's face flushed bright red. 'God. Don't tell me you didn't actually volunteer for it?'

It took Drake a moment to unclench his jaw before he replied. 'What exactly is it, Bill, that I didn't volunteer for?'

Chapter 10

Colonel Hawker strode over towards the orders group of the South Devonshires subalterns who had gathered after the briefing. He looked around at the faces and gave a short, tight smile. His eyes swept glassily onto Drake's. 'As you can see, the prodigal son has returned.'

Drake saw how it was going to be. A private affair between the two of them. He kept his mouth shut.

Colonel Hawker broke off his gaze. 'Now, gentlemen, you heard the general. The waiting ends. I'm sure you're all popping to have a go.' He swung one arm forward in a soft rendition of a punch. 'At last, we've got a chance to really sink our teeth in.'

Captain Esmonde, acting as Hawker's *aide-de-camp*, began erecting a small map board as the colonel handed out a typed flimsy sheet to each officer.

'These orders are explicit,' Hawker said. 'There should be no hesitation in obeying.'

The officers all nodded – that went without saying.

Hawker rapped his cane against the map as he rattled through the plans, indicating a sweeping manoeuvre around the city of Arras. 'The Royal Tank Regiment will advance in two separate columns towards Duisans and Dainville *here*–' and he pointed west and south-west of Arras, '—with the first objective Agny. Beaurains is the second objective–' now indicating directly south of Arras '*—here and here*. The Durham Light Infantry along with the Devonshires – that's us – will follow in close support.'

The subalterns all nodded. 'Yes, sir.'

Drake spoke up. 'The general said that small elements of the German seventh armoured division are here. In my experience, the Wehrmacht doesn't do anything in small elements, sir.'

'Ah, our resident expert.' Hawker smiled thinly. 'Be that as it may, we'll be sending a forward screen of carriers in skirmish formation in front of the machines of the Royal Tank Regiment to flush out the enemy positions so the RTR units can identify targets and engage.'

The group of officers suddenly fell silent. Bill Lucas glanced at Drake, then spoke up.

'Won't that be a somewhat unhappy situation for the fellows doing the screening, sir? If the carriers do find enemy artillery, they'll be sitting ducks. Sandwiched in the firefight between the Germans and our tanks, so to speak.'

Hawker glowered through his thick-lensed glasses. 'We're going into battle. We expect to take casualties. There's not a man here who's unaware of the risks. I knew your father, Lucas. Men of his generation were not shy.'

Bill Lucas blushed. 'Yes, of course, sir.'

The officers shared a look as it suddenly dawned on them that this was really it. After all the waiting around of the Phoney War, they were finally going into battle. Some of them would be killed today. Some of them wouldn't be here at sunset. The expressions on their faces said it all.

The first orange rays of the dawn, rising behind Colonel Hawker, cast him into shadow as he continued with the briefing. His moustache twitched as he looked around at the group of officers. 'We must all be grateful to Mr Drake here, who is gallantly volunteering to lead the carriers. Reveal the German armour, if there is any, and pinpoint enemy artillery. Give the tank boys a free run at the enemy. It will vastly increase our odds of success. Isn't that right, Mr Drake?'

Drake silently cursed the man. He was slick. Drake had no way to back out of it in front of his fellow officers without looking like a coward. The other men watched with grave faces. Despite his misgivings, Drake realised that Hawker's strategy, while unorthodox, was tactically astute. And nobody would blame the colonel if a number of his men were killed, so long as the tanks were preserved.

'A forward reconnaissance patrol, sir?' he suggested, hoping to make the best of it.

Hawker shook his head. 'No, no, Drake. Skirmish formation. You are to maintain visual contact with the tanks at all times while engaging enemy positions. You'll have no signals contact with them, so timely, visual targets are what the tank chaps need. The British armour is far too precious to be taken by surprise.'

'Do you mean, sir,' Drake said, trying to keep his voice level, 'that we will flush the enemy out by exposing ourselves and drawing fire?'

'It may come to that, Drake. It may come to that. I'm sure every man of us appreciates your valour.'

The officers murmured to one another and gazed at Drake with a new-found respect.

'Now, Gentlemen,' Hawker continued. 'Everything's riding on this attack. I'm sure you'll do the reputation of the South Devonshire Regiment proud. We rendezvous with the Durhams at Vimy, five miles north of Arras. Can't miss it, there's a ruddy great monument there. Then we make our way to the startline at Duisans. Hop to it. Kick off's eleven double-oh.'

The other officers moved off until only Drake and Colonel Hawker were left.

The colonel stood, hands on hips, and watched him through his thick glasses. 'I know what you're thinking, Drake, but you're wrong. We're desperately short of manpower, especially officers, now that Philips – as you say – is gone. I've given you a significant responsibility. You're going to have to step up to the crease. Six machines, a carrier platoon of your own to command. Half my young subalterns would jump at a chance to have a bash like this. Show initiative, and there may be something in it for you.'

Drake's stomach tightened. Any mention of medals was a sure sign that they didn't expect him back. The other officers were dispersing now. Drake studied the horizon. The sunrise was colouring the surrounding countryside in uncanny hues. The hills were red from the dawn's early rays, and to Drake they looked as though they were drenched in blood. Hawker stepped towards him and tapped his finger onto the typed flimsy sheet that Drake was still holding.

'No more skylarking. I'm giving you a chance to redeem yourself.'

Drake bit his tongue. 'Yes, sir. Thank you, sir.' *And damn you all the way to hell.*

'Dismissed,' Hawker said abruptly.

As Drake walked away, he folded the order slip and put it in his trouser pocket. His fingers touched something else in there. Something flat and smooth.

That was strange. He'd thought the pocket was empty.

Drake pulled the object out as he walked. He stopped short. It was a calling card. He'd never seen it before. Embossed on the front, in flowing Edwardian script, were the words:

Major P. T. Lyle-Smith

On the reverse, a short message had been handwritten in black ink.

Trust no one. L.S.

Drake slipped the card back into his pocket, looking for the transports that would take him to his new platoon, and he could feel Colonel Hawker's eyes boring into his back as he strode away.

Chapter 11

BEAUMETZ-LÈS-LOGES, NEAR ARRAS – 06:25HRS

FOUR MILES EAST OF the outskirts of Arras, a black Renault *Vivaquatre* police car raced down a long, straight road that bisected the rolling fields. The tyres threw up a trail of white dust in their wake. The powerful four-cylinder engine roared and the streamlined styling of the saloon car gave an even greater impression of speed. Then, with a bang, one of the tyres burst and the car violently swerved. A stream of bullets from automatic weapons clattered into the engine block. The Renault veered off the road and bounced heavily into a field of newly-growing crops. After thirty metres, it juddered to a halt on the dry, ploughed earth. The windshield disappeared behind a cloud of hissing steam.

A dozen figures in heavily-camouflaged uniforms emerged from the crops and ditches at the side of the field. They wore *Stahlhelme* – German steel helmets – under canvas covers. There was plane-tree patterning on their camouflaged smocks. Steam hissed noisily out from the car's pierced radiator. Machine guns and rifles pointed aggressively towards the vehicle. A German officer stepped slowly forwards from the edge of the field.

The driver's door of the Renault opened and a man in a civilian suit climbed out. His face was obscured by the brim of his hat. He raised a large, red silk handkerchief in his right hand, and called out loudly, '*Sie hätten mich töten können*. You might have killed me, *Herr Hauptsturmführer*.'

The German officer looked at the red silk handkerchief, then studied what he could see of the man's face.

'*Meine Männer sind gute Schützen.*' He examined a small photograph which he held in his hand. '*Nehmen sie ihre Mütze ab*,' he said. 'Take off your hat.'

The civilian carefully folded the silk handkerchief and returned it to his breast pocket. He raised his hat – a grey, short-brimmed Homburg – with his right hand, and then replaced it.

'*Heil Hitler!*' the German captain said, clicking his heels in the Prussian fashion, as he raised his arm in the Hitler salute.

'*Heil Hitler*,' the civilian responded, modestly raising his own right hand from the elbow.

The soldiers, as one, all raised their right arms, and the shout of '*Sieg Heil!*' crashed across the field.

'Come with me, please, sir,' the *Hauptsturmführer* said, and escorted the civilian through the knee-high crops as an Opel lorry emerged from a stand of trees some hundred metres away. It drove towards them slowly over the furrows of the field.

The lorry was painted drab grey, and had the double lightning strike of the *SS* on the front. A grinning skull and crossbones was stencilled in white on the cab door. The civilian noted the markings as he clambered up and in. The *Hauptsturmführer* followed and sat next to him on the bench seat, and his men clambered into the back. The driver put the lorry into gear, and pressed his boot to the throttle. The six-cylinder engine grunted heavily as the lorry drove away across the fields.

Chapter 12

VIMY, NEAR ARRAS, FRANCE – 07:30HRS

DRAKE LEAPT FROM THE back of the British Morris Commercial transport lorry as it slowed. MacTaggart jumped down after him. Officers and men began to disperse to their mustering points as the transports halted and parked beneath the trees. Drake's eye was immediately caught by the tall, stark monument of Vimy Ridge.

The Vimy Memorial was a white stone tower that stood ninety feet high, struck in two parts as though split down the middle by lightning. It stood at the crest of a high, steep escarpment, which gave spectacular views across the French industrial heartlands to the north. The memorial was made all the more remarkable by the fact that the landscape around had been kept exactly as it had been in 1917. Great shellholes, now grassed over, pitted the ground. Immense craters lay sixty feet deep, a hundred feet across, holes that seemed to suck down into the bowels of the earth. Drake knew they had been caused by the underground explosions of tunnels and mines. Some of the Great War trenches had been preserved in concrete, exactly as they'd been left. It was sobering. He wondered if anybody had thought through the effect on the morale of the men.

Vimy Ridge had been hailed as one of the great Allied victories of the last war, but Drake knew the history. Ten thousand Canadians had died in a bloody, bitter struggle, for little more than a mile or two of useless ground. After the war, the German general Ludendorff had summed it up neatly. *No doubt exceedingly important strategic objectives lay behind the Allied attack, but I have never been able to discover what they were.*

Drake walked along the escarpment's ridge with his sergeant. The grass was short. It was being cropped by a loose herd of sheep. He glanced up again at the stark, white memorial.

'Evil omens, Sergeant.'

MacTaggart nodded. 'Aye.' He pointed towards a stand of young conifers. 'That looks like our little lot over there.'

A row of Universal Carriers was camouflaged in the dappled shade at the edge of the trees. Two dozen men were milling around the vehicles. This was Drake's first real battle command. He knew he'd have to form them into a coherent, motorised unit. He felt a sense of pride, but also a darker, more sinister undercurrent. It took him a moment to recognise what it was. Hawker had set them a dangerous – almost reckless – objective, but the men were no longer the colonel's. They were Drake's men now. And he'd be the one who was leading them out under enemy fire.

The Universal Carriers, or Bren Gun Carriers, as they were better known, were fast, slack-tracked, open-topped transports for infantry deployment and patrol, armed with Bren guns and the infamous Boys anti-tank rifles. They were painted in the army's standard drab green, but a handful of the more enterprising men had found a pot of red paint, and they were in the middle of daubing names on the sides, as though they were rowing boats or yachts. Some of the names were heroic, others comic. *Hercules. Daphne. Clappers.* Drake knew the troops would be happy enough to have the machines. At least they wouldn't have to march. And marching was the bane of the poor bloody infantry's life.

A thin man was following the others with a slow, ambling walk, painting little red feathers next to the vehicles' names. *The Red Feathers* was the old nickname for the South Devonshire Regiment, and one they took pride in. In the American War of Independence, the regiment had become notorious for taking no prisoners. When the Americans had sworn vengeance on them, the South Devons had put red feathers in their Shako caps, to single themselves out from the rest of the line and dare the enemy to come.

'At the double, Private Foale!' MacTaggart barked.

Despite being a Highlander, an outsider seconded to the regiment as drill sergeant during the Phoney War, MacTaggart was above all an army sergeant through and through. His kilt, his tattoos, his scars, his bright red face and above all his thunderous Scottish voice meant that the men held him to be somewhere in between God and the devil himself. The unlucky Private Foale jumped, and set about the task of painting the feathers with renewed haste.

Drake looked over at the rest of his men.

He'd been given a list of names, but he couldn't put all of them to the faces. Some of them had been in different companies, some were new, or territorials recently incorporated into the regular battalion. He recognised Corporals Simpson and Cawsey, Privates Addems, Dobson, Butcher, Hooper, Foale, Salter, Davy, Leighton... the list went on. He saw the heavyset Stoker and the pock-faced Pritchard. Others were unfamiliar to him. He knew he ought to learn all the names by heart, but the plain truth was that he didn't want to get to know them any better. Not yet. He had an awful feeling that if the day went badly he'd be leading many of them to their deaths.

He touched the calling card in his pocket, and wondered if he should have taken up Lyle-Smith's offer. *Of course he bloody well should.* He kicked the regrets away. He had to get his little carrier platoon into shape, and not stand around daydreaming about things outside his control.

He and MacTaggart began to inspect the vehicles with their newly-daubed names. *Lightning. Dobbin.* Drake vaulted into one of the machines, sat in the gunner's seat at the front and checked the Bren gun that was mounted there. Each carrier had two Brens, one up front and one in the rear. According to British Army doctrine, the Bren was so important to the infantry section's firepower that every man – from cook to staff officer – was trained in its use, and every infantryman would carry two magazines in a pouch for the section's Bren in addition to his own rifle rounds.

'See if you can scare up some more ammunition, Sergeant. We'll need it. And more grenades.'

'Aye, sir,' MacTaggart responded. 'Bangs and crackles it is.'

Drake hunkered down in the seat and squinted along the Bren's offset sights. His right cheek pressed to the butt, right eye aligned to the rearsight, right hand to the pistol grip. One of the first things Drake had learned when he'd signed up as a young lad was that there were no left-handed men in the British Army. He gripped his left hand over the small of the butt. As a left-hooker, even after all these years, it still always felt like he was holding the gun the wrong way.

He looked up, slapped his hand against the thin steel armour. It dawned on him that they were going to drive straight at the Wehrmacht in these little machines. It seemed like madness. After a moment, he jumped down from the carrier. He patted the steel wing above the front of the track. The metalwork was warming up in the French morning sun.

'This one will do for us.'

MacTaggart looked put out. 'Do you not want me leading a section of my own?'

Drake shook his head. 'I have a feeling I'm going to need your assistance, Sergeant.' He read the name the men had painted on the carrier and suddenly laughed. '*Mickey Mouse.*'

MacTaggart raised his eyebrows. 'That about sums it up nicely, sir.'

The rest of Drake's newly-formed platoon were waiting at the treeline in front of the carriers. The evil omens of the Vimy memorial appeared entirely lost on the men. Some lay dozing in the old shellholes, helmets tipped over their eyes. Others chewed on breakfasts of dry ration biscuit, cigarettes, and endless tin mugs of tea brewed up on spirit stoves. A few were playing cards: *Knave, Queen, King*. Half a dozen men were throwing all their money in an upturned tin hat – a month's wages for some lucky bugger if he lived long enough to spend it.

'Oi. What's the difference between the French and a slice of toast?' called out one of the soldiers, Private Butcher. Butcher was a big man, and he spoke with a deep, baritone voice, and an accent from the wrong side of the Plymouth docks. He was well known in the regiment and was regarded as one of the battalion's finest shots. At six foot six, he was hard to miss. Even squatting on the ground, the man was enormous. Drake had heard he'd been a champion boxer in his youth.

'Dunno. What?' Private Leighton rasped. Fred Leighton was lean, ferrety and blond haired, with tattoos on the backs of his hands. He was only in his twenties, but he smoked so much he sounded like a sixty-year-old man.

Butcher replied deadpan. 'You can make soldiers out of toast.'

Leighton coughed out a harsh cackle, showing a set of uneven, dirty teeth as he laughed. The other men chuckled. Drake was relieved to hear that they were telling jokes. Their morale was good. *So far.*

'Good one, Butch,' said Hooper, a stocky young man with ash-blond hair.

Butcher's smile dropped from his face. 'Oi. Don't call me that.'

Butch had been his prizefighting name. To Drake, there seemed to be something dangerous about the man, not just his size. He had dark wavy hair and was good looking, in a brutal sort of way. His nose had been broken in the ring, and it was wide and flat in the middle. It only added to his stature among the men. Drake noted that when he spoke, the other men listened. And when he laughed, they all laughed too, even if they didn't know why.

'Sorry,' said Private Hooper quickly. 'Didn't mean nothin' by it. D'you want some tea, then? Brew's up.'

The men looked up and, noticing an officer's presence, most jumped up and saluted. Not Butcher.

Drake nodded. 'Easy, men. As you were.'

Colonel Hawker, like all the BEF, was so short of manpower that he'd relieved the military police of their most troublesome cases to fill Drake's new motorised platoon with volunteers. Some of the men were laughing and joking as they loaded ammunition by hand into Bren gun magazines. But others were grey, tired, and fearful, flinching at every sound.

'I think you'll find the French are on our side, Private Butcher,' Drake said. There was a grain of truth in Butcher's joke – the French conscripts had hardly covered themselves in glory so far. 'They're fighting the Germans, and dying for their trouble, same as we are. They're our Allies. Remember that, you men.'

Butcher smiled, and rose to his full height, a good few inches taller than Drake. 'You used to go a few rounds, so I'm told.'

'I used to coach the men in the ring. But I've given it up. Bad for the health.'

Butcher looked down at him. 'Too good for it now, are you?'

There was a sudden hush amongst the men. All eyes fell on Drake. Drake chewed the inside of his lip for a moment. It had been a hard step, being made up from the ranks. It meant that he was disliked on both sides. The officers thought him a jumped-up sergeant, no gentleman. They were right about that. And the men just thought he'd got too big for his boots.

Drake eyed the heavyweight Private Butcher. 'It's quite understandable to feel a bit jumpy before your first battle, Butcher. Just don't take it out on your own side.'

Butcher's gaze stayed on him. 'I ain't jumpy.'

MacTaggart stepped forward. 'That's no way to address an officer, Private Butcher! You'd be on a charge if we wasn't going into battle!'

Drake laughed it off. 'It's alright, Sergeant. No harm in a bit of banter with the men.' He looked up at Butcher, who was still staring sullenly down at him. His arms were like sides of beef, and his great hands were brutal and scarred.

'Kit inspection, ten minutes!' MacTaggart bawled out. 'Weapons cleaned and loaded! At the double, or I'll have your bollocks off quicker than a landmine! We're not here for a ruddy picnic! There's Germans to be had! Lively now!'

MacTaggart winked at Drake as the men all jumped into action and hurried away to prepare their kit. All except Private Butcher. Butcher leaned insolently against the steel side of one of the carriers, and slowly lit a cigarette. As he inhaled, he met Drake's gaze again with strange, angry eyes.

'Come on, Dan,' rasped the ferret-faced Private Leighton. 'You heard the sergeant.'

Leighton led Butcher gently away like he was an angered prize bull.

'That was bold, sir,' MacTaggart chortled. 'Bold, and very neatly done. But you've not made yourself a friend of the big laddie there. I'll put him in the rearmost carrier, in case you don't want a bullet in the back of your neck when the fighting starts.'

They watched as Privates Butcher and Leighton sauntered along the line of carriers towards their piles of kit. They looked an odd pair – the one a scrawny smoker, the other a huge slab of a man.

'You do know what he was in for, don't you sir?' MacTaggart murmured.

MacTaggart was always a mine of information. Drake had rarely known gossip from the sergeants' mess to be wrong.

'Like almost every other crime in the field regulations manual, I expect it's drink-related?'

MacTaggart leaned in close. 'Not at all, sir. He was sober as a turkey at Christmastime. You've picked a right one there, sir. They say he's got a screw loose. Been hit on the head one too many times. He was due to be sentenced for murder. He beat a man to a bloody pulp with his bare hands, over nothing more than a wee packet of cigarettes.'

'Murder?' Drake was strangely troubled by a memory, dragged back up from his coaching days. The regiment had once lost a man in a championship boxing match, hit so hard that he'd sat straight down and never got up. He shook the troubling thoughts away. 'Just point him at the enemy, Sergeant, and he'll give us no trouble.'

They looked across the ridge to see a line of British soldiers were now beginning to appear from the north, tramping along the escarpment. Soon the first echelons began to reach the memorial. A sergeant major bellowed orders. The men immediately threw themselves to the ground.

Not more than two minutes later, half of the men were already draped over the hummocks and slumped in the craters of the old, grass-covered shell holes, fast asleep.

MacTaggart gave out a low whistle. 'It appears that the Faithful Durhams have contrived to lose their transports, sir. I heard they marched forty miles to get here overnight.'

Drake shook his head. 'What a way to go to war. And they've still got a dozen miles to go.'

MacTaggart sucked in a breath through the gap between his two front teeth. 'I've been with the British Army through four years of the Western Front. I've fought in Palestine and the Middle East, Afghanistan and Waziristan too. I've seen everything the dear old Army can do. With its back against the wall, some of it was as near to miraculous as you'd ever hope to see in your life. But you must be aware, sir, that every time the British Army organises anything it's either a ruddy shambles or a total balls-up. You just have to pray the enemy is even more disorganised than you.'

'Fat chance of that,' Drake snorted. 'The Germans are organised as hell.'

He gazed around with a growing unease. By now, the ridge and the surrounding woods were becoming covered with men of the Durham Light Infantry, all stretched out on the hummocked grass.

He glanced up as a flight of Luftwaffe bombers came droning towards them, flying high overhead from the east. There was no Ack-Ack to bother them. It was just as well. The guns would never even touch the planes, but would very effectively give away their positions and invite an unnecessary raid.

'Come to think of it,' MacTaggart said suddenly, looking around, 'we havenae seen hide nor hair of the ruddy French, have we sir?'

Nearby, an air sentry cranked his handle and the air raid siren began its ominous wail.

Chapter 13

DRAKE SAT ON A pile of ammunition boxes, staring at his wristwatch, waiting. Waiting was the worst of it. It gave you time to think, and all his thoughts were turning sour.

MacTaggart marched over and handed him a flask. 'I took the liberty of boiling some tea, sir.'

Drake nodded. If there was one thing the British Army could do properly, it was make tea that was heated to industrial levels. It would take the lips off you and scorch your tongue to a stub. Drake sniffed at the scalding liquid in the flask. He liked his tea black and with enough sugar that you could bend a spoon in it, but this stuff almost took his head off. His eyes watered as he looked up and saw MacTaggart's grin.

'*Tea*, you call it, Sergeant?'

MacTaggart sucked air in through the gap between his front teeth. 'Only a wee nip in it, sir,' he muttered. 'Against the morning chill.'

Drake forced a grim smile. He took a gulp. 'A nip?' he wheezed. It was liquid fire. It burnt his throat and brought tears to his eyes. 'There's barely any tea in it. I will not ask where the brandy came from, Sergeant.'

'No, sir. Best not. Although I am led to believe that a case of Napoleon became separated from Colonel Hawker's personal effects in transit.'

Drake shook his head. 'Lucky I didn't hear that, sergeant.'

'Might as well get hanged for a pig as a sheep, if you ask me,' 'MacTaggart grinned. 'It's the good stuff.' He suddenly jumped up. 'Speak of Beelzebub, and he shall appear. Eyes front, sir!' He nodded across the ridge. A scout car was bouncing towards them over the grass. 'Where in hell did he get that Dinky toy from?'

Drake looked across the field. The Daimler Dingo scout car had a tall, lightly armoured chassis on four large all-terrain wheels, with a two-man cab that was open at the top. Colonel Hawker was standing upright in the vehicle, one hand on the rim of the frontal armour.

Drake saluted smartly as the scout car came towards them.

'He's brought his bodyguard,' MacTaggart muttered, as the heavyset face of Sergeant Cronin appeared next to the colonel, leering across from the driver's cramped position.

'What does he need a bodyguard for?' Drake hissed.

MacTaggart grinned. 'Why, sir, to protect him from the likes of you.'

The scout car drew up to a halt, engine purring almost silently. The colonel pursed his thin lips, and his moustache twitched. His eyes seemed to swell behind his thick, steel-rimmed glasses. The quiet murmur of the scout car's Daimler engine died as Cronin switched off the ignition.

Hawker spoke without preamble. 'As you know, we were expecting two French infantry divisions. There's no sign of them. It's damned bad luck. And as for the two battalions of French tanks – well, a handful of Prioux's machines is all we've got. Nothing like the hundreds we were expecting. And General Franklyn thinks that the promised divisions don't even exist.' The colonel's eyes blinked as they moved disconcertingly behind his glasses. 'However, the fellows in the Tank Corps are on their way. They've driven through the night to get here. A twenty-five-pounder battery of the Royal Artillery is en route, and the Northumberland Fusiliers are stuck in traffic but they should be arriving shortly.'

Drake thought it through. The Tank Corps, that was something. The Northumberland Fusiliers were crack motorcycle troops and machine gunners. And a battery of twenty-five-pound howitzers would be a serious addition to Frankforce. But surely they would not be needed now? Without the divisions of French infantry and armour, the counterattack simply could not go ahead. Instead of twenty-five thousand men and hundreds of tanks they'd be less than two thousand men and a few dozen machines, against the full might of the Wehrmacht. He hadn't realised just how tense he'd been, until he felt the great, washing wave of relief. *They're going to call it off.*

The colonel fixed Drake with a glare through the thick lenses of his glasses. His cheek twitched. 'So, Drake. We make and mend. The show is on.'

'On, sir?'

'Yes, Drake. On.'

In the distance, Drake noted a pair of South Devonshires practicing with their bayonets on a bale of blankets tied to a tree trunk. They were laughing, but it sounded strangely hollow. Drake looked around at the vast, rolling French countryside that was laid out before them at the foot of the escarpment. 'On, sir. Yes, sir. Right, sir.'

'Better without the Frenchies, eh?' the colonel said. He let out an odd, strangled laugh, like a fox's bark. 'No mix-ups. No foreign interference. A British force commanded by a British general!'

Drake found his gaze drawn to the lines of Hawker's boneless, sallow face. His dark moustache. Round, steel-rimmed glasses. The colonel's narrow shoulders barely filled his uniform.

He glanced up at the wide blue skies. 'Air cover will be vital against the Luftwaffe, sir. I've seen what they can do.'

Colonel Hawker removed his glasses. He drew a handkerchief from his trouser pocket and polished the lenses. Without his glasses, his face seemed sunken, and vulnerable, his eyes suddenly naked, small and strange.

'We shan't be needing air cover, Drake. This is a British Army operation. Not combined forces, d'you see?' He put his glasses back on, adjusting them on the bridge of his nose, then thrust his chin forward. 'And as it happens, the boys in blue have picked today to ship themselves back to England.'

Drake gazed straight ahead. 'Yes, sir. Back to England. Of course, sir.'

Hawker rapped his cane on the metalwork of the Dingo scout car, and the engine caught with a purr. 'Start line is at Duisans, eleven double-oh. Get your men moving. Don't be late. This is your chance to show the stuff you're made of. I'll be watching you.' He gave Drake an unnatural, thin-lipped leer.

The air siren went off again, wailing across the ridge as another flight of German bombers came droning towards them from the east. As they passed overhead, they darkened the earth with quick flicking shadows, eclipsing the rays of the sun.

Drake turned away. He exchanged a look with MacTaggart as they walked back towards their men. 'Ruddy shambles? It's a total balls-up, and we haven't even started yet.'

He looked at his watch, and his stomach tightened as the hands brought the start time closer. He watched absently as a drab green Humber Snipe drove rapidly across the bumpy grass towards them. Its paintwork was streaked with a coating of thin white dust from the unmade roads.

The car continued coming quickly towards them as if to run them over, then suddenly stopped with the bumper only two yards from their shins.

'What in Satan's name are you playing at?' MacTaggart bawled at the driver.

Through the dusty windscreen, the driver merely jerked his thumb over his shoulder towards the person in the back.

Drake walked slowly around the side of the car. He peered through the dust-stained window. On the back seat sat a small, lean officer with receding hair. Despite his age, and his broad moustache, his face had a familiar boyish look.

Major Lyle-Smith wound down the window an inch. 'Get in.'

Chapter 14

THE INSIDE OF THE Humber smelled of leather polish and cigarette smoke. Newspapers were piled on the back seat. Drake pulled the calling card from his pocket and held it up. The major made a dismissive gesture as the car pulled away across the bumpy, tussocked ground.

Drake looked at the papers that were on the seat between them as they drove slowly towards the road that ran westwards through the woods. The news was days old. On the cover of *The Daily Telegraph* was a photograph of Winston Churchill outside 10 Downing Street, wearing a tall black hat. At battalion HQ, they would have seen the reports long ago, but for Drake it was all still new.

'What?' Drake said. 'Churchill's in charge now, is he?'

Lyle-Smith flicked a cigarette out from a carton of Pall Malls, then twirled it, unlit, between forefinger and thumb. 'Do try to keep abreast, Drake.'

Drake avidly flipped through the sheets, absorbing the news from home.

On the second page of the *Telegraph*, he saw that in Paris, the French war cabinet had been changed again. Marshal Pétain was back as deputy prime minister at the age of 84.

The Daily Mirror, five days old, ran with a bold headline:

Hand to Hand in Battle for Sedan

The Times ran with pages and pages of closely-printed war reports. Drake saw that Queen Wilhelmina of The Netherlands had landed as a refugee in Britain after Holland had been overrun. The story was repeated in bold in the *Daily Express*:

THE KING MEETS DUTCH QUEEN
Arrives in London with cardboard suitcases.

Elsewhere were stories of the plucky Belgians, fighting for every inch of their soil; a picture of their king, Leopold III, riding a white horse, inspecting his troops on the front line. A smudged photograph at the bottom of the page ran with a story that the Belgian fascist party had been disbanded and their leader, Léon Degrelle, interned. Drake skimmed over it. He had only a hazy understanding of the opaque morass of European politics. Frankly, he found it dull. His attention was grabbed by a headline in *The Daily Herald,* which had a story much closer to home:

OSWALD MOSELY ARRESTED!

The British fascist and eight of his followers were going to spend the war in prison.

'Good bloody riddance,' Drake said. 'If you ask me.'

The major regarded the news with indifference. 'Quite.'

Drake found himself stroking his jaw, remembering scuffles and punch-ups with blackshirts on Union Street. Despite Moseley being a Great War veteran and a champion fencer, there was something about him that made your skin crawl. Drake tossed the *Herald* down, and glanced at the rest of the papers, then turned to the back pages.

'What's your analysis, Drake?' the major snapped.

Drake looked up. He rubbed his chin. 'A strong, agile defence will be key, sir. There's a significant threat on the flanks.' He put the sports section of the newspaper down. It was all talk of the Football League War Cup which was going ahead for the sake of morale. 'It's going to be tight. Damned tight. Rovers could nick it in a pinch, but my money's on West Ham.'

'Very droll, Drake,' Major Lyle-Smith glared. 'It appears that the French police have allowed our prisoner to escape.'

Drake turned. 'How?'

Lyle-Smith spoke with quiet frustration. 'For reasons best known to themselves, they let him see a priest. He beat the poor man unconscious and murdered half a dozen policemen on his way out, including my best source. I went to see the place for myself. They didn't let him out without a fight, I'll give them that. It was bloody. And now some awkward bugger from the Deuxième Bureau has taken charge of the case. It never would have happened if only we'd got to him first.' He poked a finger towards Drake's chest. 'If only you had done what I asked.'

'Well, I'm sorry sir,' Drake said. 'So I suppose the whole thing's off?'

'Quite the opposite.' The major observed the back of the driver's head for a moment, then he slid shut the glass panel that separated the front and back of the car. They were approaching a queue of British lorries, which lined the road here. Drake saw they were full of his own regiment, the South Devonshires. 'We know this agent ran for a safe house. SIGINT picked up another transmission on the same frequency. He must have been in a tearing hurry, because the message was sent *en clair*. Uncoded. In plain.'

Drake watched as the major put an unlit cigarette between his lips as if to smoke it, then withdrew it again. 'He transmitted just one word. *Viper*. The Abwehr has a *penchant* for dramatic codenames. Poor trade-craft, if you ask me.'

The Humber juddered as it left the track, which was blocked by the Morris Commercial transports. The suspension shuddered as the car traversed a series of hummocks and furrows in the grass.

'Viper is the same word in English, French and German,' Drake said. 'One of a very few.'

The major spun his unlit cigarette between the fingers of his right hand before he spoke. 'There's something about this whole thing that reeks. Why was his escape so bloody?'

Drake shrugged. 'Didn't want to leave any witnesses? I suppose he killed all the men who might have recognised him? Except for the priest.'

'The priest is still unconscious. They don't know if he'll ever wake up.' The major waited for a moment before going on. 'So, Drake. Riddle me this. If this Viper fellow is German, or even a Frenchman going over, why would he care about witnesses? He said the war would be over in seven days. Witnesses shouldn't matter. Why bother killing six people if he didn't have to? He could have made a much cleaner escape.'

Drake chewed it over for a moment. He realised that the major was testing him. 'To kill six armed policemen – it means he's trained. Military, then?'

'In all likelihood. Yes.'

Drake tried to remember all the information he'd been told, working the logic through. He rubbed briskly at his face, hoping to stimulate his tired mind. 'There's only one reason to get rid of witnesses. He plans to go back under cover. And I suppose that if he knows about this scheme to bring the war to an abrupt conclusion, he must be somehow involved.'

'Very astute,' Lyle-Smith said. 'You can see why it's piqued my interest. We can tell from the transmitter he used that he's Abwehr. But this is where it gets interesting. There was a reply to this man's transmission. Also a single word. Also in plain. *Obenauer*.'

Drake frowned.

The major handed him a grainy picture, a photostat obviously taken from a newsreel. Three men in grey uniforms in front of a jostling crowd. Scrawled in pen at the foot of the picture was a description:

Reinhard Heydrich. Heinz Jost. Hermann Obenauer.
August 1939. Berlin.

Obenauer seemed very much like an ordinary little German shopkeeper in a drab uniform.

'Don't be fooled by appearances,' the major said. '*Standartenführer* Hermann Obenauer is as bad as they get. A senior figure in the *Ausland* Department of the Reich Security Main Office: Foreign Policy. And a full colonel in the SD.'

Drake ran his fingers along the tight scar on his hairline. It itched like hell. He looked back at the photostat. 'Sorry sir. The SD?'

The major snorted. 'The *Sicherheitsdienst des Reichsführers SS.* The security police and intelligence service of the SS and the Nazi party. The Abwehr reports only to the *Oberkommando der Wehrmacht* and is, of course, strictly military intelligence, but the SD is a political force and reports directly to Herr Hitler himself. Quite frankly, they make the Abwehr look like a bunch of wet kittens. Highly secretive. Rabid, murderous Nazis to a man.'

Drake had a sense that whatever this was, it was going to lead to unpleasantness. A great deal of unpleasantness. He stared out of the window as they drove along a country track. He said nothing, and waited for the major to continue.

'What do you know of the *Totenkopf*?' Lyle-Smith said.

'The Death's Head Division. I witnessed one of their officers murdering a Belgian prisoner on the first day of the invasion.' Drake's stomach twisted as he thought of the Belgian woman he'd met, Axelle. How the *SS Sturmbannführer* had shot her father in cold blood. And he recalled her fanatical hatred of the Nazis, even though her mother had been German.

'Quite so. A nasty set of brutes. One of the most fanatical units of the entire *Waffen SS*.' Lyle-Smith waved his cigarette airily at the horizon. Drake followed his gaze. 'According to the Lancers, the Totenkopf are operating not five miles from here. To our knowledge, they're the only elements of the SS in this whole region. Do you see?'

The Humber drove onto a main road that led them away from the memorial, towards the village of Vimy itself. The driver in the front looked mutely ahead as the six-cylinder engine purred.

Drake said, 'I'm not quite sure I do.'

'The transmissions.' Major Lyle-Smith tapped the cigarette absently. '*Viper. Obenauer.* It can only mean a rendezvous. I'll give you even money that Obenauer is with the SS Totenkopf. If this Agent Viper is going anywhere, that's where he'll be.' He smiled, and jabbed his unlit cigarette playfully towards Drake's chest. 'And that's where you're going, isn't it? Right into the thick of it. This little jaunt that Cecil Hawker's sending you on. You'll be the first man in. It couldn't have worked out better if we'd planned it ourselves.' He prodded Drake's shoulder. 'Find the SS Totenkopf, Drake, and you'll find Agent Viper.'

Through the window, Drake saw a column of soldiers from the Durham Light Infantry who were marching along the road towards the ridge. They looked footsore and shattered.

'You bastard,' he said. 'You set me up, didn't you?'

Major Lyle-Smith shrugged. 'When we spoke at the memorial, I said I needed a commitment. I do consider a gentleman's word to be his bond.'

'You yourself made a point of saying that I'm no gentleman. And anyway, I said no.'

The major shot out a short, hard laugh. '*Touché*.' But the mirth vanished as quickly as it had appeared. 'So?'

Drake looked out through the glass. He noted that the car was descending slowly down the road towards Arras. They turned left into a narrow lane. Drake banged his fist on the glass panel behind the driver.

'Pull over. You can let me out here.'

The driver ignored him and kept going.

Lyle-Smith turned to Drake again. 'I require Agent Viper for questioning. It is not in your discretion to decline.'

Drake almost laughed. 'You're asking the impossible!'

The major held his unlit cigarette quite still and observed it as though it were some foreign, unfamiliar object. 'The entire BEF is in an impossible situation, Drake. Britain wasn't ready for this war, not by a country mile.' The car passed a line of ragged refugees, women, children on handcarts, old men with walking sticks, all shuffling, sore-footed, down the road. 'Events are moving very rapidly, and I'll admit we're clutching at straws here, but the world as we know it is collapsing more quickly than we ever imagined possible. If I'm asking for miracles, it's because we ruddy well need them.'

Drake noted the dark rings that circled the man's eyes. He was tired. They were all so bloody tired. The smooth hum of the car's engine began to strain as they followed the road. Drake saw that it wound back up the escarpment. They were circling back towards the monument.

'Listen, Drake. You'll get no thanks or recognition for what I'm asking. God knows, you may well be hated and reviled by your own side. But if I was asked to do something for my country in her hour of need, no matter what, I shouldn't be able to live with myself if I refused.'

Drake shook his head. 'I'm about to lead my platoon into battle. My first duty is to my men.'

'Your first duty is to your country, Drake. The fate of nations is at stake here. Britain's very survival is in the balance. So be a good chap, and do what you're ruddy well told.'

The fate of nations. For the first time, Drake saw that the image of the genial, boyish major was merely a pose, a façade, a cover. Beneath the impish visage was a razor-sharp mind and a glint of polished steel.

He looked out of the window as the Humber climbed the last hundred yards back up to the ridge. Eventually the car drifted to a stop. They had arrived back at their starting point. He saw MacTaggart look up from the kit inspection, staring curiously in through the windscreen.

Drake reached for the door handle. 'I don't know why I didn't see it earlier,' he said. He knew he should just get out, walk away and never look back. A bullet to the head was better than what the major was offering. 'You're not on Lord Gort's intelligence staff at all. I'll bet you're not even a major, are you?'

Lyle-Smith took the still-unlit cigarette, and flipped it over in his fingers. 'The penny drops, at last. Clunk, clink.' He struck a match. The pale flame spluttered in the sunlight that came in through the car window. He finally lit the cigarette, and inhaled.

The driver in the front seat of the car sat oddly motionless.

Drake gazed out through the glass. Out there somewhere the Wehrmacht was waiting.

Lyle-Smith wound down the window an inch. He exhaled a long, thin plume of smoke through the gap, and gave Drake a razor-thin smile. 'Bring me back Agent Viper in one piece.' He flicked the still-burning cigarette out through the narrow opening at the top of the window. 'Your cooperation in this matter is requested and required by His Britannic Majesty's Secret Intelligence Service. You are to succeed, or give your life in the attempt. Don't bloody well let me down.'

Chapter 15

MAROEUIL, NEAR ARRAS, FRANCE – 10:30HRS

THE MAJOR'S WORDS WERE still ringing in Drake's ears as the carriers raced towards the start line. He sat hunched in the gunner's seat in the front of the leading carrier, the *Mickey Mouse. Daphne, Hercules, Clappers*, and *Lightning* followed. *Dobbin*, with Private Butcher safely in the back, brought up the rear. The carriers were fast, and the Ford V8 petrol engine in the *Mickey Mouse* thrummed hotly in the centre of the rear load bay, where two privates, Hooper and Dobson, sat. The slack tracks threw up clouds of dust from the unmade road. The muzzle of Drake's Bren gun poked out through a gunslit in the frontal armour, and the stock was resting in his lap.

Drake's orders were to rendezvous with the Royal Tank Regiment, and then sweep around Arras anti-clockwise, protecting British Rear GHQ, and cutting through the overstretched German lines of communication to link up with the French in the south. But despite the heat of the morning sun on his helmet and kit, despite the brightness of the early summer's day, without the support of the French divisions, there was now a grey tinge of desperation colouring the entire scheme. *Something's rotten in the Third Republic.* Drake had a sour feeling in his guts. He couldn't help wondering if the failure of the French divisions to arrive might be down to more than just bad luck.

He glanced at his battlemap. The terrain here sloped gently downwards from the back of the escarpment of Vimy ridge. It was perfect tank country. Wide, open fields rolled across low hills on a plain that stretched as far as the eye could see.

'What the hell are we supposed to do with only two knackered battalions, Sergeant? You've seen what the Germans can do.'

MacTaggart shrugged, peering over the top of the armour as he drove. 'Ours but to do and die, sir. Ours not to criticise the damn bloody fools who run the Army.'

'Ha!' was Drake's only response.

MacTaggart gave him a quizzical look. 'So, what did your major have to say for himself, sir? There's something about that man that fair gives me the creeps.'

Drake rubbed at his face before he answered. 'Trust me, Sergeant. You really don't want to know.'

MacTaggart fixed his eyes on the road ahead. 'Try me.'

Drake turned. He was certain the men in the back couldn't hear them over the clatter of the tracks and the growl of the engine. He leaned in towards the old sergeant, and quietly explained.

He had the beginning of an idea of how he could pull it off. It was a bad idea. It was dangerous, foolhardy, downright irresponsible, and it could only lead to trouble, far more trouble than he could handle right now. But the way he saw it, they were probably going to get killed anyway. 'Might as well get hanged for a pig as a sheep, Sergeant. You said so yourself.'

MacTaggart swerved the machine past a farm cart laden with glum-looking refugees. For the fraction of a second, Drake thought he recognised a woman's hair – *Axelle's* – but it was just a farmer's wife, of course. He was imagining things. He had started seeing her face when she wasn't there. He pushed the disturbing thoughts away.

MacTaggart let out a long, low whistle, bringing Drake back to the present. 'You shoulda told that major to take a running jump,' the old Scotsman said. 'But you bloody *want* to do it, don't you? Aye, don't deny it. You're soft in the head, sir, so you are. Dinnae forget – I've seen that look before.'

Drake shrugged. A strange emulsion of fear and excitement was surging around his insides. As ever, MacTaggart had hit the nail on the head, but his brief moment of good humour faded as a black crow flew off the road ahead, startled by the sudden rattle of the carriers. Drake watched as it flapped and cawed, screeching, to settle in a nearby tree.

'Tanks!' came a loud cry from the back of the carrier. Private Hooper leaned forward from the rear compartment, pointing keenly ahead. 'There, sir!'

Drake pulled up his field glasses. Sure enough, in the distance, a line of widely-spaced tanks was advancing along a road that intersected the one they were on. They were coming from the north. The machines were long and low, painted in olive green with swirls of darker green camouflage breaking up the pattern.

'Well spotted, Hooper. You must have good eyes.' Drake stood up in the carrier, using his knees to brace against the armour. He called back to his men. 'It's alright, boys. They're ours!'

The men all cheered as they drew closer. Drake knew that most of them had never even seen a tank up close before, let alone trained with one. In typical British Army style, tanks were a closely-held secret. Combined arms training had been left to the Germans. British infantry soldiers instead had spent their time learning how to point a rifle, march, dig holes in the ground, boil tea, and get helplessly, violently, drunk.

Drake raised his arm, and the carriers slowed at the junction. The first of the tanks rumbled towards them, and the deep grumble of its engines grew louder. The other machines, to protect against air attack, were spaced out behind at the regulation hundred yards.

MacTaggart whistled again, with admiration this time. 'Them tin can warriors have gone up in the world, sir.'

They were the brand-new Mark II Matildas, British heavy infantry tanks designed to advance with the foot soldiers, heavily armoured to absorb anything the enemy could throw at them. The Matilda, despite its comical name, was a handsome vehicle. Curved, sloping frontal glacis armour swept up to the turret, and thick armoured skirting – complete with mud chutes – protected the linked steel tracks. A pair of tall wireless antennae stood up from the turret of the lead tank, and the aerials carried small flags. Drake recognised the *Fear Naught* insignia of the Royal Tank Regiment. Large bundles of canvas and other field equipment were strapped to the sides of the turret, and the camouflaged hull was streaked with dark oil and fine grey powder. Heavy steel links clanked on the dusty surface of the road as the tank slowly moved towards them. Each machine was powered by a pair of London bus diesel engines, which gave off a heavy, chopping roar.

The tank clattered to a halt right next to the carriers. The name *Gwendoline* was painted on the turret in white. A stench of heavy oil tainted the air, and the hot steel armour shimmered dully in the heat of the French sun, which was high above them now. On top of the turret, the main hatch opened like two halves of a manhole cover, and *Gwendoline*'s commander appeared. He wore the black beret of the Royal Tank Regiment, and had a headset over the beret. At his neck, he sported a bright, apricot-coloured silk scarf above his khaki overalls. He was unshaven, and had dark yellow hollows beneath his eyes.

The tank engine stopped suddenly, leaving Drake's ears ringing. The commander removed his headset and vaulted out of the turret with practiced ease. He was a small, lean man. A low leather holster, slung forward on the front of his right leg, carried a hammerless revolver. The crown and pip on his epaulettes and the "Mother" tank badge told Drake he was a lieutenant colonel of the RTR.

Drake jumped out of his carrier and saluted smartly. The tank colonel appraised Drake's uniform, then took a moment to extract a packet of cigarettes from his overalls. He lit one of the cigarettes and inhaled deeply before speaking.

'Who are you?' His voice had a grating, plummy drawl. 'Where's your ruddy CO?'

'Second Lieutenant Drake, sir. First Battalion, South Devonshire Regiment. The colonel's miles back. We're ordered to take up skirmish formation in front of your tanks to flush out the enemy. To give you your targets, that kind of thing.'

The tank colonel laughed, an irritating bray. He inhaled again on his cigarette. 'In those things? Give Jerry some target practice, eh? Very sporting.'

Drake tried to suppress a surge of frustration. The tank officer must have seen something of it, because after that he softened his tone.

'Look, I'm sorry. We're all bloody tired. We're perfectly capable of finding our own targets. I shan't say anything if you just toddle along behind and clean up any mess we leave in our wake.' He held out a hand. 'Daborn. Piers Daborn.' Drake shook it. 'What time's kick off?'

Daborn inhaled once more on his cigarette as Drake handed him the order flimsies and the battlemap they'd brought in the carrier. 'Eleven double-oh, sir. General Franklyn's orders. The attack is to start right away.'

Daborn's answer came out in a cloud of smoke. 'You're ruddy joking! We've just driven a hundred miles overnight. I've lost twenty-six tanks to breakdowns alone. All because they couldn't find any transport to bring us on. Not a single bloody train driver to be had in the whole of France, it seems. Makes you wonder whose side they're on. And anyway, my men haven't had any breakfast.'

'Breakfast, sir?' Drake felt his stomach growl. He realised that the only sustenance he'd consumed was an unhealthily large dose of MacTaggart's brandy. His eyes rested on the name *Gwendoline*.

Daborn followed his gaze. He suddenly gave out a short, sharp laugh. 'Ha! Named after the wife. Make of that what you will.'

Drake suppressed a smile. The tank colonel's remark seemed to break the ice. Daborn slapped the big machine's side armour. 'The boys are itching to see what these contraptions can do.'

'How many have you got?' Drake asked, shading his eyes and looking back down the line of tanks, so spaced apart that they disappeared into the distance on the long country lane.

'Thirty-eight Seniors, Mark IIs. A hundred-odd Junior A11 Mark Is after breakdowns. And a handful of light Vickers-Armstrongs.'

Drake looked down the long, stretched-out column once more. He took up his binoculars and drew them into focus. The front tanks were the brand-new Matilda IIs, heavily armoured with three-inch plate, and armed with the excellent two-pounder cannons. Their names were painted on the hulls and turrets: *Devil, Dauntless, Dragon, Dreadnaught* – and Drake wondered for a moment if they had all been named after wives. Behind the first echelon, the majority of the remaining tanks were the old, outdated, narrow, two-man A11 Matilda Mark I models, with exposed tracks like bulldozers, small, one-man turrets, and a single Vickers machine gun as their sole armament. It was like they had been dug up from the trenches of the last war.

Drake lowered the field glasses and watched the men of the Royal Tank Regiment as they climbed over their vehicles, stowing kit, making adjustments, checking links and drive wheels.

Colonel Daborn caught his eye. 'Between you and I, this is the sum total of all the serviceable heavy machines that the BEF has this side of the channel.'

Drake turned his gaze to the horizon. No wonder the British Army had kept their tanks so bloody secret. Somewhere out there the Germans had more than a thousand fast, well-armed, modern panzers. *Christ.*

The tank commander scanned his orders. 'We're to rendezvous with the infantry at Duisans, then split up into two columns. I'm taking the left with 4RTR. The Seventh is forming the column to the right.'

'The DLI have lost their transports, sir,' Drake said. 'So they'll be late.'

A crewman hurried towards them and spoke quickly to the tank colonel. 'We've had a message on the Morse machine, sir. We're to advance to the start line right away.'

Daborn snorted. 'Alright!' he called to his crew. 'Start her up! So much for my ruddy eggs and bacon.'

He hauled himself up onto the *Gwendoline's* turret and pivoted feet first in through the hatch. The starter motor whined, and the tank's great diesel engines juddered into life.

Standing up through the hatch, he unfurled his apricot-coloured silk scarf, raised it above his head, and cast his arm forwards, the bright cloth signalling the advance. The engines vibrated with a loud, chopping racket. The tracks clanked as the tank jerked forward.

Drake vaulted back into his carrier. He nodded to MacTaggart, then glanced back at his platoon. For a moment, he hesitated. An unfamiliar emotion took hold, as though he were watching the scene from outside himself. The whole thing seemed unreal. He felt suddenly quite queasy. He wondered if he was getting the fear.

'Are you alright, sir?' MacTaggart said.

Drake shook himself. 'I'm fine. Step on it, then. Let's go!'

The great machines of the Royal Tank Regiment rolled forwards, engines chugging loudly. Drake's troop of half a dozen small carriers raced past them in single file and then tore down a narrow country lane. Their tracks churned up a trail of dust, and Drake's mind turned back to the major's cryptic words.

The fate of nations.

The war you see, and the war you don't.

Don't bloody well let me down.

Private Hooper leant forward over the cab and pointed ahead. 'Look, sir! There's more of our tanks!'

Drake glanced up. His eye was caught by the odd, symmetrical shapes on the road ahead, in a depression before the foot of a hill. He stared.

After a second he pulled up his Kershaw field glasses. The image defined itself into two angular shapes. *Christ.* No. It was three, four, five. A flash of alarm went through him, and he threw himself across the cab and hauled the steering wheel over.

'What the Jesus—!' MacTaggart yelled, fighting for control. The *Mickey Mouse* skidded off the lane and clattered heavily into a shallow ditch.

'Disperse! Disperse!' Drake bellowed to the carriers behind. 'Get off the bloody road!'

In the distance there was the sharp yellow flare of a muzzle flash. Half a heartbeat later, something screeched up the lane towards them at impossible speed. Drake's breath was ripped from his lungs by the vacuum of the shell passing. A searing blast thrust at the back of his head. Then the enormous, raging roar of a detonation.

Drake turned and glimpsed a ball of bright, jagged light as the second carrier jumped three feet into the air. Black smoke blossomed upwards and the faces of the men inside the vehicle disappeared inside a sheet of yellow fire.

Chapter 16

'Move it!' Drake bellowed. 'Disperse!' He gazed back at the burning carrier. Not one of the men in there had a hope of getting out. He felt ice cold inside. 'Panzers! Artillery formation! Disperse! Disperse!'

MacTaggart crashed their little carrier through the ditch and out into a field. The Ford V8 engine roared. The men in the other vehicles needed no further encouragement. They gunned their motors and scattered off the road. Drake's limbs clashed painfully against the steel armour as they flew over ruts and furrows. When they came to a hollow in the field, he signalled for MacTaggart to halt.

The first Matilda tank, the *Gwendoline*, rumbled forwards along the lane, *line ahead* with the other tanks behind. Colonel Daborn was standing upright in the turret, field glasses trained on the enemy. His bright scarf flapped at his throat as the great machine surged on. The twin diesel engines thundered and the tank shoved the burning wreck of the carrier aside.

The tank colonel unwrapped the scarf from his neck and waved it in a transverse arc above him. He yelled above the racket of the engine, 'Lay on, Macduff! And damned be him who first cries, *Hold! Enough!*'

The other tanks began to fan out behind the *Gwendoline*, heavy tracks grinding the dry soil of the fields. A moment later, Daborn signalled again and the Matildas stopped. The colonel shouted into his headset microphone.

'Figures three-four-two, cannon!' The turret traversed, gun sight elevated. 'On!' the colonel shouted into the mouthpiece. 'Brew the bugger! Fire!'

A pink jet of flame shot from the cannon muzzle. The report thumped instantaneously inside Drake's chest. He found himself mesmerised by the spectacle. The two-pounders on a dozen Matilda tanks all then fired in a heavy, hammering salvo. Tracer from the shells streaked away across the fields, dipping towards the panzers at the foot of the hill. They hit in sparking flashes.

'Cannon traverse right!' the tank colonel shouted again. The turret inched around in a fine adjustment. 'On! Down thirty.' The cannon's elevation dropped. 'You've got him! Fire again!'

Drake trained his binoculars on the German tanks in the distance. An acid gleam, and one of them was engulfed in fire. Fumes billowed as a turret hatch opened, and Drake saw a small figure dancing out, sheathed in flame. A volley of muzzle flashes came from the remaining panzers.

A screech of metal. Sparks shot through the air nearby as a shell ricocheted off a Matilda's thick steel hull. The thumps of the distant firing followed on the crashing impacts. A signal from the colonel's scarf, and the heavy Matildas began to roll forwards once again.

Another volley of shells screeched across the shallow valley, tearing holes through the air all around them. A great clang slammed into the *Gwendoline*'s hull, showering the tank in sparks. But the three-inch steel absorbed the heavy impact and the tank rumbled on, untroubled by the blow. Another shell glanced off in a clashing burst of light.

Drake signalled, and the carriers hurtled out of the line of fire, bucking madly across the dry, ploughed field. The little machines were fast, and their tracks were designed to bow as they steered, making them turn rather than simply skid when they cornered, so they were much more manoeuvrable than most other tracked vehicles. It made them difficult targets, but with every bump, Drake's knees banged against the angled armour. The vehicles had no roof, meaning they were intensely vulnerable to any enemy attentions coming from above. The side armour was thin – it would protect them from rifle fire, but little else, and Drake was tall enough that his head was sticking out from the top. The carrier was no place for a big man, and he felt badly confined and yet horribly exposed at the same time.

The British tanks kept advancing, then stopped once more to take aim. Deep, cracking retorts punched through the air. Two-pounder shells screamed overhead from the rearmost British tanks. Drake caught a glimpse of Hooper and Dobson in the back of their carrier. Hooper was watching, wide-eyed as a ten-year-old boy. Dobson was huddled down as low as he could get, helmet clutched tightly over his head. Shells from the panzers shrieked back in, buffeting past them in blasts of hot, hissing air, to detonate in clashing explosions on the armour of the advancing British tanks.

Drake dropped his field glasses and lowered his head, hunching down in his seat. 'Evasive action. Get us the hell out of here, Sergeant!'

'Right you are, sir.' MacTaggart floored it. As the carrier accelerated, its front end rose like a motorboat's. The machine zig-zagged away across the field, followed by the remaining carriers.

The German machines were firing high-explosive shells now, but the heavy Matildas rolled on through the smoke, led by the doughty *Gwendoline*. Clouds of dust obscured the terrain. Diesel engines chugged and thumped. Tracks clanked as the tanks rolled on.

MacTaggart eased their carrier to a halt in the cover of a stand of small trees at the edge of the pasture. Drake watched the developing tank battle through his field glasses. Colonel Daborn was standing upright in the turret of the Matilda, exposed to the enemy fire. He waved the machines onwards with another sweep of the scarf, and the *Gwendoline* led the tanks down into the valley. Behind the heavy Matildas, dozens of the old Mark I A11 tanks spread out into a fan shape and advanced at walking pace. It was a fearsome sight, and the effect on the panzers was instantaneous. The three surviving German tanks quickly reversed, crashing backwards through a hedge. They skid-turned on their tracks and sped away, far faster than the British infantry tanks could give chase.

A British two-pounder thumped, the shot harrying the panzers' retreat, then the din of firing stopped as Daborn held up his hand. 'Cease fire!'

Drake's men looked up from their hunched positions in the carriers. It was suddenly shockingly quiet.

'Bravo!' Colonel Daborn called out in the distance. Drake could just make out his words. 'Two-nil! The Fourth RTR is blooded!'

The tank commander waved the big machines forwards. Private Hooper, in the back of Drake's carrier, cheered. Even Dobson, who had been silent and grey-faced up to now, broke out into a cackling great whoop of relief.

'Shut it, you men,' MacTaggart growled. 'There's naught tae celebrate.'

Drake glanced back over his shoulder. He saw that the second carrier from their platoon was still burning where it had been hit at the start of the skirmish. It was throwing up a tall, black column of smoke.

'You lot stay here!' Drake shouted towards his remaining vehicles. MacTaggart spun the wheel round to take them back up the hill.

For the short duration of the frantic fight, Drake's focus had been on merely staying alive, and the speed of the engagement hadn't given him time to take it all in. But now an icy claw gripped his heart as they approached the burning carrier. The steel frame was enveloped by pale yellow fire. The frontal armour had been smashed in, as if by a great iron fist. Petrol from the fuel lines hissed as it burned in the high, bright sun. Sat neatly in the front seats of the burning wreckage were Corporal Cawsey and Private Addems. Privates Foale and Sutton were upright in the back. Their helmets were still on their heads, but their uniforms were on fire and their faces were charred and blackened. Through the flames, Drake could just make out the name on the carrier's hull. *Daphne.* The men had laughed as they'd daubed it on, just hours ago, just this morning. Drake turned and saw then that the rest of his platoon had followed them. *Hercules, Clappers, Lightning.* The comical names sounded absurd to him now. From the back of the *Dobbin* the heavy face of Private Butcher glowered.

'Alright,' MacTaggart called out. 'Nothing to see here. Move on.'

Drake cast a last look back at the burning wreck, and ran a hand across his face. *There but for the grace of God, go I.*

He signalled with a turn of his index finger, and the carriers wheeled away, following the tanks down into the valley. And the grey looks on the faces of his men told Drake that they were thinking the exact same thing as he.

Chapter 17

THE VILLAGE OF DUISANS was easy to spot. It was marked by columns of black smoke. The carriers soon clattered past the slow-moving infantry tanks. To Drake, the bright morning sunshine appeared false now. The reality of what they were up against was beginning to dawn. He consulted his battlemap, then studied the terrain ahead. The full might of the Wehrmacht was somewhere out there, hugely outnumbering the small British force. Their chances of surviving the day, let alone locating a German agent in the middle of it all, seemed horribly remote and unreal.

As they passed the tanks, Drake saw that the heavy machines of the RTR were now splitting into two columns; one to head east, the other in a more southerly direction. He turned his field glasses towards Duisans. Some four or five hundred yards ahead, a line of static, smouldering lorries were burning up in the morning sunshine on the verges of the road.

Drake gestured to MacTaggart and they slowed as they approached. A sharp tang of burning caught at the back of his throat. Blackened corpses were hanging out of the lorry backs, charred, and full of holes. He noted their large, boxy steel helmets, and their *feld grau* trousers and coats.

'Germans,' he said. 'Somebody's beaten us to it.'

The sight was macabre, uncanny, ominous. There was no sign of life. Machine-gunned corpses littered the fields. Drake's men stared, faces pale. For most of them, this morning had been their first taste of death.

'And we've yet to reach the ruddy start line, sir,' MacTaggart muttered. 'The Hun was not supposed to even be here.'

Although the Germans were dead, it didn't bode well. Drake wondered what else the British planners didn't know.

MacTaggart manoeuvred the line of carriers around the body of a large Wehrmacht soldier, which was spreadeagled across the middle of the road in a pool of congealing blood. Half the dead man's brains were spilled out and an eye was dangling on its string towards the ground. Drake dragged his gaze away and forced himself to keep looking at the horizon, scanning for danger. He realised he was sweating profusely. His steel helmet was pressing down heavily now with the heat of the sun, and his woollen kit was prickling at his skin.

He saw, back over his shoulder, that the Royal Tank Regiment was a quarter of a mile behind them now, advancing at not much more than walking pace.

'Slow down,' he said to MacTaggart.

The sergeant lifted his foot and the carriers rolled steadily along.

Drake pulled up his field glasses once more and studied the route ahead. In the distance, the large, rounded shape of a tank sat at a sharp bend in the road. It was painted with thick bands of beige, green and brown camouflage stripes. The domed turret had a roundel of red and white with a blue dot at the centre.

'Somua,' Drake said. 'French.'

As the little carriers approached, there was a buzz of automatic fire. It was coming from behind a wall and through a thick hedge. Abandoned German motorcycles with sidecars stood at the side of the road. Their riders were taking cover from the attentions of the French Tank. A loud chatter from the Somua's machine gun silenced them. Drake realised, with a shock, that the German troops were hiding in a British Great War cemetery. He signalled to MacTaggart, and they moved off the road to the left to avoid coming under fire themselves. They skirted behind the French tank, and Drake raised a hand to the commander, who was visible through a hatch at the back of the turret.

'*Les chars britanniques,*' Drake called out, 'The British tanks will be here in a few minutes!' He signalled that he was going on. 'Our infantry are following close behind.'

The French tank commander, peering out from the turret, gave Drake a vague salute, then began to fire his machine gun on the German troops who were huddled behind the gravestones on the other side of the road.

The carriers rolled slowly onwards, giving the cemetery a wide berth. As they emerged into countryside once more, the vehicles separated into a broadly-spaced column, line ahead in single file. The fields all around them were wide and flat and open and eerily quiet.

Drake studied his map. They were now advancing around the city of Arras in a counter-clockwise direction. They drove on, into a strange, deserted no-man's-land. There were few signs of the enemy now. It was obvious that, due to the speed of their advance, the Germans hadn't had time to set up any cohesive defensive positions along their northern flank. Lord Gort's instinct had been right. It seemed that, here at least, there was no real front line.

The carriers rattled past an abandoned farmstead. Cows lowed plaintively in the fields. There was nobody left to milk them, and they were in obvious pain. Drake glanced at his compass and gave MacTaggart directions. At a junction of two country lanes, they swung south east.

Drake glanced at his sergeant, but the two men said nothing. They proceeded down a long, shallow slope into a valley. At the bottom, there was a level crossing over a single railway line, and the gate was closed. A small, white-painted railway cottage stood beside the track. It had roses growing by the front door.

MacTaggart stopped the carrier in front of the crossing. The other machines pulled up behind.

Drake swung around in his seat. 'Dobson, Hooper! See if anybody's home.'

The two privates jumped out of the back of the carrier and banged their rifle butts against the cottage door. After a few moments, a Frenchman in railway overalls emerged, rubbing at his face. It was obvious he'd been sleeping. Drake ordered him to open the gates, *toute suite.*

The Frenchman shrugged. '*Mais non, Monsieur*. I cannot. There might be a train coming.'

'Well is there or isn't there?' Drake said.

'I don't know, Monsieur. The telephone line is down.'

Drake glared at the man. 'There's a war on. We'll take our chances. Now open the bloody gates.'

The French railwayman crossed his arms. 'I cannot. *Non*.'

Drake felt a surge of sudden frustration bubbling up, but a deep, chopping engine sound made him turn his head. The first of the heavy Matilda tanks was catching up. Colonel Daborn was visible in the turret as the tank came rumbling slowly down the lane.

Drake shouted up, 'He won't open the gates, sir!'

Daborn gazed at the problem for a moment, then nodded. 'Like the great Alexander, we shall cut the Gordian knot!' He rapped on the microphone of his headset. 'Driver! Full steam ahead!'

The *Gwendoline's* exhaust pipes chugged, the engine bellowed and the tank lurched forwards.

'Should be in the ruddy West End, sir,' MacTaggart said with a roll of his eyes, and Drake suppressed a smile.

The tank's tracks chewed through a vegetable patch as it passed the carriers on the verge. The French railwayman stared aghast at his garden. The front of the tank hit the level crossing gates. Timber screeched, then snapped like gun cracks. The heavy machine rolled over the crossing, a moment later splintering the gates on the far side. The French railwayman held his face in his hands and let out a despairing groan.

Drake's carriers clattered across behind the *Gwendoline*, which pulled to the side of the road to wait for the slower Mark I machines, which were straggling. Daborn gestured for Drake's machines to pass with a theatrical wave of the hand.

They accelerated up a low hill on the other side of the valley, leaving the long tank column behind them. At the crest, he signalled for MacTaggart to stop. The area to the south of Arras consisted of small villages set between parallel, rolling, low ridges which ran roughly east or east-south-east. There was another of the shallow valleys ahead, and at the foot of it lay the village of Achicourt. It had a village green, a stream and a duck pond. At the side of the road stood old, low cottages, a small hotel, and a mill.

Drake pulled up his field glasses and drew them into focus. 'Bingo.'

Strung out through the village was a line of soft targets. German lorries and other vehicles were parked neatly, one behind another, nose to tail. A pair of static half-tracks were stopped at the front of the column, and they were full of sleeping German troops. Other men in field grey Wehrmacht uniforms strolled around the village, steel helmets held under their arms, smoking and talking as though they were on holiday. They obviously felt themselves safe, miles behind the front lines.

Drake passed MacTaggart the binoculars.

The sergeant gave a low whistle. 'Och, well. Christmas has indeed come early, sir.'

Drake called out instructions to his troops in the carriers behind. He raised his right arm and pushed it forward to signal a slow advance. The five carriers rolled gently down the hill towards the village, careful to keep the revs low and the noise of their tracks as quiet as possible.

Through the lenses of his field glasses, Drake watched a pair of German soldiers who were leaning on the tailgate of a lorry at the edge of the village. They had their helmets off, and they were smoking cigarettes.

The carriers were only a hundred yards away when one of the soldiers got to his feet. He looked up the lane towards them and started yelling.

Drake let the binoculars drop. A rush of intense energy flowed through his veins, as though from a needle shot. He gave the signal and the line of carriers surged forwards, engines suddenly racing. He took aim through the offset sights and squeezed the trigger of his Bren.

Chapter 18

THE CAB ERUPTED IN a stuttering *bom-bom-bom* of automatic fire. Spent cartridge cases clattered onto the cab floor, and the stock of the machine gun rocked heavily back and forth. Fumes rose from the barrel as gun oil burnt off. Hooper's Lee Enfield rifle cracked above Drake's head. Private Dobson fired the second Bren gun from the back of the carrier. As the machines tore down the lane and into the village, the two German sentries fell, punctured by multiple bullet strikes before they hit the ground.

The machines shot into the village. All their guns came to bear as they rattled alongside the first of the static German Opel wagons. Bren gun rounds ripped through the canvas backs of the lorries. Screams cut through the air. Men in grey uniforms fell from the tailgates as bullets found their marks. In moments, German soldiers were running in every direction and shouting in confusion and panic. Drake dismounted the Bren and rested the forestock on the carrier's side armour. He squeezed out burst after burst as they sped past the parked lorries. Glass shattered. Rounds clanged loudly into steel. He pulsed the trigger, firing in short, deadly bursts. The first few seconds of the engagement seemed like hours.

When his Bren stopped firing, Drake slapped out the magazine and quickly reloaded another mag of twenty-eight rounds. He fired again. A whiff of petrol, then the fuel tank on one of the German lorries went up, ignited by a tracer bullet. Drake felt the heat on his face as the *Mickey Mouse* raced past an expanding ball of fire.

MacTaggart kept his foot down, and the vehicles rushed onwards, bringing death and havoc to the enemy supply column. German soldiers leapt from wagons. They ran in all directions, mouths pulled wide in surprise. Wounded men screamed in pain. Great sheets of flame leapt from one lorry to the next, igniting the canvas, and adding to the chaos.

Clouds of oily smoke billowed across the road. Gunfire crackled all around in a deafening hail.

Drake's mind was racing now, caught up in the fury of the attack. Every gun in his troop of carriers was blazing. He looked back and saw the huge figure of Private Butcher, standing up in the back of the last carrier, *Dobbin*. He was holding a Bren gun at his hip as though it was a toy, and was raking the German lorries with unrelenting fire.

Bullets thumped into the Wehrmacht soldiers, ripping through cloth, through flesh, shredding organs and shattering bone. Heads split open, faces torn off by close quarters machine-gun fire, so loud now that it was a meaningless, deafening din. The stench of burning cloth hit Drake's nostrils, and his Bren grew so hot that oil was dripping from the wooden pistol grip as he fired and fired and fired. Shrieks from burning, dying men filled the street. A German soldier ran out in front of Drake's machine, his uniform half on fire. The frontal armour of the *Mickey Mouse* hit him with a sickening thud and MacTaggart didn't slow down.

As the carrier ran on down the street, it seemed the whole transport column was burning. But it took only seconds until German officers and NCOs were regrouping, shouting orders to their men.

A German *Korporal* pointed and his face worked madly as he tried to organise his troops. '*Achtung! Da drüben! Feuer!*'

The Wehrmacht soldiers responded quickly, professionally, the moment of panic receding as they understood what was happening. As the carrier accelerated towards a crossroads at the end of the street, a six-wheeled armoured car swung out onto the village green and blocked their path.

Drake felt a flash of fear. A single word escaped his lips. 'Shit.'

He slapped another magazine from his Bren and slotted the next one in. He squeezed the trigger. A clatter of rounds sparked and scattered off the armoured car's sloping steel plate. It appeared to have no effect. Drake watched in dismay as the turret traversed slowly towards them. The long, thin barrel of the 20mm cannon was tracking their path.

'Move it!' he yelled to MacTaggart.

The sergeant slammed the carrier into reverse, jabbed his foot to the floor and yanked the wheel hard over. The carrier slewed off the lane and tore across the village green backwards at full speed. MacTaggart spun the wheel, tracks clawing them round on the grass, when a stunning *thud-thud-thud-thud-thud* ripped through the air above them. Drake was drenched in a mist of red.

He spun around to see that Dobson's neck was gouting blood, and half his head was missing. *Christ.* In the back, Private Hooper gave a loud groan of fear.

Drake's attention snapped quickly away. The autocannon on the armoured car was tracking them again.

'Reloading!' he yelled. 'Get us out of here! Now!'

MacTaggart stomped on the accelerator pedal. The carrier lurched forwards, zigzagging at full speed through the village. Another clip of high-explosive shells thumped out from the armoured car. Detonations erupted in a violent line behind them as the shells slammed into the ground. Clods of wet earth rained down from the blasts. The carrier shot towards a cloud of black smoke that was billowing across the village from the burning lorries.

Inside the cover of the choking smoke, it was blinding. Between raging fires, German officers were screaming out commands. A stuttering glow jabbed towards them as a Spandau machine gun fired from a cottage window, then another joined in. Rounds whipped murderously through the fumes, eddying the embers of burning canvas that were floating around in the madness.

The *Mickey Mouse* shot forwards once more, and Drake gasped fresh air as they re-emerged from the smoke. He saw, through streaming eyes, that at the far end of the village, a troop of German motorcyclists was racing in from the south, sidecar-mounted machine guns blazing. Their arrival cut off any chance of the carriers going straight on and out of the village to safety on the other side.

The buzzsaw drilling sound of the Spandau machine guns was intensifying, and Drake saw that the raid was turning nasty. With no way to go forward, his carriers were getting pinned down on the green. His men fired back, Brens and rifles blazing from behind the machines' thin armour, but the carriers were not designed as fighting vehicles. They were getting sucked into a static firefight, and as the German forces regrouped, they were now becoming heavily outnumbered and outgunned.

The German armoured car reappeared from the blowing smoke, engine roaring as it sped towards them. Its machine gun flickered into life. MacTaggart swerved their carrier violently to the left. Automatic rounds clashed into the thin steel plate, and Drake kept his head down, helmet clutched to his skull. When he looked up, he saw that throughout the village, rifles and machine guns were crackling fire from doorways and windows. The German troops were really getting organised now.

The *Mickey Mouse* tore across the village green, almost colliding with *Lightning* which was going the other way, sheer terror on the faces of the men.

'Fall back!' Drake bellowed. 'Back the way we came!'

A second later they were hidden again in the fumes from the blazing lorries. Drake's eyes were burning. He rubbed his sweat-soaked face with his sleeve. He could barely see.

German sergeants were bellowing orders to their men, and deadly streams of automatic fire came scything through the smog. They were setting up positions in the village houses. MacTaggart raced the carrier back towards the lane to the north of the village, but a steel-armoured half-track was manoeuvring into position to block their escape.

'We're trapped!' the old Scotsman growled.

Through the rags of smoke, Drake saw a thin, tanned face, under a grey steel helmet, as a German soldier ran across the grass. Drake let rip with the Bren, and the man staggered back and fell with a look of disbelief on his face. Drake instantly forgot him as the armoured car barked fire towards them, tongues of flame jabbing from the cannon muzzle again and again and again.

Tracer streaked across the village. Drake forced his head down as the shells banged out, one after another, a murderous *crack-crack-crack* of heavy fire. A crashing thump, and Drake saw one of his other carriers hit. Three men bailed out as it burst into flames, but there was nothing left of the driver.

Drake bellowed to MacTaggart, 'Move!'

MacTaggart skid-turned their machine around, tracks digging into the turf as he desperately looked for an escape. There was a steep-banked stream at the far edge of the village green – but no way to get the vehicles through it in a hurry. The German motorcycles and machine guns were now set up at the south end of the village, and Drake saw with a flash of dread that the armoured car had cut off any hope of a retreat.

He grabbed MacTaggart's arm. There was only one thing for it. 'Laager!'

MacTaggart immediately understood. He spun the *Mickey Mouse* around, and headed for the crippled carrier.

'Out!' Drake shouted, leaping from the gunner's seat as they slewed to a halt. 'To me!'

'Form a circle! Laager!' MacTaggart bellowed. 'Move it, laddies! You ain't in Bodmin no more!'

The other drivers quickly caught on. The remaining carriers tore in and formed a corral, using the smoke from the burning *Hercules* as cover. The men poured out and took up positions inside the defensive circle made by the tracked machines. Drake ducked his head as bullets slammed into the carriers' thin steel armour. The rattle and clack of gunfire was deafening now, interspersed with the enemy's shouted orders. Drake threw himself to the ground behind the *Mickey Mouse* and fired the Bren between the tracks, in bursts of suppressing fire to keep the enemy pinned down.

At the southern end of the village, the motorcycle troops were dismounted now, and were carefully working their way in. Drake noted that they wore camouflaged smocks and cloth helmet covers. He watched as they ran in pairs to set up the machine guns in protected positions. Their Spandaus crackled, spitting flame, adding significant weight to the enemy's firepower. Metal fragments hissed dangerously in all directions through the air. Rounds sparked off the armour of the carriers in jangling, sparking bursts.

Drake peered beneath the running gear of the *Micky Mouse*. The element of surprise was gone and they were in grave danger of encirclement. The stream behind them, at the edge of the village green, looked like their only way out – on foot. He cursed. He didn't want to lose their machines.

There was a short lull in the firing. Drake's heart pounded hard in his chest. He used the back of his sleeve to rub ash and sweat from his eyes. He kicked himself. *Christ.* Their attack had been reckless. *Should have done a proper recce.* The initiative was all with the Germans now. They had two options. Fight it out against impossible odds, or flee and lose all their vehicles. The carriers gave them some little protection, but for how long?

A clatter of Spandau fire smacked into the side of the *Mickey Mouse*. Drake peered under the tracks. Through the smoke, he could see the Germans were changing positions, and were starting to close in.

'Suppressing fire!' he called out. 'Keep those Spandaus quiet!'

MacTaggart bellowed targets to the men, and they focused on trying to overturn the fire from the German machine guns that were now set up in covered positions, in the cottages and the hotel. British Lee Enfield rifles snapped, and the Brens chugged out short three-round bursts. If they could keep the enemy heads down, they could stop them from going on the offensive, at least for now. But the armoured car was a major threat. They had little defence against its autocannon's fast-firing, high-explosive rounds.

MacTaggart crawled over. 'We're rats in a bloody trap, sir.'

'Butcher!' Drake yelled. He saw the big man look in his direction. 'Get the Boys rifle onto that armoured car!'

The big man sneered, but did as Drake ordered. He swapped the Bren for the five-foot long antitank rifle that many of the machines carried. Drake knew the theory, but he'd never seen one fired in anger. The Boys antitank rifle weighed thirty-five pounds and fired a four-inch long hardened steel projectile at one thousand, six hundred and seventy miles per hour. Most of the men were too afraid to use it – the recoil had been known to break collarbones or worse. But Private Butcher was one of the best shots in the regiment, and he was so big that in his great hands, the enormous rifle looked like a popgun.

On the other side of the village green, the German armoured car traversed its turret. Drake followed the thin muzzle as it pointed in their direction.

'Down!' he yelled, and put his face to the ground. He pulled his helmet over his head.

The circle of carriers took the brunt of the hits. High-explosive shells slammed into the burning wreck of the *Hercules* in a quick, staccato thunder. Crashing detonations spat fire and shrapnel through the air, and left Drake's head ringing like a bell. One of his men started screaming, hit in the face with hot steel splinters. MacTaggart crawled across the grass on his belly to help the injured man.

Drake set his field glasses on the German armoured car.

'They're reloading, Butcher. Now!'

Five yards away, lying beneath the carrier *Dobbin*, Private Butcher took careful aim. Drake saw the rifle jerk back and heard the harsh *crack-thump* of its report. There was a piercing clang as the bullet struck the car's amour plate.

'Give them another one!' Drake shouted. 'Aim for the vision slit!'

Butcher pulled back the heavy bolt, took aim and fired again. He shot two more and suddenly the armoured car jumped in the air. A jet of flame seethed from its steel bonnet and smoke billowed out from inside. Private Butcher looked down at his rifle and frowned.

Out on the village street, a German lorry exploded. Drake stared through the clouds of ash and dust. Amidst the piercing din of the battle came a sudden *chop-chop-clatter*. Drake put up his field glasses. He couldn't get a clear sight past the burning lorries. Then, through the billowing, seething smog, he saw the flash of an apricot-coloured silk scarf.

The *Gwendoline* advanced slowly, clanking through the smoke towards the village. Its turret traversed, machine gun flickering. The tank stopped, and its two-pounder thumped, spitting fire from the muzzle, and a German half-track went up in flames.

'It's our tanks!' Hooper cried out. 'It's only our bloody tanks!'

Another machine – the *Dauntless* – came lumbering down the hill behind it. Cannon muzzles flashed, shot streaked through the fumes, loud reports thumped starkly through the choking air. The *Gwendoline* advanced again, engines grunting. It drove straight at the German half-track that was blocking the entrance to the village. The frontal armour hit, and it rolled unstoppably on, shunting the machine aside.

'Go on! Smash 'em!' Private Leighton called out. He cackled, and hacked up a smoker's cough, then spat phlegm down onto the green.

The faces of Drake's men stretched into strained grins, as they took heart once more and redoubled their fire.

The Besa machine guns on the lead British tanks jabbed long bursts of flickering fire from their turrets. More and more of the tanks fanned out, quickly overwhelming the German positions. Colonel Daborn stood up through his turret hatch and waved his silk scarf forward. He lifted something long and made of brass, and he set it to his lips. Across the village came the unmistakable peal of a hunting horn. And Drake's men, outnumbered and outgunned behind their little carriers, all cheered.

Chapter 19

BY THE TIME THE first dozen tanks had rolled into the village, the enemy fire had dwindled to nothing. The German motorcycle troops at the far end had mostly recovered their machines and were racing away. As the long line of British tanks kept clanking slowly in, Drake's men began to round up the enemy soldiers who were surrendering in droves.

Colonel Daborn surveyed the scene from the commander's turret hatch of the heavy tank *Gwendoline*. 'Good show!' he called down over the engine noise. 'Can't stop! There's more Jerry to be had!'

'We'll catch you up, sir!' Drake shouted back, but he was distracted. There was something bothering him about the motorbikes. He jogged through the smoke and across the churned-up grass towards the southern end of the village. A few of the three-wheeled motorcycle and sidecar combinations had been left behind, their riders and gunners sprawled dead or mortally wounded on the ground.

Drake squatted down to examine one of the corpses, avoiding the gaze of the lifeless, staring eyes. He peeled back the canvas cover from the helmet and saw the double lightning-strike rune of the *Schutzstaffel* on the painted metal below. He pulled the dead man's bloodstained smock aside, revealing the field grey uniform underneath. The collar tabs bore a shining, metallic insignia of a grinning death's head. He gazed along the road in the direction the German riders had gone.

MacTaggart appeared at Drake's side. 'What d'you want me to do with all these Hun, sir? We cannae take prisoners with us, can we now? But in all good conscience, we cannae shoot them, neither.'

Drake stood up. 'Make them strip to their underwear and burn their clothes. They'll feel a lot less like rejoining the battle then.'

'Aye, sir,' MacTaggart grinned. He saw Drake's look. 'What is it?'

Drake glanced again at the dead German motorcyclists. If he had harboured any doubts about what Major Lyle-Smith had told him, they were all but laid to rest now. 'Take charge of the village 'til battalion turns up, Sergeant. I've got a little errand to run.'

MacTaggart rubbed at his scalp beneath his khaki tam o'shanter. 'Should we not be going with the tanks, sir?'

Drake touched his finger to the side of his nose. 'Won't be long.'

He stepped towards one of the abandoned motorbikes. It was a Zundapp. He took a moment to orientate himself with the unfamiliar controls. He found the ignition by the side-mounted gear selector and flicked it on. With a blip of the throttle, he kicked the starter pedal down. The engine was warm, and it caught easily, with a thumping buzz. Drake swung a leg over the saddle, tossed his helmet into the sidecar, clunked into gear, twisted back the throttle and released the clutch. The engine thudded and the motorcycle-sidecar combination pulled him forward. As he accelerated along the road, he felt the warm wind pushing pleasantly at his face and drying his tangled, sweat-soaked hair and his kit.

He pushed on faster, working the gears, following the gravel lane southwards over a series of hillocks and humps between open fields. Eyes squinting into the wind, he searched the horizon for signs of the enemy. After a couple of miles, he came to a long, straight stretch that ran in a slight slope upwards towards a distant hamlet. He pulled in the clutch and let the motorbike coast up the foot of the hill until it gradually rolled to a stop. He raised his field glasses and drew them into focus. Scanned back and forth across the village, but there was nothing to be seen. A few red-tiled roofs. Trees. A church spire. He swept the glasses left and right once more. Nothing. And then he stopped. *There.*

Above the treeline there was a thin, almost unnoticeable spiral of smoke. So there *was* somebody there. But who? He looked again, searching the buildings with his field glasses. Something moved.

He held the glasses steady and saw the dark outlines of five men walking slowly through the village. He adjusted the focus and they came into sharp relief. They were German soldiers wearing the same camouflaged smocks, heavily armed. He moved position and scanned the village again. There were glimpses of men in the buildings, moving behind the windows. There were grey-painted lorries parked in the village square, and a command car topped by a bedframe-style wireless antenna. He couldn't see the markings on the vehicles, but he was sure.

He watched for a moment longer until a rifle round chimed off the gravel a yard from his foot, the crack of its report following a half-second later. Somebody had seen him. He spun the motorbike around on the narrow road. Another bullet streaked off the ground nearby. He yanked the throttle hard open, and the tyres kicked up clouds of dust as he tore away.

Five minutes later, he skidded the machine to a halt, back in the village of Achicourt. He leapt off and ran to find MacTaggart, who was still organising the captured German troops.

The old sergeant saw him coming, and hooked a thumb over his shoulder. 'Eyes right, sir. Battalion's here. And the colonel's looking for you. He's in a right old stew.'

Across the village, a Daimler Dingo scout car was parked on the green, and a line of drab green Morris Commercials was backed up along the narrow lane behind it. Colonel Hawker was inspecting the half-naked prisoners, swagger stick rapping against his leg as he walked. He looked up in Drake's direction, jerked around and began striding towards him with a sour look on his face.

Drake grimaced. 'Get the men back into the carriers, Sergeant. At the double. Change of plan.'

MacTaggart bellowed orders, and the men piled into the machines. Colonel Hawker marched towards them through drifting smoke from the still-smouldering Opel lorries. Drake vaulted into the gunner's seat of the *Mickey Mouse.*

He ducked his head as MacTaggart got into the driver's seat. 'Don't hang about. Go!'

The front end of the machine rose up and they accelerated in the direction the tanks had taken. Colonel Hawker strode quickly to cut them off, and held out a hand to bring them to a halt.

'I didn't tell you to take prisoners, Drake!' he bellowed. 'You're supposed to be out in front of the ruddy tanks!'

'Don't stop!' Drake hissed.

MacTaggart kept his foot down.

Hawker had to jump back out of their way.

Drake saluted as the machines tore out of the village, leaving the colonel behind in a cloud of fine grey dust. His words were lost in the roar of the flathead V8 engines.

'Put your foot down, Sergeant. We've got to find those bloody tanks. And fast.'

Chapter 20

THE *MICKEY MOUSE* TORE eastwards along a French country lane, followed closely by *Lightning*, *Clappers* and *Dobbin*, five men now crowded into each. They soon approached another village. A sign read *Agny*. It was their next objective, according to the plan. German corpses were scattered in the gutters of the streets, shot up by the passing tanks – but the tanks themselves were nowhere to be seen. Drake signalled for his sergeant to press on.

The day was really warming up now. The sun was directly above them in the clear blue sky, and Drake could feel the heat of it on his steel helmet. Beneath his kit, his skin was bathed in sweat. A welcome breeze blew over them as they jarred through the village and out into the countryside again. Down another lane, slack tracks skidding on gravel as they turned into Beaurains, a village to the south of Arras. That was the second objective, and it appeared that it was already taken. Dead German soldiers hung from the windows of shot-up buildings. Corpses littered the streets. Opel transports were burning. The tanks had obviously already been and gone.

The carriers surged onwards, rattling through the deserted village, then out into the countryside once more, slack tracks throwing up dirt until the men were all coated in dust. After half a mile, they approached a pair of German antitank guns which had been shot up and pushed into the verges of the road. The gun crew still lay across the hard-packed gravel surface. It seemed the entire tank column had rolled over their corpses, flattening them to ghastly pancakes. It was a vile sight. The track was edged with spare body parts and a layer of pink froth.

'Oh God,' said Private Hooper, from the back of the vehicle. 'I think I'm going to be sick.'

Drake's platoon pushed onwards for another mile. All they saw were German dead. They were everywhere. It had obviously been a slaughter.

From far ahead of them, distant, heavy gunfire thumped dryly through the air. Above the engine noise, Drake made out the chatter of machine guns. They passed blazing vehicles, buildings riddled with bullet holes. It was an eerie scene. The column of tanks had destroyed everything in their path.

Slowly, despite the corpses, despite the horrors, a dark euphoria began to take hold of the men. It appeared, against all odds, that the counter-attack was working.

'Them tin can warriors have been having a field day,' MacTaggart said quietly. 'Looks like we've been missing all the fun.'

The men began to chatter in the back, suddenly over-excited.

'We're winning!' Private Salter cried out. He'd joined the *Mickey Mouse* after the destruction of the *Hercules*. He was fair-haired, with just a wisp of fluff on his chin. He shouted it out. 'We're bloody winning!'

'Watch out, Hitler!' somebody else called out. 'Berlin, here we come!'

The men in the carriers started laughing, even though it wasn't really funny. Drake lifted himself up from the seat so he could see the rest of his little company. After all the defeats and reverses of the invasion so far, there was something about the ease with which they were advancing that made them almost manic with joy, and the men were all grinning. Drake began to laugh, and even MacTaggart joined in. As the four machines sped on through the French countryside, throwing up a long, high trail of dust, their laughter pealed behind them.

'Look, sir!' Hooper cried out. He pointed ahead. 'There! It's the tanks!'

In the distance, fifteen hundred yards away, the column of British tanks was climbing a series of sloping fields, advancing up the near side of a low hill. Their tracks had carved a swathe of lines through the crops. Drake heard a piercing crack of gunfire.

'Go on boys!' shouted somebody in one of the carriers, as though he were at a football match. 'Stick it to 'em! Give 'em hell!'

The other men in the carriers all whooped and cheered.

They veered off the road and into a field of knee-high wheat as MacTaggart followed the tank tracks. The young wheat was a deep, intense green, the same colour as the vehicles' camouflage paint. The stalks hissed against the tracks as they raced ahead. A cannon thumped again in the distance. Drake raised a hand and the old sergeant eased off the throttle. Behind them, the other carriers all slackened their pace.

As they slowed, Drake drew the tanks into focus through the lenses of his field glasses. He slid the range dial around. They were down to nine hundred yards now. The tanks were scattered ahead of them on the wide slope of crops. A copse of trees crowned the high ground at the top of the field. Drake gazed back down at the map. Its name was Telegraph Hill.

'Stop,' he said, raising an arm.

MacTaggart coasted the carrier to a halt.

As the engine idled and the sun beat down, Drake fixed his gaze intently ahead.

'What is it, sir?' Private Hooper said.

Drake stared through the Kershaw glasses. None of the tanks were moving. Black dots were spread out across the field, and there was a strange, almost dreamlike swaying in the wheat.

Drake's sense of euphoria evaporated. He lowered the glasses and glanced at MacTaggart. 'Something's wrong.'

The high, hot sun was pushing down on Drake's steel helmet. Sweat trickled uncomfortably down his back. He scanned the field again. Some of the tanks' turrets seemed crooked. Their guns were pointing up, down, left, right, and every which way. Drake pulled the lenses into better focus. Yellow flame, almost invisible in the sunlight, was seething out of the turret of one of the narrow A11 tanks. The commander was hanging upside down from the hatch, and his uniform was on fire.

Drake dropped the glasses, his elation replaced by a sickening dread. 'Christ! They've been ambushed. Get us up there, now! Move!'

Chapter 21

THE CARRIERS ACCELERATED QUICKLY. Drake could see it with the naked eye now, as they closed in. Burning men hung out of blazing tanks. Flames licked at static hulls, pale yellow in the bright, high sun. The black dots on the field were the berets of injured crewmen who were crawling away from their wrecked machines. Another narrow, two-man A11 infantry tank was hit. It jerked backwards, knocked onto its side as if struck by an invisible sledgehammer. The piercing thump of cannon fire followed a heartbeat after they saw the explosion. Fifteen seconds later, a blast of air shrieked past them, only inches away. The shell detonated a hundred yards behind.

'Disperse!' Drake yelled. 'Artillery formation! Disperse! Disperse!'

MacTaggart pressed his foot to the floor. The sergeant whipped the wheel back and forth, zigzagging them across the field at full speed. Drake caught a glimpse of the strained, grim faces of the men in the other machines. *Clappers* sped away to their left, *Dobbin* and *Lightning* moved out to the right. As they zigzagged towards the tanks, another shell screamed through the air to detonate in the field nearby.

MacTaggart turned his head. 'Where the Jesus are they firing from?'

A third shot, and this time Drake saw the flash. 'Copse on the hilltop! There!'

A stunning crack and a flash of heat, and *Clappers* flew sideways across the field. A detached arm cartwheeled through the air as the machine tumbled away, disintegrating in a sickening ball of fire.

The men in the back of Drake's carrier looked on in dread.

'Move it!' Drake yelled. 'Get into cover behind those bloody tanks!'

The *Mickey Mouse* flew on, engine screaming past its limit. Drake felt a nauseating *whoomp* as the air ripped apart in front of them, torn by a passing shell. But the remaining three carriers were swerving quickly across the fields now, making difficult targets. Detonations burst all around. A bright flash and a black spout of smoke leapt from the ground in front of them. A moan of fear came from the back of Drake's carrier as they thumped through the flaming crater. Soil rained down from the explosion to patter onto their helmets. Finally they crashed to a halt in the cover of the burning tanks.

Drake stared around, mind frozen for a moment by the catastrophe. *Gwendoline, Devil, Dauntless, Dragon...* they were all on fire. A smaller two-man machine was sheathed in flame, and machine gun rounds were going off inside the turret like corn in a cooker. A reconnaissance tankette lay on its side with its tracks in the air. A red-hot hole the size of a fist was punched through the armour, and a jet of flame seethed out.

Drake leapt from the carrier, beckoning his men to follow. They began to drag the surviving crewmen from the stricken, burning tanks. Engine oil, fuel and ammunition made a lethal mix. The machines were like incinerators and Drake could see shapes inside, writhing in the flames.

They pulled a couple of crewmen free before their tanks went up. The men were badly burned. Private Salter was violently sick.

'God,' said Hooper, repeating the word again and again. 'God. God. God.'

Drake felt hollowed out inside. Through his binoculars he studied the small patch of trees at the top of the hill. 'Bastards,' he said. 'You bloody bastards.'

Another shell from the German gun screamed in and hit a static tank hull with an appalling crash. Drake was almost glad of the distraction. He couldn't shake off the vision of hell that he'd seen inside the burning wrecks. He'd always hated small, enclosed spaces. He'd take a bullet to the skullbone any day of the week, but to be trapped inside, on fire... *Christ in hell.*

They found a few other injured crewmen crawling away through the crops, and dragged them into the cover of the tanks. The whine of a starter motor made Drake spin around. It was coming from one of the still-smouldering heavy machines. As the motor caught, fumes belched from the tank's exhausts and the twin diesel engines coughed into life. The tracks jolted, picking up the slack, and the tank rumbled forward, slowly gathering speed. Smoke billowed from its hull as it advanced. Another tank, a narrow, blackened, two-man A11, started up, following the heavy Matilda II. And from the small turret, its Vickers gun began to strafe the woods.

Drake bellowed to his men, 'Back in the carriers! Follow those tanks! Come on!'

Chapter 22

THEY VAULTED BACK INTO their three remaining vehicles. A flash ripped from the trees at the top of the hill with a shattering crack. The detonation hit two hundred yards behind them. The two tanks clattered slowly onwards and they followed, keeping the heavy armour between themselves and the site of the gun. Drake could almost feel the German gunners going through the motions as they loaded the next shell. They wouldn't miss a second time. The tanks were so slow they were as good as sitting ducks.

A flash, a penetrating crash, as the German gun fired from the trees once again. Drake watched in horror as the two-man tank jumped, then exploded in a searing detonation. He knew the smaller tanks, though slow and under-armed, were heavily armoured. So what the hell could do that to three-inch steel plate?

He shouted orders. 'Flank the woods! Automatic fire at the muzzle flash!'

MacTaggart pulled the wheel over. They broke away to the right, the little carrier bucking over the furrows of the field as the sergeant accelerated hard. From behind his head came the *thump-thump-thump* of Hooper's Bren. Drake fired his machine gun towards the site of the gunflash, a long burst that made smoke pour off the barrel. Rounds scythed into the trees. He heard the sharp snap of Salter's Lee Enfield rifle. To their left, the Besa machine gun on the heavy tank crackled, as the great machine crawled slowly on up the hill.

A jabbering flicker of fire from the woods pinpointed a German position.

'Take out that Spandau!' Drake shouted. 'Go for the right flank!'

The machine guns from the tank and from all Drake's men now converged on the small copse, stripping leaves and branches from the trees. The foliage began to shake, then a German artillery spotter tumbled out from a tree, still clutching his yard-wide range finder. The shredded foliage revealed a dark muzzle and the shapes of a gun crew working frantically in the woods. The gun was huge, towering over the gunners' heads, and the barrel was twice as long again. A German gunner *Korporal* screamed orders, and a loader hefted a shell to the breech. The gun layer, strapped into his seat, spun the elevation screw and another wheeled the traverse as they drew the slow, heavy tank into their sights.

'Go straight at them now!' Drake yelled. 'We've got to take out that bloody gun!'

The *Mickey Mouse* surged forwards, engine screaming, as they raced towards the treeline. Drake fired over the frontal armour. The Bren shook as it thudded out the rounds until it emptied the magazine. Drake was close enough to see the faces of the German gun crew as they hurried through their fire drill. A *Korporal* shrieked orders as the carrier jolted closer, flying across the field. The gun loader slammed shut the breech. Drake slapped out the Bren's empty magazine, and slotted another in. Fired and fired again, rounds tearing into the woods. The *Mickey Mouse* sped closer, guns blazing, until it crashed into the undergrowth. The three-ton hull shot through a thicket of brambles before thumping to a hard stop against the wide trunk of a tree.

'Out!' Drake screamed, as he leapt from the front seat. 'With me!'

He sensed Hooper jumping out after him, and MacTaggart springing forward, snatching up his rifle. Drake saw the dirty, terrified faces of the German crew. He squeezed the trigger of the Bren. The German gun layer shuddered in his harness as rounds ripped into his guts. Drake kept firing. The remaining gun crew turned to flee. Drake fired again, and the Bren rocked in his hands. He was deaf to the noise of it now. The woods were grey and everything was far off and moving in slow motion. The second carrier slammed in, and Private Butcher jumped down. The big man swung his Bren gun round. He glared at Drake for a moment with his finger on the trigger. He laughed and turned away, and emptied the magazine at the German troops who were fleeing. Then, with a shuddering roar, twenty-five tons of Matilda tank smashed heavily into the woods.

The great tank ploughed in, uprooting tree trunks, tracks churning through the soil. The machine gun in the turret fired madly, swivelling in all directions, muzzle flickering white and yellow as its rounds whipped into the woods, ripping branches from trees, and slaughtering the running German crew. Lee Enfield rifles snapped, Bren guns chugged out entire magazines. Another artillery observer fell from a high branch. He landed on the ground six feet from Drake with a nauseating thump.

The machine gun on the Matilda turret kept firing in crazed, extended bursts, long after the last German soldiers had fallen. Drake realised he was panting wildly. Some of his men were yelling, others cheering, irrational from the intensity of the short, desperate fight. The tank's machine gun finally stopped, and a wounded German gunner began to scream. Private Butcher ran forwards and silenced him with a blow from the Bren gun's butt.

'Alright!' Drake called out. 'It's done now, men. Easy, now. It's done.'

The sound of the tank engine died as the driver killed the motor, and a strange, eerie silence fell across the woods.

Drake senses refused to return to their normal state. Everything seemed out of proportion, his hands felt too large, and the treetops looked very far away. The German gun, silent now, was enormous, standing well over seven feet high. The barrel was twenty feet long, and grey. It appeared, if anything, like a giant Bofors Ack-Ack gun, and Drake realised that was exactly what it was. A large-calibre, high-velocity anti-aircraft cannon, but fired horizontally over open sights.

The heavy Matilda tank was smouldering. Kit that was strapped to the outside of the hull was still burning and giving off smoke. The commander's hatch on the turret hinged slowly open and a man clambered awkwardly out. He untied a sooty scarf from where it had been wrapped around his head. His face was red and sweating, skin blistered, eyes raw and streaming from the fumes inside the turret. He slid down the armoured hull and landed heavily on his feet. He staggered for a couple of paces, eyes far away, and he walked right past Drake like he wasn't there. It took Drake a moment to recognise it was Colonel Daborn. He walked slowly to the edge of the woods and gazed down at the fiery wrecks of his tanks.

It was a disaster. Half of the British tank force had been wiped out by a single, well-placed German gun.

MacTaggart grasped Drake's arm. 'It's not your fault, sir. Don't blame yourself.'

But for once the old sergeant was wrong. Drake knew his carriers should have been out in front, protecting the tanks, but instead he'd been dawdling, playing at spies. He only prayed that the major's mission would somehow be worth it. And down on the fields below Telegraph

Hill, the precious, priceless few British tanks burned up under the high French sun.

Chapter 23

DAINVILLE, NEAR ARRAS, FRANCE – 15:30HRS

Drake's three remaining carriers led the *Gwendoline* westwards across the rolling countryside to the south of Arras, back almost the way they'd come. Colonel Daborn and the surviving crewmen had managed to salvage a two-man A11 tank from the wrecks, and it followed, clanking slowly along behind. Daborn, with heavy heart, had ordered the retreat. There was no sense trying to hold the hill now. The plan was to rendezvous with the other tank column. Elsewhere, the fight was still going on. There appeared to be no order to the battle. From what Drake could make out, it was a series of skirmishes taking place through the surrounding hills, villages and vales. A crackle of distant small arms fire sounded above the chop and chug of the engines, and the occasional thump of far-off big guns shook the warm summer air. German spotter planes buzzed overhead, observing the British movements. Rifles snapped from the Bren gun carriers as the men took pot shots at the skies.

A roadside sign read *Dainville.* Drake studied the battlemap, his mind half-dazed. Pillars of smoke dotted the horizon, towering over low hills and shallow valleys. The fields were green, the skies were blue, but to Drake's eye, it had all turned sour and grey. Everything was unreal, slow moving, and somehow tinged with death. He felt he was removed from himself, like he was seeing it all on some terrible, hellish film.

The carriers clattered through an abandoned hamlet and his mind picked up small, irrelevant details. Ash cans left by the side of the road. Front doors bolted shut, others left wide open as if the residents had just popped out to the shops. The dark, empty doorways seemed to stare right back at him. A stray dog watched them pass with mournful eyes. Drake glimpsed a reflection of their carrier in a window, and he barely recognised what he saw. His throat was parched. He shook his head. Squeezed shut his eyes. The sun beat down on their faces and their thick woollen kit. He scratched at the sweat-soaked, matted hair beneath his helmet. His face felt papery and dry beneath a sheen of sweat.

'Tanks, sir!' came the cry once more from Hooper in the back.

Drake pulled up his field glasses. Sure enough, heavy tanks were blocking the entrance roads to a village up ahead. They were British, heavy Matilda IIs. He stood up on the seat and shouted back towards Colonel Daborn.

'It's the other column, sir!'

Daborn glared grimly ahead as they advanced towards the village. The men of the Seventh Royal Tank Regiment let them through with good-natured clapping and cheers. But the jollity faded fast when they saw there were only two tanks left of Daborn's entire column.

'Where are the rest?' called out a tank commander.

Drake couldn't bring himself to answer. Behind him, Daborn just gazed coldly over their heads, and the conversation faded rapidly away.

After halting the vehicles at a green, the officers gathered quickly by a stone-walled barn at the north side of the village. The colonel gave them his report. Drake could see their faces turn to shock.

'Good Lord,' said one of the tank commanders when Daborn had finished. He was a young lieutenant with a blond moustache.

'What about my brother Jimmy?' said another man.

Daborn shook his head, and the man turned away with a frozen look. Drake kept his gaze to the ground, his insides gripped by talons of unease.

'We're running thin on fuel and ammunition, sir,' said the major in charge of the Seventh. 'Have you had any new orders? Oughtn't we to fall back and resupply? Our Morse machines have fallen off the net.'

Sergeant MacTaggart jogged over. 'Vehicles approaching, sir!'

Drake hurried around the barn to take a look. A distant cloud of dust appeared, about half a mile off. He saw through his field glasses that it was a column of lorries, led by a Dingo scout car. *Colonel Hawker.*

'I suppose you'll want to wait for your battalion?' Daborn asked him.

'Not really, sir. My orders are clear. For what it's worth, I say we keep the momentum going. Keep attacking. That's what the Germans have been doing so well in this campaign. If we halt for a conference and allow them to reorganise, we'll lose the vital element of surprise.'

'I say we fall back and regroup,' said the major from the other tank column. 'We must while we still have enough fuel left.' The tank major suddenly saw that Colonel Daborn was staring furiously at him. 'But of course it's your decision, sir.'

'Yes it is,' Daborn said tartly. 'There are no new orders. We attack. We keep attacking until we break the German lines. And I for one shan't rest until the deaths of all my men have been avenged.'

The major glanced at his subalterns. 'Yes, sir. Of course. But where?'

Drake stepped forward intently. 'There's what looks like an entire German infantry regiment not far from here, sir. I'd imagine your tanks would have no trouble with them.'

'Show me,' the tank colonel snapped. A sudden, hard brightness glittered in his eyes. 'What d'you have in mind?'

Drake unfolded his battlemap. He ran a pencil stub over the chart, taking in the distances and the terrain.

'There,' Drake said and jabbed at the village of Simencourt with the pencil end. 'It's the Totenkopf sir. *Panzergrenadiers.* The motorised infantry troops of the Waffen SS.'

Chapter 24

SIMENCOURT, NEAR ARRAS, FRANCE – 16:15HRS

THE CARRIERS WAITED BEHIND a screen of trees to one side of the road, engines idling. Drake's jaw was clenched with tension. They were close to the village of Simencourt. Insects darted in the hedgerows. Birds fluttered from branch to branch.

Drake nodded to Sergeant MacTaggart. 'Alright. Drive like hell.'

MacTaggart put his foot down and the *Mickey Mouse* leapt forward through the hedgerow. *Dobbin* and *Lightning* came racing out after them. Drake stared through the gunslit, scanning the village buildings. There was no movement. Aside from the noise of their engines and the rattling of tracks, everything was still.

The carriers accelerated up the slope towards the settlement. Drake felt his stomach tighten as he watched the silent village ahead.

'Stop!' he suddenly called out, and MacTaggart stood on the brakes. They were only seventy yards from the first houses now, and the hamlet was uncannily quiet.

'Are you certain the Hun are here, sir?' the old sergeant whispered above the low thrum of the motor.

Drake gripped the Bren gun, pushed off the safety selector on the left side of the pistol grip, and took aim through the gunslit. 'Yes. Let's wake them up.'

He squeezed the trigger. The Bren thumped in his hands, the reassuring *bom-bom-bom* of a short burst sounding loud in the quiet village. Two seconds later, the other Bren fired from the back of the carrier. Rifles cracked from above Drake's head. The guns on the *Dobbin* and *Lightning* thumped as they opened up.

'Cease fire!' Drake shouted.

Drake scanned the village through his field glasses. There was nothing. No reaction. No movement.

He tutted. 'Reveal yourselves. Come on.'

He Drake snorted, and ran the lenses of his field glasses back and forth across the buildings. The upstairs windows on some of the houses were wide open, but there were no faces. He scanned the gardens. Went back over them again.

'Look, sir!' said Hooper from the back.

Drake looked up just as Hooper's head shattered, split open by a rifle shot.

'Jesus wept!' cried Private Salter. He was splattered in blood.

Drake ducked behind the protection of the carrier's thin steel plate armour, as a well-hidden sniper hit the vehicle again with another round.

'First floor window on the right!' he yelled, and the Brens on the carriers responded. Drake started as, behind a garden wall, something moved. He drew his field glasses up. It suddenly came into focus. A black circle, behind it a heavily-camouflaged gunshield, draped with netting and covered in branches cut from garden bushes.

'Antitank gun!' Drake shouted. 'Bloody move!'

The carrier lurched forward. Drake fired his Bren towards the gun and at the same moment saw a jet of flame. The shell fizzed past between them and the next carrier, and detonated in a field far behind.

'Clear the road!' Drake yelled. His Bren thumped as he put down a burst on the German gun crew. All hell let loose. The windows in the village houses lit up with automatic fire. Drake's men responded with rifles and machine guns. MacTaggart floored the accelerator pedal and skid-turned the *Mickey Mouse* off the lane. They jolted into a field, closely followed by the *Dobbin*. The third carrier, *Lightning* was just a second too slow.

The frontal armour punched open with a deafening clang. The carrier caught fire. The men in the front seats had no chance. Two men clambered out of the back and ran.

'Go! Go! Go!' Drake bellowed. MacTaggart gunned the engine and wrenched the wheel over, as another antitank gun cracked, muzzle jetting fire. German machine guns strafed the carriers and the men put their heads down. Bullets jagged into the thin armour plate as they lurched across the uneven ground. Finally they came to a dip in the fields and halted, out of sight of the guns.

The German firing stuttered, then stopped. A stray shell fizzed overhead. Drake was panting like he'd run a record mile. Private Hooper's body was sprawled, half in, half out of the back of the carrier. Blood ran down the green-painted armour. Colonel Daborn's tanks were waiting in the hollow. They were hidden from the village by a dip in the terrain, which gave them a covered approach – *turret-down*.

'Your targets, sir,' Drake said, glancing up. 'Light antitank guns only. But they're well dug in.'

Colonel Daborn was studying the position through field glasses from his hatch in the *Gwendoline*. 'Got them, thank you, Drake.'

Daborn lowered his binoculars and raised his right arm, holding up his scarf. 'Forward!'

The first of the tanks began to roll up the hill. There were a dozen heavy Matilda Mark II machines, then a whole line of the narrow Mark I A11s. Added to their column were half a dozen French Somua tanks that they had picked up along the way, all eager for a crack at the enemy.

A clashing salvo rocked the air as the line of heavy tanks fired their two-pounders towards the German gun emplacements. Drake knew that the antitank shells the British tanks used would be ineffective against soft targets – they were essentially just giant bullets, and for some reason best known to the Chiefs of Staff, they carried no high explosive. But the racket they made had a moral effect, and the French Somuas joined in, firing HE.

Drake looked back towards the village, wondering if Lyle-Smith had been right. If so, then somewhere in there was the German agent, and Standartenführer Obenauer of the Sicherheitsdienst des Reichsführers-SS. Drake's stomach tightened uneasily. Irrationally, he found the prospect of searching for the enemy agent more uncomfortable, more alarming than the firefight itself. If the major was right, the fate of nations would be hanging on his actions here. A detonation hit one of the buildings in the village, and it went up in a cascade of bricks and fire and smoke.

Colonel Daborn waved his silk scarf onward. Engines bellowed, and the tanks clattered up the slope. *Gwendoline*, *Thunder*, *Galahad*, *Victoria*, *Trafalgar*, and a host of others opened their formation out into a V-shape, line-abreast. The heavy tanks surged through saplings, flattening undergrowth. Tracks churned through broken stumps and branches, chewing up foliage. Machine guns rattled, spitting fire towards the village at the top of the hill.

The German positions lit up once again, returning fire as the tanks came into view. The hidden machine gun nests showed themselves. Antitank cannons thumped. Tracer shells streaked down across the field.

Bullets clanged and sparked off the tank hulls. Shells hit with mighty anvil blows, but the Matildas' three-inch thick steel armour held firm.

Behind the Matildas, the second line of A11 two-man tanks advanced slowly. Their Vickers guns flickered, spraying the German positions with indirect fire as they crawled up the shallow hill. To their left, the group of French Somua cavalry tanks went racing away, using their greater speed to chase around the flanks.

Drake's two remaining carriers followed the ponderous British heavy tanks, keeping in their cover. German bullets sparked off the machines in front and spun away to whoop madly, dangerously overhead. Drake stared into the smoke and the flickering gunfire. He steeled himself for what was coming. Ahead, the line of British machines advanced, with the *Gwendoline* at the apex of the *V*.

Colonel Daborn stood erect in his turret amid the crash and thunder of enemy gunfire. Like some great figure from a bygone age, he was leading from the sharp end. He waved his silk scarf onwards, and the tanks surged forwards up the hill.

Chapter 25

The German antitank battery fired a stinging salvo. Shells screamed down towards the British tanks and hit in staggering detonations that burst like firecrackers, but the heavily armoured machines took the punishment and simply kept rolling on. In the village, behind garden walls, or hidden in outbuildings and houses, the German gunners reloaded. Flames flashed and jabbed. The crack and thud of cannon fire shook the air. Smoke billowed, obscuring the view. Shells streaked down towards the tanks then exploded in bright, sparking flares, or spun off, howling away. The Matildas' cast steel shells seemed to be impervious to anything the light antitank guns could throw at them. And Drake's two little carriers stayed firmly in the cover of the tanks.

Bullets and shells ricocheted in every direction. The lane fizzed and hummed with automatic fire. Under the constant hits from tracer rounds and shell strikes, the stores and canvas bundles strapped to the outside of the tank hulls smouldered, then burst into flames.

Through the smoke, Drake saw that the French tanks had dashed around both flanks of the village. Another salvo of German guns crashed out and as the range shortened, the firing intensified towards the British tanks. In response, the massed machine guns from the great line of tank turrets now flickered and crackled. At short range, the Vickers guns on the A11 tanks were deadly. Cooled by water-filled jackets, the Vickers could keep up firing all day and never overheat.

Tracer bullets ripped through clouds of dust and fumes, leaving glowing, eddying trails in their wake. Machine-gun fire tore into the buildings of the village. Roof tiles shattered, stones clashed down, plaster stripped from the walls as the rounds skittered madly through the streets. The SS troopers fought doggedly, but the firepower of the tanks was overwhelming. Within moments, all through the hamlet of Simencourt, German soldiers began to fall.

Peering through a break in the smog, Drake saw enemy gun crews reloading in a frenzy. He let loose a burst from his Bren, but the smoke closed in again, glowing red as cannon muzzles spat back in desperate counterfire. Streaming lights of tracer lashed down the smoky slope, flaring into impacts on British armour. The kit on more than half the leading tanks was up in flames now. Fumes streamed out behind them in billowing black clouds, and a stench of burning canvas filled the air.

Ahead, the *Gwendoline* kept crawling on towards the village. White blasts of high explosive threw up plumes of smoke and soil in front of her tracks. Shells screeched towards the tanks, and those that missed came on, plunging and skipping across the ground towards the frail armour of the *Mickey Mouse*. Drake peered through the steel-plated gunslit at the front of the carrier and hunched down into the narrow seat. From the line of Matilda tanks, two-pounders crack-thumped in staggering volleys. Shells whipcracked, screaming, into gun pits and buildings. Bullet strikes from German machine guns peppered the tanks' armour plating. Spent rounds pinged off in all directions. Fires raged on the tank hulls from their burning stores, but still the great tanks crawled on.

Shell splinters clashed into the armour of Drake's carrier. Red-hot shards of shrapnel hissed angrily overhead. German gunners poured their fire down in a relentless fury, each crew desperately loading and firing shot after shot. Drake clawed numbly at the carrier's steelwork, hands tight as piano wire. As the tanks closed the distance, the firing grew to a mad frenzy. Bullets swarmed through the acrid fumes, and the stench of burning choked the air.

They were near enough now that the German guns at the edges of the village could fire laterally into the British flanks. Drake saw there were scores of German soldiers in foxholes and machine gun pits, peppering at the machines with flashing small arms and light weapons. Their bullets had little effect on the heavy armour, but the rounds ripped into the carrier's side, denting the thin steel plate in a hideous jangling din.

MacTaggart's eyes gleamed as he sucked air in through his front teeth. He glanced across. 'Keep your head down. It's liable to get dangerous now, sir.'

Drake would have laughed if he could have moved his jaw, but the tension had wired it shut. Ahead of them, the second line of tanks, the narrow A11s, came into their own. Useless against enemy armour, they were designed for just this kind of slow, murderous warfare. The Vickers guns arced wave upon wave of bullets at the enemy positions, shredding window frames and spraying death into the village buildings. Drake saw German soldiers diving into the gun pits for cover. The machine gun rounds followed, and for the enemy gunners it was murder. They had nowhere to run. A gun layer fell, ripped in half by interlocking streams of fire. Another crewman looked in puzzled shock as a stream of bullets tore off his hand. Despite the onslaught, the German antitank gun crews maintained their fire drill, and kept doggedly shooting back.

At the edge of the village, a German *Stabsscharführer* raced to the nearest PAK gun. He cast the dead body of the gun layer aside. He loaded the next shell himself, spun the elevation screw. Aimed over the sight wires, jerked back the firing lever, and the cannon thumped. The shell streaked into the hull of one of the leading tanks and exploded in a white-hot flash. But still the tank, blazing fire, billowing fumes from its hull, came clanking on towards the German lines. The *Stabsscharführer* watched in dismay, then grimly snatched up another shell and slammed it into the breech. The leading tanks were only fifty yards from the edge of the village now. The *Stabsscharführer* jerked the firing lever back without aiming, but the British tanks just kept rolling on.

Cannons cracked. Shells ripped through the smoke. All around the village, flame streaked from hidden muzzles. Machine guns juddered and great clashes split the air as high explosives burst in shock after white-hot shock. The British tanks were unstoppable now. Protected by almost-impenetrable armour, the machine guns traversed left and right in deadly, killing sweeps.

A German *Schütze* crawled out of his foxhole. He stared for a split second at the blazing tanks. He threw down his rifle, turned his back, and ran for his life. Drake watched him disappear through the smog. And from covered positions in buildings and behind garden walls, one after another, the dark figures of the German soldiers began to turn and flee.

'They're running!' Drake yelled. A wave of exultation surged through him. He signalled to the other carriers. 'Floor it, Sergeant. Go, go, go! We're going in!'

MacTaggart stomped his foot down, and the carrier bucked as it accelerated. From the smoking, shattered buildings, more German soldiers turned their backs and ran. Drake squeezed the trigger on his Bren and watched as the enemy fell. The cold heat of battle was on him. They were in the killing zone now. He had no time to think, just fire, fire, reload and fire again in a haze of rage and terror. Drake's finger kept clawing at the trigger until he realised the magazine was empty. He smacked it out with his right hand, slotted in a new one with his left. He squinted through the gunsight. A German gunner, face clear at thirty yards now. He's a young man, a *Standartenjunker,* an officer-cadet. The Bren chugs again, and Drake's hands seem to work it of their own accord. The man goes down in a spray of red. It's terrible. Murderous. Sickening. But it's do or die. There's no time for sympathy. *Kill or be killed.*

From the back of the carrier, Salter was firing his rifle and calling out a prayer between each slamming shot. 'The Lord is my shepherd,' he shouted. 'I shall not want'. The muzzle crashed above Drake's head. 'He maketh me to lie down in green pastures.' Salter snapped the bolt forward, charging the chamber. 'He leadeth me beside the still waters.' The harsh snap of the .303 and another SS *Schütze* fell as Salter kept on chanting out his psalm.

The stench of alkaline fumes, the tang of hot oil. Drake's blood surged. In his hands, the Bren chugged round after round after round with a thumping racket, a repeating *bom-bom-bom-bom-bom.*

The gun's butt hammered into Drake's shoulder but he couldn't feel a thing. The murderous instinct was screaming inside his head. MacTaggart hurtled the carrier towards the village, all thoughts of personal safety gone to the wind. Ahead of them, the German soldiers started pouring out of the houses and gardens and foxholes, running, fleeing for safety. The British tanks showed no mercy. Their machine guns swept pitilessly across the backs of the escaping men.

Through the swirling smog, Drake saw the dark maw of a German antitank cannon muzzle as it traversed around and came to rest, aiming right towards them. Behind the gun shield, exhausted, blackened, a face appeared through the clouds of smoke.

The German *Stabsscharführer* screamed obscenities as he loaded. Drake's teeth ground together. There was no time. Nowhere to go but onwards, faster, ever faster. MacTaggart stamped on the throttle pedal and the carrier accelerated. Drake's muscles tensed for impact. He gazed ahead, face aching with terror, staring at the hideous black circle of the cannon muzzle which was tracking their path as they sped towards the German line.

Drake fired his Bren. Sparks flew from the German gun shield. The *Stabsscharführer* slammed the breech and reached for the firing lever. No time to aim now, the target was almost at the end of his barrel. The world slowed to a split second of motion. Drake could see it all so clearly, he was staring into the enemy's red-rimmed eyes.

The German gunner jerked back his arm. Drake saw a flash of light. The carrier slammed backwards, stopped in its tracks, in a crushing, tearing din. Fragments spun off in all directions. The front of the cab punched inwards. Red-hot leaves of metal seared into the space between the two men. A split second later and the engine behind them exploded as the fuel lines caught. Drake threw himself bodily from the machine.

On the ground, he pushed himself up, then staggered to his feet. He caught a glimpse of the *Gwendoline* as the heavy tank ploughed on through the German defensive line. Daborn was still standing upright in the turret. The great machine ran over the antitank cannon, and the steel tracks bent the barrel like a straw. The tank rolled on and the *Stabsscharführer* turned desperately to flee, but in his haste he fell. A ghastly scream shrilled out through the village, then abruptly cut off as the *Gwendoline's* track went over him.

MacTaggart grabbed Drake's arm, grinning madly. 'That was a rare one, alright. You're not going to get sick on me, are you now, sir?'

Drake rubbed at his face, shaking off the spinning nausea that was going round and round inside. He looked at the *Mickey Mouse* and guessed that the armour piercing shell had gone right through the middle and lodged in the engine block. The carrier went up in a searing ball of fire. Hooper, slumped over in the back, was already dead. Private Salter stood nearby with an expression like a scalded cat, but seemed otherwise unharmed.

Drake gazed through the swirling smoke. They'd broken the perimeter, and the tanks were now pouring into the village. The Germans were on the run. The last surviving carrier, *Dobbin*, had shot ahead, following the tanks as they pushed on, chasing the German infantry into the village. He caught a glimpse of Private Butcher, standing up in the carrier's back, spraying German soldiers with bursts from his Bren.

The din of battle was moving away from them now as the tanks overran more German positions. From all around, from cottages and foxholes, came screams and groans of badly wounded men. Three German soldiers ran down a lane between the buildings. Drake let them go. The tanks would find them soon enough.

Drake stood over a German machine gunner, dead in the road, eyes staring at the sky. A gleaming skull and crossbones grinned up from the man's collar tab. *Find the SS Totenkopf, and you'll find Agent Viper.* The major's words danced around like devils in his mind.

He retrieved his Bren gun from where it lay on the ground next to the burning carrier, then he slapped MacTaggart's shoulder.

'That was the easy part,' he said, and they broke into a run.

Chapter 26

The British tanks rolled through the village of Simencourt, chasing down any signs of the enemy. Machine guns spat streams of chattering bullets at the low, single-storied houses where groups of SS soldiers were trying to hang on. The attack had seemed to take an age, but it was in reality no more than twenty minutes. Drake and MacTaggart, now bereft of transport, climbed aboard a heavy Matilda tank as it rumbled into the village.

'Salter!' MacTaggart bellowed. The young, blond-haired private was staring at the devastation as if in a dream. 'Get your backside up here, laddie. *Toute suite!*'

At MacTaggart's words, Salter appeared to see them for the first time. He ran after the tank and climbed on. His jaw was still moving, silently now, as he mouthed the words of the psalm.

The heavy tank rolled noisily along the main road into the village. They passed farm buildings, cottages and stable entrances, then veered left towards the spire of a church. A French Somua tank was firing high explosive at the church tower, trying to dislodge a machine gun nest. At the far end of the village, the main body of Royal Tank Regiment was ploughing through the German encampment, a field full of rectangular tents and *Zeltbahn* bivouacs. SS officers were screaming and shouting orders. The German troops were running madly this way and that.

Drake saw that, two hundred yards away, an aerial mast rose up twenty or thirty feet above the tents.

'Salter, stay here and try to find the other men,' he ordered. 'MacTaggart – you're with me.'

The two men jumped down, hit the ground running, and dashed along a passage between the lines of tents. They had to be careful now. British infantry tanks were steamrolling through the camp, oblivious to the flimsy shelters. Machine guns flickered, and the tracks flattened anybody unlucky enough to be caught inside the tents. Drake saw an SS trooper cranking the starting handle of an Opel lorry, in his haste getting thrown back by the sudden catch of the engine.

A Matilda tank clattered through the lines of tents. Machine guns rattled, and tracer rounds set fire to the canvas. It was chaos. Some of the British tanks still had burning stores on their hulls, and fires were catching everywhere across the field. The petrol tank on an Opel lorry went up in a whoosh of flame. A German soldier staggered across Drake's path, eyes wide in alarm, and moved to bring his rifle up. Drake shot him with a thumping burst from his Bren.

'That way!' Drake pointed to the tall aerial mast that was still visible above the fire and smoke. There was a cluster of vehicles, tents and awnings all under camouflaged netting. Signalmen and officers were frantically pouring petrol onto piles of burning paperwork in braziers and bonfires. There was an eight-wheeled armoured command car with a large, wireless frame antenna above the superstructure. From the rear of the vehicle protruded the telescopic aerial mast they had seen. There was a web of smaller antennae and tether cables splayed out from the top. The crew were frantically trying to release the cables and lower the mast. Drake raced across the grass towards them, MacTaggart at his heels.

German signalmen were running in and out of the tents, smashing up their wireless equipment with axes and rifle butts. A chain of men was passing out heaps of paper, throwing maps and charts onto the blazing bonfires, and pouring on more fuel. Flames roared six feet high. Ash and shreds of burning paper billowed skywards, and the fumes were everywhere. A German transport lorry was driving away, packed full of soldiers and signals equipment. Drake shook himself, trying to think straight, trying not to get sucked into the madness. He moved quickly towards a large, rectangular signals tent that stood next to the eight-wheeled radio car.

The tent was large, and as yet untouched by the marauding British tanks. Drake pressed the muzzle of his Bren through the flaps of the entrance. A German stick grenade came tumbling out to land beside his boots. He gazed at the grenade for a split second, then kicked it neatly back inside the tent.

He dived to the floor, pulling MacTaggart with him. 'Get down!'

The tent flashed bright green as the grenade cracked open inside. The canvas ripped and was splattered with blood. Head ringing from the detonation, Drake pushed himself back to his feet.

Inside was a slaughterhouse. The bodies of German signalmen lay strewn across tables and chairs, killed or knocked out by the burst of their own grenade. Upturned braziers were still burning, stuffed with maps and charts. Smashed kerosene lamps littered the tables and the floor. Drake's eyes burned from the acrid fumes as he looked in vain – but they were all SS soldiers, no sign of a man in civilian clothing. No sign of Agent Viper. He cursed and pushed his way past an upturned desk, but a machine pistol raised itself from behind a pile of German corpses. Drake kicked the desk over towards it and the jabber of bullets went high.

A colossal figure in SS uniform stood up, casting off the dead German soldiers that had covered him. His face was overgrown, with a bony ridge across his eyebrows and a heavy, jutting jaw. He was so tall that his helmet brushed the roof of the tent, and he was twice as broad as a normal soldier. He was the biggest man that Drake had ever seen.

The big German's belt was stuffed with stick grenades, and he held an MP40 submachine gun in one hand like a pistol. Drake squeezed the trigger on his Bren, but it clicked – empty. *Christ.* He leapt away as the German giant's muzzle flickered, and bullets tore into the furniture behind him. He scrambled out under the ripped canvas opening, ran and dived behind the cover of a burning Opel lorry outside.

The big German came rushing out of the tent. Drake saw that he was in the uniform of a *Scharführer*, a section leader, the SS equivalent of a sergeant. Throwing himself flat on the ground behind the truck, Drake pulled his sidearm from its holster and fired the revolver towards the big man's legs. The German sergeant sprung away with surprising speed, and the shots went wide.

Drake heard a loud clatter and the grunt of a diesel engine. A narrow, two-man A11 tank veered, clanking, through the gap between the lorries and a row of tents, Vickers firing constantly. The German sergeant dodged behind the slow-moving tank, pulled the cord on a stick grenade and shoved it into the smoke launcher that was fixed to the side of the turret. Four seconds later the grenade went off with a shattering detonation, and the tank stalled, spewing fumes. The Scharführer fired his machine gun again, using the armoured vehicle for cover. He kept firing until the gun stuttered, magazine empty. He cast it to the ground.

He picked up a spade, left on the grass near the tethers of the aerial mast, and came running, his rugged face snarling as he let out a roar. He swung a huge arm, and the shovel blade whipped under the Opel lorry's chassis. Drake jerked back and felt the wind of it passing only inches from his face.

'Komm raus, kleines Schwein!' the giant boomed, shoving the spade under the chassis again. It gouged into the dry earth as Drake backed away. 'Come out, little pig!'

The shovel jabbed in again and Drake rolled away just in time. With a guttural sound the huge German pulled the weapon back again for another swing. But as he drew the shovel back, MacTaggart appeared behind him and hooked it with his rifle strap. The old sergeant heaved, pulling the big man off balance, then went in for him with his knife.

Drake scrabbled out from behind the lorry as MacTaggart lunged towards the enormous German sergeant. The big man shoved MacTaggart away, jerked his spade free, and slammed the haft towards the old sergeant's face.

Drake fired his revolver as he ran, the bullet ricocheting loudly off the shovel's blade. Then, through the open flaps of the smoke-filled tent, he saw there was a small German officer inside, hastily searching through a pile of papers on the ground between the upturned desks.

The man wore *pince-nez* glasses and had razor-cut hair beneath his cap. He seemed unthreatening, like nothing more than a harmless German shopkeeper. He was stuffing a thick ream of papers into a black leather briefcase. His drab, grey uniform had a black diamond patch on its sleeve, and on the patch were embossed the silver letters *SD*.

Chapter 27

DRAKE COCKED THE HAMMER on his revolver and carefully pulled aside the loose awning of the tent. Smoke billowed out from the fires within.

'Standartenführer Obenauer, I presume,' Drake said. He gestured with the revolver. '*Hände hoch!*'

The man looked up from his crouching position. He stood slowly, keeping both hands half-raised, pale palms towards Drake's face. Behind the glasses, his eyes moved disconcertingly around the tent as though following an invisible fly.

He spoke in precise, lightly accented English. 'And may I have the pleasure of your name?'

Drake gestured with the revolver. 'No you may not. Bring the briefcase. You're coming with me.'

Hermann Obenauer smiled. That is to say, his mouth widened, cheeks stretched, but his eyes remained cold, detached, and feral. What was lacking was any semblance of human warmth. He flicked his right arm out, and a small automatic pistol appeared from the sleeve of his jacket. Drake saw the movement almost too late. The German officer fired. Flame jetted from the muzzle, oddly bright in the green shade of the tent, and only a desperate lunge saved Drake from a bullet to the face. He felt the whipcrack of the shot as it skimmed past his cheek. He stumbled back, momentarily off balance. Obenauer snatched up the black leather briefcase from the ground then fired again as he backed away out of the far side of the tent.

Drake chased after him, revolver at the ready, pushing through the tent flaps, but his face was met by the crashing fist of the huge German Scharführer. He staggered back, gasping, head lit up with tiny, flashing lights. The big German came storming into the tent after him, and hurled a typewriter from a smashed-up desk. It hit Drake in the guts, and knocked him painfully backwards. He reached out his left hand to steady himself and scorched it on a burning brazier, piled with smouldering papers. He fell, dropping the revolver. He quickly reached for it, but an enormous jackboot slammed down on his right wrist, pinioning it there. The colossal German sergeant grinned as he raised the typewriter again, ready to bring it smashing down.

Drake reached out his left hand and snatched up an unlit kerosene lamp, and hurled it at the big man's head. The glass broke and the fuel splattered over his helmet and shoulders. Then Drake gripped the leg of the burning brazier. He heaved it up towards the German sergeant's face.

The burning ash went into the big man's eyes. The spilled kerosene caught fire, and the man's hair went up in a whoosh. He stumbled back, hands beating at his face. Released, Drake jumped to his feet. He turned sideways, kicked away the central tent pole, and the material billowed down around them. The German sergeant staggered away, thrashing madly at his flaming skin. His hands caught fire. Drake backed away and crawled out under the canvas flap.

The tent collapsed, shooting out a cloud of ash. Burning scraps of paper billowed into the open air. The canvas smouldered for a moment before bursting into flames. Trapped inside the burning material, the huge German sergeant flailed around, then let out a terrible, muted bellow. But Drake's eye was caught by a movement on the far side of the tent.

Through the smoke and fire, he saw Obenauer step up onto the footplate of the eight-wheeled armoured radio car. The German officer's pistol cracked again, and the shot went by as Drake spun away into the smoke. He fired at Obenauer, too late, as the man scrambled into the interior.

The eight-wheeler's engine roared, the wheels dug in, and the radio car lurched forwards. The mast antenna was still erect and held by cable tethers which were pegged into the ground. As the vehicle moved, the cables began to strain. The tyres bit into the grass. The mast bent, then snapped away. The massive eight-wheeled car surged forwards, gathering speed, dragging cables and tent ropes behind it. Drake fired the remaining rounds from his revolver but they sparked off the steel armour. The broken antenna retracted jerkily back down.

He ran after the vehicle, but it easily pulled away from him through the burning camp. Then a machine gun snout poked from a vision slit at the rear. It jabbered orange flame as it fired. Drake threw himself to the ground and rolled into cover behind an abandoned German transport lorry. He watched in frustration as the eight-wheeler accelerated away.

After a moment, he ran back to MacTaggart and bent over the old Scotsman's prone form.

'You alright, Sergeant?'

MacTaggart stirred slowly, then rubbed at a bump on his head. 'Naught to write home about. Och, and I almost had him, sir. I was only just getting started, but he caught me off guard.'

The sergeant seemed no worse than usual. Drake shook his head and smiled.

The command tent had collapsed by now and was blazing in a heap on the ground. Drake jogged towards it, but it was impossible to get too close. There was a searing whoosh as another kerosene lamp inside exploded. Drake rubbed at his face, feeling the heat of the fire, then ran his fingers beneath his helmet, through his tangled, smoky hair.

On the grass, bonfires of maps and charts were smouldering, burnt up now, filling the air with an acrid stench. There seemed to be nothing of any value left.

'Bugger it!' he shouted. He kicked over a brazier that had been covered by a flap of smouldering canvas. The material must have stopped the air getting to the fire, because some of the papers inside were still only half burnt. Drake's gaze fixed on them for a moment before his brain slotted into gear.

The papers, exposed to oxygen once more, burst into flames. He lunged in and snatched the top sheet from the pile. He used his jacket to smother the burning edges of the paper.

'Quick, Sergeant! Put that fire out!'

MacTaggart came swiftly over from where he'd been examining something that was lying on the ground. He tried to stamp the flames out, but it was too late now. There was a stink of petrol or kerosene and, in seconds, the entire wad went up in a blaze.

Drake held onto the single top sheet that he'd saved. His head was spinning. Obenauer had got away, and there was no sign of any civilian agent. Drake was exhausted from the battle, from lack of sleep, from the strain of war. Now that the frenzied attack was over, a pounding headache was closing in.

He watched the distant shape of the eight-wheeled command car as it sped down into the next shallow valley, where the routed German troops were now also heading. He saw the last carrier, *Dobbin,* was returning, but he ignored it, and looked down and stared at the paper in his hand.

It was blackened all around the edges. But something was typed in the centre of the page in German blackletter script.

OPERATIONSBEFEHL DÄMMERUNG

Operational Order *Dämmerung*.

And *Dämmerung* meant Nightfall, Twilight, Dusk.

Drake grabbed MacTaggart's sleeve and began to pull him towards the oncoming carrier.

'We've got to catch that bloody radio car!'

As the *Dobbin* drew up next to them, Drake started pulling at the men who were crowded inside. 'Out! Now! All of you! Find your own way back to battalion!'

Leighton and Butcher clambered out, followed by Pritchard, Davy and Stoker. Private Salter seemed only too glad to be out of it. Leighton shrugged and spat down onto the ground.

Moments later, Drake was pinned back to the seat as MacTaggart stomped on the pedal. The carrier *Dobbin*, with the two men in it, shot away.

Chapter 28

BEAUMETZ-LÈS-LOGES, NEAR ARRAS, FRANCE - 17:50HRS

The *Dobbin* hurtled down the grass towards the foot of the hill. Drake scanned the terrain ahead. Half a mile away, on the other side of the valley, the routed troops of the SS Totenkopf were streaming up the next hill towards the village of Beaumetz-lès-Loges. There was a bottleneck of German vehicles where lorries, motorcycles and sidecar combinations, whoever and whatever had escaped the first tank attack, were all vying to pass through a field gate to get up the hill. There were half-tracks towing guns, and men on foot, all trying to get through the gate. Drake picked out the tall superstructure and bedframe antenna of the eight-wheeled command car, caught in the slow-moving queue.

'They're stuck in a jam,' he said. 'We can catch them.'

The *Dobbin* quickly overhauled the slowest of the British tanks. The drivers and gunners of the two-man A11 machines had their hatches open. The crews' faces were blackened by smoke, and the small tanks seemed impossibly cramped inside. The carrier's Ford engine thundered gamely as they shot past them, and MacTaggart kept the pedal to the floor.

They soon caught up with the heavy Mark II Matilda tanks, twin diesel engines chopping loudly, tracks clattering as they ploughed up the steepening hill. The routed German infantry were still fleeing. Colonel Daborn was straining like a dog on a leash, as if he could will their heavy machines to move faster. His smoke-stained silk scarf fluttered around his neck. Behind the *Gwendoline*, the *Galahad*, *Thunder*, *Trafalgar* and the others were following up the hill.

'That's the ticket, Drake! Run down those hares!' he shouted.

Drake waved a hand in a loose salute, and the carrier sped on. The *Dobbin* tore along a farm track and began climbing the hill towards the next ridge. From where they were in the depression in the valley, the top of the ridge was out of sight once more. But the retreating soldiers of the Totenkopf were not. Drake watched the field gate. Foot soldiers were running, leaping over hedges and walls in their panic to get away, as the vehicles shoved and shunted ever more urgently forward through the narrow gap. Drake saw why. The French Somua cavalry tanks were rapidly closing in from the right flank. A cannon cracked, and a high-explosive shell burst close to the eight-wheeled car. Reibel machine guns on the Somuas opened fire, and the fleeing Totenkopf soldiers began to fall.

'Faster!' Drake hissed. 'Now's our chance!'

MacTaggart pushed the carrier on, working the gears hard. The pale faces of the SS footsoldiers turned back in agonised fear, seeing the tanks in pursuit. As Drake closed in, he could see a German officer shouting orders from the top of the big, eight-wheeled command car. It had to be Obenauer. The armoured radio car rammed into a troop transport that was stuck in front, using its weight to shove the lighter vehicle out of the way. Rounds from the French tanks' machine guns skidded off the radio wagon's sloped glacis armour. With a final shove, the eight-wheeler tore through the gate, and, freed at last from the constraints of the queue, began to accelerate quickly up the hill.

German faces turned back in terror as the French tanks gave chase up through the fields, like cavalry of old, mowing the panicked infantry down as they ran. Drake grimaced as he saw one of the French tanks go straight over the form of a fallen man. Another German soldier leapt out of the way, only to be gunned down by the machine guns of the other tanks that were following. It was a slaughter, and for a moment it seemed as though the entire German army was on the run.

When they came to the wall, the French tanks simply burst through the stonework. Their machine guns scattered the routed SS troops, who ran in all directions across the hill. By now the German vehicles had either got through the gate or were burning. The little *Dobbin* raced past them, and Drake scanned the chaos up ahead.

They were gaining on the eight-wheeler now. He fired the Bren at the vehicle's tyres, but it had no effect. He sent in another burst, the rounds this time skittering and sparking off the armour. The command car was climbing rapidly up the hill ahead of them now, and it went over a crest and momentarily disappeared from sight.

Seconds later, the *Dobbin* came out of the saddle of the valley and followed over the crest, its spirited V8 engine pulling them away now from the first of the pursuing French tanks. A series of fields stretched out before them, sloping gently upwards towards a distant, tree-lined ridge. A clacking thump, and a shell shot past from a French tank to hit an escaping German lorry. It exploded in an acid-yellow flash. Seconds later, the *Dobbin* rattled past the blazing wreck. Drake's eyes were fixed only on the radio command car. He took a grenade from a box in the front of the carrier. He could feel the tension rising in his chest as they closed in.

'Get as near as you can!' he yelled to MacTaggart.

The engine chugged and shook the carrier as MacTaggart worked it past its limit, and the little *Dobbin* gave them a final burst of speed. When they were twenty yards away, Drake stood up and pulled the pin on the grenade. A machine gun fired from a pistol port in the back of the eight-wheeler's superstructure. MacTaggart swerved the carrier just as Drake lobbed the bomb. The grenade flew through the air, and dropped towards the car's open superstructure, but fell short and clanged into the metal side, bouncing twice before exploding on the ground in a hard, flat crack.

'Try again!' MacTaggart shouted, but Drake's eye was caught by a flash from the distant ridgeline. A second later, a shell exploded into the field thirty yards to their left.

Another crash of high explosive threw flames and dirt up in the air in front of them. Drake snatched up his field glasses.

'Christ,' he said, under his breath. He yelled to MacTaggart, 'Stop!'

The sergeant hauled the carrier swiftly to a halt.

As the German command car pulled away, Drake stared at the ridge through the lenses. There was an impression of movement in the treeline. He couldn't see much, but what he could see was enough to send a shot of ice cascading through his veins. There were the unmistakable silhouettes of German vehicles towing trailers into position. The dark, fleeting shapes of men moving rapidly through the trees. He focused the lenses. A line of antitank guns was being set up all along the ridge. A flash from the treeline, and Drake had the impression of a line of fire streaking towards them. A shell shrilled past, only inches from his head. A salvo followed. Detonations rocked the field.

Drake glanced back over his shoulder towards the valley, where the British tanks were still crawling slowly upwards. It was obvious they couldn't see the top of the ridge from where they were. Drake had a bad feeling. A very bad feeling. For a moment he was torn. Then he touched MacTaggart's shoulder.

'Turn it around.'

MacTaggart seemed startled. 'What about the radio car, sir?'

Another shell screeched in and exploded nearby. Drake looked from the tanks to the ridge and back again. He saw another glimpse of German antitank guns, wheeled into position, the maws of their muzzles gaping. Half-tracks, with anti-aircraft cannon mounted on the back. The German stragglers were all now racing for the protection of the distant ridgeline.

'Turn around,' Drake said once more. He sank back into the gunner's seat of the carrier with a terrible sense of deflation. 'It's a bloody trap.'

Chapter 29

THE GREAT SWARM OF British tanks came rumbling up the saddle of the hill towards the first crest. They were hidden from the German defences by the dead ground, and many of them had their hatches open, letting in fresh air. Colonel Daborn was standing up through the turret of the *Gwendoline*.

'You have to turn around,' Drake shouted, his voice half-lost in the deafening chug and clatter of the motors. 'They're waiting for you with a line of antitank guns up on the ridge.'

'Antitank guns?' Daborn contemplated the horizon. 'They're ineffective. My orders are to attack.'

Drake felt a growing sense of dread. He ordered MacTaggart to bring the carrier, *Dobbin*, closer. The tank's hull was blackened from where the canvas equipment had burned half away. The thick steel armour was pitted with bullet and shell strikes, but it was still intact.

He stood up in the carrier and shouted up to the colonel, 'They've got Flak guns, sir!'

'Calibre?'

Drake hesitated. 'Small calibre, sir. But their position. The ridge–'

The colonel held up his hand, cutting Drake off. 'We have no chance of flanking them, they'll simply watch us coming and turn their guns. That leaves only two options. Attack, or retreat.' He glanced at the pennant of the Royal Tank Regiment that was fluttering from the antenna. 'We shall not retreat.'

'They're waiting. It'll be murder, sir.'

'My orders are quite clear. If we can break through, we stand a chance of cutting off Jerry's entire advance. Whether or not we are likely to succeed, you must know that it's our only hope. You've done your job. Now we'll do ours. These machines will stand up to all but the largest munitions. So we shall press the attack.'

Drake sank slowly back down into his seat.

Up on the tank turret, the colonel barked into his intercom. 'Driver – Advance!'

The engine note of the heavy Matilda rose, and the tracks rolled forwards appreciably faster. Drake fixed his gaze rigidly ahead. The tanks were approaching the crest of the slope now. It was an impressive sight. A dozen heavy Matilda Mark IIs leading thirty or more of the smaller, two-man machines. *Gwendoline* led the advance. *Galahad* was nearby on the left of the inverted *V*, *Thunder* on the right. Directly behind was *Trafalgar*. *Lionheart*, *Victoria* and *Harry* brought up the flanks.

MacTaggart gave Drake a quizzical look. 'Sir?'

Drake shook his head, but he knew that the colonel was right. Whatever the odds, no matter how slim, they would never get a better chance than right now. A chance to beat the enemy on the field of battle. A chance to seize the intelligence that was so desperately needed. There could be no other choice. He grabbed some spare ammo boxes from the back. 'Follow them, Sergeant. Obenauer's up there. We've got to try.'

In the *Gwendoline*, Colonel Daborn turned around in his turret until he was facing the line of his tanks, and he raised a hand.

'The German guns are waiting,' he called out. Every man strained to hear his words through the noise of the engines. '*Fear Naught* is our motto! We shall not falter, and we shall strike them down!'

A shout went up from the tank crews.

The colonel turned and waved his silk scarf onwards. And as the *Gwendoline* and the other machines of the Royal Tank Regiment crested the ridge, the treeline came into view. Flashes sparked from the enemy position as the German antitank cannons fired. And the colonel put his old brass hunting horn to his lips and blew.

Chapter 30

THE PEAL OF THE horn sounded across the hillside. A blistering volley of shellfire erupted from the ridgeline. The crews ducked back into their tanks. Armoured hatches slammed shut with loud clangs. Lines of tracer streaked through the air as incoming shells rained down. Detonations crashed all around. Gouts of fire and smoke and soil shot up where the ordnance detonated on the ground. A shell clanged off the hull of the *Galahad* like the toll of a cathedral bell, and it whooped off, spinning away from the glancing blow. Drake ducked down behind the thin armour of the *Dobbin*, and yelled to MacTaggart to get into cover behind the heavy tanks.

The great machines of the Royal Tank Regiment rolled forward, engines growling, tracks clanking loudly, but their guns remained silent. Drake guessed they were more than a thousand yards from the ridge, well out of effective direct machine gun range, and the armour-piercing shells that were all the heavy Matildas carried would be next to useless against soft targets at such a great distance. In contrast, the German artillery had the great advantage of sending high explosive down in deadly, plunging fire.

Sparks flew off the British armour in deafening explosions. The fury of each impact was like a physical blow. Drake clasped his helmet tightly down over his head. As the tanks rolled up the slope, another shattering barrage of gunfire thumped from the ridge. Shells screamed in hard and fast, and detonations rocked the hillside. Impacts slammed into hulls, shells exploding in showers of sparks or crumpling into red-hot balls of steel.

Drake peered ahead through the gunslit on the carrier. Shrapnel and white-hot splinters lanced lethally through the air. The wide fan-shaped formation of the tanks was rattling slowly up the hill in front of them. A shell, overshooting the tanks, shrilled over their heads to hit the field behind them in a cracking, shaking roar. Another detonation sent up spouts of soil and smoke from the ground thirty yards ahead. Drake's entire body began to tense with the strain.

An ominous flicker of rapid Flak fire began on the ridgeline. A split second later, a stunning barrage of shells shrieked in, slamming into the tanks in front with a sound like gravel on shattering glass. The lead tanks were hit by fiery explosions, but, sheathed in clouds of smoke and impervious to the small-calibre shells, they simply rolled on.

Drake grimaced, and kept his head down behind the carrier's thin steel armour, eyes fixed through the letterbox-sized vision slit. His face was aching with the tension. The air smelled foul with oil and smoke and burning canvas as the equipment on the tanks in front of them once again caught fire.

'Satan's blood!' MacTaggart shouted through the maelstrom. 'Can they not go any faster, sir?'

Drake glanced over. His eye was caught by a glint of silver, and he saw the sergeant was wearing a shiny new kilt pin. For a moment he wondered why. Then another salvo flickered from the ridge and all rational thoughts were driven from his mind. A tremendous blast of thunder sounded as a round struck the armour of a nearby tank and screeched along the side of the hull.

Drake watched the small grey shapes of men running up the hill in the distance. The stragglers of the routed SS regiment were making for the gun line on the ridge. German vehicles were churning up the ground as they struggled up the last stretch of the steepening hill. Slowly, the formation of tanks crawled up towards them. A heavy chattering of machine guns began, as some of the two-man A11s began firing their Vickers guns now. They sent up looping parabolas of indirect area fire to rain down onto the German positions in scything, deadly arcs.

Drake snatched up his field glasses. The eight-wheeled command car was racing for the safety of the German gun line. There were flashes of light. A barrage of shells, flying fast and close together, shrieked towards him in a swarm. They hit the heavy tank *Trafalgar* and clashed off in spikes of shrilling, bright fire.

Ahead, a broken-down German lorry, stuck halfway up the hill, was hit by the machine guns of the tanks. It exploded in a fireball. Then a fusillade of jabbing flashes came from the hilltop. A great clanging sounded nearby as a heavy tank flared up in a blistering crack, but the machine just kept clanking forward. The German high-explosive shells were detonating on the outside of the hulls, and were not penetrating the tanks' three-inch-thick steel armour. But the heavy machines were slowing. The hill was deceptive, and the ponderous tanks were climbing more steeply now as they grappled with the slope.

They passed more burning German vehicles. Enemy soldiers lay dead or wounded in the grass where they'd fallen. The tank drivers didn't swerve to avoid them. A man who had escaped the machine guns got to his feet and ran madly for the ridgeline, but the machines of the Royal Tank Regiment had no sympathy. Automatic fire from a dozen tanks cut him to pieces. It was hateful, sickening work. Up ahead, the ridgeline flickered again.

As they closed in, the German cannon fire began in earnest. Shell after shell screeched down towards them. A shell slammed into the *Gwendoline's* steel hull and Drake's ears sang from the noise of the impact. His entire body tensed as small calibre rounds smashed into armoured plate all around.

Drake saw that one of the narrow A11 machines had thrown a track. It was being left behind, a static target, and the crew were crawling away across the field. Ahead, on the hilltop, a half-track mounted with Flak cannons slewed to a stop, and almost immediately the guns burst into frightful life. Flak shells shrieked down in a torrent, screaming in to clash off the tanks in bitter explosions. The weight of German fire was growing now. Shellfire scorched down upon the tanks until it seemed that nothing could withstand its fury. Hit by shell after shell, external aerials and flag masts were shot to pieces, and anything flammable on the outside of the tanks caught fire. Most of them were billowing smoke now as their lashed-on stores burned up, but the heavy tanks' steel armour held firm and they rolled relentlessly on, up the ever-steepening hill.

Flames leapt from the back of the *Gwendoline*. Shells clattered into the steelwork in an endless, agonising din. Drake tried to bring his field glasses up to peer through the carrier's gunslit. He carefully brought the lenses into focus. Something ominous was happening up on the ridge.

Vehicles were reversing. Frantic artillerymen were laying out trails. Officers and men were moving quickly, running through the smoke.

'Gun tractors!' Drake shouted out. 'They're bringing up more guns!'

He adjusted the lenses. In the treeline, enemy gun layers leapt into seats and rapidly wound elevation screws. Loaders ran from half-tracks, carrying one shell at a time. Each shell was the size of a grown man's thigh.

'Field howitzers,' Drake said. He turned to MacTaggart. The old sergeant's face took on a grim, sour look. 'Get me alongside the *Gwendoline*, Sergeant!'

MacTaggart accelerated the little carrier up until it caught the heavy tank. Drake shoved himself up from his seat and, waiting to get his timing right, he leapt from the carrier onto the engine cowling behind the turret. Smoke billowed up into his face, and flames flicked towards his trouser legs. He ignored the searing heat, and leapt forward past the worst of the fire. He drew his revolver and banged its butt onto the turret hatch.

There was no response. He slammed the gun against the metal again and again until the periscope turned. Half the hatch was suddenly flung open. Smoke poured out from inside.

Colonel Daborn peered out from the darkness of the interior. 'What in God's name are you doing?' he shouted.

'Four inchers, sir!' Drake yelled back, pointing. 'Up on the ridge!'

Daborn spun around, peering ahead through his own binoculars. 'Good God,' he said.

Drake knew that a four-inch field howitzer could lob a thirty-three-pound high-explosive shell seven miles through the air in twenty-three seconds. At that range it could blow up trenches, take down bridges, even smash through reinforced concrete walls. But these were going to be fired over open sights at the tanks at virtually point-blank range.

He cupped his hands to bellow through the din of the battle. 'You've got to turn back!'

The tank commander stared forward through the smoke for a moment. Then he shook his head. 'The rear armour is weaker!' he shouted. 'If we turn away, they'll simply pick us off!'

Drake felt his jaw tighten as he realised the colonel was right. They were committed. They simply had no choice except to meet the guns head on.

'Good luck then, sir,' he shouted.

The colonel gave him a quick, grim smile. 'I appreciate the sentiment, Drake. Now be a good chap, and get off my ruddy tank.'

Drake nodded, then ran back over the fiery engine cowling. He leapt awkwardly back down into the carrier.

'We go on,' he shouted to MacTaggart. 'Do or die. It's victory or bust.'

MacTaggart's expression hardened as the little *Dobbin* plunged on into the wreaths of smoke that were now covering the field. They kept close in, behind the heavy machines. The first of the howitzers belched fire from the hilltop. Drake stared into the glow of the smoke. A shell screamed overhead with the sound of an express train. It detonated in the earth close behind them with a terrifying, apocalyptic roar. Drake's entire body ached with the tension. They followed the tanks onwards, towards the very mouth of hell, through the flickering, thundering storm.

Chapter 31

THE TANK DRIVERS WOUND their engines to fever pitch. *Gwendoline*, *Galahad* and *Trafalgar* led the V-formation as they clawed up the hill, giving everything, but it was still too slow. There was a shattering, shocking crash. Drake was thrown back by the heat of the blast. The heavy tank *Thunder* had been hit.

At first, it just meandered to a halt. The turret hatch opened and the commander's head poked out. Then a sheath of flame erupted from inside, enveloping him in a jet of fire. Drake tore his gaze away, looking bleakly ahead. Flare after flare of German muzzle flashes lit the hilltop. The howitzers, thumping steadily now, were hitting their stride. And even through the cacophony of battle, Drake could hear the burning tank commander's scream.

A smoke canister launched from the side of the *Gwendoline's* turret and a fog went up in front of them when it hit the ground. The remaining Matilda tanks followed suit, lobbing canisters in quick succession, creating a wall of smoke between them and the enemy line. Explosions roared all around, buffeting the carrier with shocks from the detonations, but the smoke was screening their advance. The German guns could now only fire blind. The *Dobbin* followed the glow of the burning tanks through grey-brown clouds of smoke.

'Coming into MG direct fire range, sir,' MacTaggart said, his voice strangely precise and calm. 'Now we'll see.'

As the tanks drove into their smoke shield, the machine guns on the heavy Matildas began to fire. Up until now, the British tanks had been impotent, soaking up shell after blistering shellstrike, and just grinding grimly on, unable to directly strike back. But now the machine guns came into their own. The German artillerymen were at a disadvantage, unable to see the tanks in the smoke. But for the machine gunners, it didn't matter. A wall of automatic weapons flickered, plastering the

German ridgeline in area fire. The Vickers guns on the A11 tanks chattered endlessly as they came to bear directly on the enemy. All around them, through the crackling smoke, tracer rounds flashed through the air in a shimmering, growing maelstrom of fire. As suddenly as the tanks had entered the smoke, they burst out of the other side. Drake peered ahead through the line. On the ridge, under blistering machine gun fire, the enemy gunners had started to fall in droves.

Drake ducked as an A11 tank in front of him was hit by a howitzer shell, knocked three yards backwards by the impact. MacTaggart swerved the carrier around as the turret blew off and it went up in a ball of flames.

Machine guns flickered all along the tank line, and strings of tracer streaked murderously through the air. Despite the danger, the German guns kept firing. Half a dozen of the heavy Matilda tanks were still driving, on fire. Drake saw the *Victoria*, smoke pouring off the stores and equipment lashed to its armour, as she rolled gamely on. But scattered behind them, through the smoke and dust, a dozen other tanks were already knocked out. Even losing a track or an engine breakdown made them sitting targets, and that meant death under the ceaseless barrage of the German guns. Shells slammed into steelwork, searching for a weak spot. Drake's hands clamped onto his Bren and he started firing and firing again, arms aching with the strain.

A flitting, searing salvo of Flak shells screeched down from the German ridgeline. They were throwing anything and everything they had at them. The Flak shells hit the hull of the *Gwendoline* in a horrendously deafening clatter. Small-calibre antitank shells shrilled down from the treeline. The armour on the tanks was glowing red hot in patches where the shells hit again and again. Drake kept his head down, helmet clutched tight to his skull. He knew that any single one of the shells could destroy their thin-skinned carrier. A muffled scream suddenly pierced the din of the battlefield as another two-man tank lurched to one side and the engine stalled. He could smell the acrid stench of burning hair and paint.

As they passed the halted machine, Drake heard the driver shrieking. The frontal armour was so hot from repeated strikes that it was melting, caving in on the men inside. It was hell on Earth. Drake forced himself to look away.

The gap between the tanks and the treeline had appreciably narrowed. More smoke canisters shot out from the turrets, obscuring the battlefield, and both sides began once more to fire blind. They were entering the death zone, so close that each side could hardly miss. Drake saw the heavy tank *Victoria* on fire now, buckled to one side. Its nearside track was a mangled mess on the ground.

Machine guns from the British tanks rattled out streams of deadly, hacking rounds towards the trees. A cluster of anti-tank shells slammed in, to crack onto the armoured steel hulls. Drake strained in his seat, just waiting for the one that would hit them – a ricochet, or steel splinter, or a howitzer shell coming over the top. He squeezed himself further down into the footwell, pressed his face down behind the gunshield, jaw clenching, face stretched with the tension. A terrible, rending clash hit the *Galahad*'s turret nearby, but still, somehow, the thick steel armour held, and the machine rumbled bravely on.

Up on the ridge, the German artillerymen gazed in horror as the British tanks came out of the smoke once more, flames pouring from their armour. Despite everything the German gunners had thrown at them, still they kept advancing towards the treeline and the guns. Machine guns flickered from the turrets, reaping into German positions, slaughtering entire gun crews who had no protection from the interlocking, ceaseless fire.

'Keep going!' Drake screamed at the tanks, at MacTaggart, at anybody who might hear him. 'You've got to keep going!' Hunched down, his entire body was cramping with the strain.

And suddenly, one of the German gun crews broke and ran.

'They're turning, sir,' MacTaggart bellowed. 'Look!'

German gun crews began to panic now, seeing their comrades flee, abandoning their guns. Drake felt an urgent, mounting hope as the British tanks came unstoppably on. Through the flashing smoke and the thundering din, he watched as more and more enemy artillerymen began to desert their posts. The rate of shellfire slackened. It felt like the whole field was caught up in a surge of exhilaration, like killing, like victory, like nothing on earth they had ever felt before.

'We're going to bloody do it!' he cried out. 'They're running! Dear God, they're running! Come on!'

MacTaggart, fists clamped to the wheel, gave him a tight, crazed grin. Drake felt the breath catch in his lungs, his heart thudding in his neck. They were going to do it. They were going to break right through the lines. But then one of the big howitzers thumped again, a great gout of fire shot from the muzzle. A terrible *crump-crump* hit nearby and the *Galahad* jumped up in a sheet of flame.

Drake fixed his attention resolutely forward through the carrier's gun-slit. He watched, not understanding. Incomprehensibly, unbelievably, the enemy artillerymen were returning to their posts. A German officer was running along the ridge, screaming orders in a frenzy. The artillerymen were responding, going back to their guns to load and fire again.

Antitank cannons thudded. Flak shells streaked down the hill. Drake flinched as a blast skittered over the tanks in front of them, shells ricocheting in all directions. Everything else was forgotten. Drake's entire world was compressed into a single, frenzied thought: *we've got to break that line.*

On the ridgeline, the German officer was directing each gun to its targets. His actions were having an astounding effect. Instead of fleeing in terror, the German gun crews were now firing faster, ever faster, even as the tanks closed in. It appeared that the enemy, at last, had realised the seriousness of the situation. The British armour was about to break through and cut off their entire advance. After two weeks of easy victories, the Wehrmacht was suddenly under severe threat. They were waking up and fighting for their lives.

Drake pulled up his field glasses. 'Christ, he's a ruddy general!' he shouted.

He dropped the glasses and sighted the Bren. It juddered as he squeezed the trigger, but everything seemed to miss the man on the ridge as he kept running from gun to gun.

The British tanks clawed up the hill, streaming fire from their machine guns. Drake's skull ached, crazed with furious tension. All along the treeline, German artillerymen were hit by machine gun fire and fell, but others came to take their places. Drake fired the Bren, again, again, again, ignoring the overheating barrel. Under enemy fire, regulations went out the window. A German gun loader's face imploded, but a staff officer ran to replace him, picking up the shells himself. They were so close now, both sides enveloped in a rolling, roiling thunder of gun flash and automatic fire, Drake felt he could almost touch them. He saw the general's face work fanatically as he shrieked his orders. His arm chopped down again and again as he screamed out *Feuer! Feuer! Feuer!*

It was obvious that one man on the ridge was turning the tide of the entire battle. Drake emptied the Bren magazine at him but the man seemed possessed, he had a charmed life, and every bullet went wide. The Bren was seriously overheating now.

'I can't hit him!' Drake bellowed in frustration. 'Stop the carrier!'

MacTaggart gawped at him as though he'd just gone mad.

'Stop!' Drake screamed again, and the little carrier crashed to a sudden, rattling halt.

Drake reached into the back and quickly pulled up a Lee Enfield rifle. He checked it was loaded. A single shot could do it. The carrier was a static, stable base now. A single well-aimed bullet could save the battle. It could turn the course of the war around in a day.

The major general was standing next to one of the howitzers, frantically urging his artillerymen on. Flak guns fired from the back of half-track wagons. Shells screamed down and clashed into the tanks. Machine guns replied from turrets, gouging holes in the enemy line as the heavy tanks crawled forwards. Field howitzers thumped, barely able to miss at close range. The *Trafalgar* went up in a raging torch of fire, penetrated by a four-inch shell. All across the field, the British tanks were being decimated. Drake blocked it all out. It all came down to one shot. He set the range to minimum. Racked back the bolt and chambered a round. Focused his mind, pressed his cheek to the stock, and took slow, deliberate aim through the notch of the rearsight. He waited for the German general to align with his frontsight. He raised his aim a fraction to offset the slope of the hill, then exhaled.

He squeezed the trigger.

There was a loud crack and an imperceptible flash at the breech as the propellant ignited. The half-ounce bullet ripped from the muzzle at two and a half thousand feet per second as it flew in an almost flat ballistic curve across the field.

A quarter of a second later, it slowed as it passed through a human skull.

Drake snatched up his field glasses. He felt a rush of fierce joy. On the ridgeline, the German general was nowhere to be seen.

But then the general stood up, drenched in blood and flecks of bone. It seemed he'd bent down to pick up a shell at the exact moment the shot had come through. And in his arms, he held the body of his decapitated *aide-de-camp*. Through sheer bad luck, Drake had shot the wrong man.

On the ridgetop, in the line of trees, the German *Generalmajor* stared back at the British tanks. Drake saw him open his mouth as he jabbed his finger, screaming orders. Drake could almost read the words. '*Nullpunkt! Feuer! Feuer! Feuer!*'

And nearby, close to the eight-wheeled radio car, there was a man in a civilian suit and hat. Drake watched him through the lenses of the field glasses. For a split second, he was frozen with shock. There was no other possible explanation. It was him. *Agent Viper*. Had to be.

Cannon muzzles flashed from the treeline. Drake jerked back into motion. 'Evasive action!' he bellowed. 'Move!'

MacTaggart hauled on the wheel and the carrier skid-turned to the left, as all across the ridge the German guns once more began to erupt in a blistering salvo. Shells screamed in and cracked in Vulcan hammer blows onto the steelwork. A howitzer shell shrilled past the *Dobbin*, shaking the three-ton vehicle with its wind. Lightning flashed through the smoke-stained field as cannons relentlessly barked. Bursts of flame ripped through the smog. More British tanks were hit. Black pillars of smoke obscured the rays of the sun.

Close to the *Gwendoline*, the heavy tank *Lionheart* spun on a thrown track, unable to go on. Caught, static, helpless, the crew tried to bale out as the tank was hit again and again and again. All the while, the ceaseless Vickers machine guns on the two-man A11 tanks were butchering the German gunners. It was simple attrition now. Last man standing would be the victor on the field.

The steel hulls of the tanks rang, struck by a dozen hammerblows every second. Mechanical fires broke out as rubber melted from the heat of the burning hulls. Drake's mind was in a frenzy, delirious with the noise and fear and tension. He couldn't think, he couldn't breathe. All he could do was load and fire the Bren, again and again and again.

'Keep firing!' he screamed towards the tanks. 'Keep firing!'

MacTaggart's face was a mask of grim concentration now. Drake's Bren gun stuttered, overheating as he went through mag after mag. And all along the ridgeline, German artillerymen fell and the counterfire slackened again.

'Keep going! We've just got to keep going!' Drake yelled. It was hell, worse than hell, worse than anything on Earth. They were driving into the jaws of death. His skull was agony, teeth clenched in an unnatural grimace of fury and fear. But all they had to do was keep at it and they'd overrun the line. There were so few of the British tanks left now, but if even a single tank could get in amongst the guns, it would all be over, and the British infantry could follow in and mop it all up. They could still win the battle, they still could turn the war around. They just had to push on and break through. They just had to hang on.

German Flak guns fired with unimaginable speed. Tracer streaked in every direction, spears of fire tearing through the smoke. Through the swirl of dust, through the hellish screech of shellfire, detonations slammed against the *Gwendoline*'s hull. In the *Dobbin*, Drake was in agony, his spine cramped as he bent behind the thin armour plate, his ribcage aching with unbearable strain. The Bren hammered in his hands and he was barely aware he was still firing it. The field was filled with smoke, and everything was burning now. But they were almost there. There were so few men left alive on the German gun line that staff colonels were running with shells in their arms. The major general slammed a gun breech shut and pulled the firing cord himself.

Drake squinted through clouds of blowing smoke. He couldn't see, he couldn't open his lungs. There was nothing that he could do except keep firing, keep holding on. His jaw muscles compressed to wires. Teeth grinding so hard that they cracked. The clash and thunder of the battle was deafening, stultifying, murderous as they came on towards the guns.

He was straining forward in his seat, as though physically willing the tanks on, forward, to break the German line. 'A hundred yards! Ten seconds! We've got them!'

They were so close now. The smoke cleared and for a second Drake saw the face of the German major general, stretched and screaming orders. They were near enough now that the enemy guns were firing in diagonally from the flanks. Drake stared into the maelstrom, the madness, the deafening cacophony of detonations. Then the *Gwendoline* was hit in front of him in a heavy thunderstrike. The great tank shivered and seemed to glow from inside with a white-hot light.

Drake's heart flipped in his chest. He couldn't breathe. He saw a muzzle flash on the ridge with an intense and almost mystic brightness. He felt frozen, as though he should recognise the path of the shell as it came towards him. A vast, crashing, apocalyptic hammerblow hit like the end of the world, and he was thrown, cartwheeling high in the air, through a pyre of screaming incandescent flame.

Chapter 32

DRAKE CAME ROUND, FACE flattened to the ground. The first thing that struck him was the silence.

It was a shocking lack. He slowly lifted up his head. The gunfire had ceased.

His skull was ringing from the blast. Everything hurt. His entire body was numb and shocked and bruised.

It took him a few moments to take in the scene. The field was strewn with burning tanks, and the sun was sinking towards the west, just a pale red disc through clouds of blowing smoke. He pushed himself up a little, and fixed his eyes on the ridge. His heart plunged as he saw German soldiers walking down through the field. Just ahead of him, a heavy tank was burning brightly, fumes pouring from its turret. From where he lay, he could just make out the name painted on the turret's side: *Gwendoline*. And Drake knew, with a horrifying certainty, that they'd failed.

'Are you still with us, sir?' MacTaggart called out.

Drake turned painfully around. The old Scots sergeant was crawling towards him. He pointed at the remains of the carrier, the *Dobbin*, which lay on the ground, almost ripped in two. A shell had hit the rear compartment from the flank and shredded it, leaving the cab almost intact.

'Got shot in the rear end, so to speak,' the old sergeant said.

Then they heard the screaming. Drake stared at the static, smouldering, shattered machines of the Royal Tank Regiment. German soldiers were combing the field now, looking for survivors. A rifle shot rang out.

MacTaggart grabbed his sleeve. 'Time to get out of here, sir. The Hun's on the loose. Shank's Pony is the order of the day.'

Drake shook his head, then ran towards the smouldering *Gwendoline*. The screaming was coming from inside the tank. He clambered onto the burning hull and peered in through the turret hatch. The inside of the machine was like a furnace, but somebody was still alive in there. Drake grabbed a man's hand to help him out, but as he tugged, the flesh came away from the man's bones.

Drake felt sickened and he almost gagged. He covered his own hand with his battledress jacket, and reached into the scorching heat, then heaved on the man's kit, dragging him through the narrow opening. The man made a terrible screeching sound as his body hit the tank's hull outside. He was so badly burned that there was smoke coming off his skin. Drake caught the smell of roasted meat and burnt hair, but the smouldering man was somehow still alive. Charred skin had stuck to his uniform where it had seared into the cloth. His left leg was hanging by a sinew from the knee, and a strange, choking, cawing sound came from his mouth. Drake realised, with a spike of horror, that the man was trying to speak.

'K— kill me. P—p—please.'

'I'll get my rifle sir,' MacTaggart said. 'He's got no chance.'

Drake stopped him. 'No.'

He pulled his service revolver from its holster and rested the muzzle against the side of the man's head. He looked at the *Fear Naught* cap badge, and the blackened scarf around the tank colonel's neck.

'Godspeed,' he said, and he looked away. The snap of the gunshot was high-pitched, loud and hollow in the silence left since the thumping of the cannons had ceased. He fought an almost overwhelming urge to be violently sick. But MacTaggart was tugging at his sleeve again – they had no time.

German troops were returning from the ridgeline now, and swarming down the hillside in great numbers. Drake and his sergeant hurried from the scene, keeping to the cover of the burning tanks that littered the field. Behind them, the fuel tank on the *Gwendoline* went up. Black fumes billowed out from the turret. Great crackling explosions jetted fire from the hatchway as ammunition went off inside the hull.

Drake ran across the field, with MacTaggart at his side. Gunshots snapped out and they picked up the pace. The men of the SS Totenkopf had been humiliated by the British tanks, and it seemed they were taking their revenge on any surviving crews.

Drake searched for a way off the hillside. They slid carefully through the knee-high wheat, then rolled into a ditch at the edge of a field. They crawled along the ditch for a hundred yards, then cautiously got to their feet. They looked around, and ran like hell.

After half a mile, they stopped. Something made Drake turn and look back up at the hilltop. He shaded his eyes against the smoke-blackened evening sky. He pulled up his field glasses and focused on the ridge. He saw the blazing ruin of the *Gwendoline* and behind it the brave little carrier *Dobbin*, which lay so close to the gun line. The Royal Tank Regiment had been decimated. Half Drake's men had been killed, and the others were missing. Obenauer and Agent Viper had escaped. Everything was in ruins. Drake felt an awful, keening despair well up inside. They had utterly failed.

'We had to try,' the old sergeant said. He smacked a fist into his hands. 'Satan's hell, but, we almost *had'em*, sir!'

'Almost,' Drake said. He looked back at the now-distant ridgeline. They'd come so close. So unbearably close. 'We lost the fight today, Sergeant. We may have just lost the entire war. And we lost it by just a hundred bloody yards.'

Gunfire crackled from the hillside. German soldiers were working their way down now, taking back the ground they had lost. Darkness was falling.

Drake pulled the charred piece of paper from his pocket, and studied the writing once more.

OPERATIONSBEFEHL DÄMMERUNG

He looked back up towards the treeline. *Twilight. Nightfall. Dusk.*

Up on the ridge, *Generalmajor* Erwin Rommel gazed down at the smouldering battlefield through tired, smoke-dried eyes. His gaze lingered on the burning wrecks of the British tanks that were dotted all across the pitted ground in the lowering evening sun. The carcasses of the great machines were smouldering still. Dark columns of oily fumes rose up from the wrecks, drifting over the fields. The general wiped a stain of blood and bone fragments from his tunic. He knew what had been in play today. And he knew just how close – how very, very close – they'd come.

Nearby, on the hilltop, in the strange, smoky glow of the dusk, a man in a civilian suit looked on. He tipped his hat to the general, then turned his gaze coolly towards the sunset. He touched his throat, then his tie, and he felt that there was something missing there. It was no matter. He looked to the west. And he knew, with a fiery certainty now, that at last his time had come.

PART III

THE RETREAT

WEDNESDAY 22 MAY 1940

Chapter 33

HEAVY TORPEDO BOAT LA POURSUIVANTE, POSITION 50° 88' N, 01° 55' E – 01:26HRS

IT WAS PITCH BLACK in the Channel, two and a half kilometres off Cap Gris-Nez. And then it was blindingly bright. The searchlights on the Melpomène class French heavy torpedo boat *La Poursuivante* flicked on in a dazzling array, picking out – at five hundred metres – the white hull of a civilian motor yacht.

The deck of *La Poursuivante* thrummed with the twenty-thousand horsepower of her two oil-fired steam turbines as she closed at 30 knots. The vibration changed as the helm turned and the twin screws thrashed the water, laying the 680-tonne vessel in a sweeping curve to intercept.

Lieutenant de vaisseau Pierre Julien Chesneau stepped off the open bridge and onto the companionway. He raised a high-powered megaphone to his lips and his voice was projected across the water.

'*Virez!*' he ordered. 'Heave to!'

Picked out in the searchlights, the smaller vessel's bows dropped. It wallowed as it cut its motors, drifting slowly on the shifting, furrowing sea.

Chesneau stepped back onto the bridge, and spoke rapidly to First Ensign Guillou, who had the helm. '*Mettez a couple!* Lay alongside!' He turned to the young *Aspirant* Trottier, who had appeared at his right-hand. He noted the pale blond hair visible beneath the midshipman's cap.

'Board and search the vessel. And be quick about it.'

'*Ou-ou-oui, mon commandant*, the young midshipman stuttered. 'Wha– what are we looking for, sir?'

Chesneau rubbed at his face. He was exhausted, and he needed a shave. He'd been going for 36 hours straight. '*Rien.* Nothing. I suppose that they are only civilians escaping Boulogne. But find out what's happening ashore, if you can. Searchlights off!'

A moment later, the sea plunged into darkness once more. In the dimmed, red glow of the bridge lights, a seaman came up the ladder from the galley and handed Chesneau a mug. He took it gratefully. Coffee, made from his personal supply of beans.

'*Merci*, Barrat,' he said.

The *matelot* grinned and went back down the ladder. Although classed as a torpedo boat, *La Poursuivante* was, in essence, a small destroyer, and had a complement of 105 souls. Chesneau had only commanded the vessel for a few weeks, but he had made a point of remembering every single name.

He sipped the coffee. It was bitter and scalding – boiled to within an inch of its life. He didn't care. It would keep him awake. Despite the prickle of heat that lingered on his lips, his eyelids grew heavy, and he felt himself slipping away, until the shame of falling asleep in front of his helmsman jolted him back to life.

He looked into the darkness. It was a clear night. As his eyes adjusted, he could just make out the dark smudge of the yacht against the grey sheen of the water. He saw the shadowed shapes of men boarding, but was distracted as flashes of distant shellfire flickered above the looming mass of land to the east. For a moment he wondered what was happening to his parents, back home, almost five hundred kilometres away in Brittany. Would Brittany, too, be overrun? He hoped that his father would not take out his shotgun when the Germans came. He sighed, shook his head, then concentrated on finishing the coffee as quickly as he could. He could not make out the horizon. There were three hours until dawn. At dawn, come what may, he'd turn in and sleep for an entire, blessed watch.

A few minutes later, he saw the shapes returned onto deck from the yacht. The blond-haired young midshipman clattered up the companionway. He saluted smartly with an excited look on his face.

'Found something, Trottier?'

'*Ou-oui. Non*. Not something. S-s-s-someone. I think you'd b-better come and see for yourself, sir.'

Chesneau followed him down the ladder. In the dim starlight on deck, he could only make out the shape of three uniformed crewmen from the yacht, held at gunpoint by a pair of sailors with carbines. He glanced at Trottier.

'Well?'

Trottier pointed towards a man who was standing at the back of the small group, as though he were trying to hide from the light. He was wearing a dark civilian suit and a short-brimmed hat, which he had tipped down, partially obscuring his face.

'Th-that one. We saw him th-throw something overboard.' He snapped on a flashlight, and shone it into the man's face.

Chesneau stared. At first, the man seemed a stranger. 'Look at me!' he ordered. 'Take off your hat!'

The man looked up, removed his hat, and Chesneau met his eyes. Slowly, his features gathered into recognition in Chesneau's exhausted mind.

'*C'est pas possible!*' he said. '*Putain!*'

He gazed at the man's face a moment longer, then issued orders. 'Secure them in the sickbay. Take two able seamen to crew the yacht, and be quick about it.' He turned to the midshipman and suddenly clapped him on the shoulder. 'Well done, Trottier. *Enseigne intérimaire* Trottier. Very well done indeed.'

'*Merci bien, mon commandant,*' Acting Ensign Trottier replied. 'Thank you very much, sir.' He realised with a shock that his stutter was gone. In the darkness, nobody could see his bashful, beaming grin.

Chesneau ran up the companion ladder to the bridge. He pressed a button and spoke to the wireless operator. 'In three minutes I shall have a message for you to encode and send to the commodore. Come and collect it from the bridge.'

'*Oui, mon commandant,*' came the voice through the pipe.

Chesnau hung up the intercom. 'Slow ahead.'

First ensign Gillou, who was at the helm, pushed the lever forward on the engine order telegraph and a bell rang. 'Slow ahead,' he repeated.

'Bring her about. Bearing 046 degrees. Lay her on a course for Calais.'

'Yes, sir,' Gillou answered, '046 degrees, sir.' He spun the helm. The deck canted slightly as the ship manoeuvred in a half circle. He peered into the darkness of the night.

'Full ahead,' Chesneau ordered.

'Full ahead,' Gillou repeated as he sent the signal through the engine order telegraph. A bell rang in the engine room, far below.

Chesneau pursed his lips, making the curious first ensign suffer a moment longer, before eventually he spoke.

'We have an unexpected guest aboard.'

'Yes, sir,' Gillou replied. He watched the commander, who gave no further information.

Both men gazed out into the night. The stars swung around in the sky until the ship was on a bearing approximately north by east. Beneath their feet, the deck vibrated with the power of the twin steam turbines as they brought *La Poursuivante* back up to 30 knots.

Chapter 34

CAMBLAIN-CHÂTELAIN, HAUTS-DE-FRANCE – 09:30HRS

The remnants of the first battalion of the South Devonshire regiment marched in quick time, in a column three men abreast. Drake marched alongside the column. The land was hilly here, and the road ran dead straight for miles. They passed trudging bands of French civilian refugees who were strung out all along the way.

The battalion had managed to retain its small arms, but they had lost their transports. When the armoured attack near Arras had collapsed, the infantry positions had been rapidly overrun. Arras had been evacuated, and the BEF was pulling sharply back towards the Channel coast. Drake's mind kept drifting back to the battle. He felt deflated, lost, with the bitter gall of defeat stuck like a bone in his throat. Lyle-Smith was right: Obenauer *had* been with the SS. And there was a civilian. There was little doubt in Drake's mind now that it was Agent Viper. And – *damn it all* – Drake had let him get away.

He swatted at a cloud of biting flies as the battalion marched up a hill. The road ran through a forest here. Drake's helmet was heavy and clammy against his scalp. The sun was already hot and hard, and his woollen serge collar chafed at his neck. He rubbed at the sweat that was pouring from his face, and tried to think more clearly.

Operationsbefehl Dämmerung. Twilight, nightfall, dusk. But what was it? To involve a full colonel of the SD – well, it had to be political. The major had been right about everything so far, but simply kicking the front door down had failed. Without getting hold of the Viper, without knowing what *Dämmerung* actually was, they were really no better off. And with Frankforce routed, and the BEF in full retreat, he had no way of contacting Lyle-Smith. With a weary heart, Drake had to face squarely up to the truth. The entire operation had catastrophically failed.

He looked up as Colonel Hawker's Dingo scout car roved up and down the column. Hawker had been fuming when they'd been ordered to retreat, as though it were somehow entirely Drake's fault. Drake shook his head and marched on. The road ran north-westwards, towards St Omer and the Channel coast, and it was swarming with refugees – a piteous herd of humanity on foot, on farm carts, or in slowly-crawling motorcars piled high with suitcases and mattresses. Every few minutes, the marching column had to halt, or reroute past a crowd, who, despite the bawling of sergeants and the klaxon of Hawker's scout car, either wouldn't or couldn't get out of the way.

Heavily-laden farm carts were being pulled by great ponderous plough horses. In between the vehicles trudged thousands of people from all walks of life. There were old men with walking sticks, or wheeling bicycles with cardboard boxes tied to the front and rear. Women of all ages, shoving handcarts and pushchairs, bundled up high with their offspring and their possessions. There were dozens of children, walking, limping, hobbling slowly along, some led by priests, others by nuns. It was depressing to see. But far worse was the sight of hundreds of deserting French soldiers. A few scattered Belgians lurked amongst them, and their kit – or what was left of it – was almost identical. Green overcoats and long puttees, helmets and packs turned grey with dust from the long, dry march. Some still wore their *casque Adrian* helmets – the Belgian ones were the same as the French but with the crest of a rampant lion. The soldiers were anything but rampant. Their weapons had been cast down, fighting kit discarded, dumped on the verges. They were tired and dirty, they'd had enough, and they were going home.

Drake glanced up at a farm cart that was clopping slowly along as the South Devonshires marched past it on the verge. A pair of grubby children sat on the back. The little boy began to pick his nose. It made Drake think, with a smile, of his little brother back home in Plymouth, but his thoughts turned not to Hazel, his sweetheart in Devon, but to Axelle, the woman he'd—

He'd what?

He pulled himself up. He'd felt something for her, that was certain. It was pointless to deny it. They'd met on that crazed first day of the invasion in Belgium, when her father had been brutally murdered by the SS. Axelle's hatred for the Nazis had been visceral, and at times she had put Drake to shame. With everything that had happened, it seemed months, even years ago now, but it had been less than two weeks. He knew she might be out there, somewhere, in the hordes of dispossessed, shuffling away from the German advance. *Christ.* He could feel the pressure of the invasion building up behind them like an inexorable, rising tide.

As Drake marched, he grimly observed the French countryside around them. The day was really heating up now, and the road ran straight on, up and over hills and down into shallow vales. The long marching column clomped through a smouldering village. They saw a group of old Frenchmen pulling the burnt corpses of a family from a shattered house. The battalion had no time to stop and help. Back out on the open road, burnt and bullet-ridden civilian cars stood charred and abandoned on the verge.

In the distance, towers of smoke dotted the horizon. The Luftwaffe had been hard at work. Drake closed his eyes for a moment as he marched. *Left-right. Left-right.* He tried to clear his mind. He thought back to the conversation at the Arras memorial. *Something's rotten in the Third Republic.* Something was rotten alright. The French army had let them down at Arras – they simply hadn't turned up to the fight, aside from a handful of tanks. But was that accident or design? And where did that leave them now? Drake wanted more than anything to believe the French were still in the fight. If the British Army couldn't trust its greatest ally, they were doomed.

His eyes roved over the fields as they marched on through the growing heat. Dead horses lay across their path, their heavy, immovable, bellies swelling in the heat. Flies flew up in great buzzing clouds as the boots marched past. Drake's kit was drenched in sweat, and he quickly wiped a sleeve across his dripping face. His rifle strap dug in, rubbing his shoulder raw with every step, but he insisted on carrying one – an officer's sidearm was next to useless in a firefight. He could feel his feet swelling up inside his boots. But what really chafed was the sense of failure. The Germans were winning. There were dead bodies everywhere. Civilians killed by the roadside. Some buried in shallow graves marked with makeshift crosses. Others left to rot just where they fell. The Luftwaffe had been putting in a shift. Dust flew up all around from the crash of boots on the unmade road, clogging up his nose, his mouth, his eyes.

Flies followed them in great swarms, biting and stinging and getting in their faces, under their eyelids. There were mutters of discontent and anger as they marched past a group of French deserters who were drinking wine from broken bottles at the side of the road, but Colonel Hawker kept the men marching, eyes front, and there was no trouble. They marched past a little Renault car that had been shot up by the

Luftwaffe and had burned itself out. It was filled with the charred corpses of an entire family.

Drake looked dully at the road ahead, his mouth filled with a bitter taste. His mind was numbed by the *crump-crump-crump* of boots hitting gravel in time, but Lyle-Smith's words came back to haunt him. If they couldn't halt the Nazi advance, this would happen to England very soon.

They stopped for the regulation five minutes every hour, but as the day dragged on, the sun's heat and the dry air sapped their strength. They marched past an old man on a farm cart, pulled by a slow, lame horse. The man wore a 1914-issue French army greatcoat of faded horizon blue. He called out the Great War slogan of French defiance, '*On ne passe pas, mes braves!* They shall not pass!' His voice cracked as he raised a fist up to the skies.

'They've already bleedin' passed!' shouted one of the men from the middle of the ranks. Drake could tell from the dry cackle that it was Private Leighton. It drew a laugh, but the idea resonated in Drake's mind. *They had already passed.* Somebody screamed nearby and Drake lost his train of thought.

He stopped marching. A woman was lying on the verge, surrounded by infants. Her skirt was soaked in blood, and she let out another animalistic shriek. Then one of the children, a girl no more than six or seven years old, begged the soldiers for help.

'*Le bébé arrive!*' the little girl said. She kept repeating it. '*Le bébé arrive! Le bébé arrive!*'

The harsh toll of a klaxon sounded, and Drake stepped back as the colonel's Dingo scout car drew up towards them, then slowed to a halt.

'Can't the MO help her, sir?' Drake said. 'The poor woman's about to give birth.'

Colonel Hawker glared down from his scout car. 'I'm sorry, but we're here to fight, Drake, not act as ruddy midwives! We can't hold the entire battalion up because some French trollop's having a baby, can we? There's a war on. Fall in!'

The woman began screaming once more, her face red with exertion. Drake opened his mouth to speak again, but caught the rigid look on Colonel Hawker's face. Drake saw the sergeants, including MacTaggart, as they hustled up and down the columns, redressing the distracted men. The colonel was right, of course. If they got entangled in every tragedy they saw on the way, the entire battalion would disintegrate and have no value as a fighting force. Drake reluctantly stepped back into marching pace, but his heart went out to the young woman and her children at the side of the road.

'Dinnae worry yourself, sir,' MacTaggart said from the corner of his mouth as he marched briskly by. 'Looks like her fifth. It'll walk out on its own two bonnie feet.'

'Eyes front, there!' Sergeant Cronin bellowed. 'Left-right! Left-right! Left-right! Now, who's for a jolly old song?'

A tubby red-headed private from D Company, Lambton, led on his harmonica, and the men sang their own version of that popular Czech waltz, *The Beer Barrel Polka*. They ignored the screaming woman as they marched past, and their boots crashed out in time.

Roll out the barrel,
and we'll have a barrel of fun!
Roll out the barrel,
'cos we've got the Hun on the run!
Zing boom tararrel,
and ring out a song of good cheer!
Now's the time to roll out the barrel,
for the Red Feathers are here!

It was forced jollity, and it was galling, but the song seemed to distract the men enough to keep them going. A stray dog with a white patch over one eye began trotting next to them as they marched. Some of the men tossed it hard tack from their pockets, which the dog happily swallowed without chewing.

''Ere, Private Barker!' Leighton hissed, then cackled at his own joke. The dog ran up to him expectantly. 'Wanna gasper?' Leighton said, offering the dog a cigarette.

'Shut it, Leighton!' Cronin bellowed, marching alongside the column. He swung a boot at the dog, which easily skipped away. 'Now – come on. Let's have another jolly song!'

The men groaned but Lambton's harmonica screeched, and they quickly picked up a new tune.

It's a long way to Tipperary
It's a long way to go
It's a long way to Tipperary
To the sweetest girl I know –

The battalion kept marching in time, and they set a rapid pace. But as the first echelons tramped into the next village, the singing began to falter. Half a minute later, as Drake's section marched in, he saw why.

'Eyes front!' Sergeant Cronin bellowed, but the men ignored him, and stared as they marched past a bombed-out convent. Outside, on the pavement, were the bodies of ten young girls, not more than seven or eight years old. White cloths covered their faces, but their little patent leather shoes were all lined up below the hems of their dresses, pointing skywards. Drake dragged his eyes away. The mood in the marching column suddenly changed.

'The shits,' one of the men said, looking up at the sky for signs of the Luftwaffe. 'The sodding shits. If I get my hands on one of them, I tell you –'

Drake shared the man's outrage. And he knew at that moment that he could never give up on his task, he could never again be squeamish about what he was asked to do. He felt the fury rising inside his guts, his chest, almost choking his throat. *Dämmerung*. Dusk. Twilight. Nightfall. Somehow, some way, he was going to figure it out, whatever it took. Whoever he had to kill. And it was clear to him now that this was not a gentleman's fight. This was total, bloody war.

A woman, a mother, ran towards the marching men. '*Lâches! Poltrons!*' she shrieked, and she struck at Drake with her parasol as he marched past. He didn't try to avoid the blows. He understood exactly how she felt. In her eyes, they weren't fighting. They were running away. The column marched on in silence from then on. Just the *crump-crump-crump* of five hundred pairs of boots.

They marched all day until the sky began to change colour and the shadows grew long. Lambton tried another tune, but nobody felt like singing anymore. Every town or village they passed revealed new horrors, and Drake's mood plummeted, sick to his very bones. A *Fieseler Storch* kept buzzing overhead, and Drake half-expected the Stukas to come. But they only saw distant, high-level bombers, flying towards the north and west. For a moment he was puzzled as to why they'd only strafed the road, not bombed it as they did the towns. After a moment's thought it was obvious. They needed the roads to bring their panzers up more efficiently. He glanced self-consciously back over his shoulder, expecting to see tanks, but there were none. *Not yet.* But it wouldn't be long.

By evening, Drake felt like he was marching on his chinstrap, but he knew they'd covered a remarkable distance. Hawker's scout car went past once again, throwing out dust and fumes as it passed on the shoulder of the road. Drake strode on, boots thumping in time, all sensation gone from his body in the mindless, exhausting rhythm of the march. *Left-right. Left-right. Left-right.*

He gazed ahead. The countryside was growing duller and flatter as they marched into the twilight. They were approaching the flat country of the Pas-de-Calais and Flanders. He fixed his thoughts on the placement of his feet as the shadows lengthened. *Left-right. Left-right. Left-right.* And a single thought kept circling round inside his mind, in time with the thudding of the boots. If Lyle-Smith was right, the war would come to a crashing end, only five days from now. But how?

MacTaggart marched smartly past, keeping the columns of men in trim, and Drake noted once again that the Scotsman had a new pin on his kilt. It looked like a silver St Andrew's cross, glinting in the high, hot sun. Drake wondered where he'd got it from, and frowned.

Chapter 35

RIHOULT CLAIRMARAIS FOREST, NEAR ST OMER, FRANCE – 20:45HRS

THE BATTALION BIVOUACKED DEEP in a forest, making the most of the close cover. Drake stood at the edge of the trees. A ring of sentries guarded the woods. The nearest was fifty yards away, well camouflaged and barely distinguishable from the undergrowth. Drake knew that the sentries were jumpy. The whole battalion was. Nobody knew where or when they'd run into the Wehrmacht again. The early summer evenings were long and warm, and it seemed to be taking an age for the sun to edge down towards the horizon. There was a town about five miles off in a south-westerly direction. *St Omer*, Drake reckoned. It was burning. The Luftwaffe never stopped. As the sun slipped closer towards the horizon, it lit up the distant shrouds of smoke in an ominous red glow.

Drake's feet were swollen, aching and blistered, but he dared not take off his boots – he'd never get them back on again. He watched the countryside darkening. After a while, MacTaggart found him, bringing a canteen of tea. Drake sipped at the black, sweet, scorching liquid. It was fortified from the colonel's missing supplies, and, after the long, hard march, it was heaven. MacTaggart refilled the cup as soon as it was emptied, and replenished his own.

Drake looked at the kilt pin the old Scotsman was wearing. 'Where did that come from, Sergeant?'

MacTaggart's eyes narrowed. 'Och, this? It's naught but a wee charm, sir. Nothing more.'

'That's not what I asked,' Drake said. He eyed the old sergeant over the mug of steaming tea. It wasn't like him to prevaricate.

MacTaggart squirmed under his gaze. 'I found it, sir, if you must know. Just lying about.'

'Lying where, exactly, Sergeant?'

The old Scotsman sighed. 'In that German encampment, sir. It's a wee Saltire, a cross of St Andrew – the patron saint of Scotland! I suppose some other Caledonian type had dropped it on their way through. I figured we could use all the luck we could get. Did I do wrong?'

'You found it outside that German command tent, didn't you?' Drake said.

MacTaggart seemed to deflate. 'Aye, sir. I suppose I did.'

'Give it here,' Drake said, holding out a hand.

The sergeant removed it, and reluctantly handed it over. 'But it's my lucky charm!'

It was a diagonal cross in silver, but it wasn't a kilt pin, it was a tiepin. MacTaggart had had it fixed vertically, the wrong way around. The cross had rough, saw-toothed edges, unlike a traditional Saltire.

'Right, Sergeant,' Drake said. 'Come with me.'

They found Captain Lucas pacing the perimeter of the camp, checking up on the sentries. Drake raised an arm and the captain sauntered over.

'You're an educated man, Bill,' Drake said.

Bill Lucas laughed. 'Hardly what you might call educated, old bean. I took History and Languages up at Exeter. Not much of a preparation for the real world. But I can recite the Field Service Pocket Book back to front, sideways, and in French, German, Latin and Ancient Greek, if that's any good?'

Drake held up a hand. 'That's educated enough for me.' The closest he had come to university was marching past the grand entrance of St Luke's as a raw sixteen-year-old recruit, eyes fixed firmly to the front, trying not to fall out of step.

Captain Lucas eyed MacTaggart's canteen. 'And I've never said no to a drink yet,' he said, 'when offered.'

MacTaggart filled a mug for him.

Lucas took a swig. His eyes watered and he let out a breath. 'Crikey. Top hole.'

Drake held out the tiepin on his palm. 'What d'you make of this?'

The diagonal cross glinted a silver-gold colour in the late evening sunlight. The captain picked it up and turned it over in his hand. He ran his fingers over the silverwork. The edges were jagged, a repeating pattern of oblique projections and depressions.

'It looks almost like razor-wire,' Drake said. 'I don't know if it's a St Andrew's cross at all.'

Bill held it up. Squinted. 'Tiepin, obviously. Curious heraldic symbolism. Well, it *is* a Saltire, of sorts. *Crux decussata*, raguly.'

Drake peered at the pin. '*Ragu*-what?'

'*Raguly.* See these saw-toothed notches? That makes it a Cross of Burgundy, of course.'

Drake gazed at the tiepin. For a moment it appeared like some ancient treasure as the metal glinted in the evening light. 'What does that mean?'

Bill thought for a moment. 'St Andrew was one of the original disciples of Jesus, and was martyred in Patra – in modern-day Greece. Legend has it that he was crucified on a diagonal cross at his own request. He's been adopted widely, of course, and he's got little direct connection to Scotland.'

MacTaggart frowned.

Bill Lucas ignored him and went on. 'St Andrew was the patron saint of Burgundy too – among many other states. As I'm sure you know, Drake, the Valois Dukes of Burgundy ruled significant swathes of Eastern France and the Low Countries, way back in the fifteenth century. And the Hapsburgs took the Burgundy title – and this symbol – with them when they moved to Spain. In fact, it's rather controversial now.'

Drake turned to Bill, taking the tiepin back. 'Controversial? Why?'

'I suppose you've heard of the Carlists? They were a group of Spanish Catholic Royalists, supporting King Carlos of Spain.'

Drake watched Bill Lucas' face in the evening twilight. 'Can't say I have.'

'Didn't they teach you anything at school?'

Drake shrugged. 'Left arm over the wicket was my greatest scholastic achievement. And for two years I held the record for receipt of the cane.'

Bill Lucas chuckled. 'Why does that not surprise me? Well, this is the interesting bit. The Carlists threw in their lot against the Republicans in the Spanish Civil War. So it's not something to be flashing around these days. Rather poor show. And look, d'you see the hallmark here on the back?'

Drake squinted at the tiny marking, no more than an eighth of an inch across. It was a five-pointed star inside a circle. 'It's a pentagram! Don't tell me they were devil worshipers?'

Lucas grinned. 'Not a bit of it. Don't you know your hallmarks, Drake? Tut-tut. It's a Spanish silver fineness mark. That makes it rather more conclusive. Don't you see?'

Drake looked up. 'Imagine I was a poor ignorant peasant, Bill. Explain in language that even I can understand.'

The captain raised his eyebrows. 'These days, the Cross of Burgundy is mostly thought of as a symbol of the regime of Francisco Franco Bahamonde.'

'Franco?' Drake recalled what he knew of the Spanish dictator. With Hitler's help, Franco's fascist armies had won the murderous civil war against the socialist Republicans, and the killings hadn't stopped when the vanquished had laid down their arms. 'Christ.'

'*Christ* indeed,' Bill said. 'Well, the Roman Catholic Church, to be precise. So. Go on. What's all this skullduggery about?'

Drake stood in silence for a moment. 'I can't tell you. And I'm not sure you'd want to know if I could.'

The captain looked shrewdly at MacTaggart, then back to Drake. 'Come on. Spill the beans. What the devil are you two up to?'

Drake hesitated, then drew the scrap of charred paper from his pocket and passed it to the captain.

Bill stared at it in the fading evening light, which seemed to turn the paper a dull red colour.

OPERATIONSBEFEHL DÄMMERUNG

'Crikey, Drake. Wherever did you get this? It looks legit.'

Drake shrugged. 'We picked it up on our travels.' His thoughts were racing, and a horrible idea was beginning to form at the back of his mind. He took the paper from the captain and held it up in the evening light. '*Dämmerung*. I know it means nightfall, twilight, dusk. The Germans have a penchant for dramatic codenames. But could it mean anything else? Any ideas?'

Captain Lucas grunted. 'Well, of course any fool who's been to the opera can tell you that *Götterdämmerung* means twilight of the gods. Destruction. Extreme chaos and violence. In other words, the end of times. But I suppose you want something more?'

Drake looked quickly across at him. '*Is* there more?'

The captain smiled. 'Actually there is. *Dämmerung* has another meaning, in old German. It's a bit archaic, but it means the end of an era, the changing of the old guard, the passing of kings. Is that what you're looking for?'

Drake took back the scrap of paper and examined the blackletter script as the last light faded from the sky. 'The passing of kings,' he repeated. He heard the distant thumping of bombs falling in the distance. He folded the paper before putting it safely back in his pocket. 'Honestly? I don't know. I'm chasing at shadows and I need some time to think.'

'Right,' Captain Lucas said. 'Well, I'd better complete my inspections of the sentries. Don't want Jerry sneaking up on us, do we?'

MacTaggart took the hint, and with a nod to Drake, he made himself scarce.

Drake stalked along the perimeter of the forest. Above his head, the heavy drone of aero engines throbbed across the purpling sky. The Luftwaffe were out again, but his thoughts were elsewhere. Uneasy, amorphous images started whirling around inside his mind. *The cross of Burgundy. The Carlists. Franco.* Drake recalled what the Belgian woman, Axelle, had told him when he'd met her in those first days of the invasion. In the Spanish Civil War, Franco and the fascists had beaten the communist-backed Republicans only thanks to the help of Hitler's tanks and Condor Legions. The amorphous thoughts suddenly coalesced into a horribly solid shape. It struck Drake like a hammer blow, and he stopped in his tracks. What if Hitler was now calling in the debt?

He tried to calm the sour churning in his guts as he absently surveyed the horizon. It was a horribly plausible scenario. If the Germans were planning to bring Spain into the war, it would open up a whole new front in the south, collapsing the entire French army's defensive plans. It would be a disaster, a catastrophe of biblical proportions. The French army would simply fold in on itself, and the Alliance would be over. Britain would be on her own.

Drake started as a shape moved at the edge of the trees to his right. He swung his rifle round and called out sharply, 'Stop! Who's that?'

There was no reply. Drake saw a bat flit out of the woods, a quick black shadow against the deepening colour of the evening. He drew back the rifle bolt, slid it forward until it clacked.

'Who goes there?' he demanded again. 'Answer me, or I'll fire.'

Chapter 36

As the Luftwaffe bombers thrummed overhead, a scrawny, narrow-faced soldier emerged from the bushes. The man gave a nervous, rasping laugh. 'Easy, tiger. Keep your hair on, sir. It's only me.'

Drake relaxed a little. 'What the hell are you playing at, Leighton? I might have bloody shot you.' He released the bolt on his rifle and slung it loosely from his shoulder.

Leighton hesitated. 'Just come to see the sunset, sir,' he said with a high-pitched cackle. 'Same as you.'

'Bollocks you have. If you're thinking of running, don't.'

Leighton's scratching laugh burst out irritatingly again. 'Me, sir? Run, sir? The thought never crossed my mind, sir.'

Drake shook his head. 'And I'm a ruddy Welshman.' He nodded towards the treeline. 'Enjoying the view? So's Cronin. He's out with a pair of binoculars and a rifle. Colonel Hawker's in a froth about deserters. Take it from me, you won't get fifty yards.'

Leighton frowned. 'Now why would you think I'd try something like that? When we've got far more interesting business on our hands.'

'What business?' Drake felt an uneasy stirring. 'Who's *we*?'

Leighton glanced just over Drake's shoulder. Drake spun to see Privates Pritchard, Davy and Stoker all standing behind him. They were survivors from the ill-fated carrier expedition. The sound of the aero engines had muffled their approach. They were three of the worst men in the regiment, and that was saying something. Stoker was a docker, almost Drake's height, but broader and thick-limbed, with wiry blonde hair. Davy was a tall, lean man with eyes too close together. Pritchard was stocky, balding, with dry, pock-marked skin, and always wore a look of grievance.

'You'll never get away with it,' Drake said.

Leighton laughed again. 'You've got us all wrong, sir. We're not running. We're staying put. That's God's honest truth.' He rubbed the side of his nose and tossed something onto the ground. Drake saw it was a wad of ten bob notes bound with string.

Drake eyed the bundle as it lay on the forest floor in the gloom. 'For Christ's sake, what are you up to? There must be a hundred pound there, Leighton.' It was a year's salary for an experienced soldier with a trade. Almost three years' salary for a raw recruit on two shillings a day.

Leighton cackled dryly. 'We've been having a collection. The boys don't reckon they'll have much use for their pay if they all get killed. The battalion raised a prize fund, see.' He smiled in the half-light. 'Some of the boys – they like to have a flutter, know what I mean? It's yours if you win, Drake. Fair's fair.'

Drake shook his head. 'No chance. I don't want your money. Now bugger off and we'll say no more about it.' He turned quickly to look at the men who were standing behind him. They were closer now. They obviously had an axe to grind. A knot tightened in Drake's stomach.

The big man, Stoker, leaned in close, and scratched at his face. 'Too good for it, are you?' he said.

Drake weighed up his choices. Fire a shot – *not a good idea.* There was a more than even chance the sentries would fire back in a panic, and all hell would break loose. Call for help? The men would see that as a weakness, and it would be around the battalion in no time. He'd lose all chance of respect among the men. What then? It was four to one, and they hadn't touched him – so far. He wasn't going to start it. There was only one thing for it. *Play along and see where it ends up.*

'Oh, piss off,' Drake said. He was trying to sound unruffled, but the knot in his stomach was tightening into a ball. They probably blamed him for the deaths of all their comrades in the carriers. The stink of booze was on their breath, and it didn't smell good.

A flash of memories came to him – youthful days behind the barrack walls. The slaps and mockery and name-calling until he agreed to box. The sting of leather on skin. 'I'm not fighting. I've given up. It's bad for the health.'

'Bad for the health!' Leighton cackled again, then coughed, a dry smoker's hack. 'He's afraid. Runs in the family, so I hear.'

Drake saw that other men were now gathering in the dusk light, expecting an evening's entertainment. It seemed like everybody was in on it.

'Back to your duties!' he ordered. 'I'm warning you—'

He saw from the looks of the men that they weren't about to disperse. They'd paid good money. Drake's options narrowed. He could kick up a stink, rouse the senior officers, and have all these men on a charge. And have every private soldier in the battalion think he'd swerved a fight. And if it came to a battle, he might end up with a bullet to the back of the neck for his trouble.

Drake ran a hand through the tangled hair beneath his helmet. *Christ.* He had far weightier matters on his mind. He wished these bloody thugs would just disappear. But, of course, they wouldn't. Well, Agent Viper would just have to wait. He rubbed the palms of his hands together and shrugged. *Alright. Let them try.*

'Which one of you, then?' he said. 'You, Stoker? You're built like a brick shithouse, and you stink like one.'

Leighton laughed. 'Good one, Drake. But Stoker? No, not 'im.' He turned around. 'Come on, Dan.'

The huge form of Private Butcher stepped out from the cover of the trees. Drake shook his head. *Of course.*

'You think you're better than us, don't you Drake?' the big man muttered in a deep baritone growl. 'But you're just the same as we are. A nobody. A piece of shit. That pip on your shoulder don't fool me.'

Drake saw more shapes moving in the gloom as the light faded incrementally further. Men were gathering to watch in ever increasing numbers. By now the whole bloody battalion must have known. They had him cornered. He could still bellow for help, and MacTaggart would come running, but he'd lose the respect of the men forever. Butcher would beat him without landing a single punch.

'Alright,' he said. 'One condition.' He felt the familiar rage rising inside and began to unbutton his jacket and shirt. The rage that had forced him to run from home at the age of fifteen, and into the army as an underaged recruit, avoiding the long arm of the law. He spoke through gritting teeth. 'I'll give you an exhibition match, no more. Just a bit of sparring. Sportsmanlike. No scrapping or monkey business. Agreed?'

Butcher nodded. 'Sparring.' He grinned. 'Sportsmanlike, then.'

Drake turned to give Leighton a deadpan smile. 'Did you never hear why I gave up boxing? Of course, it was before your time. Last time I boxed was for the regimental cup. I hit the other man under the chin. He sat down and he never got up again.' He scanned the men's faces, and saw just a hint of doubt come over them. 'Like I said, it's not good for the health. But this is just for sport, so you don't have to worry. Strictly Marquess of Queensberry Rules.'

Chapter 37

Drake pulled his shirt over his head, then his dirty singlet vest, stripping down to just his trousers and boots. After two weeks at war, always on the move with barely a decent meal, he was leaner than he'd ever been. His muscles showed through his skin like tight, dry knots. The fields were growing darker, but a red light from the sunset glowed from the sky. It was one of those nights where the twilight lingered and it seemed it would never get dark. And from throughout the forest, still more men of the battalion were now sneaking through the trees to watch the fun.

Private Butcher stripped down too. His torso was thickly muscled, his chest and shoulders like slabs of meat. His arms were as wide as another man's legs. His bare fists were the size of turnips. It was years since Drake had fought. But that gave him an advantage. Few, if any, of the men here had ever seen him in the ring. Drake was a left-hooker, and Butcher probably didn't know that. He'd soon find out. In the scrappy world of army boxing, taking control was everything. Drake observed Butcher's motions as he flexed his fingers, then balled them into fists. He knew that the big man, with his reach and height, would be able to pummel him to nothing if he let him have the chance. His best, his only chance was to take the initiative and keep it. Strike fast and hard, and keep at it, 'til the bastard went down. Because he knew he wouldn't be able to withstand Butcher's sheer strength for long.

Drake saw MacTaggart coming towards him, about to bellow the house down, but he shot him a glance and the sergeant's cry died before it left his lips.

MacTaggart pressed in through the throng. 'Don't do it sir. Are you mad?'

'Just wait in my corner, Sergeant,' Drake said. 'Alright! You men, link arms and form a ring. And for God's sake keep your voices down. Don't forget there may be Germans around. Or even worse, Colonel Hawker.'

That got a small laugh. Drake knew he had to get the crowd on his side, or run the risk of them tearing him limb from limb.

After a moment, he and Butcher were propelled into the newly-formed ring. The men started whispering, pointing, those forming the ring pushing back, those behind them pressing forwards to get a better view.

Drake spat on his hands, and slapped them together. He called out, over the murmur of the crowd, 'Three-minute rounds! A minute rest in between. No biting, wrestling, butting, gouging, kicking, and nothing below the waist. No hitting a man when he's down. We've got no gloves, so bare fists it is. Count of ten and you're out. Three round limit. Just a bit of sport, nothing more. Shake on it, Butcher? Agreed? Marquess of Queensberry Rules.'

Drake held out his right hand. Butcher reached out his big paw to grasp it. Drake gripped, but Butcher gripped harder, trying to crush Drake's knuckles in his iron grasp. Drake looked up at him and smiled. He had far more important things to worry about than wasting time with oafs and thugs with grudges. They might have heard that Drake used to box, but they obviously didn't know he'd also coached all-in fighting. Drake held Butcher's right hand firmly, and punched him in the face with his left. He yanked his right arm back, pulling the big man forwards, off balance. He swung his left leg up with the full force of his bodyweight and kicked Private Butcher in the balls.

Private Butcher's eyes opened wide, then closed. He let out a sickening groan and sank down slowly to the floor.

'Oi! That ain't Queensberry Rules!' Leighton shouted.

'Foul!' cried the crowd.

Drake glanced around at the ring of men, arm in arm, who were all staring at him now, faces turning angry. They'd been cheated. 'Serves the bastard right!' somebody called, and another group laughed started counting Butcher out – *one – two – three.*

Drake saw that a band of armed men were hurrying towards them through the trees. And with them was the thin form of Colonel Hawker.

'What the bloody hell are you playing at, Drake?' Hawker's piercing voice bellowed through the gloom. Sergeant Cronin and Captain Esmonde came next to him, weapons held at the ready in their hands.

For once in Drake's life he was pleased to see the colonel. He raised his palm in a friendly greeting. 'The men asked for a demonstration, sir. How to deal with the enemy at close quarters. Private Butcher here was playing the German sentry. Thank you Butcher, you can get up now.'

Butcher glared at Drake, and rose slowly to his feet.

'Is this true, Butcher?' Hawker demanded.

Butcher glared at Drake, hesitated, then nodded to the colonel. 'Yes, sir.'

Hawker gave Drake a piercing look, and seemed about to question him further. He appeared almost disappointed.

Drake nodded to the colonel, then turned his back and spoke to the crowd. 'First rule of combat, men. If you're in, you're all in. We're at war. Fuck Queensberry Rules. Anything goes. The only thing that matters is to win.'

THURSDAY 23 MAY 1940

Chapter 38

RIHOULT CLAIRMARAIS FOREST, NEAR ST OMER, FRANCE – 04:40HRS

Drake was still half asleep when he heard a word going through the battalion like wildfire. *Dunkirk.*

He sat up. He'd bivouacked under the trees, near the edge of the forest. The sun was nudging the horizon, and the battalion was waking up.

MacTaggart came over. 'The BEF is retreating to Dunkirk, sir! The whole job lot.'

Drake shook his head and got to his feet. 'Where did you hear this, Sergeant?'

MacTaggart pointed to a group of men, gathered a few yards into the forest. 'Don R came in this morning, with battalion orders. The colonel's hopping about like a sodding flea.'

Drake watched as the Don R, the Despatch Rider in question, sauntered over. He saw Private Leighton was lurking at the edge of the trees.

As the rider came closer, Drake saw that his goggles were up, and his face was grey from the road. His features were obscured by dust and smuts, except for white patches around his eyes where the goggles had been keeping the dust out. The rider looked at Drake and sidled up to him. He gave Drake an odd searching glance, eyeing him up and down.

'Your battalion's been ordered north, sir.' The man had a broad Yorkshire accent, stretching his vowels and shortening his *T*s. 'Everybody's off t' Dunkirk, up t' coast. Seems like you're t' last lot to find out.'

'Dunkirk?' Drake knew Dunkirk was an important port, a far larger harbour than Calais or Boulogne. But the whole BEF? 'Why? What's at Dunkirk?'

The despatch rider shrugged. 'No Germans.'

Drake heard Leighton cackling. 'No Germans! I like it! Good one!'

'Sod off, Leighton,' Drake said, and the scrawny private disappeared into the trees.

The despatch rider rolled his eyes. 'Jerry's everywhere else. The whole place is swarming wi' the buggers.' He nodded towards the horizon. 'Things are not looking too grand out there, sir. Take it from me. South Devons are t' fall back and join t' defensive line.'

Drake shook his head. 'How d'you know all this? You read the sealed orders, didn't you?'

The man laughed. 'Course. Always do, Squire. In case I lose 'em. I've got slippy fingers, but I can remember them messages pretty good up here, mind.' He tapped the side of his head. 'Goes wi' territory, see.'

A German spotter plane buzzed over the woods above them. Drake saw it was a Fieseler Storch, with its high wing, protruding nose and mosquito-like legs. It circled, letting out a trail of grey-brown smoke. That didn't bode well.

The Don R followed Drake's gaze. He shook his head and tutted. 'They're bloody everywhere. Watching. Seeing everything. *Spying*.' He turned back to stare at Drake's face. His voice changed register. ''Ere. You're Drake, are you not?' He extended the vowel so it sounded like *Drayek*. 'Tennyson Drake?'

'Second Lieutenant Drake, to you chum,' Drake said, then he frowned. He studied the man's kit, noting he had no regimental markings. That set alarm bells ringing. 'How the hell do you know my name?'

'Talk of t' town, so you are, sir,' the despatch rider said. He raised an eyebrow and pulled a packet of Players from his bag. He offered one to Drake.

Drake shook his head.

The rider lit one, sucking hard on the end. He took off his goggles and wiped them carefully with a rag, cleaning off the dust. Eventually he placed them back on his head.

Drake heard an urgent shout from the edge of the woods. 'Stukas!'

An air sentry was pointing upwards, binoculars focused on the sky. Everybody turned to look that way, and a ripple of fear ran through the battalion. They'd been lucky. They hadn't been bombed for days.

The air sentry shouted again. 'Twenty! No – make that twenty-four Stukas!' He had no siren now – it had obviously been lost along with everything else in the retreat. 'Circling at twelve thousand feet!'

Drake could just make out black dots, high up against the blue. 'Christ,' he muttered. 'That's all we need.'

'Well, *Second Lieutenant* Tennyson Drake,' the Don R said. 'I'd best get on, before Johnny Luftwaffe have something to say 'bout it. But I'd go to Cally if I was you. Not Dunkirk.' He winked. 'Cally, got it?'

Drake stared at the man. 'Go to Calais?' That was how some of the men pronounced it, *Cally*. 'What the hell are you talking about?'

The despatch rider held up his hands. 'Don't shoot the messenger.' Then he let out an idiotic laugh.

Drake was in no mood for games. 'What do you want with me?' he hissed. 'How do you know who I am?'

'Easy, duck.' The man spoke in a low tone now. 'No need t' tell whole battalion.'

Drake studied the man's worn-down overalls, his battered boots, his chipped goggles. 'Who the bloody hell are you?'

'Go to Cally,' the man repeated. 'Report to Brigadier Nicholson. Them's your orders. Different from *battalion* orders, see?'

Drake was stunned into silence for a moment. His mind started racing. He glanced at the other men nearby, but they were all staring up at the sky.

The despatch rider began to saunter away. 'Right you are. Must be off.' He slapped his satchel. 'Messages to deliver. People to see. T' fate of nations is in your hands now, so to speak, Mr Drake.'

High up above, the sky was filled with a rising moan as the first Stuka tipped down into a dive.

Drake followed the rider. *The fate of nations*? 'What do you mean? Who sent you?' He spoke in an urgent, hushed tone. 'Was it Major Lyle-Smith?'

The despatch rider turned and laughed again. He touched the side of his nose. 'Oh no. Not 'im. Not even 'is boss. This comes from 'is boss's boss.' The man bent from the waist as he gave Drake a tidy, practised little bow. 'This message is delivered by courtesy of T' Chief.'

Chapter 39

THE WAIL OF THE Stuka sirens grew louder. The woods were filled with men staring up at the sky. Some ran this way and that, looking for cover in the trees. Others started hastily digging slit trenches, although it was far too late for that. Drake watched as a black cross with crooked wings grew larger against the pale morning sky. The distant, high-pitched moan swelled into a hideous howl, but the despatch rider's words were circling around inside his mind.

'A whole bloody squadron!' a soldier shouted as he ran past Drake and into the woods, helmet clasped tightly over his head.

The shriek of the divebombers wailed ever louder as more and more tipped into their dives. Drake shook himself into action.

He yelled out orders. 'Disperse! Take cover! Get some Brens on that first Stuka. Now!'

He watched the shapes of running men as the battalion scattered through the trees. He gazed up at the sky, for a moment transfixed by the hideous silhouettes as they came shrieking down, closer and closer. The sirens screamed louder, ripping down towards them, the sound clawing horribly through the morning air.

'Get down!' Drake yelled again, and the men threw themselves to the ground behind the cover of tree trunks. Bullets snapped through the branches. Drake heard the judder of machine-gun fire from the aircraft as it strafed the woods. Somewhere not far off, a man screamed as he was hit. Then there was the groan and the changing pitch of the siren as the first Stuka released its bomb and began to pull up from its dive.

Drake heard the sickening whistle of organ pipes as the bomb sped towards them, shimmering black, as it plunged on, down, down, down. He pressed his face into the soil and his entire body tensed. A blistering light tore through the woods as the detonation burst. The blast ripped branches and entire boughs from the trees. The impact of the pressure wave hit Drake like a London bus, bowling over him in a crashing wall of wind. Wood splinters shot murderously through the forest, whistling inches above his head. From the corner of his eye, he saw two men as they were catapulted through the air. Drake pressed his face to the earth. Underpressure sucked air back into the bombsite, and he was pulled up off the soil, then slapped back down.

A moment later, it was over. Drake's head was tolling like a church bell. He finally lifted his face and looked around.

A corporal from A Company was lying on the ground. Drake wasn't sure if he was dead, or simply frozen in shock. The legs of another man were hanging from a tree. The wail of the next Stuka siren screeched closer and closer, down and down towards them again. Drake instinctively pulled his feet up, curled into a ball, convinced for a moment that it would land behind him. The bomb hit further away than the last, the detonation cracking sharply through the trees.

Drake kept in the cover of the treetrunks as another howling Stuka scream filled the air, another bomb whistled down and hit the forest a hundred yards away, blasting hard and shattering timber. He heard a man screaming for help, and another shouting for the medics. More Stukas howled down in their awful shrieking dives. Smoke billowed in between the trees.

The wail of Stuka sirens grew louder. Bombs whistled down and hit the ground in thunderous, brutal crashes, exploding through the woods in hard, fast, roaring blasts. Fire and smoke shot up into the sky. A bomb detonated fifty yards away, a flash of white and yellow and red, silhouetting the trees.

Drake got to his feet and ran through the forest. Bren guns chugged out bullets from the edge of the woods as they fired up at the next wave of divebombers. A series of howls, then the ominous whistles as the bombs fell. Trees blew apart in great, catastrophic bursts. A man shrieked as Drake ran by, jagged wood splinters stuck into his body from a shattered tree stump. Drake dodged through the smoke, and saw that the colonel's Dingo scout car was parked beneath the canopy, hidden under a camouflage net. He stopped, then climbed up onto the step and peered inside.

There was a Bren mounted at the front, and an antitank rifle standing at the back, behind the commander's seat. He examined the controls. It would be a cramped, awkward space for a tall man. The seat was set at an angle to allow the driver to look easily over his left shoulder to reverse.

He saw the petrol tank was positioned right behind the driver's seat. One spark, and he'd be toasted to a crisp at a thousand degrees.

Drake suddenly felt a hand clasp his leg, and he was jerked from the scout car's step. He tumbled awkwardly to the ground and a boot went into his kidney. He gasped with the sudden, lancing pain. Big hands pulled him up from the dirt and he saw Butcher's grinning face, leaning down over him.

'Queensberry Rules, is it? Hold him!'

Drake felt hands grip him from behind, pinning his arms back, and from the smell of old cigarettes, he guessed who it was. Private Leighton was lean and wiry, and much stronger than he looked.

Drake had no way to protect himself.

Butcher took a step back, then kicked him hard in the balls.

A searing ache shot up from his groin, erupting in his stomach in a volcanic explosion of nausea and pain. He doubled over, gagging, and retched. The world was blotted out by a mushrooming wave of agony that sickened his entire being. He sank down to his knees.

Leighton jerked Drake's arms up behind his back into a full Nelson grip. Another wave of nausea churned Drake's stomach, and he heard himself groan. He clenched his eyelids shut as red-hot stars of torment shot in front of his eyes.

A bomb went off in the forest. Butcher ignored it and grabbed Drake's hair. He pulled his head up. Grabbed his face in one giant hand, and grinned. 'Fuck Queensberry Rules.'

Chapter 40

Drake gasped and opened his eyes again, forcing himself to look up at the big man. He tensed himself to brace for the next heavy blow. He knew what was coming. A murderous kicking, and, in the chaos of the Stuka attack, nobody would ever know about it or come to his aid. The shriek of Stuka sirens grew louder. Bombs whistled down and hit the ground in thunderous, brutal cracks all through the woods.

Butcher glared down at him, then suddenly turned to Private Leighton. 'Let him go.'

Leighton frowned. 'What?'

Butcher growled at the little man. 'Just bloody let him go.'

Leighton released Drake's arms, and Drake forced himself back up to his feet. He brought his arms up, fists clenched in a guard position. So the big man wanted to make a fight of it after all.

Bombs whistled down into the woods, exploding in hard, fast, roaring blasts. Fire and smoke shot up into the sky. Shell splinters thudded into the surrounding trees. Drake watched Butcher as the detonations went off all around. The big man didn't even flinch.

After the blasts, there was a momentary quiet.

'You're alright, Drake,' Butcher said in a deep, baritone growl. 'For an officer.'

Drake shook his head, as if he hadn't heard him right.

Leighton winked. 'We're coming with you.'

'No you're bloody not,' Drake said.

'We heard what that Don R said,' Leighton rasped. 'You're going to Cally. So we're coming too.'

Drake felt a rising sense of alarm. 'You don't understand. The BEF is pulling out. You're going back home.'

Butcher tore the camouflage netting off the Dingo scout car. He shot a dark look back at Drake. 'I'm on a murder charge if I go back to England. I'll take my chances in Cally.'

A bomb crashed a hundred yards away, a flash of white and yellow and red, silhouetting the trees. Drake ignored it. He stared at Butcher in stunned surprise.

Private Leighton leapt into the scout car and sparked the wires. Beneath the cowling behind the cab, the Daimler six-cylinder petrol motor thrummed vigorously into life.

Stukas screamed down from the sky. The forest shuddered as a salvo of bombs detonated, one after another, thundering towards them through the trees. Branches crackled, catching fire.

Leighton revved the engine and the car inched forwards. 'Well, get in then,' he said.

Another divebomber screamed down. The bomb shrilled overhead. It hit the forest fifty yards away in a tremendous blast of fire. Drake took a moment to gather his thoughts. He rubbed at his hairline, felt the itch of the healing scar. *In for a penny, in for a pound.* Might as well get hanged for a pig as a sheep.

He vaulted in through the scout car's open top. Stukas howled down, bombs whistled into the forest, exploding brightly all around in ripping peals of thunder.

Drake nodded to Leighton. 'Go!'

The scout car shot forward. Then came to a sudden stop, as Colonel Hawker stepped out to block their path, flanked by Sergeant Cronin, Captain Esmonde, and half a dozen armed men. Hawker pulled his sidearm from its holster. Rifles bristled. The colonel's shrill voice cut through the din of the attack.

'Deserting under enemy fire, Drake? Don't move another bloody inch.'

All around them, trees were blazing now, flames leaping from branch to branch. Smoke was blowing thickly through the woods.

'I've got orders to report to Brigadier Nicholson in Calais, sir!' Drake shouted back. 'Special orders!' He had no time to stop and explain.

Leighton revved the engine and the Dingo edged forwards again.

'Balderdash, Drake!' Hawker cried out. He raised his pistol. 'Come out of the car at once!'

Butcher grinned and got a footing on the scout-car's step. He reached into the open cab, then spun around and pointed the Boys antitank rifle at the colonel.

'Get out of the way,' he said.

'You're not going anywhere!' Hawker bellowed in sudden fury.

Drake nodded to Leighton. The Daimler engine roared and the scout car surged forwards. Hawker and Cronin dived out of the way.

'Stop him!' the colonel screeched as he fell to the ground. 'You're a dead man, Drake! The penalty for desertion under enemy fire is death!'

Cronin fired his rifle from a prone position, but the shot clanged off the armour. The other men just stepped back as the scout car thundered past, seeming loathe to fire on a comrade. In the cab, Leighton jerked the wheel hard right and swerved in between the trees. The six-cylinder Daimler engine was fast and powerful. The exhaust note thrummed as they accelerated away through the burning woods.

A bomb detonated in their path, and Leighton wrenched the wheel over. They hurtled through the smoke, then bounced onto a rough track that led out of the forest. Another shot cracked out, spinning off the armour. Drake twisted round to see Hawker, now clutching a rifle, taking potshots at them as they went.

'Room for one more?' boomed a Scottish voice as they tore towards the edge of the trees. Drake signalled, and Leighton slammed on the brakes. Sergeant MacTaggart ran out from between the trees and leapt onto the side of the scout car.

'Fire on that car!' Hawker's shrill command pierced through the forest. 'Those men are deserting. Stop them!'

Leighton stuck his foot to the floor.

Drake ducked down, expecting to feel the clatter of bullets. But instead he heard a voice call out from the woods, 'Three cheers for Lieutenant Drake!'

He looked back over his shoulder, bemused. Bill Lucas was standing in the shadow of the trees. Instead of opening fire, the men at the edge of the clearing cheered and threw their helmets in the air.

'Hoorah!' they yelled. 'Hoorah! Hoorah!'

Drake turned to MacTaggart as the scout car raced away. 'What the hell was that all about?'

The old sergeant clung on to the side, one hand keeping his khaki tam o'shanter pinned to his head. 'You may not know it, but you're becoming something of a legend among the men of the battalion, sir. And may the good Lord forgive me, but I might have fanned the flames with a well-placed rumour or two.'

Leighton slammed through the gears and pressed his foot to the floor. The engine thrummed and the scout car jolted forward down the track. High above them in the sky, another wave of Stukas began to scream down into nosedives, dark wings flickering as their machine guns strafed the road. The Dingo engine thrummed and the wheels pummelled along on the narrow, unmade track.

Drake shot MacTaggart a look. 'You told them what exactly, Sergeant?'

MacTaggart hesitated. 'I said you was on a secret mission to save Britain from the Nazis.'

'You did what?' Drake stared at the sergeant in disbelief. 'You're a bloody fool.'

MacTaggart pulled himself up on top of the rear engine cowling. 'Your thanks is graciously accepted, sir.'

They all ducked their heads as machine gun bullets strafed the road. Drake glanced up. The next divebomber was tracking their vehicle. The Stuka howl grew into a wailing, mind-numbing scream. Drake waited for the groan as the plane pulled up and the bomb released, then yelled, 'Left!'

Leighton yanked the wheel hard over. The Dingo lurched leftwards into a dry, crop-filled field. The bomb whistled down to explode where they would have been had they stayed on the track. It seemed as though the entire Luftwaffe was on their tail.

'Christ in hell,' Drake said as Leighton crunched higher through the gears, pounding his foot to the floor. 'Where did you learn to drive like that?'

Leighton cackled. 'I may have liberated one or two transports from the docks when I was back on civvy street.' He looked suddenly worried by his confession. 'But I'm on the straight and narrow now, sir, I swear on my mother's grave, bless her soul.'

Drake slapped the armoured steelwork. 'Alright. Let's see what this thing can do.'

The Daimler engine thundered and the Dingo picked up speed. Leighton swung the wheel right, and the men clung on as they bounced back onto the track. They hurtled along, tyres throwing up a long trail of fine, grey dust in their wake.

Drake flashed a look back up at the sky. Another Stuka was giving chase. Private Leighton pressed his foot flat to the floor and fixed his eyes on the narrow road ahead. Drake's jaw was clamped tight, but his mind was racing. *Calais*.

Next to him, MacTaggart knocked on the steel plate of the scout car's armour. He slapped down a wad of ten bob notes into Drake's hands, and gave him a gap-toothed grin. 'I took the precaution of securing your winnings, sir. Now, where in Satan's dark realm are we going in such a damned hurry? What the hell have I missed?'

PART IV

CALAIS

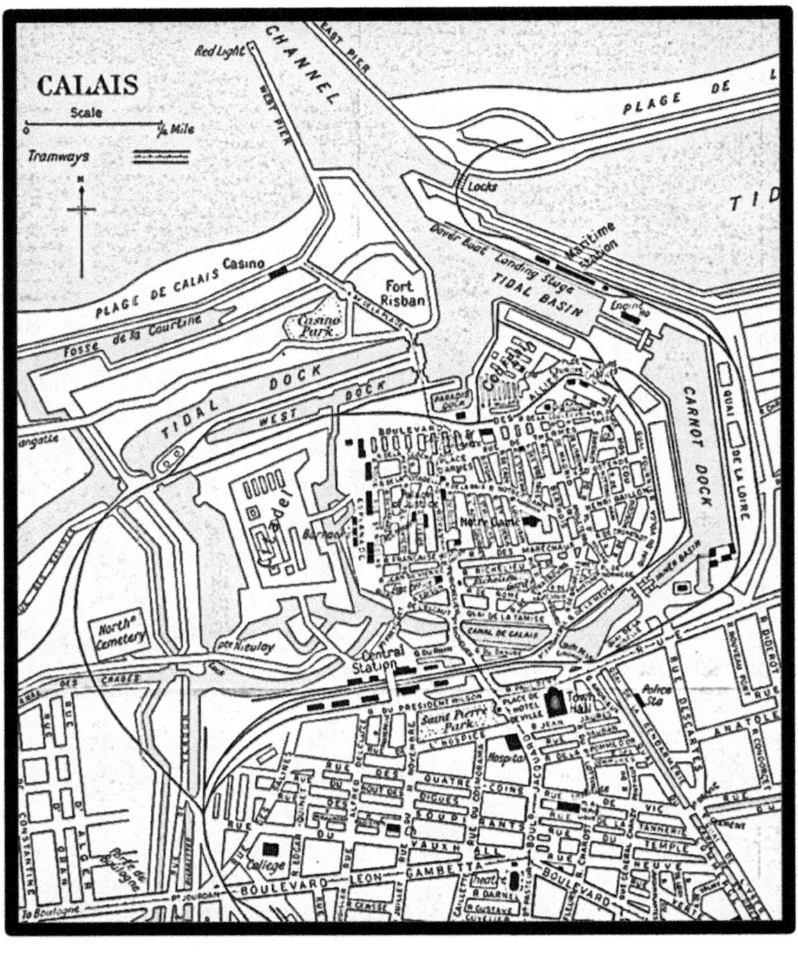

FRIDAY 24 MAY 1940

EMPIRE DAY

Chapter 41

RUE DU CHEVAL GRIS, ST-PIERRE-LÈS-CALAIS, FRANCE – 09:00HRS

DRAKE PULLED THE LACE curtains aside and peered out of the window, which overlooked the railway lines on the outskirts of Calais. An urgent thudding of distant artillery rattled the glass. The chugging *bom-bom-bom* of a Bren gun sounded loudly from the room next door. Two seconds later came the whistles of shells as they landed in the city. Drake dived to the floor as the glass shattered and a blinding crash went off outside.

He took a moment to catch his breath. His ears were ringing from the detonations. They'd arrived at Calais as dark had been falling the night before. They'd run the gauntlet of the panzers, which had closed an iron ring around the city to seal off the British garrison. Drake reckoned they must have been the last British soldiers to get into Calais by land.

When they'd arrived, fierce skirmishes were being fought around the outskirts in running battles. The British had been fighting desperate and one-sided rearguard actions, falling back from bridge to bridge. Night had fallen, and in typical German fashion, the attack had ceased, allowing the British forces some respite overnight, but Drake and his men had had no luck finding Brigadier Nicholson in the darkness, in the chaos of the blackout. Tank attacks and shelling had picked up again just after dawn.

The British forces were now defending a perimeter of canals and railway tracks that looped around the outskirts of the city. MacTaggart, Butcher and Leighton had taken up positions behind window frames, weapons pointing out. Drake got to his feet and moved through the house, boots crunching on broken glass. His focus now was simply on finding the brigadier.

Men of the Green Jackets rifle regiments were stationed alertly around the doors and windows of the house. Their kit was strangely clean, and Drake realised they must be fresh off the boat. He saw from the Maltese cross on their cap badges that they were the King's Royal Rifle Corps –

the best-shooting regiment in the British Army, if their reputation was to be believed. Many of them had the crossed-rifle badges of marksmen. But half of them were only reservists, and they seemed to have left all their heavy weaponry at home.

Drake listened for a moment to the sounds of battle. Heavy artillery tubes were thumping in the distance. Calais was in for a hammering. Glass shattered, and somebody started swearing loudly. Drake heard the distinctive sound of Spandau machine guns and the muted thudding as their bullets struck at the building's walls.

Drake looked outside, and tried to get his bearings. The house was in the newer, southern part of Calais, known as St Pierre. Behind them, the northern edge of the old city of Calais was on the channel coast. But even with the sea at their backs, and the Royal Navy on it, there remained a grave danger of encirclement. Drake didn't envy Brigadier Nicholson his command. If the Germans could work their way all around, they'd lay siege to the city and squeeze.

Drake rubbed at his face. He'd spent time in Calais during the Phoney War, and knew that the city had evolved by having to defend itself from land and sea over hundreds of years. Its network of canals and fortifications would make it a tough nut for the Germans to crack. And these riflemen, he reckoned, would put up a very stiff fight.

MacTaggart tapped him on the shoulder. 'If we're going to meet the brigadier, might I recommend the use of my razor, sir?'

Drake found a bathroom mirror and had a quick shave, scraping away at his battered chin. He studied the image the mirror reflected. He seemed to have aged ten years in the fortnight – how could it only be a fortnight? – since the invasion had begun. He shook himself, rubbed fingers over his freshly-scraped jaw and through his matted, dark red hair. He wondered why he'd been sent to Calais. He didn't know. But he'd nailed his colours to the mast. He'd burned his bridges with Colonel Hawker. There was only one way now, and that was forwards at all costs.

He reached into his battledress pocket and pulled out the charred sheet of paper they'd saved from the brazier. He studied the typescript.

OPERATIONSBEFEHL DÄMMERUNG

Twilight, Dusk, Nightfall. He held the paper up to the bathroom window to examine it, then froze.

There was something there. Something he could just make out against the morning sunlight that was streaming in through the glass. Suddenly he saw it, clear as day, almost like a watermark on the page. Something had been written by hand on another page on top of this one, and it had left an indent. It was just a few words, and the weak outline of the German cursive script was hard to read.

Outside, the sound of gunfire suddenly intensified, Spandaus and Mauser rifles clattering. Drake knew that an attack would be coming soon.

He hurried out of the bathroom. He snapped his fingers. 'Pencil, Sergeant!' he said.

MacTaggart frowned, then fumbled through his pockets and pulled out a stub.

Drake flourished the scrap of paper. Held it up against a window pane at the south side of the house where the glass was still intact. They could just make out the indent of the handwriting.

'What's the date today, Sergeant?'

MacTaggart looked at him, surprised. 'Och, well, did ye not know? It's your ruddy Empire Day today, sir! Thursday, twenty-fourth of May. Though I doubt there'll be much dancing in the streets back home.'

Agent Viper had said the war would be over in seven days, and that had been on Monday. It seemed astonishing to Drake that it had only been three days ago, with all that had happened in between.

'Well I'll be damned,' he said. 'Come over here. Look!'

He traced the markings on the page with the pencil. Then he had it. He showed it to MacTaggart.

Stunde Null. 28. Mai.

MacTaggart gave him a quizzical look.

Drake tapped the paper. 'Zero Hour, Twenty-eighth of May.'

MacTaggart counted forwards on his rough fingertips. 'Four days, sir. Four days until this – whatever it is – happens?'

Drake shook his head. 'Not quite. To the German way of thinking, zero hour on the twenty-eighth would be literally double-oh, double-oh. That's midnight on the night of the twenty-seventh for us. Which leaves three and half days. Three and a half days until Operation Nightfall, whatever the hell that is. Christ.'

MacTaggart gave a low whistle through the gap in his teeth. 'Well, I'd have given the BEF a fortnight, tops, the way things have been going. But three days?'

'It speaks of a complete collapse,' Drake said. 'But how?'

It didn't bear thinking about. There were three or four hundred thousand men of the BEF on the continent, the best part of the British Army.

One of the riflemen spoke up then, and said the King was going to make a speech on the BBC that afternoon. The announcement was met by a loud, sarcastic cheer. All through the house, more and more of the riflemen were being called to man windows and rooftops with rifles and Brens. A wounded corporal, splashed in bright red blood, staggered down the stairs, held up by a comrade. A medic rushed to help him. Shells crashed into the surrounding streets. Small arms fire began crackling around in a mounting din. The German attack was starting in force once again.

MacTaggart interrupted Drake's thoughts. 'I was about to tell you. The MO reports that Brigade CP is a mile away, sir. In the basement of a medical clinic on Boulevard Gambetta.'

Boulevard Gambetta. Something stirred at the back of Drake's mind, there was something in what MacTaggart had just said, but he couldn't put a finger on it. He shoved the thought away. They had to get to Nicholson – and fast. Time was pressing. Drake pulled on his helmet and snatched up his rifle.

'Butcher! Leighton! On your feet! Let's go!'

Chapter 42

In the streets, the crash of shellfire was deafening. They ran along behind a low railway embankment while riflemen were taking up positions on the tracks. Piles of rubble were evident on every road now. Drake stared for a moment at a great tower of smoke that was rising darkly from the harbour. It seemed the oil tanks were on fire. Nearby, German mortars *whumped*, and the bombs came down in sickening cracks into the railway ballast, throwing up great spouts of crushed stone into the air. Moments later, a rain of gravel began to spatter down. Through the din, Drake could hear orders being yelled, and the sound of heavy motors. A pair of British Cruiser tanks accelerated up from a side road to fire across the tracks before quickly reversing away. The German attack was intensifying. Small arms fire crackled and snapped across the rails. Drake and his men hurried on behind the railway lines, ducking back behind a street of terraced houses as the pressure began to build.

It took them a long time to find Boulevard Leon Gambetta in the chaos – a broad, cobbled road with tramlines in the centre, and trees along the walkways for shade. In better times, it would have been a pleasant place to stroll, but now there was no sign of any civilians. Drake kept hard over to the edge of the pavement nearest the buildings as stray shells and bullets whipped down the middle of the road.

They walked under a pharmacist's sign, a green cross with a symbol of the cup of Hygeia. Next door to the pharmacy, was a large, *fin de siècle* building – *Clinique Gambetta*. A shell struck the boulevard to the west in a great, shattering racket, throwing out flames and debris. Grasping his helmet to his head, Drake hurried through the smoke and went inside.

A pair of runners came thumping towards him, clutching order slips.

'Where's Nicholson?' Drake called out. 'Where's the brigadier?'

The two men pointed at the stairs to the basement as they ran out of the building, then headed in opposite directions along the street.

'Wait here,' Drake said to MacTaggart, and he leapt down the steps three at a time.

He found a colonel of the Royal Artillery directing operations in a room lit by two bare electric bulbs. The basement room was flanked by maps, with a dozen or so officers and NCOs crammed in. The thudding of the detonations was muted down here. The room was gloomy, and it stank of unwashed men. The colonel was bent over one of the city maps, giving orders to an adjutant for the placement of barricades.

'Excuse me, sir,' Drake said hurriedly. 'I'm looking for the brigadier.'

The colonel barely glanced at him. 'He's gone to see the situation at the front for himself.'

Drake quickly scanned the maps that were placed around the room. The front seemed to stretch in a great semi-circle, from Fort Risban by the harbour, all the way around the outskirts of the city, following battlements and railway tracks, circling back to the port on the eastern side – a distance of some half-dozen miles.

'I'm sorry sir, but I've got to find him. Do you know exactly where?'

The artillery officer stood up. His eyes were bloodshot, ringed with black shadows. He looked utterly spent. 'He left ten minutes ago on foot, heading for the western wall. You might catch him if you hurry.'

Drake raced out of the room. With his men in tow, he ran back westwards along the boulevard, heading towards the sound of fighting. The gunfire grew heavier as they hurried towards a bridge that spanned a dark canal. Bullets were flying in all directions and pinging off the cobblestones. Moving forward became slow work. They crossed the bridge carefully, keeping to the cover of the parapets. Up ahead, they could see the backs of British riflemen firing doggedly over the ruins of an old city wall.

Darting from cover to cover, Drake eventually found a young second lieutenant of the King's Royal Rifle Corps who was taking shelter behind the ruins. The young man had a broad moustache. A sweep of thick, dark hair was barely concealed by a helmet tipped back from his face. He was directing his men to shoot rifles at German armoured vehicles which were only a hundred yards away. The gunfire cracked and clattered in a hammering din.

'Where's the brigadier?' Drake yelled.

The young officer shook his head and shouted back. 'He just left.' He pointed north towards the harbour and the port. 'Went that way I think!'

A British two-pounder antitank gun thumped loudly nearby, its Royal Artillery crewmen each in the regulation position on one knee behind the shield. A moment later, yelling came from the crew as the shell scored a direct hit. In the distance, a German tank brewed up, billowing smoke. Drake left them to it. Keeping their heads down, they made their way carefully northwards, crawling or bent double at times, staying in the cover of the old city walls.

Shells slammed into the stonework in deafening concussions. Splinters flew in all directions. Clods of earth shot into the air. The deadly chatter of Spandau machine guns spattered constant fire into the brickwork, but the thin line of riflemen fought professionally, shooting staunchly back, not giving an inch of ground. Drake and his men worked their way on, through the clash and fizz of the crossfire. A Green Jacket section leader was firing a Bren gun over the wall towards the enemy positions. Short bursts jabbed from the muzzle in stuttering thumps. Every now and then the louder crack-thump of an antitank rifle went off. They ducked down as a series of screeching detonations splintered into the walls, fired from German autocannons. Overhead, heavy ordnance shrieked across the city as the German assault began in earnest. Large calibre shells landed behind them in the old town, with thick, thudding crashes that they all felt in their chests. They pushed on, panting now, bent over, kit soaked with sweat in the heat of the morning sun.

After half a mile, Drake came to a turn in the canal. They followed its course, and the sound of fighting faded a little behind them. They dashed along the overgrown banks, and the Citadel of Calais rose up before them, great ramparts on an island of waterways and canals. Standing upright at last, Drake ran over a bridge that led towards the high embankment walls. The main gate and the top of the ramparts were guarded by British troops, but there was no enemy in sight here yet. A British sergeant with a Tommy gun stood at the gate. A whine of Stukas cut through the air from high overhead.

'Where's the brigadier?' Drake shouted through the din. 'Where's Nicholson? I was told he came this way.'

The sergeant shook his head. 'Left over an hour ago. Try the CP in Boulevard Gambetta.'

'Christ in hell! We've just come from there.' Drake looked around in despair. 'Are you sure?'

The sergeant scowled at him. 'Yes, sir. Course I'm sure.'

Drake gazed upwards for a moment as the first Stuka came plummeting down towards the city, down and down, siren wailing. It pulled up, groaning, from its dive and the tiny black dot of its bomb began to fall.

Drake turned around. 'Alright, men. Back the way we came. He must have gone the other way.'

Fred Leighton rolled his eyes and groaned.

Drake glanced at his watch. The morning was slipping away from them. As they made their way back through the fighting, he became increasingly frustrated. Under fire from land and air, the city was descending into chaos. He tried to find a motorcycle, a bicycle, any transport at all, but there were none to be had. Everything that could be moved had been requisitioned already or piled into great heaps in the streets to make barricades. Whenever they approached the perimeter, they kept getting bogged down by unpassable streams of gunfire, or intense, punching German attacks that were defiantly repulsed. Drake grew increasingly desperate as the time ticked past and the sun crept slowly through the sky above them. It was galling. They were unable to move for minutes or even hours at a time as the battle raged around them. Bombs fell in deafening flurries to land all across the city. Fires began to burn. Everywhere they went, it seemed the brigadier had just been and gone.

'Christ!' Drake yelled out, kicking at the debris that blocked one of the roads. 'He's got to be somewhere!'

By mid-afternoon, they were back in southern Calais, in the outskirts of the city, not far from where they had started. There, at a series of railway junctions, the Green Jackets were coming under heavy pressure from German panzers. Shells screeched in as the tanks fired on their positions. Against the bigger machines, the infantry's antitank rifles were useless, and the British two-pounder guns were few and far between.

Drake found a captain of the QVR – the Queen Victoria Rifles.

'You've missed, him!' the captain shouted. 'Have you heard? Fort Nieulay has fallen!'

Drake groaned inwardly. *Bloody hell.* It was ominous news. Fort Nieulay was a great bastion on the western edge of Calais. If the Germans had taken it already, it was a very bad sign.

Drake surveyed the defensive positions. The riflemen were still firing stubbornly from behind the embankments, but panzers lurked in between the buildings on the opposite side. Squadrons of Luftwaffe bombers dotted the sky, flying over at high altitude.

Drake watched a pair of British tanks advance to the railway embankment. They fired a few shots on the German positions, then reversed away. It was a clever tactic. By springing up and disappearing, only to appear again some distance off, the British armour gave the impression that they were there in great numbers, and made it impossible for the enemy to know what he was up against. And for the same reasons it did wonders for the infantry's morale.

Drake beckoned his men back behind the cover of a blasted building. He took off his helmet and scratched his fingers through his sweat-soaked hair. 'We're going round in bloody circles! Where the hell is the brigadier?'

Leighton spat out a half chewed cigarette butt. 'Don't ask me, Guv.'

Drake spotted a wireless lorry in an alleyway to the rear of the British position. He ran towards it. Inside, a wounded major was giving instructions to a signals sergeant.

'I need to find Nicholson,' Drake said. 'It's urgent.'

'He's surveying the entire front line personally,' the major shouted back over the din, then held up a hand for quiet. 'Hush now! It's the speech!'

The signals sergeant turned up the volume on the amplifier, and it took Drake a moment to realise that what he was hearing was the tinny, stilted tones of King George.

It is not mere territorial conquest the enemy is seeking.
It is the overthrow, complete and
final, of the Empire and of everything for which it stands,
and after that the conquest of the world.

Drake saw that his men had followed him. A German armoured car appeared at the far end of the alley. The air cracked as Butcher let off a shot from his antitank rifle.

There was an ominous whump from the other side of the tracks.

'Trench mortars!' MacTaggart bellowed. 'Into cover!'

Drake dived behind a crumbling garden wall.

The bombs fizzed down to burst forty yards away among the line of riflemen, causing terrible injuries and throwing up railway ballast. The stones whipped through the air, crashing into walls and vehicles. There was a sudden intensification of firing from the enemy positions all along the embankment. A medium Mark III Panzer advanced. The grey turret traversed as the engine bellowed and the tracks jerked and skidded over railway lines. A British two-pounder thumped and a shell struck the underside of the panzer's frontal armour with a shattering din. The tank shuddered to a halt. A moment later, Drake could hear the muffled screaming of the crew inside. Elsewhere, the assault was pushing on with renewed intensity. German machine guns rattled out streams of bullets. Shells and mortar bombs detonated all around.

'We're getting flanked,' MacTaggart yelled. 'We'll have to fall back, sir! They're breaking through!'

Drake knew that fighting armour with rifles was a lost cause. The Germans seemed to have an endless supply of armoured vehicles of all descriptions, from panzers to six-wheelers, and for each one that was knocked out, two or three more appeared. Enemy tanks were now pouring over the railway tracks to the east of their position. Riflemen were falling back in echelons in good order, but it was brutal, hard and bloody fighting. A line of wounded men were laid out behind a building, waiting for stretcher bearers. And now the German infantry were infiltrating in between the panzer thrusts. It was clear that they'd never find the brigadier in all this chaos.

'That's it,' Drake said. 'Come on. Time to go.'

They retired with the riflemen, firing in short hard bursts whenever the enemy came into sight, then dashing, bent double, from wall to wall, alley to alley, road to road. They stopped at a street corner to cover the retreat of a wounded man. Drake lay on the ground, rifle butt pressed to his cheek, and fired into the haze at the fleeting shapes of German infantry. The rifle cracked loudly again and again. At the far end of the street, a large, dust-stained panzer emerged from the smoke, machine gun flickering, and accelerated towards Drake's position. It hit a row of mines that were strewn across the road. A track blew off and two steel running wheels scythed through the air to clash into rooftops nearby. The turret hatch flew open and a face came out in a funnel of smoke. Drake squeezed the trigger and the head snapped away. He felt nothing inside.

'Fall back!' he shouted, jumping to his feet. He signalled his men to withdraw.

Side by side with the riflemen, they fought a desperate, rearguard, running battle. The riflemen shot carefully, never wasting their rounds, and each street was littered with German bodies before it was taken, but road by road, junction by junction, the Germans were advancing, and the riflemen were getting pushed back, slowly, yard by bloody yard. Drake's frustration was growing. They were no longer looking for the brigadier, now they were just fighting to stay alive.

The sun edged towards the west, and the shadows in the city grew long. Butcher scavenged among the heaps of British dead and found some more ammunition for his antitank rifle, which he'd taken to using in an antipersonnel role. When the German soldiers came running down the street towards them, Butcher fired three rounds from the great gun, and his hits almost tore the enemy soldiers in half – with great effect on the morale on both sides of the fight.

MacTaggart fired his Thompson submachine gun in short bursts, conserving ammunition. The spent casings pinged away in arcs across the street. But despite their best efforts, it was obvious now that the city was surrounded by an overwhelming German armoured force, and, without support, the British infantry had little hope of hanging on. The enemy assault pressed hard, fighting street by street, corner by corner. They desperately wanted Calais, but the riflemen were making them pay in blood for every inch of ground.

In a momentary lull, Drake called to MacTaggart, who was lying behind a pile of rubble. 'We've got to break contact and get away!'

MacTaggart nodded and whistled to the other two men. Hooked a thumb over his shoulder. 'You go first, sir. I'll hold here 'til you get to the end of the street.'

Drake ran like hell, diving into cover at a junction. He covered the street with his rifle, then waved to MacTaggart to come. The old sergeant came running and skidded down beside him. Butcher and Leighton followed a few seconds behind.

The Scotsman stared up the road, breathing hard from the run. There were no enemy in sight. 'All clear, sir.'

The sun was lowering towards the horizon now, and they still hadn't found the brigadier.

'Alright. Back to the command post. Move it!'

Drake got to his feet and ran.

Chapter 43

DRAKE AND HIS MEN pounded back through burning streets. A flight of Stukas screamed down from the sky, machine guns jabbering sparks. Bombs fell from beneath their wings and hit in devastating blasts, sending earthquake-like shudders through the ground. The perimeter defences had crumbled. Houses were catching fire all across the city now, filling the air with smoke. A stiff sea breeze was picking up, but instead of fresh air it brought heat, fumes and ash from the fires. Drake was surprised to see the sky colouring with sunset. In the intensity of the fighting he had lost all track of time.

A Mark IV heavy panzer rolled across the intersection of Boulevard Leon Gambetta and Boulevard Pasteur. Its 75mm howitzer thudded. A sharp flash and crack of explosion followed, and an entire section cascaded down from an apartment wall. Drake and his men took the backstreets, keeping away from the German armour. British riflemen were retreating, still fighting desperately in the chaos, firing from windows, doorways and street corners. From the ruins, a Bren gun chugged bullets towards the tank with a dogged *bom-bom-bom-bom-bom*.

Drake skidded around a corner, and onto Boulevard Gambetta.

'This way!' he called out to his men.

They ran towards the clinic, where they found the command post was being evacuated. Men were coming out of the front doors at a run, clutching maps and papers and telephones or wireless equipment. Riflemen and engineers were dotted across the boulevard, firing up streets and alleys at German infantry, who were slowly advancing towards them. A British officer in service dress was shooting gamely with a revolver in each hand. A motorcycle despatch rider, still in his leathers, was lying behind his motorcycle, firing a sidearm. German soldiers shot with rifles from the streets that ran obliquely to the boulevard. A burst of automatic fire shattered cobbles as it zipped across the road.

Drake ran to the officer, who was reloading his revolvers now, at the corner of the buildings. He recognised the man as the artillery colonel who had been running the command post.

'Where's Nicholson?' he shouted through the madness. 'Where's the brigadier?'

The colonel stared at Drake, then pointed north, towards the old city, the port and the sea.

'Fall back across the bridges!' he said with a groan. 'Brigade HQ's moved to the citadel. You'll probably find him there.'

'Come with us,' Drake said. 'St Pierre's been overrun.'

The colonel shook his head. 'I won't make it. The bastards got me. I'll take my chances here.'

When the colonel had finished loading both revolvers, he staggered a little, then walked towards a side street which was brimming with German infantry. Drake saw a stem of blood spreading across the centre of the colonel's service jacket. It was uncannily pink in the strange evening light. He'd been shot in the guts, and was trying to mask the pain.

'Go on. Get your men back,' the colonel gasped. His face was drawn and pale. 'The name's Grenville. Tell my wife I'm sorry, I won't be coming home this time. Now go!'

Holding himself up with extraordinary strength despite the wound, the colonel stepped around the corner and fired both pistols at the German troops, who scattered, finding cover. A tank clattered forwards down the street, and its turret traversed slowly around.

The colonel called back over his shoulder, 'Don't just stand there. Bloody well run!'

Drake grabbed MacTaggart. 'Take Butcher and Leighton. Meet me at the citadel. That's an order. Go!'

The sergeant signalled to the two men, and they sprinted across the boulevard. Drake ran back to the clinic, where the motorcycle despatch rider had holstered his pistol and was straddling his machine.

'I need your motorbike,' Drake said.

The rider gave him an incredulous look. 'Sod off. Get your own.'

Drake smiled and reached into his pocket. 'I'll give you a hundred pounds.'

The Don R's mouth fell open as Drake thrust the wad of money at him. 'Take it! Now get the hell out of here! Go on. Scram!'

The rider took one look at the advancing German tanks. He grabbed the money and ran.

Drake slung his leg over the saddle, switched on the ignition. It was a Triumph 350cc single, and he kicked the starter down. The engine popped and burbled into life. He took a last look at the artillery colonel who was facing the tank and firing both his revolvers like it was high noon. *Grenville*. Drake would remember the message. *Christ*, he'd never forget. He tore his gaze away, opened the throttle and accelerated hard down the darkening street.

He shot towards a cobbled road that ran northwards from the boulevard, heading for the old town of Calais Nord. He rode hard, exhaust note thumping, narrowly avoiding a group of running British soldiers as he whipped around the turn. Bullets whizzed and cracked through the air as he sped on, followed by the exhaust note's howl. At the end of the road, he skidded to a halt. A row of tall iron railings blocked the way. Behind them was a civic park. He turned right, but the main thoroughfare was thick with fighting. A British light tank was burning, giving off clouds of acrid fumes. Dead riflemen and territorials lay scattered on the cobbles in pools of blood. A Cruiser tank was firing at the advancing enemy's positions. The sky was gradually darkening above the city, flickering with shells and bombs and small arms fire.

Drake stopped again, and turned the handlebars, mounting the pavement and riding through a narrow gateway into the park. He ripped the throttle open. The back wheel tore up turf and the engine thumped as he flew across the lawns.

He came out of the park, and saw the way ahead was clear. Turning into another boulevard, he was momentarily lost – and then in the dim light he saw the bridge. He wrenched the throttle back and rode like hell towards it. Retreating British riflemen fired all around him, and burning streaks of German tracer ripped through the air.

As he raced on, flat out, he could see that the entire crossing was blocked by a barricade. The Germans hadn't reached it yet, and retreating British troops were scrambling back over the top. Drake hurtled towards the barrier. It was made from lorries, Bren gun carriers, cars, and drums of steel cable from the docks. Iron girders and great timbers were interleaved through the vehicles. Bricks and rubble and broken tiles had been piled up to fill the gaps. The Triumph's engine roared. Drake flattened himself across the petrol tank and flew towards the obstacle, but, at the last moment, he saw there was no way through. He pulled up sharply on the brakes. The tyres shrieked on the cobbles as the motorcycle skidded, sideways, to a halt. Drake leapt onto the saddle, and used it as a springboard to launch himself over. His boots thumped to the ground on the other side. Tossing his helmet down to the ground, he ran on.

Dodging through the narrow, smouldering streets of the old city of Calais Nord, he sprinted in the direction of the Citadel. It finally came into sight as he rounded a corner. Even in the dusk light he could see the rampart had been heavily shelled, but the Germans were still being held on the other side of the canal. The Citadel was secure, for now at least. Drake saw the same sergeant with the Tommy gun, still standing at the gate.

He ran up to him.

'Is Nicholson here?' he gasped, sucking in in deep lungfuls of the smoke-filled air.

The sergeant nodded. 'You're in luck, chum. He's just arrived. Brigade HQ is in the cellars under the northern ramparts.'

Drake ran on. The ramparts were twenty foot high and half as thick again, the citadel's grounds protected behind the massive earth and stone walls. He slowed to a jog, and in the gloom, he finally found a door that led inside the great walls.

There was an old table propped inside the door, and a harassed-looking staff captain looked up at him. 'Yes?'

'I've got to see Nicholson.' Drake heaved in another deep breath. 'Is he here?'

The staff captain gave him a wan, tired smile. 'Name?'

'Drake. Second Lieutenant Tennyson Drake. South Devonshire Regiment. It's urgent.'

'South Devonshires? I don't think we have any South Devonshires.' The man scanned a list on a clipboard. 'I don't see your name. Are you sure?'

Drake felt the frustration boiling up. 'Am I sure what my name is? Or my regiment? Yes, I'm bloody well sure. Forget the sodding paperwork. It's urgent that I see him. Right away!'

The staff officer raised his eyebrows then let out a long, tired sigh. 'Be my guest,' he said, waving Drake into a corridor with a sweep of the hand.

Drake stepped quickly in, then stopped. There were about fifteen other officers in the corridor, some standing, others sitting and fidgeting, still others fast asleep on the floor where they sat. Every single one of them outranked him. Every single one of them was the worse for wear or wounded. Every single one of them looked exhausted, and shot to hell.

Drake glanced at his watch again. Time had lost all meaning in the madness of the battle. It was almost ten o'clock in the evening.

Drake turned to the staff captain. 'But I've got orders to report to him right away,' he said, hope suddenly fading. 'It's urgent. Really urgent.'

The staff captain gestured towards the other officers. 'The city's on fire, Jerry's throwing everything at us. It's all urgent, don't you see? Everything is urgent, and everybody wants to see the brigadier at once. I can assure you that we're all doing our level best, but I'm afraid you're going to have to join the queue.'

Drake groaned.

SATURDAY 25 MAY 1940

Chapter 44

BRIGADE HQ, THE CITADEL, CALAIS, FRANCE – 07:55HRS

Drake started as a hand shook his shoulder. 'You can see him now.'

He gazed around, wild eyed for a moment. It took a second to remember where he was. A dull light was coming in from the exterior door. *Christ!* It was morning now. He'd been out cold, and he'd lost an entire night. The crash and thunder of artillery had been going on for hours already. The other men who'd been waiting were gone, but by now there were new ones behind him in the queue.

Drake got up stiffly from the cold stone floor where he'd been sitting, and the staff officer showed him down a dark staircase and along a lamp-lit corridor to a doorway twenty feet below the ground.

Drake pushed it open and slowly stepped inside.

The captain announced him. 'Second Lieutenant Drake. South Devonshires.'

Brigadier Claude Nicholson was sitting at a wooden desk in a gloomy, vaulted chamber beneath the ramparts. His face was lit by the glow of a paraffin lamp. His strong-looking fingers massaged his temples as he stared down at a stack of papers on his desk.

After a moment, the brigadier glanced up briefly. 'For Christ's sake, take a seat man. I'll be with you when I can.'

Drake eased himself into an old wooden chair that stood opposite the desk.

He waited, watching the senior officer. Brigadier Nicholson looked supremely tired. His long neck was bent forward as he studied the papers in front of him. His fingers pinched the narrow bridge of his nose. His eyes were ringed with black circles, and Drake could almost feel his headache. Nicholson's hair was dark and wavy. His top lip was obscured by a thick moustache, but the skin of his cheeks was drawn, pallid and grey.

The shudder and groan of the German shelling suddenly stopped. In the silence, Drake noticed that the four paraffin lamps that lit the room were hissing quietly. He peered up at the ceiling, and so did the brigadier. They had grown so used to the ceaseless, numbing din that it seemed preternaturally quiet.

The brigadier returned to his paperwork. Above his head, the arched ceiling showed centuries-old brickwork. Drake wondered if a direct his from a bomb would make the ceiling collapse. Uneasy thoughts began circling around. The dank terrors of being buried alive. He clenched his hands into fists, pushed away the oppressive fears that dogged his mind.

'Alright,' Nicholson said finally, pushing away his pile of papers. 'You've got three minutes. What is it exactly that I can do for you?'

Drake was taken aback. 'I was told to report to you, sir.'

'How many men d'you have?'

'Three.'

Nicholson looked blankly at him. 'Three men? Then why in God's name are you taking up my time?'

Drake rubbed at his face. 'My orders come from the Chief, sir. If that means something to you.'

Drake waited and watched. Nicholson stared into the dark spaces of the underground chamber. For a moment it seemed that the brigadier had forgotten him, his mind taken up with a thousand more pressing matters. Then the man's dark eyes came back to rest on Drake's.

'So you're this chap from the service, are you?' He took in Drake's battered face, his filthy uniform. 'You don't look the MI6 type.'

'I'll take that as a compliment, sir.' SIS, although reporting to the Foreign Office, was more commonly known by its departmental name: *Military Intelligence, Section Six.*

Nicholson placed both hands on the table. 'Now listen to me, Drake. I am not a fan of all this cloak and dagger stuff. What we do *not* need is more witchcraft and quackery to frighten the politicians stupid. Hard military intelligence is what we desperately require.' He rapped his knuckles on the tabletop as he repeated the words. 'Hard. Military. Intelligence. The latest reports tell me at between two and four entire panzer divisions are advancing against my four thousand poorly-armed men. Rome is burning, and you're chasing after shadows. Peddling sensations in a war of nerves is a very dangerous game.'

'Yes, sir,' said Drake. 'Nevertheless, I was ordered to report to you, sir.'

Nicholson sighed, then shook his head again. 'I'm sorry. I haven't slept for three days. I don't suppose many of us have. I'm told they have a person of interest to your inquiry. He's a Roman Catholic priest.'

Drake sat bolt upright in his chair. 'A priest?'

Nicholson didn't bother to repeat himself.

'Who sir?' Drake said, eventually. 'Who has the priest?'

Nicholson's face twitched into a humourless smile. 'The French, Drake. The French. Always the bloody French.' He looked at his notebook, and flipped through the pages. 'One Commandant LaPointe. Another of your ruddy voodoo merchants, if you want my opinion. LaPointe's from the Deuxième Bureau.'

Drake stood up abruptly, scraping back his chair. 'Excuse me, sir. I have to find him at once. Do you know where he is?'

'No I don't.' The brigadier snapped shut his notebook. 'Try the port. The French seem to be heading there as fast as their feet will carry them. That'll be all.'

Drake nodded. 'Thank you very much, sir. I hope that this will help me find the hard military intelligence you're looking for.'

Before Drake reached the door, it opened from the other side and the staff captain came in. He led in a civilian – an old man with silver hair, dressed finely in coat and tails. He wore a *Tricoleur* sash of office across his chest, and had a blindfold over his eyes.

'Monsieur Gershell, sir,' the captain said, ignoring Drake. 'He is the mayor of Calais. He's come to ask if you will agree to terms with the Germans.'

The adjutant untied the mayor's blindfold, and the old man blinked open his eyes.

'For the sake of the civilians, Monsieur,' the old mayor said, addressing Brigadier Nicholson. 'The Germans are threatening destruction of the entire town. They say they will raze Calais to the ground if you don't surrender. They have offered a ceasefire for one hour for you to consider.'

'That's why the guns have stopped, sir,' the staff captain said.

Brigadier Nicholson put his hands together, interlocking his fingers as he rested them on his desk. 'No,' he said stiffly, 'I shall not surrender.'

The old mayor gazed at the brigadier. 'There are ten thousand women and children here, *Monsieur*.'

Nicholson gave him a humourless smile. 'Nevertheless, you can tell the Germans that if they want Calais they shall have to fight for it.'

The old man nodded, slowly, once.

'Oh for God's sake, send him packing would you?' Nicholson snapped.

'Yes sir,' said the adjutant. He hurried the old Frenchman out of the room.

Nicholson noticed Drake once more. 'Why are you still here?'

'Sorry sir, I was just leaving.'

As Drake reached the door, the brigadier grunted, then waved a hand in his direction. 'Are you married?'

'No, sir.'

Nicholson lowered his gaze and began to organise his paperwork. 'Well, don't make any plans.'

'I'm sorry, sir?'

'You might want to write a letter, Drake, if you've anybody to write to. Send it on the next ship out. The navy's still sending small boats in, strictly for the wounded and supplies.'

Drake felt the damp walls of the room closing in. *Write a letter.* So that's how it was.

Nicholson rubbed a hand over his face and held up a slip of typewritten paper. '*The eyes of the Empire are on you.* This comes from the Prime Minister himself.'

The walls loomed in closer. Drake had a sudden urge to run outside and gasp big lungfuls of cool, fresh air. 'I see.'

Nicholson shook his head. 'I'm not sure that you do.' He picked up the typewritten note and read from it again. '*Every hour you continue to exist is of the greatest help to the BEF. Government has therefore decided that you must continue to fight. Have greatest possible admiration for your splendid stand. Evacuation will not (repeat not) take place. Winston Churchill.*'

The brigadier looked up. 'The German army is pressing in with great force from three sides. We're effectively surrounded on the island of Calais Nord. We're under siege. My men are trying to hold the bridges because the Chiefs of Staff omitted to send me any explosive to destroy them with. We are fighting German tanks with rifles, and I'm reduced to sending cooks and clerks and stretcher-bearers into the front line. It's open season for the Luftwaffe, who come at us almost unopposed during every hour of daylight. There's no way in and there's no way out except by boat. There are five Royal Naval destroyers outside the harbour, but for reasons that remain obscure, they are ordered to stand out to sea and watch us fall.'

Brigadier Nicholson let the paper drop. 'We're to fight it out to the bitter end, to show solidarity to our French Allies.' He slammed his hand onto the desk with a loud, sudden slap. 'Our French Allies, who are evacuating themselves from the harbour in their thousands and refuse to fight!'

Suddenly Drake understood the haunted look that sat like an aura about the brigadier. He could sense an almost overwhelming sorrow behind the man's dark, hollow eyes.

After a moment, Nicholson once again composed himself. He clasped his hands together wearily and sighed. 'Do your job, Drake. Find whatever intelligence it is that you're looking for. But as neither you nor I shall ever leave this island, I cannot possibly say what good it will do.' Although not much over fifty, the brigadier suddenly looked very old. 'There is to be no retreat, no surrender. Last bullet. Last man. My task here is to arrange for the death of all my men in the most stubborn manner possible. So do forgive me if I seem a little obtuse.'

Chapter 45

Drake emerged from the depths of the citadel's cellars into what looked, at first, like snow. For a moment he felt lost, then saw that the ground was in fact littered with sheets of white paper, dropped from the skies. He picked one up and took it with him as he exited the citadel. It was a German propaganda leaflet in French and English, showing how Calais was surrounded, and calling on the Allied troops to surrender. At least the garrison would have no shortage of toilet paper now. Drake scrunched the sheet up and threw it to the ground.

Butcher and Leighton were sitting on the grass embankment nearby, taking advantage of the truce. Leighton was lighting a Woodbine cigarette from the dog end of his last.

'Our next stop will be the Deuxième Bureau, Gentlemen,' Drake said. 'We have to find one Commandant LaPointe.'

MacTaggart jogged over. 'I did a wee recce, sir. The rifles have pulled back to a short perimeter behind the bridges on the island. And the Frogs are all buggering off to the port.'

Drake nodded as they hurried out of the citadel gates. *The port.* He considered the layout of the town. Smoke was pouring from burning buildings. Glass and tiles lay shattered on the road, but it was all still quiet. The truce was holding, for the moment at least. He tried to make a mental map of the terrain. The whole of Calais was dissected by canals, and the old town of Calais Nord was effectively an island about a kilometre in diameter, cut off from the land by an almost-circular waterway. From what he could recall there were seven bridges connecting with the mainland, including a land bridge by the citadel. Seven bridges to defend against the panzers. *Christ.*

Drake told the men what was happening. Suddenly, the ground trembled beneath their boots. A heavy thunder rolled in the distance.

'Ceasefire's over!' MacTaggart called out. 'Now we're in for a scrap.'

Seconds later, a black line screeched down into a terraced house a hundred yards away. Flame spewed out and the house shuddered with a terrible crash. Drake and his men flung themselves to the ground in the middle of the road. The blast of the detonation buffeted over them, as a tower of smoke and dust shot up, disgorging bricks and rafters into the air. Debris began to clatter down around their heads.

The rumble of heavy artillery grew like a storm on the horizon. Another shell screeched in, then another, another, another on top of that. They hit in bright, shattering explosions, each one with an impossibly loud crash like the end of the world. Across the street, a shop wall erupted into a cascade of bricks, which surged outwards in a circular wave straight towards them, as though for a moment gravity didn't exist. Fire blistered from the ruin and the bricks tumbled down, narrowly missing Drake and his men, covering them in a cloud of dust.

Drake coughed his lungs clear and got to his feet. 'Come on! Follow me!'

They ran.

All across Calais, the German assault resumed, but now with an even greater fury. As though angered by Nicholson's refusal to give in, the Wehrmacht launched a frenzied attack. Machine gun bullets thudded into barricades. Small calibre shells slammed into the brickwork of canalside houses, while distant heavy artillery pieces rained down hell on the centre of the old town. Rifle rounds whined madly off pavements and walls. Fires took hold throughout the city. Civilians and French deserters huddled underground.

They saw a dozen British servicemen dive away from a barricade into basements and holes dug into the rubble of collapsed buildings. Drake knew they weren't ducking the fight – they'd left a sole lookout, and would be out again as soon as the barrage stopped. The British troops knew that the meticulous German army would not move up troops through their own bombardment, so there would be no direct advance until the artillery onslaught ceased.

Drake and his men ducked from doorway to doorway, building to building. The ground trembled as they ran through the choking dust and fire and smoke. Shells cracked in, heaving great surges of debris across the streets. Waves of cobblestones flew into the air as heavy ordnance exploded, piercing deep into the roads. The day was really warming up now, the sun's heat adding to the house fires. Rifles snapped out, the buzzing clatter of German Spandau machine guns strafing British positions. Bren guns of the rifle regiments returned fire, stubbornly thudding their familiar thumps in short, well-disciplined bursts.

They stopped, and Drake took a moment to get his bearings. He ran a forearm across his sweat-soaked face. Mortar bombs fizzed up and clashed down in tight, fierce detonations. He signalled and the four men ran on, bent over double, past a smouldering barricade where a section of Green Jackets were holding the old city walls against a torrent of enemy fire. He knew that, soon, enemy infantry assaults would try to breach the canal lines. The big guns thudded in the distance. Booming detonations rocked the ground.

'Alright, this way!' Drake yelled.

Hurtling around a corner, they were confronted by the odd sight of French soldiers pushing bicycles and carrying suitcases towards the harbour. Drake's men pounded past them and through the ancient fisherman's streets of the Courgain district. French sailors wearing striped jerseys and bell-bottom trousers were firing rifles and carbines from ruins and blockades. Drake found it strange that the French navy was still fighting on while the French soldiers were all hiding in basements, drunk on brandy and wine, or running for the port. Of course, the sailors were professionals, and the majority of the French army were unwilling conscripts. A few dozen Belgian troops, recognisable only by their helmet badges, just sat around in doorways and shops which had been broken open, as though waiting. *Waiting for what?* A shell whined overhead to crash into a nearby building, but the soldiers still sat there, merely pulling their helmets down as ash and dust enveloped the street.

Drake ran on, passing the shattered glass front of a café, where a group of drunken French conscripts were helping themselves at the bar. A nearby pharmacy had been smashed open, and another crowd of French soldiers were inside the wrecked shopfront, sweeping armfuls of pills and medicines from the shelves. The French soldiers all seemed to have gone mad with the pressure of the barrage. Either that, or they were out of their heads on booze and pills. Drake looked again into the chaotic scenes inside the pharmacy, the smashed sign with the ancient symbol of the apothecary, the shattered windows, and the broken pill bottles. Something stirred at the back of his mind.

'We're in France, aren't we?' Leighton rasped through the din of the shelling. 'So why aren't they fighting, then? It doesn't make sense.'

Drake watched the Frenchmen for a moment. Some of the French soldiers in the café were singing, others openly weeping.

'They're a bloody rabble,' MacTaggart growled. 'Whose side are they on?'

There was something in what MacTaggart said. But Drake shook his head, clutching his helmet. 'The only difference between them and us is that they know they're beaten. We're just too damned stubborn to give in.'

A shell slammed into a rooftop over the road, and a searing blast of heat whipped across the street. Drake threw himself into a doorway as a cloud of flying masonry tore through the air. A great black tower of smoke stood over the port from burning oil containers. The cloud, like a giant anvil, reached all the way up into the sky.

Drake peered through the dust as debris spiralled down over the roadway. From where he was, he could now see out into the great harbour. The water was jostling with French ships – trawlers, cutters and even destroyers. On the far side of the waterfront stood the quayside station, the *Gare Maritime*, and the dock was crowded with hundreds of French soldiers, all pushing to board the next boat. Drake felt a sudden surge of anticipation. The answers had to be there in the port. He got to his feet and beckoned to his men.

'Come on. Run!'

Chapter 46

DRAKE SPRINTED ACROSS A pair of narrow swing bridges that linked the island of Calais Nord with the port on the eastern side. The boots of his men thumped behind him as he stared around. Half a dozen boats were sunk around the quays, submerged or capsized, some still burning, one standing on end, its smouldering stern lifted right out of the water. Bodies floated on the surface and the shipping had to manoeuvre through the wreckage. Shells screeched overhead and shot down into murky water, bringing up great frenzied mushrooms of mud, dead fish and boiling seawater. On the dock itself, the torn-up railway tracks of a goods yard lay adjacent to the loading quays. Carriages and rolling stock stood on the tracks between smoking craters. Piled up everywhere were heaps of abandoned equipment. French soldiers were sheltering on the platforms, waiting for the boats to take them off.

A French naval trawler steamed right up to the waterfront and men began leaping onto her deck with no semblance of order. A French torpedo boat, the size of a small destroyer, sliced away through the waters of the harbour mouth, her bows throwing up a great crest of foam. Drake saw the name on her bow – *La Poursuivante,* The Pursuer. She was leaving under full steam and her decks were overcrowded with French troops. Other craft stood out to sea, trawlers, cargo boats and minesweepers. Drake ducked, clutching his helmet, as a shell shrilled in and burst into the station buildings, exploding with a deafening boom.

From out to sea came the heavy *thump-thump*, *thump-thump* of the naval great guns. Allied destroyers fired four-inch shells, which shrilled overhead towards the advancing German lines. Heavy ordnance crashed and cracked all across the city. Smoke billowed from burning buildings and the air was acrid with a bitter stench. A heavy, dark smog blew through the factories in the industrial area on the eastern side of the port, which was still under British control. There, the fuel depot was burning, with flames a hundred feet high. Above it, a great black pillar of smoke reached up to the clouds. From overhead came the hideous drone of German divebombers as they swarmed down to prey on the ships out to sea. The ships fired back with popping Ack-Ack and machine guns. Drake ran towards the station of the Gare Maritime, and leapt over the rails.

He pushed his way through crowds of Frenchmen onto the platform, which, in the French style, was level with the tracks. They sidestepped a line of stretchers that were laid out on the ground, blankets pulled over dead soldiers' faces. The air was hot and dry, and a ragged wind was eddying through the smoke. Fires raged from street to street in the old town, and was getting blown towards the harbour buildings. And in the heat, the corpses were beginning to stink.

Another salvo of shells shrieked in. The men threw themselves to the platform. Shells burst among the loading cranes, or boiled up, spouting geysers, in the deep waters of the harbour. A mile out, a British destroyer, struck by Luftwaffe bombs, was sinking fast. Drake felt a flash of dismay for the men on board, trapped beneath the waves. From the city came the crackle of small arms fire. Then a great cloud of black smoke billowed across the entire port, hiding everything from view.

'Commandant LaPointe?' Drake called out, loudly. '*Où est le commandant LaPointe?*'

The French soldiers ignored him. Drake kept calling out the question. Men pushed past, heading for the harbourside. Others just gaped up at the sky and pointed to the planes.

Drake jogged alongside the railway carriages, boots thumping on the concrete that lay between the tracks. Broken glass littered the quay and platforms. Parts of the tracks had been ripped up by bomb craters. Small fires were breaking out everywhere now. Flaming vehicles and overturned trucks blocked the lines.

'Where are your officers?' Drake shouted at the French soldiers who were sheltering in the station buildings. But shrugs, grunts and shaking heads were their only replies.

Eventually a French *sergent* answered him. The man was stretched out on a bench, wounded, with a bloody bandage around his head.

'*De l'eau* – I must have water,' the man croaked. '*Ils sont partis*. The officers have already gone.'

Drake gave him the last few drops from his own canteen. He glared at a crowd of young French conscripts who were drinking looted wine while ignoring their own wounded. He angrily kicked at an empty bottle on the floor, which went skidding away to shatter on the railway lines. An evil wail began to shriek towards them from the sky.

'Not them again,' Leighton muttered, eyes turning up to the heavens. He was smoking another Woodbine. 'I hate them bloody Stukas.'

The divebombers screeched towards the narrow streets of the old city, sirens of Jericho screaming as they hurtled down. The bombs slammed to the ground a quarter of a mile away amid the already-burning buildings, casting rafters and tiles into the air like strange confetti. Somebody whistled. Drake's gaze snapped around.

An officer, descending the steps of the train, called out to him in a cultured English tone with a hint of a French accent. 'You! You're looking for Commandant LaPointe?'

The officer turned, climbing back up onto the train, beckoning. Drake touched MacTaggart's shoulder, then hurried across the tracks. He pulled himself up the steps and into the carriage. It was a hospital train, jam-packed with wounded French and Belgian soldiers. A man groaned, blood seeping from a bandaged leg. Another man was screaming, thrashing in a makeshift bed. The compartment stank of urine, faeces and blood.

The officer who'd beckoned him in was tall, wide-shouldered, fair-haired, clean-shaven, and behind his gold-rimmed glasses he had bright blue eyes. Drake guessed he was in his late thirties. He was a medical officer, an army doctor. Instead of a helmet, he had a barracks cap on his head, sporting the insignia of the *Composante Médicale*.

'You have business with the Deuxième Bureau. May I ask why?'

Drake had no time for the niceties. His gaze took in the compartment and the terrible injuries of the wounded men. There were blinded faces wrapped in gauze, amputations, horrific burns. 'Where is he? Where's LaPointe?' he snapped.

The medical officer was tying on an apron, which was already stained dark with dried blood. 'He had me look at one of his prisoners.'

Outside, a Stuka screamed down towards the harbour. Seconds later, the bomb went off in a blinding flash, rocking the entire carriage. One of the windowpanes of the compartment split with a sharp, defined crack.

The officer ignored it. Judging by the state of the men aboard the train, they had come from an area of fierce fighting on the front.

'As a medical man, I cannot condone the methods of the *Bureau*,' he said. 'I ask again, what do you want with Commandant LaPointe?'

Drake looked out through the train's dirty window. The officer was like an infuriatingly pedantic schoolboy. On the platform, MacTaggart was staring in at him through the smoke.

'He has a prisoner that's of interest to us. I urgently need to question him.'

'What prisoner?'

Drake tried to contain his growing irritation. 'What does it matter? But he's a Roman Catholic priest.'

The tall doctor cocked his head to one side. 'I had no idea that he was holding a priest.' He considered Drake, then shook his head. '*Écoutez-moi*. Listen. I won't be party to any more witch-hunts. His methods are a far cry from the honourable traditions of the military academy. Just because we're losing the war doesn't mean that we have to persecute innocent men.'

'I need to find LaPointe,' Drake fumed, frustration boiling over. 'Why don't you just tell me where he is?'

Outside the carriage, above the smoking streets of Calais Nord, another wave of Stukas wailed down. They dived in twos and threes. Bombs whistled then exploded in hideous detonations. The carriage rocked with the impact of the blasts.

The doctor turned his back as he scribbled on a notepad. 'I cannot help you, unless you tell me why.'

Drake grabbed the doctor by the shoulder, and spun him round. He shoved him up against the compartment wall. He was tall, but inch for inch Drake knew he outmatched him. He seized him by the collar and pressed his face up close. 'Save yourself a lot of bother, Doc, and just tell me. Where the bloody hell is Commandant LaPointe?'

A woman spoke in French from behind Drake's back.

'*S'il vous plait* – would you please put the good doctor down?'

Drake felt a shiver tingle down his spine. He spun around.

Chapter 47

SHE STOOD NOT SIX feet away, in a blue nursing dress tied with a clean white apron. Her dark hair was fashionably short in a war cut, pushed back from her face behind a high white nursing cap. Drake started to say something, but the way she looked at him – coldly – made him doubt himself. He stopped.

She spoke again in French, this time directly to the medical officer. 'I believe we are all on the same side, *Docteur* Lambert.' A bomb crashed outside, further up the docks, as though to reinforce her point. 'Why don't you just tell the English officer what he wants to know?'

Lambert straightened his collar and adjusted his gold-rimmed glasses. He cleared his throat. 'You'll find LaPointe in the arsenal below the shore battery at Fort Risban,' he grunted. 'But you'll need to be more subtle in your methods, *Monsieur*. You're lucky I am a medical man, or I would have put you in your place.'

Drake felt the urge to wallop him, but he restrained himself. He glanced at the unfamiliar insignia on the man's epaulettes and he realised he'd just assaulted quite a senior officer. He turned to see that the nurse was now watching him. Her dark brown, shining eyes seemed to be trying to tell him something. But what? He opened his mouth to speak, but the chill in her gaze made him close it again. Along the carriage of the wounded, somebody groaned.

The doctor frowned as he adjusted his ruffled apron. 'Do you two know each other?'

The nurse gave a single shake of the head. 'No.'

Drake shrugged. 'Sorry. I just haven't seen a woman in a long time. Not a beautiful woman, anyway.'

The doctor put his hand on her arm. She smiled.

Drake felt his stomach tighten. *So that's it.* They were lovers. The short haircut made her look a little Tomboyish. He supposed the doctor was even handsome, in a bookish kind of way. They'd have made a lovely couple if they hadn't been slap-bang in the middle of a raging war. *Christ in bloody hell.*

Outside the static railway carriage, another storm of German shells thundered into the harbour. A wounded man in one of the compartments began shrieking and he wouldn't stop. Drake turned away.

He felt the ground move beneath his feet and had the oddest sensation that the train carriage was moving, dragging him, as if in a nightmare, towards an unknown destination. He gazed through the cracked glass of the window, seeing a glint of his own reflection. He was filthy, and he knew he stank. He barely recognised himself at all.

'Fort Risban. Thank you, *Docteur,*' he said, and he climbed out of the carriage, down to the platform.

Above the old town, Stukas dived. The sea breeze whipped smoke across his path. MacTaggart emerged from the station. Butcher and Leighton followed. A press of French soldiers was milling on the quayside now, waiting for another boat. Drake pushed his way through the throng, shoving men aside if they didn't move fast enough.

'Come on,' he said to MacTaggart. 'The priest's being held in the arsenal.'

He pushed on through the crowd. He stared ahead, barely seeing what was in front of him. Strange emotions swirled uneasily around inside.

MacTaggart hurried after him. 'Are you quite yourself, sir? You look like you've seen a ghost.'

Drake pressed on, eyes fixed on the ancient ramparts of Fort Risban.

'I have,' he said. 'Axelle.'

Chapter 48

THE ARSENAL, FORT RISBAN, CALAIS, FRANCE – 11:15HRS

COMMANDANT THIBAULT LAPOINTE OF the Deuxième Bureau paced the small storage room in the arsenal below the naval yard at Fort Risban. Above his head was a ceiling of reinforced concrete five metres thick, which protected the magazine, and above that were the heavy coastal guns of the Calais shore battery. The guns thumped and the entire structure trembled. The battery had been designed to protect the harbour from sea attack, and to control shipping in the Channel. But now they were traversed to their full extent, and aimed back inland towards the advancing German lines. LaPointe stroked his thin face, and gazed at the grey, featureless walls. The great guns thundered again. Down here, in the armoury of the battery, the prisoner at least was secure.

LaPointe spun around as the heavy steel door of the magazine slid back on greased wheels, and a British officer in a battle-stained uniform burst in.

LaPointe withdrew his sidearm from its holster.

Drake ignored the weapon and gave a casual salute. 'Second Lieutenant Tennyson Drake, *mon commandant*.'

Above their heads, the naval battery thudded again with a deep, resounding bark, shaking the room.

LaPointe gave Drake a scathing, suspicious look. 'This is a French position, Lieutenant. You have no business here.'

'We are on the same side, Monsieur.'

LaPointe narrowed his eyes. 'So you say.'

Drake scowled. His hands clenched into fists. 'Brigadier Nicholson sent me.'

He had a thousand burning questions about Axelle – what was she doing here? Why did she pretend not to know him? Why could nothing ever be straightforward? – but he pushed them all firmly away. He forced himself to stand at ease, fighting down his frayed and rising temper, remembering the major's words. *The French are as jumpy as cats.*

'I report to Major Lyle-Smith of the British Secret Intelligence Service. I'm to interrogate the prisoner.'

The French commandant's eyes searched Drake, taking in his ragged uniform from head to toe. 'The prisoner belongs to France. He is a traitor. The matter is closed.' He gestured to the door. 'You may go.'

Drake stared uneasily around the underground chamber. It had a sour, dry stench, the sharp stink of stored ammunition. This room was empty, but he knew that hundreds of thirty-kilogram high-explosive shells would be stored in the adjacent vaults. He suddenly imagined being stuck down here, locked in, unable to breathe. He had an urge to turn around and flee, but he kicked the claustrophobia to the back of his mind and forced himself to concentrate on the matter at hand.

'I must see the prisoner. He has information vital to the outcome of the war.'

LaPointe watched Drake carefully. 'I know,' he said. 'You're telling *me*.'

The Frenchman holstered his pistol, and fumbled in his pocket, then stuck a cigarette between his teeth. He glared at Drake as he lit it with a petrol lighter. He seemed to thaw a little. 'Dark forces are all around us. They are circling now, closing in for the final kill.'

'I don't think you should be smoking in here, sir.'

LaPointe gave him a singularly gallic shrug. 'What does it matter? The traitors have already won.'

'Which traitors?' Drake studied the concrete storeroom. 'What do you mean?'

There was almost nothing in the room. A wooden table, bare save for an overloaded ashtray. A chair, with LaPointe's jacket hanging on the back of it. An electric bulkhead lamp on the wall that flickered slightly when the guns went off above.

LaPointe exhaled a long, thin plume of harsh tobacco fumes in Drake's direction. 'France has been betrayed. Are you blind, Lieutenant? The war is already lost, and it has been thrown away on politics alone.'

Something moved at the back of Drake's mind. He knew that France was riven by opposing factions, some wanting to fight, others keen to make peace. The officer class had an abiding fear of the rise of communism among the workers and the discontented conscripts. A rebellion didn't seem far-fetched among deserters and disillusioned men.

'Rather Hitler than Stalin, is that it?' he said.

LaPointe regarded Drake for a moment, then slowly turned away, stubbing his cigarette out into the overflowing ashtray on the table. 'That is the stark new reality of European politics, *Monsieur*, as England would do well to recognise. There is no time for wavering or dawdling in the middle ground. Democracy is too weak. Look around you.' He gestured, as though seeing through the concrete walls to the devastation beyond. 'At the merest puff of wind, democracy crumbles and fails.'

Drake tried again. 'Be that as it may, *mon commandant*, it is imperative that I speak to the priest.'

LaPointe turned slowly around to face him. 'The priest?' he muttered.

Drake nodded. 'I believe the priest was an accomplice of Agent Viper.'

LaPointe looked strangely at Drake for a moment, and the dry skin of his thin face wrinkled as he gave him a fleeting smile. 'Ah!' he said. He waved his shortening cigarette in the air. 'Agent Viper. The man who got away.'

The Frenchman stalked the room, lighting another cigarette from the embers of his first. He inhaled harshly. 'Now we see eye to eye, you and me. So. The priest, of course, is a man of the cloth, bred to secrecy. You won't get anything out of him this side of the grave.' Smoke trailed from his nose and mouth as he spoke. 'I would have had him shot, but my men are a superstitious bunch. They would not lay a finger on him. With the one hand, they snatch at rights for the working man. And with the other, they grasp for the salvation of their eternal souls.'

Drake felt a surge of hope. 'So I *can* see him?'

LaPointe glanced at his wristwatch. 'As you wish. It makes no difference now. You have 15 minutes, Lieutenant. Room Five.'

Drake spun on his heel and strode to the heavy steel door. The concrete bastion shook and the air thumped in a terrific blast. A hot wind buffeted the door as Drake grabbed hold of it. The docks were getting pounded above the ground. It seemed that the naval guns were now in the German artillery's sights for counterbattery fire.

As Drake was leaving, the French commandant called out after him. 'Lieutenant!'

Drake turned.

Another alarming crash shook the fort. Drake felt the hard floors shudder beneath his boots as high-explosive shells struck the reinforced concrete. In a vivid flash he imagined his final gasp as the walls caved in. Steel doors slammed shut in his mind.

Commandant LaPointe braced himself against the concrete. The Frenchman met Drake's eyes and gave him a strange, dangerous look. 'The whole world is going to hell, my friend. Let his God save him if he is innocent. The priest is yours. I do not require his return.'

Chapter 49

DRAKE'S MEN WERE WAITING in the narrow concrete corridor, which was lit by flickering electric bulbs. Drake glanced up at the ventilation pipes as they walked the tunnel. An acrid stink of cordite and ammonium nitrate caught in his nostrils. *If this lot goes up...* A sudden, resounding crash shook the entire structure. The lights failed. It was black as hell, and Drake fought a rising surge of panic. Then the lights came slowly back on. He exhaled.

Commandant LaPointe stood with his back to the wall as two French sailors trundled a heavy trolley along the narrow passage towards them. It was loaded with high-explosive shells, each the size of a grown man's thigh. The French commandant fumbled for another cigarette, hands shaking, and struck a match. Drake watched with stark unease. It would only take a small accident to blow up the entire docks. *The bloody fool.*

A series of concrete storerooms opened off the corridor behind steel bulkhead doors. A man in the blue uniform of a French marine stood outside one of the doors. He saluted.

LaPointe nodded. 'Room Five,' he said, then turned away.

The marine unbarred the door.

'Sergeant,' Drake nodded. MacTaggart went in. 'You two,' he said to Butcher and Leighton, and pointed to the stairs. He didn't want Leighton lighting up in here as well. Anything could happen. 'Wait up there. Outside in the fresh air.'

Drake stepped into the storeroom and slid the steel hatch shut behind him. The small room was lit by an electric bulkhead light on the wall. The chamber had been cleared of everything except two rows of empty ammunition racks. Against the far wall, the black shape of a man rose slowly from where he had been crouched, squatting on the floor.

He stood up, and in the dim light, Drake could see that beneath his robes, he was short and rotund. He had grey hair, grey stubble on his jowls and chin. The man fumbled inside his cassock, then placed a black biretta cap on his head. His temple was yellow and purple in the dim electric light. A faded bruise.

The priest studied Drake's uniform. 'You are British, I see. The Good Lord knows no boundaries.' He spoke English, accented with French intonation, in a practiced, sonorant tone. 'We must all pull together to prevent the devil's work on Earth. May the Lord grant us peace.' He gave Drake a small bow. 'Monsignor Gillaud. How may I be of service?'

A terrible, shocking clash jolted through the room, and the priest flinched. Grey powder spiralled down from the concrete ceiling. The monsignor hacked out a cough.

Drake placed a hand on the wall, as though to keep it from caving in. He drew in a sharp, shallow breath between his teeth. *God*, but he hated being underground. He stared at the large crucifix that hung from the man's neck on a long silver chain.

'You helped Agent Viper go free. So the Viper is involved with the Catholic Church. Exactly how?'

The priest finished coughing. A thin line of spittle hung from his lip. 'I don't know what you are talking about.'

Drake thought of the little girls, dead in a row by the side of the road, their shoes pointing up towards the sky. He no longer had any time for the niceties of civilised behaviour. He had to get this over with as quickly as possible. He stepped across the room and jabbed his right fist into Gillaud's face. The priest cried out, and fell back against the wall.

Drake went in after him, and slammed a short hook with his left arm up into the priest's soft sternum. The man choked, almost spewing, and slumped down to the floor. His face turned purple as he struggled to breathe.

Drake looked down at him. 'Get up.'

The priest groaned and sucked in air.

Drake kicked him, hard, connecting his boot with a shin that was hidden beneath his cassock. 'I said get up.'

MacTaggart raised his eyebrows. 'I take it you're not a religious man, sir?'

Drake ignored him. Using the wall as support, Monsignor Gillaud pushed himself, slowly, back up to his feet.

The building shuddered with another heavy shell strike. The light faltered, then came back on. Drake felt the floor sway beneath him.

It seemed as though the walls were shifting, cracking. As if the ceiling would cave in and bury him there. He wanted to get out and run.

'*Te absolvo,*' the monsignor said. With two fingers of his right hand he made the gesture of a small cross. 'I forgive you your sin.' He wore an ecclesiastical ring on his third finger, bearing the sigil of a crown. It glinted in the chamber's dim light. 'According to the Gospel of St Matthew, Jesus tells us: *do not resist an evil person. If anyone slaps you on the right cheek, turn to them the other cheek also.*'

The monsignor turned his face away.

Drake punched him in the guts.

The priest sank, gagging violently, towards the floor.

MacTaggart stepped forward and put a hand on Drake's arm. 'Easy sir, you'll kill him.'

The bulkhead lamp flickered as the guns thumped above their heads. Drake was aware of men marching along the corridor outside, and the sound of a sob. He shrugged off MacTaggart's arm and leant forward. Knocked the cap from the priest's head and pulled him up by the hair. Pressed him against the wall, and drew back his fist.

'Who is Agent Viper? Where is he and what's he going to do?'

The priest looked at him in puzzlement, then his watery eyes closed for a moment. Drake thought the man was going to cry. In the dim, flickering light he saw the man's dirty, uneven teeth as his mouth opened, but nothing came out.

Then the old priest smiled. His lip was badly cut. Blood and spittle ran freely down his chin. 'I don't know what you mean.'

Drake punched him in the kidney with a short left hook.

Phlegm choked out of the old man's mouth, and some of it landed on Drake's face. He wiped it away with the back of his sleeve. The priest sank down again, gasping for breath, but even in pain, his face was still clenched into a maddening smile.

Drake staggered as another crack shook the deep foundations of the building. A hot wind slammed open the steel door of the vault, and the electric light buzzed and flickered out.

In pitch darkness, Drake fumbled forward and touched the cloth of a robe. He dragged the priest up again.

MacTaggart switched on his flashlight.

'Knife,' Drake said, holding out his open hand.

MacTaggart withdrew the short *sgian-dubh* dagger from his sock, and tossed it in Drake's direction. Drake caught it by the bog oak handle. He ran a thumb along the razor-sharp blade.

'How long does it take to cut a man's throat, Sergeant?'

MacTaggart's eyes gleamed through the darkness. 'Och, it's harder than you'd think sir.' He made a vicious sawing motion. 'You've got to really hack your way through the cartilage, if you want to do it properly. It's a very messy process. I'd say it takes about a minute for a man to die, if you do it right. But if you make a mess of it, it could take all day.'

The priest stopped smiling. He made the sign of a cross. 'I am a man of God! I pray only for a lasting peace. I serve only Christ the King!'

Drake pressed the dagger point into the man's pale, fleshy throat. A small, dark sphere of blood welled up. It ran down the gleaming blade. The monsignor gurgled in alarm.

'What's *Dämmerung*?' Drake growled. He pressed the blade in a millimetre further. 'Last chance. Tell me now.'

The walls shook, and a crash of thunder slammed into the vault. A crack shot through the ceiling and dust spilled down, clouding the torchlit cell.

Drake pressed the knife harder until the priest cried out in pain. He felt the blade vibrate against the cartilage as the man finally spoke.

This time, the arrogant, condescending smile was gone. 'I don't understand,' the old monsignor said. 'Why don't you ask the man himself?'

Drake released the tension on the dagger. He glared down at the priest, his mind awhirl. 'What do you mean?'

'That maniac LaPointe has fooled you,' the monsignor said, then laughed.

Drake struck him hard across the face.

The priest smiled again, with blood on his teeth. 'Leave me and I will pray for your forgiveness.' He reached up and wiped away the blood with the sleeve of his robe. 'You are asking the wrong person. The man you seek is being held in one of the other cells.'

Chapter 50

DRAKE BURST OUT THROUGH the steel doorway. The corridor lights were off. It was pitch black, aside from MacTaggart's torch. The French marine guard was gone.

Drake slammed the door shut, and slid the locking bolt, leaving the priest in darkness. Above them, guns thundered, the muffled thud of shellbursts on the surface. None of the other rooms were guarded.

'They've buggered off, sir!' MacTaggart said into the gloom.

Drake ran down the corridor, sliding the heavy steel doors open. The rooms were all empty. The whole place was deserted now.

He ran to LaPointe's room, shone the torch in. It was empty, too, his jacket gone, just a cigarette butt still smouldering in the overflowing ashtray. The walls crashed, concrete shuddering. The ceilings spilled dust as a loud, rending blow hit the fort.

Drake kicked the desk over. 'Bloody LaPointe! He's taken the Viper and gone!'

They raced up the smoke-laden staircase, blinking into blinding daylight. Butcher and Leighton were waiting in the cover of Fort Risban's walls. Drake looked around at the destruction of Calais. The Wehrmacht's grip was tightening. It seemed the whole city was now on fire. Stukas screamed down from the skies. Bomb debris flew through the air from vast explosions. Shells burst in blinding flashes. The rattle of automatic weapons filled the air, but still the British troops clung on.

Two French sailors from the shore battery were running back with the ammunition trolley, which bounced and clattered behind them. Although the French army had seemingly given up, the French navy was still very much in the fight.

'*Où sont-ils allés?*' Drake shouted. 'Where did they go? Commandant LaPointe and the marines?'

'That way,' said one of them, pointing.

Drake tried to see through the smog that covered the quay and harbour. There was no sign of them. '*Où aller?* Where to?'

One of the men made a pistol shape with two fingers of his right hand, and pretended to shoot. '*Pan! Pan!*'

For a moment Drake just stared at him, and then he understood. 'Shit,' he said, 'He's going to execute the prisoners!'

He started sprinting back along the quay towards the burning city. Another shell whined in to hit the harbour in a shattering din. Spikes of flame shot from the impact site. Splinters of brick and concrete whizzed crazily through the air.

'At the double!' MacTaggart yelled, and the other men came after him at a run.

They ran towards the Gare Maritime, where French sailors were carrying stretcher cases to small boats that plied the harbourside. Tearing into the station, Drake leapt up the rungs and into the nearest compartment of the hospital train. Some of the carriages were on fire now, and the injured men had been bundled into ever-more cramped conditions. Drake ran down the compartment corridor, leaping over the wounded who lay moaning by the dozen on the floor.

He barged into the next carriage. 'Doctor! Doctor Lambert!'

Lambert was bent over a man on a makeshift surgical table. The compartment had been turned into an operating theatre, and Axelle glanced up at Drake from where she was bandaging the stump of the patient's shoulder. An amputated arm stuck up grotesquely from a bucket on the floor. Its former owner on the table stirred and groaned.

Drake caught Axelle's gaze for a moment, then averted his eyes. He had no idea what she was doing there, but he had no time to get into it now. All that would just have to wait.

The doctor looked up, cleaning his blood-spattered spectacles with a handkerchief. Drake noted that his epaulette was marked with one broad band and two narrow ones, inscribed with the international medical symbol. He was a Lieutenant-Colonel of the Medical Component. And Drake suddenly realised he was Belgian, not French.

'You again! Can't you see I'm busy?' Lambert said angrily.

Drake felt the urgency in his stomach. 'It's LaPointe. You said you didn't approve of his methods. Well, he's taken the prisoners out for a firing squad.'

'He's going to execute them?' Lambert said, looking aghast.

Drake nodded. 'There's a German agent. It's imperative that we keep him alive. He knows something vital to the outcome of the war.'

Lambert shook his head. 'The Allied armies fight only for honour, now. The war is already lost.'

'Not yet it bloody isn't. I need your help. You outrank LaPointe. You can make him stop.'

Drake could see the doctor weighing up the consequences. Tend to the wounded, or save the lives of the prisoners. 'There are women, too, from what I understand,' Drake said. 'He's going to shoot them all.'

Lambert considered for a moment longer, then shook his head. 'My first duty as Medical Officer is to the wounded soldiers.'

Axelle turned on him with a sudden flash of anger. '*Non!* It's not true. Your duty as a doctor is for everybody! How many of them may be innocent, caught up in this hysteria? How many of those prisoners have had a fair trial? You will save all their lives if you only intervene. These men here are stable for now. I can look after them for a short while. You must go!'

The doctor turned angrily towards her, but he saw the passion in her eyes and the rebuke died on his lips. Instead he turned to Drake.

'*Merde,*' he said. 'Alright. I'll come.' He put a hand on Axelle's arm. 'You can manage? I'll see to the others when I get back.'

Lambert quickly untied his bloodstained apron. 'He's going to execute them, you say? We'll see about that!' He set his barracks cap back on his head and strode towards the door. Drake mouthed a silent *thank you* to Axelle, then, following the tall Belgian doctor, he hurried down the steps and off the train.

Chapter 51

THEY SPRINTED ACROSS THE bridges, back towards the old town. The artillery barrage intensified. French soldiers were hurrying in the opposite direction, towards the harbour. A few still carried suitcases, packs, occasionally a rifle, but for the most part they were dishevelled, disarmed, and in disarray. Drake was forced to slow down, having to elbow his way through the mob. It struck him that there was no sense of command amongst the French soldiers. There were no officers at all, of any rank. It wasn't just a few bad apples, it was a collective giving up, as though the seeds of defeat had come from the very top. He held onto that thought as he broke free of the crowd, and sprinted along the narrow, old streets. Lambert followed, Drake's men behind. It was hard going. The heat from the fires was intensifying. Dry, acrid fumes tore at their throats. The cobbles were strewn with burning rubble, slowing them down.

Shells shrieked in, tearing through walls and rooftops. Houses, factories, whole streets now raged into seething, blistering infernos. Civilians were crawling up through piles of debris from the cellars where they'd been sheltering, driven to flee the searing heat. Out in the open, they gazed around in horror at the annihilation of their city. It was a vision of hell on earth. A young boy stood on his own, clutching a ragged, soot-stained teddy bear in his arms. An old woman, tears streaming down her smut-blackened face, dropped to her knees to pray. Drake ran on, feeling sickened inside. He had only one way to help them, and that was to find out what *Dämmerung* meant – before it was too late. He retched as his lungs filled with ash and smoke from the dry, hot wind. He was finding it harder and harder to breathe.

He stopped at a shattered junction, and climbed the wrecked staircase of an apartment building that stood above the ruins, only partially surrounded by walls. It gave him a grandstand view. From the vantage point he scanned the streets all around, desperately searching for LaPointe. He could see the cathedral nearby to his left, seemingly unscathed by the shelling. Further off, on the German side of the canal, the high, pointed clock tower of the Calais town hall stood head and shoulders above the other rooftops. The tall belfry seemed to be floating above the smog. On the ground, cannons thumped. Artillery shells crashed into the old city, throwing up towers of debris and ash. All along the canalfront, machine-gun fire crackled as the Germans pressed in their assault.

Drake heard the hollow cracks of British two-pounders firing from the rubble every time a German tank appeared. Lee Enfield rifles snapped in rapid volleys from canalside buildings, making the bridges impassable. The territorials and riflemen were still holding the perimeter of the inner canal and sea lock, but, however stout the defence, there was only so long that men with rifles could hold off the tanks. The Wehrmacht was tightening its strangling grip on the siege.

Lambert appeared at the bottom of the staircase. 'Can you see them?' the doctor shouted up.

Drake shook his head, and gazed around in growing despair. LaPointe and his prisoners had vanished into the chaos of the battle. He shielded his eyes from the sun's glare as it shone down through the drifting smoke. He scanned the burning streets. Heavy ordnance screamed in from the ships of the Royal Navy, stood a mile out to sea. Their great guns thumped shells at the German army on high trajectories above the old city. Towards the citadel, Stukas screamed down, dropping huge bombs. Heinkels and Dorniers of the Luftwaffe droned through the air high above. Black sticks of incendiaries began to tumble from their undersides, flashing phosphorous-green when they landed. British Bofors guns kicked up bursting shells as the Ack-Ack pumped up into the sky. A pair of British cruiser tanks advanced up the back streets towards the barricades on the nearest bridge to support the infantry positions, and a mob of French soldiers, milling in the sheltered alleys, scattered out of their way.

As the tanks came into the open, German shells screeched in, and one of the machines brewed up in a seething ball of flame. Drake heard the rattle of panzer tracks from the other side of the canal. The stutter of German machine guns, the crunch of high-explosive shells. On the street, a rifle shot rang out, and a French soldier fell. Across the canal, on the German side, Drake glimpsed the outlines of German soldiers moving along the roof of the clock tower's belfry.

'*Tireurs!*' he shouted down. 'Snipers!'

The men on the streets began to scatter. Drake saw a Bren gun firing from an upstairs window, lace curtains billowing surreally next to the smoking barrel as it thudded bursts towards the tower. A gust of wind blew in from the sea, fanning the flames of the burning buildings. Drake's view was obscured as the streets were clogged once again with thick clouds of ash and dust. The high sun beat down through the smog, and the city was heating up like an oven. The parched air and the fumes had given Drake an intolerable thirst, but he shoved any thoughts of personal comfort aside. Then the wind picked up again, and blew a clear path through the smoke, and all other thoughts were gone.

Across the square, a group of French marines were forging their way through the chaos, formed into neat ranks that enclosed a short line of civilians. They were heading towards a distant clump of trees.

Drake leapt down the steps, almost tumbling in his haste. 'There! They're heading for that park!'

Jardin Richelieu stood at the southern end of the old town of Calais, close to the canal that formed the front lines. LaPointe's marines were hurrying a line of prisoners in through the wrought-iron gates at gunpoint. There were two women and half a dozen men, all in civilian clothes. Drake could just hear LaPointe's shrieked orders above the din of battle as he ran.

Tearing in after them, Drake saw that it was a large park, dotted with trees, with a wide area of grass near the middle. The marines were marching the prisoners into the centre of the lawn, and were forcing them to stand in a line. One of the women was begging for mercy, and she sank to her knees, but the smoke closed in again before Drake could see their faces.

When it cleared, LaPointe was standing in front of the line of prisoners. Drake ran towards him through the smog. In front of the civilians, the marines now formed up crisply into a line. As LaPointe called out the orders, they raised their carbines in precise time, and pulled back the bolts, thrusting them forward again, chambering the rounds. They were ready to fire.

'*Arrêtez-vous! Ne tirez pas!*' Drake yelled. 'Stop! Don't shoot!'

The marines halted momentarily, eyes flicking over towards him. Drake skidded to a halt in front of them, between the muzzles of their carbines and the line of prisoners. He held up his hands.

LaPointe's thin face spun towards him with an angry glare. '*Que diable* – What the devil do you think you're doing?'

Drake ignored him and turned his back on the marines. He searched the faces of the prisoners. 'Where is he?' he said. 'Which one?'

They were an odd assortment of types. There was a peasant woman, stocky, her head wrapped in a scarf. A short man in a waistcoat looked like a bank manager but he had a split lip and a black eye. The other men were in shabby suits, bareheaded or with berets, except one who seemed to be a baker, still wearing an apron tied around his waist. His face was swollen from a beating, and his white cotton apron was spotted with blood. At the end of the line, the last man was wearing a well-cut, dark double-breasted blue suit, dark shirt and dark red tie. A short-brimmed Homburg hat was drawn down over his eyes. He held himself as though he was the only important person there.

Drake beckoned to Doctor Lambert, who was panting as he caught up. 'That's him! I'm certain of it. I need that man alive!'

Doctor Lambert took a moment to catch his breath, then strode up to Commandant LaPointe. He spoke quickly in French. 'As the senior officer here, I demand that you stop! *Nom de dieu!* In the name of God, you have no authority to murder civilians!'

'They are not civilians.' LaPointe turned angrily towards Drake. 'They are fifth-columnists, snipers, assassins, and traitors. Under military law, for crimes against the Third Republic of France, there is only one sentence. Death.' He withdrew his automatic sidearm from its holster and pointed it directly at Drake's face. 'So unless you wish to join them in their fate, do not try to interfere.'

Chapter 52

At the command of a tough-looking master of marines, the French sailors moved to the left then raised their carbines again, and aimed them at the prisoners. One of the women screamed and tried to run, but was shoved back into line. Some gazed at the weapons in grim dismay, others wore a miserable detachment on their faces that suggested they had given up all hope. But at the end of the line, the man in the Homburg hat seemed unperturbed.

'*Mon commandant!*' Drake stood his ground between the marines and the prisoners, looking back at LaPointe. 'I need to speak with that man!'

Butcher and MacTaggart came jogging up through the smog. MacTaggart frowned, taking in the situation. The two men held their weapons at the ready – a Bren and a Boys antitank rifle. Drake knew they looked a fearsome pair, and LaPointe's eyes darted in their direction. Leighton sauntered up behind them, cigarette end and rifle in hand.

LaPointe moved the aim of his pistol from Drake's face to Lambert's and back. Drake noted the *MAB* markings on the handgrip. The French commandant was wavering. 'This is not your jurisdiction. It is a French matter. These prisoners are the property of the Deuxième Bureau.'

Stukas began diving over the old city, their deafening wails meaning everybody had to shout to be heard. Bombs crashed and thundered through the old town behind them. Towers of smoke and debris blew up into the air. Drake's men and the marines stood in the centre of the park in an uneasy stand-off.

Drake tried to placate the French officer. 'Listen, sir. We need that man alive for questioning. The fate of nations is at stake here. You can have him back, once we're done with him.'

The man in the Homburg hat turned towards them. His chin was darkened with a thick shadow of black stubble. He regarded Drake with calm, dark, wide-set eyes. There was something disturbingly familiar about his face. Drake wondered if he was the man he'd seen on the ridgeline outside Arras, through his field glasses. *Perhaps*.

'The fate of nations?' LaPointe scoffed. 'It is too late for playing games, Monsieur Drake.' The Frenchman gestured with his sidearm. Detonations rocked the streets all around. The sky had turned a livid, smoky red. In the strange glow of the burning city, LaPointe's eyes gleamed with an almost fanatical light. 'The world as we know it is coming to an end. Calais will fall soon, and then these traitors will walk free and celebrate their crimes with their Nazi masters. *Je dis non*! I say no!' He spat on the ground, his voice rising as he continued. 'These *capitulards* know their crimes and they will pay the ultimate price!'

Keeping his pistol trained on Drake, LaPointe barked orders at his marines, and they raised their carbines once more and trained them on the prisoners. Drake refused to budge, so the marines simply stepped to one side, so they could shoot past him. From the corner of his eyes, Drake saw Lambert stepping up next to him. He glanced appreciatively across.

Lambert held up his hands and spoke in quick-fire French. '*Je suis médecin* – I am a doctor, and I am the senior Allied officer here. I order you to stop! We are not *boches*. We are not Nazis! A man is innocent until proven guilty, even in a time of war!'

The men with the carbines hesitated, looking to their petty officer. They seemed unwilling to shoot the doctor, at any rate. The prisoner who looked like a bank manager began to sob and fell to his knees.

'Please,' the man begged. 'The doctor is correct. I am no Nazi. I have done no wrong. I have a German mother, that is all.'

'*Traître!*' LaPointe sneered. He reached out with his sidearm and stepped towards the captives. A shot cracked, a puff of smoke, as LaPointe gave the kneeling bank manager the *coup de grâce*.

The man fell forward, a mist of red dispersing in the air behind his shattered skull. A woman screamed. The man next to him looked on in dread. The other prisoners began to back away.

'*Halte là!*' bellowed the master of marines. The prisoners stopped, frozen by the threat of the carbines that were trained on them once again, in earnest now.

MacTaggart cast Drake a glance. Drake shook his head. He knew his men wouldn't hesitate if called upon to fire. But it was a dangerous situation – nobody would win a firefight between allies. Drake slowly took up his revolver from its holster. The petty officer pointed a machine gun at his belly and watched him like a hawk.

Drake felt sickened. A shuddering *crump-crump-crump* of bombs thudded ominously closer through the streets. Dorniers and Heinkels droned high overhead, and strings of small black dots were tumbling from their fuselages, wreaking a path of destruction through the close-packed buildings of the old town. The bombs were coming closer, and the pressure blasts thudded inside Drake's chest. Explosions detonated in the streets nearby. Clouds of debris fountained ever closer, in gouts of smoke and fire. Doctor Lambert edged forward towards LaPointe.

LaPointe stepped over the dead man on the grass, his close-set eyes burning with rage in his narrow, pinched face. He turned to the next in line. It was the woman who looked like she worked the land. He raised his pistol.

'This woman is a Nazi puppet!' he announced, preparing to squeeze his finger on the trigger.

Lambert launched himself across the grass with surprising speed. The doctor's fist came up and connected with LaPointe's jaw, and the shot went wild. Lambert swung a long arm again and hit him hard in the side of the head, so hard that the impact of the blow sent his own glasses spinning off his face. LaPointe staggered back and sank down to the ground. In moments, the doctor, blinking wildly, had wrestled LaPointe's pistol off him, and tossed it away.

'*Putain!*' the petty officer barked. 'What now?'

Drake saw the look. They wouldn't shoot an army doctor, it was clear. He ran over and helped restrain the stunned LaPointe.

'Well done! I didn't think you had it in you, Doc,' he said.

Lambert looked up over his shoulder and gave Drake a nod. 'It appears they did teach us something useful in the Military Academy after all.'

The man from the Deuxième Bureau struggled on the grass under Drake and Lambert's grip. 'Shoot them! Open fire! That's a direct order!'

Doctor Lambert looked up to the master of marines. 'I suggest you take the prisoners back to their cells. They will be safer there than anywhere else in this city.'

Great, crashing thuds of the German bombs drew closer to the park. The marines lowered their weapons and shook their heads at each other. The petty officer turned to his men and shrugged.

Lambert tutted. 'The commandant has cracked,' he said, in a calm but forceful tone. 'He's lost his reason. It's the pressure of the war.'

'*Eh bien*,' the marines' petty officer said. His men began to gather the surviving prisoners together. The French commandant, held firmly on the grass by the doctor, had lost all authority now.

Drake raised his revolver and moved towards the man in the Homburg hat. He twisted his arm into a half Nelson, and shoved the muzzle into his ribs. 'You're coming with me.'

'*Imbécile!* Fool!' LaPointe called out. Held down by Lambert, the French commandant struggled, and let out a raging, maddened howl.

Drake spoke to the man in the hat. 'Let's go.'

At that moment, a bomb hit a building at the edge of the park in a blinding flash. The burst of pressure hit Drake like a solid wave of air, and he felt himself lifted up then thrown to the ground.

Dazed, he peered up over his shoulder a moment later as another bomb hit the edge of the square. A building erupted and the trees in front of the blast were shredded in the blinding detonation. Rafters from the houses flew into the air. Rubble and splinters spewed across the grass in a hideous blast. A woman in the line of prisoners screamed, impaled by a stake of wood. The French marines dived for cover as the next stick of bombs whistled down. And as the smoke from the explosion billowed across the park, the man in the Homburg hat was the first to get back to his feet. He staggered a few paces, then picked his hat up from where it had blown across the grass. He looked at Drake and shrugged, then tore away, breaking into a run.

Chapter 53

THERE WAS A WHITE flash and a stunning thump as another bomb hit the lawn in the centre of the park. Somebody screamed. Drake saw the prisoner making for a gate on the far side of the park, holding his hat in one hand as he ran.

Drake went after him. 'Cut him off!' he yelled.

MacTaggart and Butcher raced across the park. Private Leighton raised his rifle and fired.

'For Christ's sake, don't shoot him!' Drake shouted back. 'We need him alive!'

A series of awful impacts hit the nearby streets as bombs detonated one after another in a quick succession of deafening blasts. The planes had passed over them, and the explosions were getting further and further away. Drake sprinted on, head ringing from the detonations. MacTaggart and Butcher were nearing the park gate now. The man with the hat, in full flight, saw them, and changed direction. He ran straight towards the fence and leapt for the railings. His dark blue suit caught for a moment on the spikes at the top, before ripping free as he tumbled to the other side.

Drake rushed at the fence, and for an instant, the man was staring at him through the railings. Drake stopped. *That face.* The man had a broad, distinctive jaw, and his mouth was slightly downturned at the corners. He had thick, dark brown hair that was almost black, and it had been blown in all directions by the bomb blasts. The dishevelled state of it could not hide a striking widow's peak. It was disconcertingly familiar. A thought flashed through Drake's mind – had they met before, perhaps a long time ago?

He aimed his revolver at the man's stomach. 'Stay where you are.'

From beneath the hat he was holding, the man revealed LaPointe's automatic pistol. He stepped back a little from the railings, and levelled the weapon at Drake's chest.

'*Touché*,' Drake said. He stared at the muzzle of the automatic.

For a moment, the man didn't answer. Drake heard screams from behind him in the park. He heard the explosions from the Luftwaffe bombs as they fell further away over the burning city. The din of battle receded as he gazed into the face of his quarry.

The man seemed elated, having just escaped death. He spoke English with a thick French accent. 'You saved my life from that madman. So – are you one of us or one of them?'

Drake used his thumb to click back the hammer on his revolver. He observed the man's red tie. 'That depends,' he said. Who *are* you?'

The man suddenly laughed, and his small, very dark brown eyes glistened beneath arched eyebrows. '*Je suis l'homme de la situation.* I am the man of the hour. The man of destiny.'

'You're Agent Viper,' Drake said. He lunged forward, trying to snatch hold of the man's clothing through the ironwork.

The man leapt a yard back, out of reach. He turned and sprinted away along the street. Then he stopped once more and cried out, 'I am the King of Burgundy!'

The King of Burgundy? For a moment, the words resonated around inside Drake's mind. He shook himself to break the spell. The man was getting away. Drake hauled himself over the railings and dropped to the pavement on the other side. MacTaggart and Butcher were thumping up the street now, having gone the long way round through the gate. Leighton was gasping, lagging some way behind.

'Come on!' Drake yelled, 'We've got to catch him!'

He ran, boots crunching over rubble strewn across the road from the bombs. Fires were burning in the houses beside the park, and smoke blew in thick black shrouds across the road. At a street corner, the man stopped. His pistol cracked. Drake felt the bullet whisk by. He dodged into the cover of a burnt-out British lorry that was upturned on the road. The man fired again and a round slammed into the chassis. Drake leaned through the cab, where the blackened figure of the dead lorry driver had been burnt to a crisp. He saw that on the street ahead, the man with the widow's peak was running again. Drake sprinted up the roadway. From a high, groaning flight of Luftwaffe Dorniers, another string of bombs began to fall.

Detonations sent shockwaves through the paving. Buildings erupted in great sheets of fire. Walls buckled and bricks fell in thundering cascades. Drake pounded along the burning street. He was gaining. His mind reeled with the speed of events as his boots pounded the cobbles. *The King of Burgundy.* He recalled his conversation with Bill Lucas – but he had no time to stop and think it through. Ahead, the man ran across a junction and vaulted a gate into the front yard of a smouldering house and dived in through a broken window.

Drake pummelled across the road, closing the gap. Ran up to the house and tumbled through the shattered glass after him. He was met by screams of civilians, women and children who were sheltering in a basement doorway. Drake got to his feet and ran through the parlour, then a corridor that led to the back. Through the kitchen window he saw the man escaping out of the back yard. A gunshot cracked, close by. He kicked the back door open, hurtled out of the yard and skidded into an alleyway. He leapt over a British soldier, laid out on the cobbles, dying fast, his helmet full of blood. Drake looked quickly up and down the alley. The man of destiny, the man with the widow's peak, the King of Burgundy was gone.

Drake heaved great breaths, smoke tearing at his throat. All around him, Calais was burning. Another wave of Stukas began to howl down, sirens wailing, towards the old town. It was hell on Earth. Bomb blasts rocked the streets. Big guns thudded and shells screeched in. The clatter and crackle of small arms fire was growing closer. Drake realised he was near the front lines now. *The front lines. Of course.* He sprinted down the alleyway behind the back of the houses, towards the sounds of the fighting. At the end of the alley, he came to another open road. He glimpsed the man going flat out across another rubble-strewn street, and he had a sixty-yard lead.

Drake pelted after him, taking a shortcut down a narrow passageway. The lane ran towards a warehouse, four or five stories tall, which backed onto the canals. Stukas shrieked down onto the city. Bombs crashed, walls crumbled, buildings exploded into fireballs. Machine gun bullets ricocheted and tumbled across factory yards. German artillery thumped in the distance. Fires were raging everywhere. Shells screeched in, smashing walls into showers of flying masonry. Drake saw the figure in the dark suit, running flat out. It was a footrace now. Drake leapt over the bodies of dead British soldiers as he ran. Agent Viper, the man of destiny, the

King of Burgundy – whoever the hell he was – was getting away, fleeing for the German lines.

Chapter 54

A British rifleman glanced up from a pile of rubble as Drake raced by. The man was wrapped in bandages, bright red with blood, and was firing across the canal.

'Watch it!' he shouted. He had a Kentish, country twang. 'There's Germans over there, boy!'

Drake barely gave the man a glance. He ran towards the crackle of small arms fire. German sniper shots snapped and echoed between the high walls of factories and warehouses. British riflemen, under cover on the ground, returned fire. Mortar bombs *whumped* up into the air, and fell, slamming open on the streets and in the factory yards in deadly, hard-hitting bursts. Drake sprinted on, ducking down as bullets whipped past his head and ricocheted off the ground. He saw the Viper try a side door of a warehouse, then run on, and try another. It opened. He flung it wide, then it slammed shut behind him as he disappeared into the darkness inside.

Drake ran up, ten seconds behind him, breathing hard. He shoved. The door wouldn't budge. He reckoned it was bolted from the inside.

He took three steps back, then lunged forward and kicked. The door tore open, coming half off its hinges. Drake chased into the warehouse. The sounds of gunfire were muffled by the thick concrete walls. It was oddly quiet and still inside. He slowed.

Tools and lunchboxes were scattered all around, as if the men who worked there had evacuated in a great hurry. Packing crates lay empty at the foot of high steel shelves. Drake hurriedly searched the cavernous room. There was nobody there. Footsteps rang out, and Drake ran through a machine room. The sound was coming from a staircase at the back. Drake thumped up it, boots clashing on the concrete steps. He pounded up five flights, legs aching, lungs gasping air, then as he came spilling out through the door at the top of the stairs, he glimpsed the suited figure. A shot cracked out from a pistol, and the bullet slapped into the wall near Drake's head. He quickly looked around.

Up here were the offices, rows of desks and telephone sets for warehouse clerks. It was untouched by the shelling. Everything was in its place as if for a day of work. Glass and wood partitions divided the space into a warren of corridors and small cubicles and offices. A shadow moved, at the end of a corridor. A glimpse of a dark blue suit.

Drake jogged along the passageway, more warily now, keeping the head of the stairwell to his back. The man saw him, and dashed away towards the southern end of the building. Drake ran after him, but it seemed he'd disappeared.

At the end of the offices, a large, deep window looked out over the waterways and edifices of the warehouse district. Drake stepped cautiously towards the glass. He had an impression of the whole of the east side of the city outside the window – the industrial port, factories, distant dunes, towers of smoke, and British ships standing far out to sea. When he turned, he saw the man come out from behind a high clerk's desk. He had a sheen of sweat across his forehead. He raised his right arm and aimed LaPointe's pistol at Drake's face.

Drake smiled and stepped towards him. He nodded to the pistol in the man's grip. '*Manufacture d'Armes de Bayonne*, Model C. I'm afraid to say it only holds six rounds.'

The man pulled the trigger. It clicked. Drake lunged forward to grab him, but quick as a snake, the man picked up a clerk's wooden stool and swung it. The seat of the stool crashed into the side of Drake's face. He staggered back from the blow, head reeling, lights flashing before his eyes. The man turned, stool in hand, and tried to hit him again. Drake was ready this time, and caught the leg of the stool, twisting it away. It catapulted into the window, and the glass shattered with a high-pitched crack.

Drake stepped back. Pointed his revolver at the man's belly. The man slowly raised his hands until they were halfway level with his face. Drake noted once again the pronounced widow's peak, the thick hair which was hanging about his face in disarray. Drake felt a sensation of great mental energy from behind his dark brown eyes. He stepped towards him, and the man edged back, closer to the window.

'You don't shoot me,' the man said. 'So you need me. Why?'

Drake smiled, and lowered the aim of the weapon. 'I could shoot you in the kneecaps, and you'd still be of use.'

He shrugged. '*D'accord.* Alright. So what do you want from me?'

Drake fished in his pocket. He held up an object in his hand. 'You left this behind at Arras,' he said.

The man frowned at the silver cross of the tiepin. 'Arras? I have never been to Arras.'

Drake hesitated, suddenly uncertain. 'Then who are you?'

The man frowned. 'Do you really mean to say you don't know?' He gestured towards his own breast pocket. 'May I?'

Drake nodded. 'Slowly.'

The man carefully extracted something red from his jacket. He flicked it and it fluttered open. It was a large, red silk handkerchief matching his tie, of the kind a stage illusionist might use. For a moment, Drake had the impression that he was going to perform a magic trick.

'I thank you for saving my life,' the man said, 'but I think we're finished here.' His eyes caught Drake's for a moment and he suddenly launched himself backwards. There was a shattering of glass as he went out through the high, cracked window and disappeared.

Drake felt a momentary sting of disbelief. He stepped to the frame and looked out in time to see the man falling, arms and legs flailing through the air, the red handkerchief fluttering in the wind. Then – a tremendous splash as he hit the dull grey water of the canal far below.

Five seconds later, the man resurfaced and thrashed for the far bank, sodden red handkerchief held up in one hand.

Drake launched himself onto the window ledge, ready to go after him, then stopped. A swarm of German troops was running toward the water's edge on the far bank, and they began pulling the man in the suit from the canal. One of the soldiers raised his face to look up at the window and began to fire. Rounds slapped into the building's concrete walls. Drake hesitated for a moment, then quickly realised it was hopeless to try to follow. He ducked back inside as debris from the bullet strikes zipped through the air.

He stared down through the shattered window at the canal. Smoke billowed across the water. Shells thudded in the distance. The German soldiers were leading the man away and he was leaving a dark trail of water in his wake.

'Satan's hell, what happened, sir?' came MacTaggart's voice, the old Sergeant gasping from the chase.

'Recognition signal of some kind,' Drake said, slowly shaking his head. He smacked his hand against the wall. 'They were expecting him. Damn it!'

MacTaggart shook his head. 'So we're back to square one.'

'Not quite.' Drake stooped down, picked something up and held it to the light. It was oval in shape, about five inches long. It must have fallen from the man's pocket when he'd pulled the handkerchief out. It was some old-fashioned kind of playing card. In fact, it seemed ancient. There was a picture of a joker, a fool in medieval dress. He had a hideous, gargoyle-like face, and held a staff in one hand. In the other hand, the ancient joker was dangling a noose. Drake felt a stab of unease.

'Who's the King of Burgundy?' he said.

MacTaggart shrugged. 'Don't ask me, sir. I'm just a poor sergeant. I've got no bloody idea.'

Chapter 55

QUARTIER DE LA MEUSE, CALAIS NORD, FRANCE – 19:00HRS

THE SUN BEAT DARKLY down through the smog that hung over the city from the fires. The blowing smoke dimmed the light, but it seemed only to intensify the heat. Drake lay on the rooftop of the warehouse, behind a concrete parapet, surveying the German positions. *Two steps forward, half a dozen back.* All around him, Calais burned.

Hot winds funnelled the flames along the streets, and the ash-laden air was so arid that Drake's throat was raw and parched. There was no fresh water on the island of Calais Nord now. Either the bombs or the besieging German army had cut off the supply. The noose was tightening around British throats. On the far side of the harbour, to the west, black fumes spewed up as though from a volcano where the port's great oil containers burned. The blazing fuel sent up roiling black clouds that towered into the sky.

Drake reckoned half the streets of the old town were now on fire. He could see it all from here. Entire terraces of houses and apartments blazed. Panzer cannons thumped at crumbling buildings on the canal banks. British small arms fire crackled back across the canal. Shells screeched in from German artillery and Flak guns, firing over open sights down alleyways and lines of sight along the roads. From out to sea came a deep, regular thumping as four- and five-inch guns from British destroyers hurled shells high overhead towards the German positions in constant, harassing fire. It appeared that the German advance had stalled at the canal bridges. Their probing attacks were dogged, relentless, insistent, but against all the odds, the barricades were still holding and the small British force was clinging desperately on. The riflemen were holding the island of Calais Nord, for now.

Drake's gaze fixated on the German side of the canal, where the man with the widow's peak had disappeared. He turned over the tiepin in his left hand. He held the playing card in his right. The Saltire cross, raguly. The medieval joker dangling a noose. What was the connection? Agent Viper. The man of the hour. The King of Burgundy. Burgundy was a province in the centre of France, southeast of Paris. So why were they in Calais? How did it fit? Slowly, as the images spun around in a kind of dreamlike *danse macabre*, a meaning began to emerge. Drake had a hunch they were on the right trail. Everything pointed to a fascist conspiracy. The Hapsburgs, the Carlists of Spain. Franco's army, poised just over the southern border of France, already battle-hardened from the bitter struggle of the Spanish civil war, where fascists and republican communists had battled hand to hand in the streets.

Communists. Drake thought of the deserters, the sullen faces of the working-class French conscripts. It wouldn't take much for them to revolt. Something was rotten in the Third Republic alright. The French officer class seemed to have simply vanished into thin air.

Drake's eye was caught by a movement on the pavement below. A group of civilians emerged from a cellar, all coughing and with cloths held to their faces, evidently driven out by the smoke. They had nowhere to go, the whole street was aflame. They gazed around in dread. But just across the road, a section of British soldiers were wheeling an upright piano out of a café doorway and onto the street. Drake watched in amazement as one of the men began to play, and the syncopated melodies of ragtime drifted up through the background clatter and din of the battle. The soldiers cavorted madly around the piano, dancing across the ruins. One clutched a bottle of wine in his hands.

Drake shook his head. There was something you couldn't fail to love about the British soldier. Their morale in dire straits was simply a wonder. It was hard to credit that men would fight so fiercely, and yet keep up their good spirits with little hope of escape. Outnumbered, outgunned, with their backs to the wall – and the atmosphere was like a bloody cup final. He wondered how much it had to do with the vast stores of booze that were to be found in almost every café and house in every street. Drake heard footsteps behind him on the rooftop, and he quickly spun around.

'The world is going to hell,' Axelle said. 'And the British Army dances in the streets.'

'Something to do with the rainy climate,' Drake said, turning back to watch the men below. 'We come into our own when the chips are down.'

The whipcrack of a bullet went by, and Drake pulled Axelle into cover, where he was lying on the flat roof behind the parapet. 'Snipers. In the clocktower. What are you doing here? Are you trying to get yourself killed?'

Axelle shrugged. 'Doctor Lambert told me what happened with the prisoners and said you came this way. Your sergeant let me past. He's guarding the staircase. He's very loyal to you, you know.'

Drake looked at her face, her deep brown eyes that always seemed to be lit with a spark from within. 'I meant why are you here in Calais.'

She shrugged. 'I came on the hospital train.'

Drake saw that she was still wearing the nursing uniform but had removed the hat. Her hair was pushed back behind her ears, to keep it from her face. Her skin was smudged with ash smuts and soot, now. Nobody was immune

'I'm sorry,' he said. 'About what happened before.'

She cut him off. 'Don't let's talk about the past.'

Drake turned away in a sudden flush of irritation. 'Alright, the present then. So, the doctor is your boyfriend now.'

'Don't be a child, Drake,' she said. 'Édouard can be a little formal with strangers, but his heart is in the right place. He was a distinguished private physician in all the best circles before the war. And all this,' she waved a hand towards the fighting, 'has been something of a shock.'

Drake held up the playing card. 'Who is the King of Burgundy?' he said.

Axelle let out a startled laugh as she took in the image of the medieval fool. 'There is no king of Burgundy! There has not been one for 800 years!'

Drake rubbed a hand across the dry skin of his face. 'Well it seems that there is one now.'

Axelle turned away for a moment, contemplating the burning skyline of Calais. Stukas were diving at the British destroyers, which were keeping station out to sea. 'It is like the Day of Judgement,' she said. 'For all our sins, the apocalypse has come.'

'You don't strike me as the religious type,' Drake said.

She caught his gaze, and threw it back. 'I'm not.'

For a moment, they stared together out over the burning city. There seemed to be a lull in the fighting now. The sun was lowering towards the horizon, and Drake knew the Germans didn't like to fight in the dark. 'You can get out. On a boat with the wounded. You're a nurse. They'll let you go.'

Axelle shook her head. 'I'm needed here.'

Drake felt suddenly angry at her. 'Don't be a bloody fool. Get on the next boat from the dock. You'll still be saving lives, your own included. Everybody who stays here is going to die.'

Axelle gave him a sorrowful smile. 'This is my fight too. I can't run away. Would you?'

Their eyes met. Drake pushed down the unwelcome feelings that it brought to the surface. He had a job to do. He'd be damned lucky if it didn't kill him, and he had no right to start—

He stopped himself. *Forget it.*

'I don't believe in coincidence, Axelle. What are you really doing here in Calais?'

She said nothing. Drake thought back to how he had met her on the first day of the invasion. Her dealings with Jack Philips. The way he could never seem to shake her off. Then it clicked.

'*Staatsveiligheid*,' he said.

Axelle shrugged. 'At last.'

Drake shook his head. *Veiligheid van de Staat – Sûreté de l'Etat,* also known as *VSSE* for short, was the Belgian security service. Finally, it all began to make sense. 'You've been playing me like a piano all along.'

She picked up the tiepin he'd been idling in his hands. She held it up in the light. 'Perhaps I've been looking for the same thing as you.'

'Agent Viper. The King of Burgundy. Who is he?'

Axelle frowned. 'He's gone to see his masters,' she said, gesturing towards the newer part of the city, Calais-St-Pierre. 'There are ways to get in there, after nightfall. But I don't want you to go.'

Drake sat suddenly upright. 'Why not?'

'There's no time, Drake. Let us not deceive ourselves.' She paused and looked away, through the smoke clouds, towards the sea. 'If I tell you where he has gone, you will follow him there and you will never come back. And I want you to come back. Don't you know?'

She gazed at him for a moment, then leaned in close. He suddenly found that she was kissing him and he was kissing her, oblivious to the danger of the snipers. When they touched, it felt so strange and so natural all at once, as though his entire life had been leading up to this one, mad moment. He pressed his face against hers, and he felt her body push into his, driven by a sudden, urgent desire.

They held each other as though the world was ending, and lay together above the burning gables of the old port city, oblivious to the sound of the bombs, as hot, dry, ash-laden winds blew over their skin. And eventually, the sounds of battle receded. The last light of the day was gradually replaced by the twilight's fiery glow.

Afterwards, in the strange dusk light, Drake touched her face. He studied her features. She was the same, but different now, as though they'd both been somehow transposed. He experienced a dizzying sensation, the strangest feeling that he'd always known her, as if they'd been lovers in the time of the Pharaohs and they'd only just been reunited now.

Night reached across the sky, pulling away the last of the sun's bloody rays. Bombs fell, carnations of fire exploding around them in the city's burning streets. Spiralling ladders of Ack-Ack traced up into the heavens. The crackle of gunfire was punctuated by deep thumping booms. Together they watched the firecrackers and Roman candles of the battle. Far off to their left were great beams of white light, criss-crossing the sky. Drake realised they were the searchlights of Dover. It brought him strange, new sensations to think of home. So near and yet so far away. He gazed on Axelle's face, bathed in the glow of the fiery city. So this was what it felt like. *Christ.* Why now?

'When I come back, we'll get out of here,' he said. 'We'll find a boat. We'll go to England—'

She put a finger to his lips and he stopped talking. 'You and I both know that is not possible,' she said.

Of course, Drake thought. Because of her mother's nationality, she'd probably be interned. He felt an uneasy churning of shame inside. And what about Hazel, back home? He pushed the feelings away. He couldn't think about that now. He'd be lucky to live through the night, so there was little point in worrying beyond that short horizon.

He stirred himself. 'It's time,' he said. Buttoning his shirt, he reluctantly got to his feet. 'Come on. I must go.'

He held out his hand to pull her up. A salvo of heavy guns flashed far out at sea and a moment later the shells whistled high overhead. Drake saw the flares of the shellstrikes as they hit the German lines in the darkness of the new town of Calais-St-Pierre. Half a second later the sound of the detonations thumped like heavy heartbeats in the dark and smoky air.

Chapter 56

GRAND THÉÂTRE DE CALAIS, PLACE ALBERT, CALAIS – 23:00HRS

A LINE OF PANZERS rumbled across the town square towards the old city of Calais Nord. The street was dark, lit only by the glow of the fires that was reflected from the clouds of smoke. Drake stood on the corner of Rue Darnel and Rue Antoine Bénard, watching them go.

Crossing the canal had been the difficult part, but once across, Drake had found dead Germans of all shapes and sizes. He'd unearthed an *Unterfeldwebel*'s uniform that was a decent fit, and had wiped off most of the blood. The uniform stank from weeks on the road. He ran his hands unconsciously over the kit. It was a little loose, but that was not unusual now – after endless days of fighting, rapid manoeuvre and little sleep, everybody had lost a lot of weight. He had the strap of an MP40 *Maschinenpistole* over his left shoulder, and a pair of *Stielhandgranaten* were shoved into his belt. He was now just one more German soldier in an army of German soldiers in the dark.

The Grand Théâtre de Calais was the most striking and elaborate building in the city. It stood on the opposite side of the road and dominated the wide square of Place Albert. Above the triple entrance doors, enormous double columns held up a stone façade complete with ornate statues. Elaborate busts were set in front of three twenty-foot-high arched windows. Their glass reflected the dim red glow of the burning old city, a kilometre to the north. The distant fires only added to the building's sense of majesty. A great red and black banner was being unfurled from the roof by engineers. The Wehrmacht's high command had wasted no time in setting up shop. It was a stark, political message that nobody could fail to comprehend. Nazi Germany was here to stay.

Drake waited until the column of tanks had passed, then strode across the square. Irrationally, he felt more afraid now than in the midst of battle. To hide the obvious strain, he set his face to look sour and grim. A high tension, pianowire tight, constricted inside his chest as he marched up the steps and went in.

The Wehrmacht sentries stiffened as he strode purposefully past. Technicians and *Unteroffiziere* of the Corps of Signals were laying power and communication cables across the theatre's marble foyer. A group of mid-ranking officers, led by an *Oberst* of the 90th Artillery Regiment, were talking with animated gestures at the foot of a curving staircase. Drake walked past them all, ill-fitting jackboots thudding on the floor, and went quickly up the steps. He emerged into a wide, green-carpeted passageway which opened to a grand foyer on the right, which in turn led to the first circle of the theatre to the left. He stopped a *Funker* – a signalman – with a brusque demand.

'*Standartenführer Obenauer vom Sicherheitsdienst?*'

'*Konversationszimmer, Herr Unterfeldwebel!*' the signalman replied. He pointed. '*Dort unten. Links und dann rechts.*'

Drake nodded and followed the directions. The electric lights were on as he descended another staircase. The German pioneer corps had quickly got the generators running. He walked on, along another quiet corridor, the unfamiliar uniform feeling strange against his skin. The sporadic shelling sounded distant and muffled from here. Eventually he came to a door. A sign on it read *Foyer des artistes.*

Drake glanced up and down the passageway. There was nobody in sight. He slung the MP40 machine gun around to the front and engaged the action. He turned the door handle and stepped inside.

The interior of the room was lush, furnished in velvet curtains and lounge chairs, bright, bulb-lit makeup mirrors, rails of theatrical costumes and eerie-looking mannequins. On a chaise longue at the end of the room sat a small German officer in a drab grey uniform. He was wearing *pince-nez* glasses and his hair was razor-short in a Himmler cut. Drake's eye was drawn to a black briefcase, stuffed with papers, which was on the low table in front of him. Chances were that it was the same black briefcase he'd seen in the tent – and the significance was obvious. On the sleeve of the man's jacket was a diamond-shaped black patch bearing two simple letters: *SD.*

The officer looked up. There was something predatory, animalistic about the set of his face. His eyes, behind the lenses, shifted like fish behind thick aquarium glass as his gaze moved uncannily around the room.

Drake aimed the machine gun at him, finger poised on the trigger. 'Standartenführer Obenauer.'

Obenauer's gaze finally came to rest on Drake's face. He spoke softly, almost mockingly. 'Good day, Herr Drake.'

Drake stiffened, and a flash like ice went through his veins. The German officer gave him a reptilian smile.

Drake saw a glint of movement in the brilliantly-lit mirrors and he turned, too late, too slow. It seemed that one of the mannequins had come to life and was rushing towards him. A stunning crack of light went through his brain as a giant paw crashed into the right side of his head. His legs turned to milk and he crumpled. A knee slammed into his spine, causing the machine gun to fly from his hands. A boot kicked him in the ribs as he fell, and he saw the monstrous face of a great golem leering down at him as he slid to the floor.

Drake blinked, lying on the ground in a daze. He must have been knocked out, because Standartenführer Obenauer was standing over him now. The officer spoke in soft, precise English in an oddly high-pitched voice. 'You recall my sergeant, *Unterscharführer* Gunther, Herr Drake? He certainly remembers you.'

Drake looked up. He saw purple, glistening skin, the hair burnt away from the flesh of the raw scalp. The mouth, lips burnt back from teeth that stood out like small grey pegs. The giant golem grinned, and his skin split, drawing blood. It was the great German sergeant who he'd set fire to in the command tent, back at Arras.

An enormous jackboot came swinging towards him. Drake tried to protect himself, but he found he couldn't move. The boot connected with his head in a shock of light and pain. He collapsed into a splintering darkness. And he had just enough time to wonder how Obenauer knew his name.

Chapter 57

Drake clawed his way back up to consciousness. Shards of fire bloomed inside his brain. The dressing room was bright, too bright, lit by brilliant bulbs. He tried to move his arms, but couldn't. He realised he was naked, arms and legs lashed to a stout wooden chair. A sick cramp of anxiety gripped at his insides. He'd walked right into a trap. But how? He shook his head in a vain attempt to clear the fuzz, but it just drove the throbbing deeper. He forced his eyes to open properly and observe.

To his left was a line of mirrors that ran the length of the entire, strange room. There was a countertop running below the row of mirrors. Each mirror was surrounded with bare bulbs – makeup lights. At the far end of the room was a second door, covered by a soundproofed curtain. Drake guessed it must lead to the stage. He turned his head and saw from the corner of his eye that the rear wall was lined with costumed mannequins, robes, and dummy heads bearing wigs. A corner was enclosed by tall dressing screens. The German uniform he'd worn to get into the theatre was now draped over a forlorn-looking figurine. From the back of the room, the burnt face of the giant German sergeant glared at him from eyes made stranger by eyelids seared by hideous burns. His head was purple and pink and glistening, and Drake could smell the sharp, medical reek of the salve.

Standartenführer Obenauer was sitting on the chaise longue at the far end of the room. His eyes roved over Drake's naked body with a sinister caress, then flicked away. Drake suppressed a shudder. He could see the man's scalp through his razor-cut hair. His *pince-nez* glasses reflected the bright glare of the bulbs. Behind the glasses, the man's eyes wandered around the room, then his gaze finally landed back on Drake's face.

Drake felt a starburst of shock as Gunther smashed a fist into his temple. Despite the swirling stars inside his head, Drake coldly noted the technique. Hit first, ask questions later. Start with fear.

His brain thumped painfully inside his skull. His throat was dry and sore. He could hear the muffled thunder of artillery thudding, somewhere far away. He watched as Obenauer got up and slowly paced towards him. The German officer's eyes rested on Drake's for a moment before they slid away to drift around the room once more.

Obenauer extended his index finger and ran it down Drake's naked chest. It was horribly disconcerting.

He spoke softly. 'The *Künstlergarderobe* – how do you say, the dressing room? – is below the level of the stage, which means it is naturally soundproofed. And in my line of work, that is a very convenient feature.' His face moved into a cold, feral smile. 'But I am not a *monster*.' He said the word with a sinewy caress. 'I am not a *monster*, Mr Drake. We can be friends, if only you will give me the information I require.'

Drake strained his arms and legs against the cords that held him to the chair, but the bonds were tight. Obenauer watched him struggle. Drake was transfixed by the seemingly random movement of the man's eyes as, from behind his narrow, armless glasses, the officer's gaze wandered around the room again, unsettled, as though following the progress of an invisible fly.

Obenauer bent down next to him. He put his lips close to Drake's right ear. He whispered, 'Is it compromised?'

Drake felt the urge to shudder, but he shut it down. He ignored the question. He was looking at the briefcase that lay on the table in front of the chaise longue. It was black calfskin leather, embossed with *SS* runes and the *Reichsadler* – the Nazi eagle and swastika.

The German SD officer walked behind Drake's chair and ran a pale finger over his shoulders. 'We can avoid unpleasantness. So! Tell me.' He leant forward, like a fellow conspirator. 'Is it *compromised*?' His breath, so close, was warm and scented with lavender.

'Is what compromised?' Drake said.

Obenauer's strange eyes slid away to look over Drake's shoulder. He pouted and said, 'Tut-tut.'

Drake saw a flash of movement in the mirrors. A great fist flew towards him and he had no way to dodge the blow. He tried to lean his forehead into it, but the huge fist slammed into the side of his head like a jackhammer. The grotesque giant spun the chair around, and punched him in the solar plexus. All Drake could do was tense his muscles and try to absorb the blow. He gagged, and heard himself let out a groan.

If his stomach hadn't been empty he would have vomited, but another great fist smashed into his skull. The chair tipped over and he slammed to the floor. A size fourteen jackboot thumped into his guts. His mind was imprinted with the sight of Gunther's enormous head, scorched bald except for a few frizzled tufts of hair, lips blistered and melted into a permanent rictus grin.

Drake lay on the floor, barely conscious. The room was swimming around him now. Obenauer squatted down so he was looking into his eyes, as though from upside down.

The German spoke gently, like a kindly doctor at a bedside. 'Come now. Is it compromised?'

Drake blinked up at him. He tried to speak, but his voice was faint. Obenauer leaned in closer.

'What did your mother do to you?' Drake said.

Obenauer's face twitched slightly, then the animalistic smile returned. He stood up, leaving Drake on the floor.

'*Strom*,' he said to Sergeant Gunther.

The burnt skin on Gunther's lips ripped a little, showing a trickle of blood, as his enormous, glistening face split into a hideous grin.

Chapter 58

A GUSH OF COLD water jerked Drake back awake. He blinked his eyes open, and found himself upright in the chair once more. On the other side of the room, the huge form of Sergeant Gunther was refilling a bucket from a washstand.

Obenauer ran a hand through Drake's dripping hair. 'Such an unusual colour,' he said. He pulled at Drake's locks, trying to force his head back. Drake resisted.

'You're not a Jew, are you Mr Drake?' the German officer hissed.

Drake ignored the question. He needed vital seconds to think. As his spinning head slowly settled, he realised he *had* learned something, something of real value. Whatever it was that they were up to, Obenauer was worried. That meant it *could* be compromised. It was not yet a *fait accompli*. Drake still had a chance.

He glanced at the mirror. Standing behind him, Sergeant Gunther gave a lipless grin. The man's left ear was shrivelled to the size of a walnut. One eyelid was stretched wide open, and the other pulled tight. His forehead sloped back from the jutting bones of his eye sockets. Pink and purple mottled flesh was stretched tightly over his enormous, heavy-boned skull.

Obenauer moved towards the countertop. He picked up a slim leather box, the size of a flute case, and opened it. A long, thin wooden implement lay in an indented velvet bed inside. He lifted it up. Drake heard the *thud-thud-thud* of big guns rumbling somewhere in the distance. He stared at the object held in Obenauer's pale, soft fingers. It was a wooden rod, about fifteen inches long. At one end was a leather handgrip. At the other end, two short metal prongs stuck out an inch or so in parallel, like a pair of blunted nails.

Obenauer's gaze rolled around the room and came back to fix itself on Drake once more. 'You will tell me what I want to know, Mr Drake. We could have been friends, but you force my hand.' He rotated the rod, examining the end where the prongs stuck out. 'As a young man I travelled the world. Our cousins in the Argentine gave me such *interesting* ideas.'

Drake stared at the odd instrument in the officer's hands. He felt a sense of creeping dread, rising through the entire room, as though coming up through the floor.

Obenauer smiled again, as his eyes drifted lazily across Drake's face. 'The *picana* is a simple instrument which, when correctly utilised, can cause the subject an exquisite sensation.'

He nodded to Gunther, who produced an electrical transformer from a wooden case. He plugged a cable into the wooden rod, then, using a cloth, he then removed a lightbulb from next to one of the mirrors, and plugged a second cable from the transformer into the bulb's electrical socket.

'*Elektrizität*,' the big man said in a deep baritone grunt. He switched the transformer on. A dial at the front lit up, and it hummed.

'*Zwölftausend Volt*,' Obenauer said. 'Twelve thousand volts,' and the sergeant's great hand turned the dial.

Obenauer chuckled. 'A thousandth of an amp. At such high voltages, a larger dose would kill you instantly. And we don't want that, do we? Not yet, Mr Drake. Not yet.' He leaned forwards and gave Drake a conspirator's smile.

He prodded Drake in the chest with the metal ends of the rod. A searing flash tore through Drake's brain and his limbs leapt against their bonds. Snakes of fire pierced his ribcage and shot straight to the centre of his skull. He was shouting, yelling, involuntarily screaming and howling with all his strength, and his heart thudded wildly, dangerously in his chest. It went on for what seemed a lifetime, but it was only a few seconds. Then Obenauer removed the picana and the electric shock abruptly ceased.

Drake slumped down in the chair, gasping and shattered. Bile rose in his throat. He gagged. The room spun around him. Sweat burst out across his skin. His entire body was aching, cramped all over. He was aware of the German sergeant's deep, grating laugh. Drake peered down at his chest, expecting to see some terrible wound, but was surprised to see his skin was barely marked. There was just a small, branching redness reaching out beneath the flesh from the point where the electrodes had touched. He groaned and spat blood onto the floor from where he'd bitten into his tongue.

'Oh, Mr Drake, you must take your medicine!' Obenauer chided, wagging a finger, as though talking to an errant child. He used the wooden shaft of the picana to lift up Drake's chin, and Drake found himself flinching instinctively away from it. The officer pressed upwards with the wood-covered wand until Drake was looking up into his eyes.

'So?' Obenauer said. 'Is it compromised?'

'Go to hell,' Drake said.

Obenauer's gaze drifted away. '*Vierzehntausend Volt.*'

Gunther turned the dial to fourteen thousand. The lights in the room dimmed as Obenauer thrust the electrodes into the side of Drake's neck.

A flash of lightning exploded inside his brain. A terrible burning filled his nostrils. His entire body racked on the chair, muscles rigid and spasming, unable to move. His jaw clamped shut so hard he heard one of his teeth crack, and his legs and torso shuddered violently against the restraints. He heard an animal keening and realised it was coming from his own throat. The pain was so intense that it seemed the entire world was one great splintering candle of burning white light. Then Obenauer removed the device, and the shock stopped, and the room lights brightened once again, but Drake's body stayed rigid for ten seconds longer, his muscles seized in agonising tremors and contractions against the ropes. When the spasms finally eased, his guts wrenched and he vomited on himself.

Obenauer shook his head. 'It's a simple question, Mr Drake. Is it compromised?'

Drake's head sagged down. He gagged again. Drool was spilling from his mouth. He couldn't seem to control his jaw.

Gunther threw another bucket of water on him, washing away the vomit. The floor was soaking wet. But the water revived Drake a little. Gunther filled the bucket again and set it down near the chair.

'*Sechzehntausend Volt*,' Obenauer said.

Sergeant Gunther's face lit up. He turned two notches further.

Obenauer smiled and his eyes rolled down to look at Drake's genitals. He leaned forward with the wooden rod and pressed the electrodes in.

Drake's world exploded into an unbearable screaming, as though some wild beast was tearing strips from his insides. The shocks going through his muscles were so strong that it seemed the cramps must surely break his bones. The spasms went on and on, and the lights in the room flickered. Drake started shaking uncontrollably, caught in an iron tower of seething, excruciating, unbearably flaming torment. An unearthly screech was coming from his throat, and his arms and legs felt like they were going to shatter into glassy fragments. The force of his convulsions was such that the chair was jumping and skittering forwards across the floor. Waves of pain blossomed into an impossible concentration of agony and he let out a scream, a cry, a roar to bring the rafters down, as if to obliterate the terrible suffering, but it just went on and on and on until he imagined he was being crucified from the inside out. Eventually, long past the time when it could go on no longer and he must surely die, Obenauer pulled the instrument away.

The jagged lightning stopped. Drake's entire body stayed stiff, locked in a rigid, tormenting spasm which lasted for a whole minute, before his limbs, no longer subject to his will, slumped down against his restraints once more.

Drake choked up a spoonful of bile, and it dribbled down his chin. He closed his eyes and colours swam across his vision as he struggled for breath.

'Now, Mr Drake. Will you reconsider my offer of friendship?'

Drake found that he couldn't get his vocal chords to work.

Obenauer glanced across at the enormous Sergeant Gunther. '*Achtzehntausend Volt*,' he said.

'Yes,' Drake finally whispered. His voice was little more than a croak. 'It is compromised.'

Obenauer's eyes narrowed suddenly. 'So!'

Drake shook his head. His entire body was aching so badly from the spasms that he could hardly breathe. The pain was driving him deep into himself, so that the room, the men, the whole world became a blur, silhouettes against the shining spears of agony that locked his muscles into horrible, jolting cramps. He felt like a marionette being jerked by its strings. He spat bile from his mouth but it landed on his chest. He knew he had only one shot, one chance to make a play.

'*Operationsbefehl Dämmerung*,' he said, and his words came out as just a broken wheeze. 'Zero hour is 28th of May. But it will never come off.' He sucked in a shuddering breath. 'Agent Viper has betrayed you. We have turned him to work for our side.'

Chapter 59

THE ROOM SPUN SILENTLY around inside Drake's head. Obenauer was watching him with those pale, uncanny eyes. They were extraordinarily mobile, like those of an animal in a cage. The German smiled, but his lips were as thin as the blade of a knife. He walked slowly towards the chaise longue at the end of the room. From a coat pocket he produced matches and a packet of cigarettes. He came back and offered one to Drake.

Drake shook his head. His voice came out in a croak. 'I gave up. Bad for the health.'

Obenauer gazed at him for a moment, then laughed out loud. 'Very good, Herr Drake. Very good!' He struck Drake's head with the side of the wooden rod, a sharp crack that Drake heard as much as felt. A jolt of pain fired across inside his skull.

Obenauer pointed the picana's iron prods towards Drake's face. 'Tell me more.'

Drake found his body was shaking uncontrollably. He felt as though he'd been in a motor accident, as though he'd fallen from a high building, but the torment was all inside. He tried to gather himself. He knew little of interrogation techniques or how to resist them, but he had one idea, and one idea only. *Interrogate the interrogator*. Give something, and win something in return.

'*Dämmerung* is a plot to bring about the downfall of the Allied armies,' he said.

Obenauer shrugged. He caressed the picana with his pale, soft hands. He brought the rod towards Drake's groin once more. Drake tried to squirm away. He did not have to feign the fear.

'You will observe what a little thing it is that we have done so far,' the German officer continued. 'Tell me everything you know.'

Drake grunted, trying to flex his fingers. 'Untie me.'

Obenauer watched him closely. 'Tut-tut, Mr Drake. Information first.'

'I met the King of Burgundy,' Drake said.

Obenauer observed him oddly. 'The King of Burgundy? There is no King of Burgundy, and there has not been one for 800 years.'

A shaft of ice slid through Drake's veins. He had heard those words before. He forged on, trying to make something from the scraps he knew. 'You have taken over from the Abwehr, because *Dämmerung* is a political matter involving the Roman Catholic Church.'

Obenauer's face remained impassive. Drake watched him as he moved slowly around the room.

'More,' the German officer said. 'I need more.' He turned to Gunther, who was watching with an almost greedy look on his face. '*Zwanzigtausend.* Twenty thousand volts.'

'No!' Drake shouted.

Obenauer thrust the picana into Drake's solar plexus. Drake shrieked as his body leapt against the restraints. His being was subsumed in a world of shattering white flame, and his body juddered in uncontrollable, bone-breaking contractions that shook the chair so hard it jumped forwards. Muscles jerked in rupturing, tearing spasms as a prong of unbearable agony forked right through his body and threatened to tear apart his soul. The wet ropes cut into his flesh, and from somewhere he heard a snap as loud as a gunshot and he knew it was his right leg because it was jerking agonisingly, spasmodically from side to side, and he felt his heart racing as if it would burst and he'd open up and break apart from the insides.

Obenauer removed the prong.

The fire went out, but Drake's body continued in a terrible seizure, heart pounding, jaw locked tight, every part of his entire body burning with the strain. His right leg flopped loosely, and he feared, in his agony, that somehow it was broken, but he glanced down, and saw that it was not his bones that had snapped, but the chair leg. He kept very still and tried to loosen his jaw enough to speak.

'You will explain to me precisely what *Dämmerung* is,' Obenauer said.

'Nightfall. Twilight. The end of an era. That's really all I know.'

Obenauer watched his face carefully. He looked disappointed. He sighed.

'I believe you, Mr Drake.' He examined his hands, as though looking for traces of blood. 'It is most unfortunate. You no longer hold any value to the Reich.' He gave the picana to the colossal sergeant. 'I don't want to see him anymore.'

A smiled broke across the big man's disfigured face.

He turned the transformer to the maximum. '*Vierundzwanzigtausend Volt*,' he said in a deep baritone grunt. *Twenty-four thousand volts.* It hummed, and for a moment the lights flickered and dimmed. '*Fünftausendstel Ampere.*'

Obenauer shrugged, and moved towards the chaise longue where he picked up the briefcase. '*Ja, ja.* As you please.'

Drake turned to Gunther. '*Du bist zwar groß, aber hässlich wie ein Schweinearsch*,' he said. It sounded very satisfying in German.

Gunther's eyes narrowed in rage and he stepped forward towards the chair, picana outthrust towards Drake's face. Drake kicked his right foot forward, hard. His foot, still tied to the broken chair leg, connected with the bucket of water that Gunther had left on the ground.

The bucket flew up and pitched over, covering the sergeant in a wave of water that engulfed the humming electrical transformer. There was a flash and Gunther jerked back. His face stretched, spine bending, limbs seizing as he was electrocuted. For a moment he spasmed and crackled and his skin began to smoke, then the transformer flared up and exploded. All the light bulbs blew out in a shattering flash and the room was suddenly doused in black.

Chapter 60

Drake lunged to his left, his bodyweight tipping the chair over in the pitched darkness. The muzzle flash of a deafening pistol shot momentarily lit the room. *Obenauer.* In the background the distant thumping of artillery tubes rumbled on. For a moment Drake could hear his own ragged breathing in the inky black of the windowless room.

Drake's limbs were stiff and aching, but he ignored the pain as he worked at his hands. He knew he only had seconds before Obenauer found him with a shot. The wet ropes had stretched with the extraordinary stresses of his seizures, and it had loosened the joints of the sturdy wooden chair.

Drake wriggled his hands until finally his left came loose. Another speculative pistol shot crashed across the room, for a split second illuminating the standing shape of Obenauer, and the massive form of Gunther laid out on the floor. Drake pushed and pulled at his bindings, bending to try to get at the rope with his teeth, and finally, after what seemed like eternity, his hand came free.

Bootsteps sounded as Obenauer stepped across the wet floor, then a match struck. In the small orange flare of the flame, Obenauer stood over the chair, pistol ready to deliver the killing shot. But the chair was empty. Drake, barefooted, stepped up behind him. He swung the heavy rod of the picana and struck Obenauer hard on the back of the head. Obenauer grunted and dropped the match. It fizzed out on the wet floor, and everything was dark once more.

Drake heard a swish of cloth and by instinct he ducked. Obenauer's pistol fired blindly, bullet whipping past his face. In the muzzle flash he saw the officer's position. He lunged up and with the full force of his entire body, plunged the pronged end of the picana towards the German's face. He felt a sickening squelch on contact. Obenauer screamed.

Fumbling in the darkness, Drake picked up the pistol and book of matches, then found his German uniform. He struck a light and saw Obenauer lying on the floor, with the picana handle protruding from one eye. The man was moaning softly. Drake quickly dressed himself in trousers and jackboots and pulled on the shirt. In the last light of the burning match, he saw that on the table in front of the chaise longue lay Obenauer's briefcase. He moved towards it, stepping carefully over the body of the giant Gunther, but before he could reach it, the match went out. Then a dazzling light shone into his face and somebody stepped in through the curtained-off doorway. Drake caught a glimpse of a rapid movement. He dived to the floor as another pistol shot flashed and cracked, illuminating shapes in the room. In the split second as he fell, he saw the outline of a man in civilian suit and a hat.

Drake rolled rapidly across the wet floor, then fired Obenauer's pistol towards where he thought the man must be. There was no return fire. Had he got him? He scrambled to his feet and ran towards the table, but he couldn't feel the briefcase. He listened. The sound of running feet, moving away quickly over wooden floorboards. He risked striking another match, and stared at the table. The briefcase was gone.

Behind him, Obenauer started shrieking for help, stumbling blindly through the darkness, trying to find the way out. '*Hilfe! Helft mir!* Help me! Guards!'

Drake left him to it. He hurled himself through the curtain after the footsteps of the running man.

Chapter 61

DRAKE STUMBLED ALONG A pitch-black corridor, feeling his way, fighting the stiffness and the cramps in his legs. His footfalls echoed closely, then he was out into what sounded like a large open space. The lights were out all over the building. His jackboots thumped loudly onto hollow boards. He stopped to listen. It was dark as hell, but to his right there were pinpricks of orange light that seemed to waver strangely before his eyes. He wondered if it was the aftereffects of the electricity. It was quiet, then he heard a cough, and footsteps thudded away in the direction of the tiny orange dots.

Suddenly Drake was dazzled by glaring beams of light. He held a hand up to shield his eyes. It took him half a second to realise the power was back on, and he was shocked to find himself caught in the limelights in the centre of the Grand Theatre's great stage. Peering through the painful glare, he saw that the auditorium was vast. Below the stage was an orchestra pit, then endless red-backed stall chairs. Four tiers of seating circles towered high above. Rows of German officers and men were smoking in the stalls, or sleeping, now rudely awakened by the return of the lights. Shading their eyes from the sudden brightness, they stared up at Drake who was standing on the stage. He was caught for a moment, like a deer in the headlights. Then Obenauer, flanked by German soldiers, staggered out through the curtain and onto the stage, clutching a blood-drenched hand to his face.

'Haltet ihn auf!' Obenauer shouted. 'Stop him!'

Somebody in the audience booed, then another man laughed. They shouted obscene comments. Then one of the soldiers next to Obenauer raised his rifle and Drake opened fire with the Walther pistol. He leapt from the stage, crashing down to the stalls as the onlookers looked on in confusion, as though they had found themselves caught in some mad Brechtian drama. Drake ran through the rows of seats, saw a figure dashing up the aisles away from him. Another gunshot clacked through the auditorium, followed by shouted protests from the men in the stalls. Drake saw the figure going for one of the exits, and he ran up the aisle, pounding up the shallow steps in pursuit. He slammed out through the door into a dim corridor. A light ahead showed stairs going upwards. He launched himself up the steps, two at a time.

A shadow moved. Drake followed it at a sprint. He found himself running back out into the auditorium, this time at the back of the chamber, which was now in uproar. Men were running from the darkness of the seats towards the bright stage, where Obenauer was yelling orders, and a medic was attending to his face.

'Haltet ihn!' somebody yelled, only adding to the confusion.

Drake saw a door flung open on the far side of the auditorium, and a figure in a civilian hat slid through. He ran across the chairs in pursuit. A German officer drew his sidearm and tried to fire, but Drake was already dashing through a throng of German soldiers, who hadn't quite grasped what was happening. He burst through the double doors, and charged down the stairs into the grand, brightly-lit foyer. A corpulent German signals engineer looked up at him in shock from over a telephone exchange he was working on. Drake pointed Obenauer's Walther at him, and put a finger to his lips.

'*Dein Mantel!*' he hissed, pointing to a field grey overcoat slung over a stool. The man slowly passed it over. It was a loose fit, and it was short, but Drake hastily buttoned it up. *'Stahlhelm!'* he said. The man passed his steel helmet over, and Drake put it on. He stepped quickly through the foyer. A man in a dark civilian suit was walking calmly down a dim passageway towards the rear of the theatre. Drake walked quickly after him, just another German soldier among the many.

'Halt!' a voice cried out in German. It was Obenauer again. 'Stop! Everybody stay exactly where you are!'

Everybody stopped moving, turned to look at the speaker. Everybody except Drake.

Drake ran.

A shot cracked down the corridor towards him. Then Obenauer, clutching a cloth to his face, appeared across the foyer and started screaming orders.

Drake sprinted after the disappearing figure of the civilian. The stage door at the rear of the theatre was still banging shut when Drake reached it. He shoved it open and ran out into the night. The stench of burning hit him. The fires in the old town of Calais were still raging, lighting the entire sky in a terrible red glow. He ran from the theatre, heading north, then east, finding himself in a large, gloomy square. He scanned the shadows for any sign of the civilian in the hat.

Shouts came from the theatre's rear exits as German soldiers spilled out. They started combing the streets behind him. Drake ignored them and ran on through ragged wisps of smoke which were blowing on a hot, dry, ash-laden breeze. A black shape moved fifty yards away, dark against the glow from the burning sky. Drake set off towards it at a sprint. The shadow stopped for a second to look back, then ran on.

German military vehicles rumbled across the square, bathed in blood-red light from the fiery skies. Drake dodged across the road, in between a pair of heavy half-tracks with Ack-Ack cannons on the back. A crash of artillery jarred the air as a battery elsewhere in the city opened up, lighting the sky above the rooftops for a moment with jagged white spears of fire.

Drake ran on, stumbling on the cobbles in a narrow lane, chasing the shadow. His legs still ached stiffly from the shocks, but he ignored the pain, and forced himself to keep going. The sounds of the soldiers from the theatre were fading now. He saw a dark shape move ahead of him, and brought up Obenauer's pistol and fired. The clash of the report, the blinding flash, and he was sprinting through the streets again, night vision stained with flares of purples and greens.

Gradually his sight cleared, and he saw the shadow head east, cross a main road into another narrow street that he guessed led towards the factories and warehouses by the port. Drake ran after the man, cursing the uncomfortable boots, and the badly-fitting German overcoat that flapped about him. He had no time to stop. He threw down the helmet. It clanged onto the road behind him. The dark shape ahead ran on, then skidded to a halt and dived into a doorway. A German patrol marched past, jackboots crunching on the ground, heading for the main road.

Drake ignored the patrol and ran across the street. The smell of salt water was in the air. A sea canal was obviously close. He pounded on, then paused. He'd lost sight of the man. To his right he could see the faint outline of what appeared to be a crane. He ran towards it, then thumped across a footbridge that spanned the waterway. A thought flashed in his mind. *He's heading for the docks.* From the silhouettes of the buildings against the fiery sky, he could see they were in an industrial quarter now. He stopped, listening hard.

Christ, he'd lost him. The man in the civilian suit had got away. Then Drake saw a shadow move. He set off again at a run.

Chapter 62

Drake raced through the darkness. The streets were deserted. Through the distant crash of artillery, he heard the thud of running footsteps. The shadow ahead swung left, and then right. Machine guns crackled in the distance. Rifles snapped. Drake saw the sparks of muzzle flashes, quarter of a mile away. He heard the *bom-bom-bom* of Bren guns. He was near the fighting lines now. He figured they must be close to the canal that surrounded the island of Calais Nord. Through the drifting smoke, Drake picked up the stench of wet concrete, seaweed, and estuary mud. He tried to get his bearings. They must be on the eastern side of the harbour. Above the smell of the sea was a sharp, resinous reek. A black shadow moved again, and Drake chased it as the man ran into an industrial yard, piled high with what looked like stacks of timber, thirty feet high. Drake ran around a corner and was met with the flash of pistol fire. A bullet twanged off a stack of pine logs, illuminated for a split second by the flare from the muzzle.

Drake kept going. He ran counterclockwise around the logpile, and threw himself to the floor as he passed the opposite corner. A dark shape moved, the sound of a shoe striking on the concrete floor. Drake fired the Walther twice in loud, successive shots. The flashes illuminated the scene for a fraction of a second. A man in a hat, in a civilian suit, was running away from him between the stacks of logs. Drake heard a sharp cry. The shadow staggered. He had the impression the man had fallen to the floor. *Got him.* The Walther 9mm was a medium powered handgun, enough to do serious damage at close range, unlike some of the smaller weapons in common use. He leapt to his feet and ran on.

A muzzle flash, and Drake felt the crack of a bullet passing close to his face. He stopped, tried to control his breathing, and listened hard. Through the background noise of the burning city, he thought he heard the man getting to his feet and running away. The steps were uneven.

Wounded. But he could only have winged the man, or else he'd never have got up. Drake followed, but carefully now. He knew a wounded man had little to lose, and was more likely to stand and fight than run.

Drake moved swiftly from one log pile to the next, trying to keep his footsteps silent, breathing as calmly and quietly as he could manage. He was sweating heavily in the hot dry air, boiling inside the German overcoat. Despite the aching stiffness in all his limbs, he felt the high anticipation of the chase, and a rising second wind. He was close.

The man ran into a cavern of darkness, a space that seemed in Drake's heightened state to be a giant black maw. He quickly realised it was the entrance to an enormous factory. The stink was overwhelming here; sharp, sickly, overpowering. It was the resinous, oversweet stench of a cellulose factory. He followed the man in, slowly now, keeping to the corners, and avoiding the trap of making himself a silhouette against the red glow from the burning city behind.

Drake stared around in the darkness of this strange, stinking underworld. Great vats towered up all around him. He ran a hand across his sweating face. It was hot in here. Hot as hell. *If this lot goes up – Christ.*

A muzzle flash and a crack. A bullet whipped through the material of his sleeve, missing his arm by a fraction of an inch. Drake ran forwards, firing the Walther again towards where the flash had come from. *Nine shots,* he thought. There must have been one chambered. He heard the man fall, cursing, then get back to his feet and stumble away. Drake chased after him, throwing caution to the wind, crashing past great machines in the darkness, obscure in the strange orange glow from outside. Then his boot slipped on something on the ground and he fell hard, sprawling on his face. He whipped the pistol up to fire again at the sound of the departing man, but the bolt clicked. He was right. The magazine was empty. He had no more ammunition for it. He was effectively unarmed.

The sound of footsteps grew further away. Drake cursed and started to get back up, but his outstretched hand touched something in the darkness. There was something solid there. It was slippery and warm and smooth. He put the pistol in his overcoat pocket and picked the object up. It was heavy. Surprisingly heavy. He ran his hands over the surface, and it had an earthy, iron smell. It was slick with blood. Drake stopped where he was. The wounded man must have dropped it when he fell.

Kneeling over the object, he felt his pockets for the matches. Struck one. In the light of the flaring phosphorous he wiped the blood away from the object with his hand. Beneath the blood was a metal clasp, and a shape that could only be the *Reichsadler,* the Nazi swastika and German eagle. It was a briefcase. No – it was *the* briefcase. *SS* runes were embossed on the black leather. Drake prised the clasp open with one hand, holding the burning match in the other. In the small, flickering light of the flame, he opened up the leather lid flap and looked inside.

The briefcase was close-packed with a stack of paper, three or four inches thick. He reached a hand inside, part of his mind listening to the sound of uneven footsteps that were staggering away into the distance. Agent Viper – *and it must be him* – could burn in hell now, for all Drake cared. This was what he'd been looking for, it had to be. He felt a surge of vindication. *Dämmerung. The fate of nations.* Whatever *Dämmerung* was, he wasn't the only one who wanted it, but it was finally in Drake's hands. He went to pull out the first sheets of paper, but the match burnt his fingers then spluttered out, leaving him in darkness. Then Drake heard a sound behind him. The clack of a semi-automatic pistol being charged. He froze.

A flicker of confusion and anxiety went through him. Whoever was behind him, it was not the man he'd been chasing, because he could still hear the distant footsteps hurrying unevenly away. He quickly picked up the briefcase and slid it out of sight, then rose and turned around slowly in the darkness. The vast space of the factory floor was dimly lit by the hellish red fires of the burning city across the harbour. A torch came on, played on his face, half-blinding him in the gloom. Drake raised his empty hands and squinted into the torchbeam as it played over him.

'Show yourself,' he said. 'Whoever you are.'

There was no answer. The torch shone on the ground, picking out a large smear of blood by Drake's boots. There was a flash of light from a pistol muzzle. To Drake, it seemed to happen so slowly. The hard snap of the gun's report, simultaneous with a sledgehammer blow to his ribs. He staggered backwards, gasping, as the air thumped from his lungs. The crash of the gunshot echoed across the vast factory chamber.

Another flash ripped the darkness, another hill-cracking blow to his chest. Drake stumbled away, the taste of blood welling up in his mouth. He couldn't breathe. He was blacking out, his heart felt like it had stopped. He staggered as he tried to keep his feet. For a moment he felt nothing but shock. He tried to inhale, but his lungs wouldn't work. The pistol fired again and a third blow slammed into him, knocking him backwards. He fell, all strength gone from his legs. His head crashed down onto the concrete floor and splinters of light flashed blindingly through his skull.

As consciousness faded, he gazed up into the darkness, at the opening of the factory's cavernous entrance, at the red, burning sky, and it was like staring into the mouth of hell. He was aware of a shadow moving towards him, inhaling on a cigarette. The bright torch beam shone into his face, and then the light went off.

The orange ember of the cigarette end flew towards a great metal tank that was oozing resinous liquid, and footsteps moved slowly away in the darkness. The cigarette end glowed for a moment where it fell, and then the liquid in the tank of resin began to smoke.

SUNDAY 26 MAY 1940

NATIONAL DAY OF PRAYER

Chapter 63

10 DOWNING STREET, LONDON, ENGLAND – 09:00HRS

THE WAR CABINET MET unusually early. Winston Churchill's private secretary read to him from a list as he shuffled towards the Cabinet Office.

'—and there's a service at Westminster Abbey at ten o'clock, sir.'

Churchill sighed. 'Very well.'

King George VI, in recognition of the dire situation on the continent, had requested that today should be observed as a National Day of Prayer. Everybody in the British Isles was to go to a place of worship and beseech the Lord's intervention. It was all the hope they had left. Long queues had already formed outside cathedrals, and congregations were overflowing in churches, chapels, synagogues and other holy sites. A live broadcast was to be made on the BBC.

Churchill took his seat at the long, green baize-covered oval table in the cabinet room.

'Gentlemen,' he said. He observed the gathered faces. Neville Chamberlain, Lord President of the Council. Clement Attlee, Lord Privy Seal. Viscount Halifax, Foreign Secretary. Arthur Greenwood, minister without portfolio. Sir John Anderson, Lord President of the Board of Trade. The Chiefs of Staff: General Sir John Dill, General Edmund 'Tiny' Ironside, Admiral of the Fleet Sir Alfred Pound, Air Chief of Staff Cyril, 1st Baron Newall. Vice-Chief of the Air Staff Richard Peirse and a number of other grey-faced ministers and civil service officials sat in attendance.

Neville Chamberlain broke the grim silence. 'This is the blackest day.'

Each place at the table was set with notepad, pens, pencils, and a War Cabinet paper, entitled *British Strategy in a certain eventuality*.

Churchill looked up. 'A certain eventuality?'

Members of the cabinet glanced at one another.

'The fall of France,' said Dill.

Winston Churchill began to scan the paper, reading quickly. It bore dire tidings.

Lord Halifax spoke. 'The situation on the continent is hopeless. Britain's prospects are perilous. We must pursue, with the utmost vigour, the possibility of a negotiated peace through the services of Mussolini!'

Churchill gazed at him for a moment, before turning to Admiral Pound. 'Have the useless mouths been repatriated?'

Pound nodded gravely. 'The evacuation of non-fighting personnel from those channel ports that are still functioning is ongoing, sir. But yes, it is largely accomplished everywhere to the north of Le Havre.'

Churchill rose from his seat. He went to the window. 'Rain,' he muttered. 'Good.' It was the first rain in a very long time.

'What about Calais?' said Neville Chamberlain. 'Is there any hope?'

Churchill stared for a moment at the streams of water that were running down the glass. By his actions, he had condemned thousands of men. It was a decision that was bitter and galling to him, yet one, he felt, that had had to be made. He had heard that small crowds had gathered on the white cliffs at Dover. From there, they would be able to see the smoke and hear the guns on the other side of the Channel. Some of them would have sons, brothers, fathers fighting over there. So near, and yet so far. He had been Prime Minister for only sixteen days, and already Britain was on the brink of utter ruin.

'Our responsibilities are grave,' he said. 'The eyes of the world are upon us.' He returned to the table, and lowered himself slowly into his chair. 'Above all, we must keep the French in the fight. To the last man standing, Calais must be held.'

There was a moment of quiet.

General Ironside cleared his throat before speaking, referring to the cabinet paper he held in his large hands. 'To sum up, our conclusion is that – *prima facie* – Germany has most of the cards; but the real test is whether the morale of our fighting personnel and civil population will counterbalance the numerical and material advantages which Germany enjoys.' Ironside paused, and raised his eyes from the paper to meet Churchill's gaze. 'We believe it will.'

Churchill studied the members of the war cabinet, his eyes travelling slowly around the room from one man to the next. The exhausted military chiefs of staff. The doubtful, wavering politicians. He met Ironside's gaze, and a microscopic nod was exchanged.

Finally, Churchill spoke. 'We believe it will,' he said. He tapped the table in front of him with a forefinger to emphasise the point. He repeated the words in a low, pugnacious growl. '*We believe it will*. There you have it, Gentlemen. We'll have no more talk of a negotiated peace. We fight on.' He set aside the paper, pushed back his chair, and the members of the War Cabinet all rose.

'We are required at the Abbey. I would ask you to make a particular petition for the men in Calais.' He looked again at the faces around the table as the men prepared to leave, and he spoke in a quiet undertone. 'May God help them, because I no longer can.'

Chapter 64

CALAIS NORD, FRANCE - 10:00HRS

THE SUN HAD RISEN from the English Channel that morning as though from a bath of blood. The coast of Kent was a smudge on the distant horizon. Great oily clouds of black fumes hung over the water. At ten o'clock sharp a German barrage started with a searing, ground shaking din. The bark and thunder of artillery battered angrily at the atmosphere. British destroyers fired back with their great guns, lobbing shells hard and high towards the German lines.

On a rooftop in the old city, Sergeant MacTaggart gazed at the sea, remembering bloody mornings from decades earlier. Daniel Butcher lay on the tiles, shaken by the noise from his sleep. Fred Leighton smoked a rolled-up cigarette, which he had scrounged from a wounded man. And all around them, the city of Calais burned.

Shells crashed into the old town in a blazing salvo. A stiff sea breeze whipped flames from building to building. The air blew hot and dry and was loaded with ash and smuts of soot. Stukas howled down from the sky to shatter the streets with high explosive and incendiaries. Civilians in basements shuddered, too tired to weep. The British stragglers, the West Kents and the Riflemen, the old men of the Searchlight Regiment, and the part-time soldiers of the Queen Victoria Rifles clawed on to their barricades with broken fingernails, and waited for the bitter, inevitable end.

Bodies, German and British, were strewn on both sides of the harbour; corpses crusted with blood, or beginning to blacken and swell. Thick fumes belched from the entrance of the colossal cellulose factory. Inside, oily black smoke spewed from a resin tank, and twenty-foot-high flames shot into the air in a blinding flash.

A moment later, on the concrete factory floor, one of the bodies, in a German uniform drenched in blood, began to stir.

Chapter 65

Drake awoke in a haze of seething heat and agony, but his first thought was the shattering realisation that there had been two men. Two civilians, both searching for the briefcase. One he'd wounded, and the other had shot him. His hands went up to his overcoat, and he found it already unbuttoned and opened. He patted his chest, which was thick with congealing blood. The briefcase he had hidden there, inside his shirt and overcoat, had gone.

Drake tried to sit up, but his chest was on fire. He prodded the wounds. They were tender, inflamed, agonising, but superficial. He felt three deformed slugs of lead protruding from the flesh of his chest. They seemed to be caught shallowly in between his ribs. The briefcase, stuffed with a thick ream of paper, had slowed the bullets enough to save his life. But now it was gone.

Sharp stabs of pain shot from his ribs – they must have been cracked. As his head began to clear, he felt the press of heat. The vat of resin was burning fiercely now, searing at his skin. He rolled away, and bolts of pain shot through his chest, but he got to hands and knees and began to crawl out of the factory, choking, coughing on the fumes, and each time stifling an agonised groan.

He staggered, bleeding, away through the ruins of Calais. A great pall of smoke hung over the city. Fires raged on, fanned by a stiffening wind. He was followed by an acrid stink as the cellulose factory went up behind him in sheets of flame a hundred feet high. He didn't look back. In his bloodsoaked field grey uniform, he stumbled through the German lines and kept his gaze fixed firmly to the ground.

Heavy field howitzers barked out in a terrible chorus. Antitank cannons thudded, sending shells shrilling into the buildings on the other side of the canal. From covered positions, panzers shot high explosive into the inferno of the old town of Calais Nord. Flak cannons fired in ear-splitting staccato from the back of tracked vehicles. The Wehrmacht was throwing everything at it now. German soldiers massed in squads, platoons, companies, by echelon, filling street after street, road after road, ready for the big attack. Rifle fire clashed back from the far side of the waterways. Drake took a grim sense of comfort from that. Somehow, against impossible odds, the British riflemen on the defensive perimeter were still hanging desperately on.

A German artilleryman called out to him as he stumbled past, '*Brauchst du Hilfe?* Do you need help?'

Drake shrugged him away with a wave of the hand, and staggered on.

He was heading towards where the fighting was the fiercest. The British were still holding a bridge across the docks. The harbour was narrower there. Machine-gun fire crackled and ripped from both sides, the harsh drill sound of the German Spandaus, the more steady, thumping *bom-bom-bom* of the Brens. British two-inch mortars kept the German assault at bay. Rifle fire swept the quay clear. It was impossible to cross the open ground and hope to live.

Drake stared around, in a daze. The spire of the cathedral was all that was visible above the haze of fire in the old town. Behind him, to his left, the clock tower of the town hall appeared to float above the blowing smog like something from a dream. As he stumbled on, the artillery fire increased in sudden intensity, as more and more tubes barked and thudded until it became a non-stop, earth-cracking din. Soot and ash blew hot from across the canal. From above the old city came the shriek and wail of diving Stukas. Through the shelling, through the mad maelstrom, their howling rose to scream upon scream upon mind-bending scream, dropping incendiary bombs which whistled as they fell.

Drake staggered on towards the raging furnace that was Calais Nord. Shells screeched in. Bombs crashed. Roaring waves of flames burst towards the sky. He lurched past more German troops, the first wave mustering now for the final assault. He pitched on down the street. At a corner, he came to a stop in front of a shattered pharmacy. He pushed past the ancient chemist's sign – the cup of Hygieia – which was broken and hanging askew across the door.

Slipping unsteadily inside, he found the place had already been looted. Boxes and vials were spilled open, shattered glass was everywhere. He kept searching, and eventually found a bottle full of likely-looking tablets – *phosphate de codeine*. He chewed and swallowed a few. They were bitter, hard and dry. He found another drawer, smashed open the lock.

Benzédrine. He took three, and gulped them, his dry throat rasping as he tried to get them down.

Stashing the pill bottles in his pocket, he swayed weakly out of the shop. A flash of white behind a shard of glass in a basement window caught his eye. A little girl was staring out, a look of terror on her face. He tried to smile, but the child screamed and was snatched away by an adult hand, and the curtain was hastily drawn. Drake saw his own reflection superimposed on the glass as he moved away. Covered in blood and stained with smuts, bruised and blackened, he had the face of a ghoul.

He staggered on, chest aching, an agony of shooting pain with every breath. Across the water in the old city, infernos raged beneath a broiling mountain of smoke that filled up half the sky. Eventually, he slumped against a broken wall, close to the water's edge. He tried to breathe, through the dust and fumes and ash that clogged the air. Everything was burning now. Every breath was a stab to his ribs. Beneath the blackened skies, the fires of Calais burned, and ash fell back down to the earth like snow. But he could feel the medicine taking hold now. The ache was dulled, and he felt a sudden welling of elation as the Benzedrine kicked in.

He painfully took off the German greatcoat, pulled off what was left of the bloody shirt. Kicked off the jackboots. He slid, unseen, into the cold, salt-stinging waters of the harbour basin, and under the cover of smoke, began slowly, painfully, to kick his way across to the other side.

Chapter 66

Drake came to, slowly, painfully. His mind was hazed and foggy, weak from loss of blood, but at the same time he felt suddenly wide awake. He was in a dark place, but a paraffin lantern hissed greasily next to his head, casting strange shadows and light. Another was suspended above him. A medic was bent down over him, examining his chest.

'*Forceps*,' the man said in French.

Drake realised he was on an operating table. He tried to get up, to speak, but the surgeon pushed his shoulder firmly down.

'*Bougez-pas!* Don't move!'

A hand passed the implements out of the darkness. Drake felt an awful wrench on his ribs, and the doctor stood upright. In the light of the hissing lantern, Drake saw the mangled slug of a bullet. It was dripping thick, red blood. *His* blood.

The surgeon, wearing a strip of cloth across his face instead of a mask, peered down at Drake. He spoke in English with a light French accent, and had a small golden crucifix on a chain, visible in the lamplight at his open collar. 'The bullets are lodged between your ribs, but it's just a superficial wound. However did it happen like that?'

Drake squinted into the bright lantern light. His head banged with an awful, throbbing pain that wouldn't go away. He explained. 'Briefcase. Full of paper. Under my coat. Must have all but stopped the pistol rounds.'

He moved his head and looked about. The rest of the space was in darkness, but he could see that he was in some kind of cellar, a tunnel full of badly wounded men. The vaulted ceilings were damp and dark. Outside of the circle of light from the lanterns, the wounded men cried out and moaned. He felt a deep uneasiness, the crawling agitation of claustrophobia. He tried to shove it from his mind.

'Where are we?' he said. He went to sit up, but he was weak and the doctor pushed him easily back down again.

The man's gold-rimmed glasses reflected in the lantern light. His apron was bathed in blood. Blond hair shone like a halo around his head from the suspended lantern.

'Oh,' Drake said. 'Doctor Lambert. It's you.'

Drake peered around the tunnel again, his eyes now adjusting. He couldn't wait to get out, back into the fresh air and the German bombs. There must have been fifty or sixty men in there. Weapons were leaned up against the wall near the operating table. Rifles, bayonets, ammunition boxes. The stench of blood was overpowering. Drake didn't envy the doctor his task. A one-legged man nearby, laid out on the floor, whimpered, then cried out. Another man sat against the black and dirty wall, clutching his bandaged head and rocking back and forth, letting out inhuman groans.

Lambert wiped a smear of blood from his face with an already blood-soaked sleeve. He was drenched in the stuff.

'We're in the vaults under Bastion One,' he said. 'On the eastern harbour, behind the Gare Maritime. They said they pulled you from the canal.' He leaned in close and gave Drake a sharp look. He spoke quietly. 'And wearing field grey trousers?' He stood up straight again. 'They said you were raving. Lucky for you that you were raving in English. They would have shot you otherwise. What the devil were you doing in there, anyway?'

Drake grunted. 'I fancied a swim.'

The cellars shuddered as shells struck into the harbour walls. The distant wail of Stukas penetrated even down here. Bombs hit in hard, rumbling crashes that brought dust and sand drifting down from the ceiling.

The doctor looked up, shook his head and sighed. 'I can see the bullets. It is only a shallow penetration, but it's going to hurt. There is no anaesthetic. You're lucky I don't have to amputate a limb. All I have is a rusty saw. Now lie still and don't try to talk.'

Drake lay back down. The vaulted ceilings were damp and dark. Outside of the circle of light from the lanterns, the wounded men cried out and moaned.

Drake tensed as the doctor probed the second wound. A tearing, ripping sensation, and his chest flashed with pain. It seemed unbearably hot in the tunnel. Sweat-dripped from his forehead in sheets. He clamped his teeth together, face tightened as he forced himself to keep still.

Lambert tugged. Drake stifled a groan. The doctor pulled again, and for a moment Drake thought he was going to faint or vomit, or maybe both at the same time. Then, with a sucking pop, another bullet came out, gritting from between his ribs.

'You're in good company,' Lambert said as he held up the forceps for Drake to see the distorted round. 'Roosevelt Senior, uncle of the American president, was shot while giving a lecture in 1912. The bullet was slowed by a fifty-page speech, which was folded up in his breast pocket, and it lodged in his chest without piercing the lung. He finished his speech before going to hospital. We studied photographs of the X-ray in the medical college of the Royal Military Academy in Brussels, but I never thought to see one like it.'

He tugged the third bullet, and it came out with a jerk. Drake suppressed a moan.

'*Et voilà*,' Lambert said, and held the bullet up. He dropped it into Drake's open palm.

'The Academy,' Drake said, recovering his breath. 'What year?'

The doctor fished agonisingly around in the wound, looking for traces of cloth or other material to bring out. 'Class of '22.' Eventually he began to stitch Drake up. He nodded towards the bullets. 'You might want to keep those as a souvenir, you know. You're a very lucky man.'

Drake snorted. 'Lucky to be shot three times?'

'Lucky to have been shot with a .32 calibre pistol. I've seen more corpses today than I'd expect to in a lifetime of civilian practice. You'll be fortunate if you don't get an infection after bathing in the canal. There's nothing I can do about that now. You must have the wounds properly dressed when – well, to be frank, you must ask the German doctors, when they take over. Which will be soon. Now sit up – easy does it. Get yourself dressed.'

Drake sat slowly, painfully, ignoring the vicious stabs that bit into his ribs, but it was better than before. At least he could move freely now, if he ignored the pain. An orderly wrapped a bandage tightly around his chest then put out items of British uniform.

Lambert cleaned his instruments using petrol. He shrugged, catching Drake's look. 'It is a good disinfectant. So, where is this infamous briefcase?' he smiled. 'It would make a fascinating study for the Journal when this is all over, which won't be long now. I cannot imagine that the British can hold on here even another few hours.'

Drake shrugged. 'The briefcase is gone.'

'Gone? Where?' Lambert quickly smiled again.

'Don't know,' Drake said. 'Whatever happened to LaPointe of the Deuxième Bureau?'

Lambert turned his hands out in a continental gesture. 'I have no idea.'

Stabbing pains shot through Drake's chest as he tried to button a dead rifleman's shirt over the bandage. He bent over, face clenched, waiting for the spasm to pass. He found the old German trousers he'd been wearing and recovered the bottle of Benzedrine tablets. He reached for the British kit and pulled it on, then grimaced as he worked his feet into a used pair of British ammo boots. He bent agonisingly forwards to tie the laces. He didn't like to think what had happened to their previous owner.

Lambert brought out an ampoule of morphine. 'Here, let me give you something for the pain.'

Drake carefully buttoned the shirt. He felt a sudden uneasiness, and he didn't know why. 'I thought you said there was no anaesthetic? Give it to somebody who needs it.'

'There *is* no anaesthetic. Morphine is not an anaesthetic, just a palliative. I was saving for the serious cases, but—'

Drake grabbed Lambert's arm to stop him. Lambert winced and pulled away.

'Sorry,' Drake said. 'Are you alright? Give it to some other poor sod. I just don't want it, that's all.'

'Suit yourself,' Lambert said. 'I'm fine.'

Drake's eyes were now level with the doctor's shoulder, as he prepared his table for the next patient. He gazed absently at the insignia on the epaulette, the symbol of the Belgian Medical Component. It was nothing out of the ordinary, just a pair of branches, one of olive and one of oak leaves, flanking the Rod of Asclepius, all set beneath the Belgian crown.

Drake peered more closely. The thought struck him like a blow to the head. *Of course.* The Rod of Asclepius. The Caduceus. The cup of Hygieia. They were the universal symbols of medicine in the western world, and they all had something in common. A cold knot began to gnaw at his insides.

Like everybody else, Drake had seen the signs and badges everywhere throughout his whole life, but he'd never given a moment's thought to what they meant. But the sick realisation began to crawl through his guts. He stared at Lambert's service badge again. His head was spinning, his thoughts fuzzy from lack of sleep and from the batterings he'd taken. One too many blows to the head. Perhaps he was imagining things. He scrunched his eyes shut for a moment, rubbed his hands up and down on his face, and forced his jaded mind to think it through.

'Who's the King of Burgundy?' Drake said.

Lambert shrugged. 'There is no King of Burgundy. There has not been one for 800 years.'

Drake looked slowly up. The chances of getting the same answer from three different people must have been close on a million to one. He ran through it in his mind one more time.

When he'd first met Doctor Lambert, he'd been sniffing around La-Pointe's prisoners – and he'd risked his own life to ensure that they weren't killed. Now, he seemed to be carrying an injury of some kind – and Drake had wounded the man he'd been chasing. To top it all, Lambert was very interested in the briefcase. But Lambert was Belgian, not French, so that didn't add up. Axelle had vouched for him. And Axelle was VSSE.

Drake glanced at Lambert's medical insignia again. *Poor tradecraft*, the major had called it. He was right. The Rod of Asclepius was a staff entwined by the symbol of a thin white serpent.

'You're the bloody Viper,' Drake said, turning to grasp the doctor's sleeve.

Lambert laughed. 'I'm the bloody what?' Then quick as a snake he stabbed the morphine ampoule down through Drake's trousers into the flesh of his left leg, and with his other hand he slammed the plunger in.

Chapter 67

DRAKE REACHED OUT, TOO late to stop the needle sinking into his thigh with a painful sting. He felt the cool, hard swell of the liquid entering his flesh before he managed to wrestle the syringe away.

Lambert ripped his arm from Drake's grasp. 'Hold him!' he cried to his orderlies. 'He's having a seizure!'

The two stretcher-bearers lunged in.

The doctor yanked down the lantern from above the operating table before striding away down the tunnel. 'Restrain him!' he ordered, as he departed. 'Don't let him leave.'

Drake wrestled with the orderlies, but he was weak from the wounds to his chest. 'Stop him!' he yelled. 'The doctor! He's a German spy!'

He struggled up, chest seized with stabbing pains, pushing off the orderlies who were trying to pin him down. He got off the table and landed on his feet.

Feeling light-headed, and suddenly disorientated, he stumbled forward and tried to run through the tunnel. His legs felt oddly dissociated from him, and the left one was like rubber. Lambert went out of the doorway, taking the lamp with him. The tunnel was immersed in darkness, lit only by the one remaining lamp by the table. Drake didn't care. All thoughts of claustrophobia were gone.

Somebody lit another paraffin lamp, and as Drake staggered towards the exit, he saw the terrible injuries of the wounded men. A man with his jaw blown off, swathed in bandages, who was trying to speak. A man with an arm and leg missing, propped up against a wall, looked blankly at the floor where his leg should have been. Another lay groaning, clutching a belly wound. A British soldier with a bandaged face got to his feet and crashed into Drake, clinging on to him in a desperate frenzy.

'Help me! Help me!' he cried. 'I can't see! I can't bloody see!'

Drake pushed past, ignoring the man's pleas. He had to stop Lambert. Everything else was driven from his mind. He stumbled towards the smoke-filled doorway and burst out into blinding daylight, but he saw that the Viper was gone.

Drake took a moment to get his bearings. He saw the tunnel he'd been in was on a promontory between two harbour channels. He was at the seaward end of Calais' eastern harbour. The entire waterfront was wreathed in ash and smoke. All over the city, the bombs crashed down. Shells screamed in and hit in blast after crushing blast. As he squinted into the fumes, he was almost overwhelmed by a feeling of euphoria as the morphine worked its way through him, easing the crippling pains of the electrocutions, and the warm buzz of the narcotic started to cloud his brain.

The mental effects of the morphine were surprising, not what he'd expected. Drake felt like he was falling backwards, into himself, as the drug took hold. He found he was smiling. He was going to catch the Viper, and everything was going to be alright. He felt quietly, wildly, deliriously happy, as though he had suddenly drunk ten straight pints of beer. He felt like he was floating on air, inflated with helium, and he struggled to walk straight. He could never remember having felt so fine. Some part of his mind fought the sensation, but it was almost overpowering, like some crazed dream from which he couldn't wake up. He found the bottle of Benzedrine he'd kept in his pocket. Chewed and swallowed another handful of tablets. In the chaos of the burning city, machine-gun fire clattered from all sides. The Wehrmacht's iron fist was tightening, and the siege was closing in.

Drake felt dizzy and faint, and his vision was blurred. A great tiredness was welling up inside him as the drug took over, and he fought a consuming urge to lie down. He forced himself to concentrate, fighting the morphine's narcotic effects. He slapped himself hard on the face in an attempt to clear his mind. By running, Lambert had confirmed his identity as Agent Viper. Drake tried to put himself in the man's shoes. So, where the hell would Agent Viper have gone? He stared back across the harbour towards the old city. Stukas screamed and the bombs rained onto the inferno. Another thought struck him, a question pressing in, demanding to be answered. If Doctor Lambert was Agent Viper, then who in God's name was the other man – the so-called King of Burgundy? Drake pushed the idea aside. He couldn't possibly answer that now. All he did know was that wherever Agent Viper was, he was gone from the promontory near Bastion One. That could only mean he'd gone back in towards the burning city. Drake forced his numbed left leg to work, and broke into a stumbling, intoxicated run.

Chapter 68

Explosions rocked the factories. Chemical fires erupted in flaming geysers that spewed foul fumes into the air. Smoke blew thickly across the waterfront. Drake snatched an automatic pistol from the hand of a dead French officer, then ran on through the maelstrom. He was chasing a shadow. A serpent. *A Viper*. Shells screeched into the harbour. Stukas dived, wailing, down onto the burning city, dropping bomb after bomb after bomb.

Drake guessed, from the ever-growing din of the battle, that the situation of the British troops had significantly worsened. The Wehrmacht was pressing the attack, throwing everything at it in one final assault to gain a foothold on the island of Calais Nord. The machine-gun fire was intensifying. German infantry were attacking from the beaches on either side of the city, trying to work their way in. Dead and wounded Allied soldiers were lying everywhere. British troops and French sailors were fighting on with contempt for the danger, trying to hold untenable positions in the dunes and on the stone-clad quays. Drake saw two British marines set up a Vickers gun to fire across the harbour towards the other side of the water. A French naval lieutenant ran madly towards the German positions, shooting with a pistol. Stretcher-bearers and signals officers were firing rifles and Bren guns. Machine guns chattered, and bullets left strange eddies and whirls as they ripped through the smoke. Old men of the Searchlight Regiment were still fighting doggedly on. A man in a cook's apron ran with three rifles towards the docks, where he took up position next to two French sailors in white caps, bell-bottom trousers and striped jerseys. There was nowhere to go, no place to hide. They were all fighting for their lives, and the siege was making heroes of everyone.

Drake sprinted across the wharf. Up ahead, the concrete of the quayside burst in vicious fragments as German mortar bombs landed in a series of cracking detonations. He ran on, every step jolting the wounds in his chest, but the pain was just a distant, dulled ache now, his head still thrumming with the high hit of the morphine. His feet pounded numbly against the stones as he lurched on back towards the town, past the part-time soldiers of the Queen Victoria Rifles, who were crouched behind harbour walls, firing, firing, firing again amidst the blazing ruins.

Drake saw a figure in the smoke, wearing Belgian military green. He was bareheaded, and had a crown of fair hair. He sprinted towards the man, and grabbed his jacket, spun him round. But it wasn't Lambert. It was a young Belgian soldier, taking potshots at the enemy. By the smell of him, he was drenched in litres of French wine. Drake was struck by a realisation. He'd prodded the Viper, and Axelle could be in deadly danger now. He had to get to Lambert first. He pushed the young Belgian soldier away and ran on.

He ran past the bomb-flattened station, the Gare Maritime, as a new vigour began to fizz through his limbs. *Benzedrine.* Great heaps of abandoned kit and weapons were strewn on the harbourside, dumped by the evacuating French. Lines of vehicles were on fire. A half-submerged minesweeper was sticking, tail-end up, from the harbour water. Drake looked around, searching everywhere for Lambert. He watched a trawler burning, belching smoke as the waters exploded all around it. He heard cries behind him, and saw British riflemen retreating, unable to hold their positions any longer. Many were badly wounded and they were dragging their weapons back to form a new, shorter line. The British troops were being squeezed past the limit of endurance, but they still unflinchingly fought on. Entire sections of the old city were continuous, wild conflagrations now. Everything was burning. It was an apocalypse, a nightmare, all the fires of hell on earth. Calais would inevitably fall in the next few hours, and the siege was closing in. It was now just a matter of time.

Drake glared across the harbour in frustration. The Viper was here, somewhere. He had to be. The old city was encircled, surrounded, closed in now. Ferocious fighting had engulfed the entire perimeter. British warships stood out to sea, their great guns thudding as they rained shells on the German lines. But they did not come in to relieve the stranded men. Drake recalled Brigadier Nicolson's words. *There's no way in and there's no way out except by boat.*

A hail of shellfire streaked in, screaming across from the factories. Piercing cracks resonated hard from the harbour walls as Flak shells burst into warehouses on the waterfront. The Wehrmacht was attacking in great force, but still the riflemen held on. They fired from cover, sniping at the enemy and slowing their advance. They couldn't hope to win, or even escape. But they'd make the Germans pay with their lives for every street, every building, every stone.

Machine gun bullets skittered across the docks, interlocking fire from advancing German positions. The way ahead seemed impassable – a quayside enfiladed by German sniper fire. Drake sank down behind a solid iron capstan as the rounds sparked off the metal. To the west, he could see the citadel, wracked by horrific explosions, the thick walls engulfed in violent sheets of flame. Nothing could withstand this kind of onslaught for long.

Dark clouds of blowing black fumes were blocking the sun until it was just a grey disk against a darker, red and black sky. It cast the entire city into an unearthly twilight. The streets glowed amber as the fires rose ever higher from the burning buildings. Only the cathedral tower stood out above the smoke, as though rising from a mist, bathed in an ominous red light from the flames. Axelle had been right. It was like the end of the world. *Dämmerung. Twilight. The end of an era. Chaos and destruction. The passing of kings.*

Drake gazed around the great harbour now, lightheaded, and everything was as strange to him as though it was all some fevered dream. Across the water, he glimpsed a man emerging onto the far side of the waterfront, on the old fisherman's wharf of the Courgain. The man was wearing a civilian suit. He looked so out of place amidst the slaughterhouse of the city's ruin, so absurd, as if he were going to work at a bank. He wore a short-brimmed hat on his head, and was carrying a black briefcase in one hand.

Chapter 69

SMOKE BLEW ACROSS THE harbourfront, and the man on the quayside disappeared. Drake sprinted across the docks to find a way around. An intolerable thirst raged in his throat, and his breath was coming hard and fast and dry. As he ran, boots pounding over the rubble, he choked on the cinders and ash in the air. Then a sudden hush fell upon the city. The German artillery bombardment abruptly ceased, and the Stukas were growling away towards the east. Drake staggered to a halt amidst the flaming ruins. It could only mean one thing. The final push of the ground assault was about to begin.

Drake stumbled on through the furnace of the blasted streets. The only way to get through to the other side of the harbour was through the burning old town itself. Roads were blocked by fallen buildings. More than once he had to turn back from the seething heat and find another route. Faces of unarmed French troops stared blankly out at him from black pits of cellars where the buildings had not yet collapsed. The Frenchmen had either missed the evacuation, or they were just too drunk to care. MacTaggart's words came back to him. *The rabble*. In the narrow alleys of the Courgain district, a woman stood in the road, tugging at the arm of a child. The rest of the child was buried under a pile of stones. It was a terrible sight. But there was nothing Drake could do for her, nothing he could do for anybody, except find Agent Viper and bring *Operationsbefehl Dämmerung* to a grinding halt.

Drake ran on, frantic now. Incoherent thoughts, jumbled by the fuzz of morphine, were racing through his mind. The pieces were struggling to fit together. There was something obvious he was missing. *The destruction of the BEF. The fall of France, of Europe, of Great Britain herself. Don't bloody well let me down.*

He skidded to a halt. Amid the roaring, crackling of the fires, he heard the clatter of tank tracks. He staggered over the wreckage of a shattered street, shrouded in blowing smoke, then without warning, the smog cleared. He'd taken a wrong turn, somewhere in the chaos, in the blocked and broken alleyways. A barrier of burnt-out lorries and industrial reels of steel cable blocked the road. Half a dozen bodies in British uniform lay motionless behind the barricade. A panzer clanked forwards through the swirling smoke and dust, followed by two lines of advancing German troops. The tank's machine gun stuttered fire, and Drake threw himself to the floor.

Christ, the Germans were inside the old city already. Calais was falling around him. Nicholson's massively outnumbered brigade could no longer hold on. But then, from cellars and windows and doorways and piles of rubble, hidden by clouds of dust and fumes, a section of British riflemen emerged. They fired into the smoke. A two-inch mortar whumped, and the bomb fizzed down to land near the tank. Drake felt a surge of pride in these men, fighting on when there was no hope left. Rifles snapped, and a Bren gun chugged out solid bursts. Behind the barricade, the advancing German soldiers began to fall.

The panzer cannon thumped a staccato burst of shells. In a gust of wind the smoke blew ragged, revealing the entire street. The shells slammed into a cottage wall with a jarring *crack-crack-crack*. Splinters of jagged masonry whizzed through the air at eye level, but the riflemen were deeply dug in. They responded with another well-aimed mortar bomb that fizzed up and clashed down into the German troops. Drake saw the remnants of the German platoon where the bomb had landed. It was bloody murder.

The panzer crew, saved by thick steel plate, crashed the tank straight towards the barrier. In the chaos of the fires, the riflemen charged the tank with bayonets, rifles cracking in a running volley. They somehow managed to drive the German infantry back to the other side of the barricade, and climbed onto the tank, hammering at the hatches with rifle butts. The tank was thrown into reverse and, engine bellowing fumes, it rumbled quickly away.

Drake ran on, leaving the riflemen to mop up the survivors. He saw in the sky above that a new flight of Stukas were now attacking the citadel with great, heavy, high-explosive bombs that slammed and thundered as they fell into the flames. Close by, German heavy mortars pounded the British positions in a relentless, sickening din. A tremendous battle raged all through the streets as the German divisions brought more and more pressure to bear, but somehow the riflemen were still fighting on, retreating inch by inch, but in good order. As Drake ran out into an open junction, he looked up as he heard a mighty, rushing roar. A pair of Hurricanes came tearing through the skies, seemingly only inches above the fiery rooftops. The 12-cylinder, thousand-horse-power Rolls-Royce engines thundered as they suddenly climbed and set about the Stukas, bringing two down in short order. The German planes, blowing smoke, slammed into the sea. Ecstatic faces of British soldiers turned up towards the ragged, soot-stained sky. They were so close to England that the fighters were coming in from across the channel now.

So close to England. Drake was momentarily transfixed by the thought. Why was Obenauer in Calais? What had Calais got to do with Spain and Franco's Fascists? High above them now, one of the Hurricanes seemed to come to a dead stop on a shilling piece. The pilot snap-rolled and dropped in behind another diving Stuka. The Hurricane's Browning machine guns flickered, and black fumes trailed from the Stuka's wing. It was too little, too late, but it was something – and that gave them hope. The men on the ground who were watching all screamed and cheered.

Drake rubbed the dust and ash from his face. He ran on through the inferno, past blasted cellars, past huddles of hiding French soldiers and refugees. Mortar bombs hissed in and buildings broke open. Walls collapsed all around him as he dodged through the rubble. The sky above was full of aircraft now, in a circus of mayhem and destruction high above the citadel. It seemed like a hundred Stukas were shrieking down, dropping bombs in flights of threes. The sirens were endless, screaming, delirious. On the ground, rifles and machine guns hammered in every street. Fires, raging, leapt across the roads, and entire buildings, bone dry from the heat of the blaze, exploded into sudden towers of flame.

Hard, bitter shocks cracked from every side as bombs hit. Debris rained down onto the streets. A man came stumbling towards him, kit ragged and his skin oozing blood, obviously caught in a blast. Drake saw that his arm had been stripped of flesh by the explosion, and the bare bones of his forearm were exposed to the air. The man just stared at it in front of his face, in disbelieving shock. Drake stepped past him. There was nothing he could do for him. He pressed on, hugging the gutters, and dashed from one searing doorway to another, from ruins to mountainous piles of smouldering rubble. He forced himself on. He was almost there now. And at the end of an alley, he finally caught a glimpse of the sea.

Chapter 70

DRAKE HURTLED AROUND A corner, and ran hard into a man coming the other way. It was a German soldier. The man's eyes grew wide, and he tried to bring his rifle up. Drake fired the automatic pistol into his face. Suddenly an entire German patrol was in the street. Drake's heart thudded violently with the force of the amphetamines in his blood. He turned and bolted, ducking away down an alley to find another way around.

He ran through the furnace, backing away from the citadel. It was impossible to even get close. The streets all around had been the hardest hit, and the old walls were surrounded by sheets of fire sixty feet high. Every house was blazing now. To his left – the west – the German attack pressed in again. Machine-gun fire, panzer cannons, Flak guns firing through broken streets, the flitting shapes of German infantry running through the smoke. German flamethrowers belched fire to scour the citadel ramparts of its defenders. The citadel was being outflanked, the canal had been breached. Calais was falling, and the pressure was mounting. The scorching wind was relentless, blowing ash and flame and soot. It rasped at Drake's throat. He ran a hand across his forehead, but the sweat was already dry in the searing heat from the flames. *God in heaven*, he could hardly breathe.

He shoved the pistol into his pocket as he ran through the destruction of the city. He hurdled over piles of rubble, dodged past half-seen glimpses of close combat fighting, the British riflemen everywhere outnumbered as German assault troops and panzers advanced, street by burning street. It was hand-to-hand with bayonets and grenades now. It was brutal, bloody killing. From out to sea, the great guns of British destroyers thumped on, shells stretching overhead to crash into the German positions at the rear.

Finally, through the dark, swirling smoke, Drake emerged onto the old harbour front. Streams of automatic fire swept the dock walls. Amongst burning and overturned cars along the wharves, British marines and French sailors were dug into shell holes in the ground, firing Vickers guns and rifles at the seaward end of the harbour. Groups of young riflemen still doggedly fought on, shouting encouragement to each other as though they were at a football game. A mass of German troops were trying to storm the positions from the sand dunes to the north of the harbour. Machine guns crackled, rifles snapped, men fell.

In amongst it all, amid the chaos and destruction of the port, Drake saw to his amazement that British boats were still plying the waters to take the wounded off. A trawler heaved up to lay alongside the quay. Badly injured men were being lowered to the deck by ropes, but a Stuka howled down towards the harbour. A Bofors gun fired, but the dive-bomber was coming too fast and the shells burst too high. The bombs released as the Stuka pulled up, and the black dots sailed, whistling down, towards the trawler. Three bombs hit the water alongside the hull, and a surging mushroom of seawater erupted. The boat heaved and the deck was washed clear by a wave twenty feet high. Wounded men flailed into the churning harbour, unable to swim. The port was strewn with wreckage and the sinking, steaming carcasses of ships. A British yacht, the *Conidaw*, steamed away, piled so high with wounded soldiers that it threatened to capsize.

The fear in the air was palpable now. French volunteers, led by a trainee priest, were firing madly from the harbour across the basin at the distant German soldiers. Every man was fighting for his life. But it was more than that – they were fighting for everything that made life worth living. Drake pushed himself on. He would never give up while there was breath in his lungs, but he was struggling to breathe in the ash-filled air. Despite the drugs fizzing around inside his veins, he was weak from his shock, from his wounds. The black clouds above the harbour made everything dim as dusk. Dark figures flitted through the twilight, muzzles flickering fire. Drake felt he was in a nightmare, running after something he couldn't quite grasp. Obscure associations, like soldiers in a fog, kept sliding just out of his reach. *A political matter. The cross of Burgundy. The passing of kings.*

He staggered to the waterfront. The first rush of the morphine was starting to fade, and his ribs ached like hell, but he couldn't stop now. He paused, gasping air, and swallowed more Benzedrine tablets. The smoke blew clear, and he saw the outer wall, and the fisherman's wharf. He saw a signalman, sending Morse signals from a wireless truck that was on fire. The man inside kept broadcasting as it burned.

Drake scoured the railway yard and the quay as another salvo went up, another frenzy of explosions rocked the city. A shattering barrage of mortar fire crept along the dockside, sending shards of old stone hissing through the air. Drake rubbed his eyes, smarting from the burning fumes and the heat. Tore his fingers through his tangled, sweat-soaked hair. He looked again, and a gust of wind for a moment cleared the smoke. There was a half-submerged steamer by the dock, its superstructure blackened and smouldering. In the shelter of the wreck, the man in the dark suit, with a black briefcase held in his hand, was standing on the waterfront nearby, gazing out to sea.

Drake ran towards the lone civilian, then as he got closer, he slowed to a stumbling halt. The pieces of the puzzle shifted inside his mind.

A short-brimmed hat. A high-cut trouser suit in a dark material. Drake saw that it wasn't a man at all.

His throat was dry. His heart thudded madly. His voice croaked as he called out in shock.

'Axelle?'

Chapter 71

Axelle's eyes flashed as she turned. She watched Drake closely, carefully as he approached.

At the last moment she threw her arms around him. 'I thought you were dead,' she said.

Drake ignored the knifing pains in his chest. He wanted to hold her, to tumble into her embrace, but his mind was whirling, his insides torn with battling emotions. His gaze flicked to the black calfskin briefcase in her left hand. It was stained with old blood, but he could make out the swastika and German eagle. And although it had been wiped down, Drake could clearly see three dark bullet holes through the leather. It made his ribcage ache to look at them. His head was beginning to clear now. Axelle had the briefcase. It could only mean one thing.

'You betrayed me,' he said. He pushed her off.

Axelle stepped back. She was holding a pistol in her right hand. She'd removed it from his pocket. 'If you say so. Now turn around. *Sors d'ici.* Get out of here if you want to live! Go!'

'It was you. At the factory.'

Axelle shook her head. 'You don't understand anything, do you?'

'Maybe I don't,' Drake said. He stepped towards her, ignoring the sound of the gunfire and the screaming of divebombers overhead. 'But I'm trying.'

Axelle fired a shot between his legs and he skipped smartly back.

'*Je ne plaisante pas,*' she said. She raised the pistol to point towards his face now. 'I'm not fooling around. Get out of here. Go and find your sergeant. Go!'

A Stuka bomb fell into the city nearby. It slammed down with a hideous bang. Debris flew through the air, but they were sheltered from the worst of it by the hulk of the half-sunk steamer. There were few craft still afloat now. All around them, heavy German artillery pounded the city. Shells screeched in and hit with hard, crashing blows that brought down walls and gouged deep smoking pits into the cobbles of the dock. Soaring waves of flame, fanned by the wind, leapt from building to building all across the island of Calais Nord. Above it all, the great guns of British destroyers thumped shell after shell overhead, to hit in crushing, shuddering blows behind the enemy lines. The shouts of the British soldiers came across the water as they refused to give ground and died where they stood. Drake tried to block it all out. It was as nothing to the maelstrom of emotions inside. The answer to the riddle was in front of him. He had to force himself to think straight, to push aside the buzz of the morphine and Benzedrine that was racing through his blood. The key to the whole puzzle was Axelle.

From the corner of his eye, he saw a small naval motor launch racing into the harbour, throwing up a steep bow wave as it came. He stepped closer towards Axelle, holding out his hand for the pistol.

'What's in the briefcase,' he said. 'I want the truth.'

Axelle glanced at the boat, then back at Drake. 'You wouldn't believe me if I told you.'

A Stuka howled down towards the sea outside the far harbour wall, and the Ack-Ack guns on a British destroyer peppered the sky with Flak. The Stuka let its bomb fall, then began to pull away into a climb. Drake watched the scene play out. The tiny black dot fell towards the British warship, as another Stuka hurtled down, a third one on its tail. Closer, inside the harbour, the motor launch swept around in a curve, spraying up sheets of water, and raced towards the dock. It appeared to be a French Coast guard vessel, but it was flying no national flag.

'Tell me,' Drake said, raising his voice above the din of the fighting. 'What's in the briefcase?'

Axelle looked him in the eye. 'Women's magazines.' There was something desperate in her look. 'Please believe me. Just women's magazines. Now in God's name, go!'

Drake's gaze was dragged away as a flash of brilliant white came from outside the harbour wall. Then a terrible, muffled detonation followed three seconds later. He saw the destroyer break in half, its boiler room exploding. The ends went up and it folded, and started to go down into the sea. He could just make out the black dots of men throwing themselves from the deck. Even the Royal Navy couldn't stop them. The cold, hard, bleak reality hit him. Britain was losing the war. The world was coming apart at the seams, and there was nothing that he could do.

Inside the harbour walls, the coastguard cutter sheered around. Its engines thrummed heavily, screws powerfully churning water in its wake as it came towards the dock.

Drake stepped closer towards Axelle. 'You're a liar. You've always been a liar. Now give me the gun.'

She shook her head and backed further away, hand tightening around the grip. 'Get out of here!' she begged him. 'Or so help me God, I'll shoot you.' She held the gun out towards his chest. 'I will!'

'That won't be necessary, my dear,' said a cultured voice, with a hint of a French accent. Drake spun to see the bespectacled face of Doctor Lambert as he came walking towards them across the quay. The cutter drew up next to the harbourside, in the lee of the half-sunk steamer. The heavy vibrations of the engines throbbed loudly as it closed to the harbour wall.

Lambert walked awkwardly up to Axelle and kissed her on both cheeks. Drake felt sickened inside.

Drake saw that, on the deck of the boat, two uniformed men of the coastguard were aiming an Oerlikon cannon down at them. He stared up at the deck gun. The Oerlikon could throw out 20-millimetre shells at a rate of 450 rounds per minute. They hadn't a cat's chance in hell of escaping that, if the sailors chose to fire.

Drake caught Axelle's eye and tried to force her to listen. 'Doctor Lambert is Agent Viper,' he said urgently. 'He's a traitor.'

Lambert tutted. 'Not a traitor, Drake. A patriot. What I do, I do for the good of my country.' Axelle passed Lambert the pistol, which he turned to point at Drake. 'Now put your hands in the air,' he said.

Drake slowly raised his arms and looked despairingly at Axelle. 'Your boyfriend works for the Nazis. But I see you already know that.'

Axelle met Drake's gaze, and there was something mocking in her eyes, something that made him want to crawl away. 'Don't be a child, Drake. Doctor Lambert is not my boyfriend. He's my boss.'

Chapter 72

A GANGWAY CRASHED DOWN from the boat to the dock, and Lambert stepped up quickly onto the deck. Axelle held Drake's gaze a moment longer, then she followed Lambert up the plank.

Drake was reeling. Nothing made sense any more. It seemed as though the entire harbour was whirling around him at dizzying speed. He felt unsteady and he was rocking on his feet.

Axelle looked down at him from the top of the gangplank. 'You're caught up in things you don't understand.' She glanced at Lambert. 'Walk away, Drake. They might just let you go.'

Drake's gaze travelled from Axelle to Lambert. Studied his bespectacled, almost-handsome face, his fine blond hair. It was hard to picture him as a German agent because he appeared so like an honest schoolboy.

'It's true, I don't understand,' Drake said. 'But I know what's right and what's wrong. And anything you do to help the Nazis win is wrong.'

Axelle turned away. Lambert reached from the deck and held out his hand to her, to help her aboard. She passed him the briefcase. Lambert took it and smiled.

Axelle looked back over her shoulder. 'Forgive me, Drake. Do, please, try to forgive me.'

Drake shook his head. 'I can't.'

'I should shoot you Drake,' Lambert said. 'But Standartenführer Obenauer wants you alive. An eye for an eye, eh? Better for you to die fighting, because if he finds you I am certain that he won't be kind. Either way, that is not my business anymore.'

He put his left arm, holding the briefcase, around Axelle's shoulders, and kissed her on the lips. She kissed him back. Then his right hand moved towards her navel, and Drake saw the gun.

'No!' he shouted. But it was too late. A muffled crack, her mouth opened wide with the shock of the impact. A film of blood shot from her back. She stumbled, clutching her belly. Drake leapt forward, but Lambert kicked Axelle down the ramp towards him. Drake caught her in his arms.

Her eyes met his, and her face was pale with shock. 'Axelle,' he said.

'*Larguez!* Cast off!' Lambert yelled from the deck. Briefcase in one hand, pistol in the other, he kicked the gangplank down into the churning water. 'I'll leave you two sweethearts together. You make such a handsome couple. I can assure you there will be no recovery from such a wound in a city under siege. It will be a slow and very unpleasant death for her, I'm afraid. If she means so much to you, you can hold her while she dies.'

The two sailors at the cannon moved to cast off a mooring rope, and the boat began to move.

Drake gazed back up at Lambert, thoughts spinning madly. He felt a heavy, crushing pain in his chest, as if his heart was collapsing inwards. He could barely open his mouth to speak.

'Why?'

The Viper stared down at him from the deck as the boat engines thrummed, churning water from the screws below him. 'The weight of destiny, Drake. The fate of nations. History leaves no room for the little people. And if you were not so blind you would see that *she* is the traitor to her country. Not I.'

Drake stood on the quay, just holding Axelle as she slumped down in his arms. The coastguard cutter began to slip away from the dock. On board the vessel was the briefcase, *Dämmerung*, and the fate of nations was inside it. As the boat began to slide away from the dockside, he lay Axelle gently down on the stones of the quay.

'Hold on,' he said. 'Just try to hold on.' She blinked her shining, dark brown eyes. Then Drake ran five paces to the edge of the dock and leapt across the churning water. His hands grasped the gunwale of the coastguard vessel and his full weight crashed into the boat's iron hull. The shocking impact on his ribcage almost made him lose his grip. His feet were only inches above the water, which was frothing from the powerful boat screws. The engines roared now, kicking out smoke and water from exhaust pipes in the transom as it manoeuvred away from the quayside. Drake managed to strengthen his grip and began to haul himself up. He had just got one elbow onto the top of the iron rail when a searing pain shot through his left hand.

Lambert looked down, his boot crunching onto Drake's fingers. He signalled to the crew. The men, now on the bridge, reversed the powerful engines. The water churned up beneath Drake's feet, and the boat began to reverse back. Drake glanced over his shoulder. He saw that they were going astern towards the dock and he was about to get crushed between the ship's iron hull and the seaweed-strewn wall. He clung on with his right hand as Lambert's bootheel tried to grind his fingers into the iron gunwale.

Lambert stamped his weight through his boot, grinding the rugged, hobnailed heel into Drake's fingers, and Drake's grip began to give. He looked hurriedly down at the agitated water below and clung on, trying to haul himself up on his fingertips. The boat closed with the harbour wall to crush him. In desperation, Drake pushed his feet back against the stones to try to shove them off. He groaned with the effort. The boat was too heavy, the screws too powerful, and the space was getting tighter by the second. But as his boots scrabbled against the wall, Drake suddenly found he could kick himself up off the rough stone blocks. He sprung upwards, hauling himself half over the rail to scrabble aboard.

He launched himself at Agent Viper and hit him hard. Lambert staggered backwards, wincing, and he stumbled over the black briefcase, which was lying on the deck. He managed to right himself and came forward again, picking up the case. Drake took two quick steps towards the doctor and shoved him hard in the chest. Lambert went backwards, flailing his arms. His feet hit the low gunwale and he slowly leaned backwards towards the sea. His right arm windmilled as he toppled, trying to regain his balance. His left hand was holding the briefcase, but his feet were caught in a rope coiled on the deck, and slowly, inexorably, he began to fall. Drake grabbed the briefcase, and Lambert clung grimly onto its handle – it was the only thing preventing him from going over into the churning sea.

Holding the case with one hand, with the other the Viper brought the pistol up. He pointed it directly at Drake's face.

'Pull me back up,' he said, straining to hold his bodyweight on the handle of the black briefcase. 'Otherwise we both will die.' His feet were still on the gunwale but he was hanging precariously back over the stern of the boat. 'I'll give you the briefcase. I'll explain everything. Pull me up or I'll take you with me! Do it, man! See sense!'

Drake watched the doctor for a moment, as he hung, leaning back from the deck, his weight suspended by the case that they were both holding onto. Drake let out a frustrated sigh.

What was in the case was far more important than Drake's personal feelings. The fate of nations hung in the balance. The destiny of France, of Britain, their only hope to stop the Nazi war machine. After everything Drake had been through, there was no way he could let it go now.

'You didn't have to kill her,' he said. He released the briefcase and stepped smartly back from the stern.

He saw the golden crucifix at Lambert's neck as the man fell towards the water with a cry of alarm, pistol firing harmlessly into the air. Lambert splashed into the churning water, briefcase still clutched in one hand. His face, in mortal terror, appeared above the foam for an instant as he tried to flail away, then he was sucked down, screaming – then silent – into the boatscrews. Bits of clothing and a torso surfaced then sank again. The water turned to a bloody pink froth, and Lambert's body sank down amongst the dead fish which had been disembowelled, organs turned inside out by the underwater detonations of the bombs.

Drake shook his head and rubbed a hand across his face. Agent Viper was gone.

'You again,' a familiar voice from behind Drake said.

With a dreamlike sense of *déjà vu*, Drake slowly turned around.

Chapter 73

A MAN STEPPED OUT of the cabin, flanked by the two sailors, who were now armed with Bergmann *Mitraillette* submachine guns. The man was wearing a different civilian suit, dark blue with a white shirt and grey tie. He was clean shaven, and his thick, dark brown hair was neatly slicked back from the unusual widow's peak. He placed a short-brimmed Homburg hat on his head and frowned.

'Monsieur Drake. What do I have to do to get rid of you? You really are becoming quite a nuisance, you know.'

Drake hoicked a thumb over his shoulder. 'It's over. Agent Viper's dead. The briefcase is gone.'

The man in the Homburg hat shrugged. 'The Germans, of course, are terribly efficient. They made more than one copy. My only concern was that the contents should not fall into the wrong hands.' He drew a small pistol from his suit pocket. 'Yours.'

The crewmen pulled back the bolts on their machine guns.

Drake felt a terrible sense of deflation. The morphine and amphetamines were wearing off and his chest was aching every time he breathed. His gaze was drawn to a Stuka as it screamed down over the burning city, quarter of a mile away. The thunderous crash of its bomb threw waves of smoke across the waters of the harbour. Flames belched from the waterfront's blazing buildings, great clouds of fumes and billowing ash. Drake looked again at the man. There was still something oddly familiar about his face. He glanced at the pistol, and saw it was a Ruby.

'That's a .32 calibre. It was you who shot me at the factory. There is no King of Burgundy. So who the hell *are* you?'

The man shook his head with a wry smile. 'Are you really trying to tell me that you still don't know?'

The engines growled in the motor launch as the boat churned away from the dock. One of the crewmen had taken the helm now, the other was still covering Drake with his machine gun.

Drake shook his head. 'No.'

The man smiled. 'The wheels are in motion. The die is cast. Destiny is upon us, and great undertakings are afoot. I am the man of the hour, Mr Drake, while you are nothing but an inconvenience. The true enemy lies in the Godless east.' He nodded to the sailor with the machine gun. '*Tuez-le.* Kill him. Do it now.'

Drake hurled himself backwards off the stern as the sailor opened fire. As he fell, he sucked in air, rotated into a dive, and hit the cold water hard and almost vertically. He shot down deep into the frothing water, praying he'd have enough momentum to get past the suck of the propellors. He kicked hard, fearing to feel the bite of the boatscrews on his feet as he desperately swam down, arms pulling, legs kicking, down, down, as far as he could go. His chest ached with the shock of the cold on his wounds. He opened his eyes and stared through the murk as machine gun bullets spiralled into the sea around him, quickly robbed of their force by the dense salt water. Above his head was the dark silhouette of the boat's hull. The surface glowed red from the tinge of blood and the fiery clouds above.

Drake, a Plymouth boy, had always been a good swimmer. The seawater here was just as cold and murky as it was back at home. He swallowed to equalise the pressure in his ears, and dived deeper, down into the gloomy depths. He saw a black shape among the swirling seaweed on the muddy sand of the bottom, and kicked down towards it, feeling the pressure growing on his lungs. He exhaled, letting out half his breath to reduce his buoyancy. The din of battle was muffled, odd, down here, the clicking whirr of the boatscrews coming through the water, and the strange, distorted thud of guns. Hampered by his kit and boots, he kicked and dragged himself further, further down. The water was cold here, very cold, twenty feet below the surface. He pushed aside the billowing seaweed, grasped the briefcase, and pulled. It was stuck. He tugged harder, and it finally gave. Up with the briefcase came the ghastly sight of Agent Viper's corpse, or what was left of it. His hand was stuck through the handle, his face lacerated by the boatscrews, eyes staring blindly at Drake, and the water below was murky and pink, and squirming with his entrails.

Drake shuddered, tore the case free of the dead man's grasp, and kicked him away. He swam for the surface, blood crying out for oxygen now. The dark hull of the boat had moved off, propellers thrashing the water behind. Drake let himself slowly rise. He knew the longer he could stay under, the greater chance he had of not being shot. After what seemed an age, veins boiling, his entire being screaming for oxygen, he broke the surface, and gasped in great wide lungfuls of air.

The sound of battle came crashing back in on him. All around the harbour, Calais was burning. Shells cracked in, machine-gun fire incessantly clattered, and the great orange pall of smoke filled half the sky. Drake saw the crooked-winged crosses of Stukas falling on the city, sirens screaming, dropping their hellish bombs in deadly swarms. There was a cry from the motor launch as one of the sailors spotted him, and as the wheel went over the boat quickly circled round. The two sailors leant over the rail with machine guns and opened fire.

Drake dived down into the depths again, and he heard the scream of a Stuka hurtling down towards the harbour, the sound distorted by the water. He kicked down, and felt a thump as something hit his back. A bullet. But more than six feet under, the bullets from a light machine gun were robbed of their power, and no worse than blows from a stone. Through the water he saw the screws of the boat thrash into life, and the craft surged towards him, trying instead to run him down. He dived deeper, and the launch rushed forwards, propellers churning the water behind it. Drake spun upside down, and kicked off the hull as the boat went over him, only to be buffeted by the whirling, sucking stream of the screws as they swept past. When he came up for air, the boat was circling around again. But the Stuka's scream was deafening now, and its machine guns strafed the waters as it dived towards the harbour. He saw the men in the boat pointing up at the divebomber and shouting in alarm. Drake remembered the fish and was hit by a sudden dread that sliced through him like a jackknife blade. If a bomb hit the water while he was still in it—

He dropped the thought and swam for the harbourside, thrashing through the water like fury.

One of the sailors ran to the Oerlikon cannon on the boat's foredeck and fired it up at the diving Stuka, while the other cranked the motor to full throttle. The bow of the launch rose, throwing up a sheet of water as it sped away. At a thousand feet, the Stuka's nose came up and it released its payload. The black dot of a bomb began to whistle down. Drake gasped through the last few yards, pulling frantically for the harbour's edge, the briefcase clutched between his thighs. His arms went round in a frenzy and he stretched for the sidewall of the harbour. At the last moment, as the bomb plunged down, he grasped the rusty ladder on the quayside and heaved himself up.

The bomb went into the water behind the launch and the detonation hit a fraction of a second later. The sea boiled up into a surging, glowing tidal wave. Drake clung to the ladder, briefcase in one hand, and was nearly torn from the rungs as a huge wave of mud and sand and water pummelled over him. The surge crushed him against the wall, surging onto the quay, but somehow he hung on.

As the seawater slowly drained back into the tidal basin, Drake wiped his eyes and looked back over his shoulder. The port was full of wreckage, but the coast guard launch was still afloat, and going hell for leather, its sharp bow cutting a line of spray as it escaped from the harbour mouth. The man in the Homburg hat, the man of destiny, the King of Burgundy, was standing at the stern rail, watching him. He was getting away. But Drake had the briefcase, and in it, the secrets of *Dämmerung*. The fate of nations was in his hands. He pulled himself up the encrusted ladder rungs, and prayed that it wasn't too late.

Chapter 74

Drake heaved the waterlogged briefcase onto the stones of the quayside. He clung there, gasping painfully for a moment, then forced himself up to his hands and knees. *Time to move.*

He staggered along behind the harbour wall, bent double, following the waterfront. Machine-gun fire still crackled across the port. Dead and wounded were lying everywhere. The German troops were closing in on the few remaining British and French defenders who were still holding out, against all odds. A pair of French marines were towing a Hotchkiss gun on a wooden sled as they tried to fall back under fire. Drake saw a Bofors Ack-Ack gun crew firing over open sights at the advancing German lines. The long barrel barked out six-foot sheaths of flame with an ear-splitting *pom-pom-pom-pom-pom*. Young men of the territorials and old men of the Searchlight regiment were mixed in with riflemen and French sailors, all fighting a last-ditch rearguard action. Somehow, amid the waterways, bridges, the ancient bastions, and the cover of the rubble and burning vehicles, the Allied troops were still, impossibly, holding a perimeter and keeping the Wehrmacht at bay.

Drake pressed on, through air that was dry and full of acrid fumes. Stinging ash billowed in clouds on the scorching wind. Smoke and flames leapt ever higher over the city, and he could feel the pressing heat even here, even in his sodden, dripping kit, which was already steaming now. It was the Day of Judgement. It was the end of times.

There was no shortage of discarded weaponry lying around, and Drake snatched up a sidearm from a dead French naval officer. It was a Pistolet SACM automatic. Drake checked it was loaded, then searched the body and found an ammunition pouch. Then he ran to where Axelle lay bleeding weakly onto the ground.

He lifted her gently a few yards into the shelter of a low harbour wall. She groaned. He knelt down next to her, and ripped open her blouse to examine the wound. There was a hole, blackened at the edges of her finely-coloured skin. *Gutshot.* Blood and clear fluids were oozing out. Drake felt a sudden hollowness inside his chest. It was bad. Very bad. A stomach wound was one of the worst ways to die, slow and agonising, and it was a crowded field. Men who'd been shot in the gut could last for hours, even days, if it hadn't hit an artery or major organ. But Drake felt an overwhelming sense of helplessness wash through him. He'd killed the only doctor in the whole harbour area. In desperation, he tore clean strips from her blouse and packed them into the wound to try to staunch the bleeding.

'You're going to be alright,' he said. The wreck of the steamer, the harbour wall and a huge iron mooring bollard shielded them from the worst of the crossfire, but stray rounds still flew dangerously close overhead.

Axelle blinked her eyes open, then struggled to speak. 'I— I am dying and you know it. You must find your sergeant now.'

'We'll get you to a doctor,' Drake said. 'A German doctor. I'll give myself up.'

Axelle tried to smile, but it turned into a grimace of pain. Her voice came out as a husky, grating whisper. 'Don't be a fool. You know what they would do to both of us. When I found you—' she spoke slowly, gasping breaths in between the words '– with the briefcase. I thought you were— already dead.' She closed her eyes, trying to hold in tears of pain. 'I have already grieved for you. And now it is your turn.'

'The man who was on the boat. The man with the widow's peak. Who is the King of Burgundy?' Drake said.

Axelle spoke again, slowly, not much more than a whisper. Drake had to put his head near her mouth to hear. 'His disciples – call him that.' She sucked in a ragged, painful breath, and closed her eyes. 'Christ in Heaven and the – the King on Earth.'

A shell screeched into the quayside, not fifty yards away. Drake held Axelle close as hissing, red-hot shrapnel splinters whipped overhead. Bullets flew through the air, or clashed dangerously off the harbour stones. Detonations crashed in the city. The smoke blew across them in rags and shrouds. Drake looked at the black calfskin briefcase. Dirty seawater was seeping from the bullet holes in the leather. He opened the clasp, and pulled out a ream of waterlogged papers. He spread a sodden wad of it out on the harbour stones. It was a soaking wet collection of housekeeping journals, fashion periodicals, and poetry reviews.

He glared at Axelle. 'What the bloody hell is this?'

Her eyes flickered open, and she gave him a faint, tired smile. 'Like I told you,' she gasped. 'Just women's magazines.'

She watched him for a long moment, and their eyes met again. She gave him a sad, regretful smile. Beneath her hands, blood seeped slowly from the wound in her guts. It trickled down to the quay, where it mixed with spilled oil in a swirl of dark patterns on the stones. Drake rubbed at his face, scratched his fingers through his wet, tangled, salt-matted hair. He felt like he was running through a dream where his legs wouldn't move. Like trying to touch something that was just beyond his grasp, and you felt you could do it if only you tried that bit harder – but it was always just tantalisingly out of reach.

Part of him wanted to squeeze the truth out of Axelle, but he knew it would only hasten her end. Instead, he pressed his hand on her stomach in an effort to stop the bleeding. But the truth, like her blood, was slipping through his hands and seeping away.

A burst of machine-gun fire clattered into the quay nearby. Stone splinters flew through the air. Drake watched Axelle's face, her shallow breath. She was still beautiful, but now she was deathly pale. Drake ran his rough, blackened fingers across her cheek. A damp sheen was forming on her face. She was dying.

'What's *Dämmerung*?' he said. He felt the frustration rising. 'The Germans are winning the bloody war! I need answers, and I need them right now! And all I've got is women's magazines! What does it all mean? Who are you working for?'

Axelle shook her head, in obvious pain. She looked at the blood on her hands. Her eyes began to dim. She blinked and spoke painfully, slowly. 'What do you believe in, Drake?' She had to stop to catch a breath. 'Your country, right or wrong? Who will you die for?' She gasped in sudden pain, struggling even to whisper now. 'Your parliament – your god – your king?' Axelle weakly lifted up her hand towards him, and it was drenched in her own, red blood. She let out a long, slow breath. 'Th – there is a better way.'

A moment later, the hand dropped, and Axelle's bright eyes were no longer bright. They gazed up into nothing, reflecting only the red clouds of the burning sky. All around them, shells slammed into the blazing city, exploding in thunderous detonations. Rifle rounds shattered on the harbour quay. Tracer from automatic fire hissed through the air. The harbour was racked by a series of jarring detonations. Drake ignored it all. None of it mattered now. He put his hand over Axelle's still, pale face and closed her eyes, and the world seemed to lose a little of its light.

Drake gazed blankly across the harbour as the bullets whined overhead. His tongue was thick with the taste of saltwater and ash. He picked up one of the damp women's magazines and hurled it into the sea. The pages flapped as it flew. It splashed down and began to sink into the dark, murky water. As the city burned, the waterlogged magazine drifted away just below the surface of the slowly-ebbing tide. Drake frowned.

He jumped to his feet and stared at it. That was odd. Very odd.

As the crossfire flew over the harbour, Drake bent over and picked up another sodden magazine. He examined it. It was an old edition of *Marie Claire*, from 1939. It had an illustration of a woman with a beret and a turtleneck sweater on the front. Drake opened the soggy pages, mystified. He looked at the waterlogged briefcase again. The leather case had three bullet holes on one side, and three on the other. The magazines had no holes at all. It could only mean one thing. *Christ in hell.* The contents of the briefcase had been replaced.

Drake felt a sharp, wrenching pain inside, and he realised that he'd got Axelle all wrong.

Chapter 75

Shells rained fire onto the burning city as the German artillery pounded in the distance. No street, no house on the island of Calais Nord was left untouched. The old town burned in great, roaring conflagrations that engulfed lane after lane, alley after alley, street after street. Whole areas of the city were nothing but ruins now, but still the Stukas came screaming in, dropping more and more incendiary bombs. On the far side of the harbour, British riflemen fought on with dwindling ammunition. There were no more boats coming in to the port now. The water was crowded with wrecks and floating fish and corpses, and the tide was dropping swiftly. Drake sat motionless, staring out towards the sea. *Axelle. Lambert. The King of Burgundy.* He was trying to piece it all together, but he simply didn't have enough information. *There is a better way.* What the hell did she mean?

In the Channel, a flight of Stukas dived towards a British destroyer. Her Ack-Ack guns flickered, and puffs of smoke appeared in the sky, but still the Stukas howled down. The whole thing seemed suddenly impossible and pointless. The Germans were winning, and there was nothing he could do to stop them. The warm fuzz of the morphine had gone now, and Drake's spirit was sinking into a colourless, sunken morass. His heart thudded hard in his chest, and he looked at the unfamiliar French pistol in his hand. Then he jumped as he heard a warm Scottish burr.

'What are you planning to do with that peashooter? Put yourself out of your misery, sir?'

Drake looked up. MacTaggart was standing in the shelter of the upended steamer by the dock, khaki tam o'shanter on his head. He was cradling a Thompson submachine gun in his arms.

It took a moment before Drake answered. 'The thought had crossed my mind.'

Nearby, Butcher was squatting behind the harbour wall. He had a five-foot antitank rifle over one shoulder it as if it were a child's toy, and held a Bren gun in his other hand. Leighton, as ever, was smoking a cigarette end. A shell crashed into the harbour wall fifty yards away, and they all ducked as debris flew in crazy spirals through the air.

'The situation's hopeless, Sergeant.'

MacTaggart snorted. 'Ha! I never took you for a quitter, sir. Would never have followed you this far if I'd known.' Then the old Scots sergeant seemed to notice Axelle for the first time. 'Satan's hell, is that not the poor wee lassie, sir? You was fond of the girl, was you not?'

Drake looked away. The water of the harbour reflected the red of the boiling sky. Drake's head ached with the detonations, the great skull-cracking explosions that were coming from the old city streets.

'You think you know someone, Sergeant, and it turns out you don't.'

'Is that so?' MacTaggart shook his head. 'Seems to me the wee lassie knew what she was letting herself in for, sir. We ran into her this morning. She put this in my charge, see, to give you when we found you. We've been searching hell and high water for you ever since.'

The old Scotsman fished something out from his haversack and held it up. 'I was to tell you that it makes better reading than women's magazines, but I'm damned if I know what in buggeration *that's* supposed to mean.'

The old sergeant held out a wad of typewritten papers. Drake stared. The wad was almost four inches thick and had three bullet holes right through the middle. At the back, it was stained dark with blood. *His* blood. 'I had a wee look,' MacTaggart went on as he handed it over. 'It's all in foreign, sir. But perhaps you can figure it out.'

'Give me those papers, Sergeant,' Drake growled.

On the front page, between the edges of the bullet holes, were two words typed in blackletter script.

OPERATIONSBEFEHL DÄMMERUNG

Chapter 76

DRAKE EXAMINED THE DOCUMENT. This was it. This was what he'd been searching for all this time. But instead of triumph, he felt empty inside. *Christ in hell.* He'd got her all wrong. Again. She'd crossed the double-crossers and walked, eyes open, into a trap. She'd knowingly sacrificed herself. All to keep the Germans from recovering the documents. And she might well have still been alive if he hadn't turned up and ruined her plans.

Drake blanked out the clashing din of the fighting all around the harbour. A surge of dark anger was welling up inside. He flipped the cover page of the document over, and quickly began to read.

The sheets were covered in densely-typed blackletter script. He flipped through the pages, struggling at first with the Nazi typescript. He translated in his head as rapidly as he could. He chewed two more Benzedrine pills – he needed to be supremely alert – then turned his attention back to the papers. This was the real thing. This was the hard military intelligence that Lord Gort and Brigadier Nicholson had been looking for. There were movement orders, logistics, diagrams and maps. There were battle orders, supply schedules, deployments for entire regiments. No – more than regiments. He swallowed, despite his parched, dry throat, as he quickly flicked through the papers. It seemed to contain the order of battle for the entire German Sixth Army. Even more than that, he saw with astonishment. Army Groups A in the north and B in the south had orders to advance rapidly to the coast. It was astonishing. The briefcase contained the order of battle for the entire German land army.

Drake glanced up at MacTaggart. 'We've got to get this to Nicholson right away. He can cable the gist of it to London.'

The sergeant shook his head. 'Nae chance of that, sir. The situation is less than pleasant over there. The citadel's on fire and entirely surrounded. The brigadier may well be dead. All I know is he ain't in command no more.'

Drake was buffeted by a blast of air as a mortar bomb cracked onto the wharf. 'Then who is?'

'Nobody, sir. It's sheer bloody chaos out there.'

'Then we need a boat,' Drake said. But there were no boats. Everything left in the harbour had been sunk, and there was nothing coming in now. And the wireless lorry, he remembered, had been on fire. He let out an involuntary groan. 'That's sod's law, down to a bloody tee. We've got the information at last and there's nothing we can do with it.'

He stared at the papers again. As far as he could see from the first look through, they contained military intelligence of great value. It was gold dust. The chiefs of staff and the army planners would give blood for a find like this. But was it *Dämmerung*? He leafed through the pages – and there were hundreds. It was typical German staffwork – efficient, detailed, scrupulous, but there was no great plot or conspiracy detailed here, as far as he could tell. And there was something about it that simply didn't add up.

'Why, Sergeant, would a full colonel of the Sicherheitsdienst, a political organisation, be sharing Wehrmacht military plans with a foreign agent, a spy? They'd have everything to lose, and nothing at all to gain.'

MacTaggart shrugged. 'Dinnae ask me, sir. I'm just a poor sergeant.'

Drake heard a rasping cackle. Private Leighton was pulling on his cigarette and laughing. 'Ain't it obvious? It's a trade.'

Drake and MacTaggart spoke as one. 'A trade?'

Drake considered the scrawny soldier. Perhaps Fred Leighton wasn't as daft as he looked.

'A trade for what?' he said. He started racking his brains, thinking out loud. 'He's only going to trade a jewel like this for something bigger, something better. Something that his master wants above all else.' He thought back to the major's words, spoken in Gort's GHQ, only days before – although it now seemed a lifetime ago. 'Herr Hitler wants only one thing. Total victory.'

MacTaggart scratched at his tam o'shanter. 'They're not far off that already, are they not, sir?'

A thundering, cracking detonation hit the warehouses on the far side of the harbour. Drake's gaze lingered on it for a minute, watching the smoke blowing out in great clouds. 'They're winning, no doubt about that. But what does total victory mean to you, Sergeant?'

MacTaggart lifted his tam o'shanter, and scratched at his thick, grey hair. 'Not just winning the battle, sir. The complete destruction of enemy forces.'

Drake jumped to his feet. 'Correct,' he said. 'And zero hour is only—' he figured the dates in his mind '*Christ.* It's tomorrow. They may be winning, but they are nowhere near total victory yet. Unless there's something big that I'm missing. *Dämmerung.* What the hell can it be?'

He sank back down to his knees and began to spread the papers around, sorting through them on the harbourside flagstones as the battle for the city raged around them. He knelt on the pages as he set them down, placed his pistol on another pile so they didn't blow away in the stiffening sea breeze.

'Well? What is it, sir?' MacTaggart said. 'D'ye think it's a fake?'

Drake shook his head. Why bother with a fake if you were already winning? Machine-gun fire chattered across from the far side of the harbour, to ricochet off the huge iron mooring bollards that were nearby. Drake ignored it, blocking the noise from his mind. The more he read through the papers, the more he was sure that the orders didn't make sense.

'We've got –' Drake glanced at his watch. It was three o'clock. '– exactly thirty-three hours. Thirty-three hours before the curtain comes down. And we're still missing a vital piece of information.'

They could hear German voices now, shouting across the harbour. The soldiers of the Wehrmacht were already in the port. It seemed they had flanked the British defences, encircling the defenders from both land and sea.

'Forget your thirty-three hours,' MacTaggart grimaced. 'Unless I'm badly mistaken, Calais will fall in the next hour or so, no more.'

Drake caught his sergeant's eye. 'That's it!' he said. 'Why are we here in Calais? Why sacrifice an entire brigade in a hopeless fight?'

Butcher shrugged. MacTaggart shook his head.

Leighton frowned. 'The whole sodding BEF was going to Dunkirk,' he rasped. 'Except us poor buggers.'

'Why?' Drake said.

'Ain't it obvious? They're going home.'

Drake scanned the harbour, taking in the rapidly deteriorating position, staring through the smoke and dust and flames. The sound of a mortar whumped, and they all ducked as the bomb fizzed overhead. It cracked onto the quay near the Gare Maritime. The enemy were closing in, fast.

He snapped his fingers. 'That's it! That's why Nicholson's been ordered to hold Calais. To allow time for the BEF to embark from Dunkirk.'

MacTaggart closed his eyes for a moment, thinking hard. 'So – this thing you've found –' and he pointed at the wad of paper '—it's meant to stop the BEF getting away.'

'Damned right it is,' Drake said. 'The destruction of enemy forces. But how?'

MacTaggart scratched at his head again. 'The Lord alone knows sir.' Then he pointed to the opposite side of the harbour, where German infantry were already breaking through the disintegrating British lines. 'Satan's hell. We've got to move.'

Drake jumped to his feet and grasped MacTaggart's shoulder. 'Sergeant MacTaggart, you're a bloody marvel.' He began to regather the papers, stuffing them quickly back into the briefcase as automatic fire from German machine guns skittered all around their position. Butcher opened fire against the German guns with his Bren.

MacTaggart looked astonished. 'I am, sir? What have I done now?'

'*The Lord alone knows*, Sergeant. Come on now, quick! Divine guidance is exactly what we need.'

The two men started running along the waterfront, ducking through the flames and explosions, with Privates Butcher and Leighton thumping along at their heels.

'Where are we going, sir?' MacTaggart grunted as they raced back towards the city.

Drake ran on, bent double to avoid the crossfire that was skimming along the waterfront. He shouted through the growing din of gunfire. 'The arsenal at Fort Risban. He knows far more than he's been letting on. We're going to ask that sodding old shit of a priest.'

Chapter 77

STUKAS SCREAMED DOWN TOWARDS the old town. There were no anti-aircraft crews left to respond. From the streets came the crackle of small arms, and the thump of two-pounders. The clank and squeal of panzer tracks as the besiegers relentlessly advanced. A German Very Light fired, the flare hissing high and white above the harbour. Drake guessed it was the signal for the final stage of the assault.

The Stuka attack broke off. The flare hung in the smoke-laden air as Drake's men hurried through the narrow, shattered streets of the ancient fisherman's quarter. They clambered over burning piles of rubble, but were driven back again and again by the heat from the towering flames. Shells whistled in to burst on the wharf, shattering the remaining buildings. Drake saw a French marine vanish in the blinding flash of a detonation. Finding another route, they ran across the harbour front, braving the automatic fire that was now strafing any open space.

As Drake ran, the stitches in his chest felt like they were tearing with every breath. His ribcage was on fire, but he couldn't stop. There was far too much at stake. They ran on, back around the jagged perimeter of the harbour towards the *Port de l'Ouest*. Bullets clashed off the cobbles and thick stone walls of the quays, and spun away in mad revolutions. They came to a British position, where the soldiers were fighting a rearguard action on the other side of the bridges, near the harbour bastions and Fort Risban.

'Come on,' Drake gasped, signalling to his men. 'Hurry! We've got to get across.'

They went doubled over, ducking behind the bridge palisades as rifle fire fizzed through the air around them. Mortar bombs crashed down on the thick, high walls of the ancient fort up ahead. The shore battery in the fort was silent, unable to traverse far enough to fire inland at the Germans now, but a handful of French sailors and an officer were dug into grass on the top of the fort's walls, and from up there, their rifles had a commanding field of fire. For the moment at least, they were holding the assault off.

On the ground, the cries and shouts of the British defenders were desperate now. Drake saw they were the territorials, the part-time soldiers of the Queen Victoria Rifles. A young lieutenant leant around the corner of the thick fort wall, and fired a revolver towards a smoke-filled park. He didn't look old enough to shave. Machine gun bullets from well-placed German Spandaus kicked crazily off the heavy cornerstones.

'We've been outflanked!' the young lieutenant yelled. 'Get out of here! We're going to fall back!'

Drake sprinted the last dangerous yards until he could shelter in the lee of the old fort's wall. His ribs were cramping up as he gulped at the dry, scorched air, and his heart was thumping fit to burst in his chest.

'There's a prisoner inside,' he gasped. 'It's vital that I speak to him. Can you hold them off for five minutes?'

The young officer looked oddly at Drake and his crew. 'We'll do our best, but I shan't be answerable for a single second more. We're about to be overrun.'

Drake clamped his hand on the young officer's shoulder, then dived in through the fort's steel door. He hurtled down the series of steps and into the tunnels. It was dark now. Pitch black. The lamps had all gone out. MacTaggart switched on his flashlight, and the beam lit the corridor weakly. Drake took it from him, and the four men moved forward. The corridors seemed narrower, darker, even more airless than before. Deep underground, the sounds of battle were muted, and it was quieter, but the floor still trembled with the impacts of shells. Drake once again had the horrible sensation that the walls were shifting, threatening to cave in.

He forced himself to concentrate. '*Monseigneur*!' he called out. '*Père Gillaud*?'

There was no answer. Just the *thud, thud, thud* of mortar bombs cracking down outside. They pushed on along the dark tunnel and counted the storerooms. At number five, Drake tried the door. It was locked with a large brass padlock. Drake pulled out his automatic pistol, and aimed it at the lock.

MacTaggart put a hand on Drake's arm. 'We're in the ruddy arsenal, sir. There's an entire shiteload of shells stored here.'

Drake's eyes went to the weapon in the torchlight. MacTaggart was right, of course. There only needed to be a trace of cordite powder on the ground and the whole thing would go up.

'Here,' Leighton said. 'Give me that torch.' He pulled a pair of heavy-weight paperclips from his pocket, straightened the first one then folded it over until it was almost flat like a hairpin. He bent the last half inch of it in the lock, and stuck it inside, using it as a tensioner to put torsion on the barrel. With the end of the second pin folded out at ninety degrees, he raked the inside of the padlock. Drake heard a series of clicks.

Leighton pressed on the tensioner with his thumb and the lock sprung open. He cackled. 'Piece of cake.'

'I won't ask where you learned to do that, Leighton,' Drake said.

'No, sir,' Leighton grinned in the darkness. 'Best not.'

Drake slid open the heavy metal door. He stared into the cell, and swung the torchbeam round. The dark form of the priest was standing against the far wall.

'Father? *Monsignor?*' Drake said once more. There was no reply. As he moved forward, the dim beam of the torchlight hit the priest's face. It was purple and grotesquely swollen.

'Satan's blood,' MacTaggart spluttered. 'He's dead!'

Chapter 78

THE PRIEST'S SOUTANE ROBE was touching the floor, but his feet were suspended a few inches off the ground. His weight was held by a purple cincture, a belt-like cord, which had buried itself into his plentiful neck. The top end of the cincture was tied to a high steel bracket on the wall.

'Hanged himself,' MacTaggart said. 'Although, to my way of thinking, Catholic priests are not normally in the line of suicide. Bad for their immortal souls, and all that.'

Drake looked at the height of the bracket. The way the purple belt was tied, the darkening features of his swollen face. 'Ha. Murdered, more like. Because of what he knew.' He swung round to face MacTaggart. 'Have you still got that playing card, Sergeant?' He'd handed it over for safekeeping, before he'd crossed the canal the night before.

MacTaggart drew it from his battledress pocket. Drake saw, in the torchlight, the picture of the medieval fool who was dangling a noose. 'I don't believe in coincidence.' He thought back to the first days of the invasion, when they had been chasing down a German agent. Could the cases be somehow connected? 'Why's it always a bloody priest?'

He took the flashlight and played it over the form of the dead man. The monsignor's hands hung at his sides, pale and hairless, palms forward, as though asking forgiveness. Something glinted in the torch beam. It was the golden ecclesiastical ring on the priest's third finger that Drake had noticed before. He turned the priest's hand over. The skin was cool to the touch.

'He's been dead a while.' The ring had a strange symbol on it. Drake held it up in the torchlight. He tugged, but the ring was stuck.

'Give it here,' Butcher said. His great fist closed around the signet ring and he pulled sharply down. Drake heard a sickening crack.

Butcher opened his fist, and the ring was there.

'Done that before, have you, laddie?' MacTaggart said.

Butcher shrugged.

Drake held the ring up in the light of the torchbeam. The symbol at first was hard to make out, then he saw what it was. A crown, a crucifix, the letters *RX*, all intertwined. He examined the pattern, then rubbed at his face and scratched his fingers through his hair. It made him think of what Axelle had said before she'd died. *Christ in Heaven and the King on Earth.*

'The Catholic Church. The King of Burgundy. The SS. They all have something in common. And somehow it ties in with *Dämmerung* and the German army orders in the briefcase. How?'

MacTaggart took the ring and examined it in the dim beam. 'I couldnae tell you, sir. But I, for one, have never seen it's like.'

Drake took back the ring, and looked at it again. He slipped it into his pocket and made for the door. 'There's bound to be another priest at the cathedral, if we can get there. They must know what this means.'

They emerged back into daylight – or twilight, more like. The clashing din of the battle was deafeningly close outside. Drake scanned the dusky, smoke-raddled city. The men who had been defending the bridge were dead or gone. The young lieutenant was lying on the cobbles, shot through the face. Drake grabbed his service revolver. It was good to have a familiar weapon. Bullets ricocheted loudly off the fort's thick walls.

'Look out! They're coming, sir!' MacTaggart yelled. 'The Hun!'

Sure enough, a handful of German soldiers were running hard towards the fort. The old sergeant opened fire with his Tommy gun. The muzzle flickered and the enemy soldiers went tumbling to the ground.

Drake saw there were more on their way. He jolted around the corner of the fort's wall as a high-velocity round hit the brickwork near his head.

'Snipers! Watch out!'

Mortar bombs cracked in to the stonework of the old fort's walls. The Germans were so close now, Drake could hear the officers shouting orders.

'Let's go!' he yelled.

He bent over double, sprinted back across the bridge and raced towards the narrow streets of the flaming city. His men followed close behind. All around them, under the increasing pressure of bombs and shells and small arms fire, the streets were turning into piles of rubble. Bombs exploded, shells from German field guns crashed in. The fire was all now focused on an ever-dwindling part of the old city, which was engulfed in towering flames. And right in the eye of the storm, above the clouds of smog and ash, he saw the tell-tale spire.

'The cathedral!' he yelled. 'Come on!'

The narrow alleyways and side streets were disintegrating as fires raged and detonations shook the ground. Drake and his men ran towards the blazing heart of the inferno, and all around them, the city of Calais burned.

Chapter 79

THEY RAN THROUGH THE fiery streets of the old town. Shells slammed overhead from German guns. Stukas dived once more, screaming, dropping destruction into a tightening circle of British defenders, who clung on in ever more desperate street fights in the ruins.

Dust-covered soldiers of the Wehrmacht were pressing hard in numbers from the port now. Machine guns clattered. Rifles snapped. British riflemen and French volunteers were falling back, street by street, and there seemed to be no overall command. Bombs detonated with explosions that sent burning debris flying murderously through the smoke. Mad shudders shook the paving beneath Drake's boots as he pounded through the rubble. He heard the screams and bellows of desperate men. The *crack-crack* of rifle fire. The judder of machine guns. Bullets whipped dangerously close down flaming streets. And through it all, the ominous rumble of engines and the clank of panzer tracks, as the German tanks rolled in, squeezing the last few British defenders ever more closely in the siege.

Drake hurried down a road of shattered houses, ducking from cover to cover. Ahead of him, a panzer with machine gun flickering crashed through a makeshift barricade, opening a breach for the German infantry to follow through. Volleys of gunshots broke out in a vicious firefight, as the British riflemen tried to slow the inevitable advance. A two-pounder cannon thumped, hidden in the wreck of a fallen building, and a streak of flame erupted from the end of the barrel. The shell slammed into the panzer's armour, opening a glowing hole in the metal the size of a small tin can. The tank gave off dark fumes, stalled, then burst into flames. But there were more machines behind it. Drake's mind was focused on just one burning thought. The fate of nations was in the balance now. He had to find out what *Dämmerung* meant before the entire city – and everyone in it – was destroyed.

'Over here!' he yelled, and he ran on, ever deeper, towards the centre of the blazing old town. He spotted a wounded man, being helped by his comrades through the thick smoke of a ruined street. Their faces were blackened with soot and dust. The wounded man had lost his left arm. He was clutching the stump, which was wrapped in field dressings that were bright with blood.

'Which way's the cathedral?' Drake called out.

'I don't know, boy,' one of the men answered in a Kentish accent. 'They've left us 'ere to die, haven't they? And the Frogs've bloody run off.'

Drake ran on, but something the man had said snagged at him. Up ahead, a ragged gap blew through the smoke, and he saw the cathedral's spire rise in front of them once again. What would in normal times have been a short walk had become a nightmare of blazing rubble, crossfire and detonations that made progress next to impossible. Drake redoubled his efforts and pounded on through the swirling ash and fog and unbearable heat, making their way step by step through the wreckage of the streets.

The four men thudded down flaming alleyways, gasping in fumes from the dry, ash-laden air. Drake's ribs were a drumbeat of agony with every step. The whole of the old city was on fire, flames fanned by a strengthening wind that was blowing in off the sea. It was so hot that his wet kit was already dried and crusted with salt. The old city centre was now like some biblical rendition of a flaming apocalypse. It was like doomsday, the end of times. The day of reckoning had come. Drake stared into the fiery hell.

He stopped. Tried to get his bearings as a wall of smoke blocked their path. Pockets of men were holding out, battling bitterly on, or digging in again, waiting for the next attack, fighting purely by instinct, without orders, yard by yard, stone by stone.

Drake ran along a narrow gap between bonfires in what had been a terraced road. Flames leapt out from collapsing walls, searing his uniform and his skin as he sprinted by. A mortar bomb whistled in, and he threw himself to the floor.

'Down!'

The hideous crack burst into an already-devastated terraced house. Burning debris rained down into the street.

'Bloody Norah!' yelled Leighton, emerging from under a pile of rubble. He was white as a miller, covered in a thick layer of ash. 'That was close!' He cackled and coughed and pushed himself back to his feet.

Drake took in the surroundings for a moment. A bitter struggle was taking place on the road ahead of them. Somebody was firing a Bren from behind a pile of blocks and bricks. Spandau machine guns and Mauser rifles responded, sending bullets in the opposite direction. From an adjacent street, a cannon on a medium panzer fired, and the machine gun position went up in a scathing detonation. Buildings were erupting, breaking open. Walls fell flat or cascaded down in sheets. All the roofs were gone, fires reaching up like grasping fingers towards the smoke-blackened sky. Drake lay for a moment in the ash and rubble, clutching the briefcase to his chest. Stabs of pain shot through him every time he gasped in a breath. Charred paper and textiles blew down the street like autumn leaves, only they were all on fire.

MacTaggart crawled up next to him. 'It's coming sir. The end. We can't hold on.'

A blast of hard white light went over them, then a shock that shuddered up through the paving as another shell slammed in nearby. A wave of masonry toppled outwards from the houses, cascading down in a cloud of burning dust across the road. German machine-gun fire swept the streets ahead, but a thudding Vickers gun fired back from the British lines, only adding to the racket. They were caught in the crossfire. Two German soldiers ran into the rubble-strewn road. Drake saw them raise their rifles in his direction and felt a stab of alarm. Before they could fire, MacTaggart gave them a dose from the Thompson submachine gun. The shell casings flew from the weapon in an arc as it emptied the magazine in two seconds flat. The enemy soldiers fell, riddled with bullet holes.

'Not bad for a pensioner,' Drake gasped through the smoke and dust-laden air.

The old sergeant's face was blackened with soot and ash, but he gave Drake a sardonic, rictus grin.

Drake heaved himself painfully back up to his feet. 'There's no way through here. Fall back. We'll have to work our way round.'

Chapter 80

Drake ran up to where the Vickers machine gun was firing from. A lieutenant of the West Kent Regiment was holding a barricade against the panzers with half a dozen badly wounded men. His face was pulled back into a sneer of agony and determination. His loader was dead at his side. The young officer had lost one eye, and was bleeding from his left arm, but he was firing the Vickers non-stop over the barricade as enemy fire kept pouring viciously in.

Drake felt a whicker of wind going past his left ear, and a split second later heard a sharp crack. He spun around. There was a sniper out there, somewhere, and Drake had the oddest sensation that he was a particular target in the sights.

'Come on!' MacTaggart bellowed, dragging him out of the line of fire.

They worked their way through the battle-torn streets, crawling, running, diving ever closer to the cathedral. A clatter of German machine gun rounds drilled into a wall at Drake's side, suddenly driving all thoughts but his immediate survival from his mind. He darted across a road, followed by a line of bullets stitching across the paving behind him. He sank, panting, against a broken wall, exhausted, trying to catch his breath. MacTaggart, Leighton and Butcher tumbled down into cover next to him, sweating heavily and breathing hard. Their faces were barely recognisable now, stained as they were in layers of ash and dust and soot.

There was a screech of metal on brickwork. A Mark III panzer, piled with bricks and rubble, was bulldozing its way through the ruins towards them. Drake glanced quickly around. Listened. They could all hear more of the squealing, clanking tracks. There were tanks on the next street over. A corner of a grey steel hull crashed through the ruins of a terraced house. As the bricks cascaded from its armour, Drake saw it was a Czech-built 34t, commandeered by the Germans when they'd taken over that country. He shook his head grimly, silently cursing Neville Chamberlain. *Peace in our time,* my arse.

From the smoking ruins, a British soldier from the West Kents ran towards the tank, right arm pulled back and holding a grenade. The machine gun in the tank turret flickered. Bullets kicked up off the cobbles, hitting the man's leg, but the man continued running on the stump of his ankle, for a few seconds unaware his foot had been shot clean off. He threw the grenade, then was cut to pieces by the fire from the panzer's turret. He fell in a shuddering bundle before the grenade blew open in a hard, flat detonation right next to the tank tracks, stalling the machine.

Drake got to his feet. 'Come on!' he yelled. 'Run!'

They sprinted over piles of rubble, half-blinded by smoke and swirling ash. Drake had no time to think now. He just had to get to the bloody cathedral. His three men dashed after him across the shattered road.

They raced through the roar and crackle of the blazing streets. Through the billowing clouds of dust and fumes, Drake again saw the cathedral's spire rising up above them, much closer now. They were almost there, but there was a barricade barring the way ahead. A handful of British soldiers were shooting gamely over the top.

'Hold your fire!' MacTaggart bellowed. 'Do I look like a bloody German?'

'Sorry Sarge!' somebody shouted.

'Hurry up, Jock!' another man cried out.

The barricade was five foot high, made from broken furniture and rubble, old prams, bicycles, and anything that came to hand. They sprinted towards it. From behind them, German machine gun bullets skittered insanely off the paving. Drake hurled himself onto the barricade, clawing his way up, then tumbling over the top. He saw, with a ghastly shock, that piled-up corpses of British soldiers had been used to reinforce the barrier, and the survivors were firing over the bodies of their dead comrades. Drake rubbed the burning smoke from his eyes, and stared around at the carnage as he sucked in deep, agonising breaths.

The panzers were closing in, breaking open roads for the German infantry to follow through. Somewhere a two-pounder gun barked shot after flaming shot through the smog. Machine gun bullets thudded wetly into the barricade. Small groups of riflemen were firing, standing or lying behind the barriers. Machine-gun fire stuttered, and rifles shots clashed in. Men fell to the ground, silenced, or screaming wounded. Others ran this way or that in the chaos, looking for cover. At one edge of the square, behind the ragged gap of a broken wall where the bricks had tumbled into the street, Drake spotted a pair of French sailors in white summer uniforms and blue berets, as though on parade. They were firing a deck gun that had been dismounted and dragged into the city streets. The gun chattered out burst after burst of 20mm shells. Drake ran on.

A German soldier tried to leap over a barrier that was made of bricks and tiles and a burnt-out car. He was met by the bayonet of a rifleman, and impaled as he fell. The rifleman fired, point blank. Another British soldier was writhing on the ground, screaming for death, hit by incendiary bullets and burning up inside. Drake rushed towards the cathedral and tried to shut the horror from his mind.

Soldiers lined the stone walls of the church gardens and fired grimly out at the advancing German hordes. The ominous growl of the panzers was creeping closer every second. The city burned all around them and the air crackled in an apocalyptic, shimmering haze. A lone piper stood in the middle of the square and began to play *Amazing Grace*, curling wreaths of ashen fog wrapping around him like a Highland mist. Drake felt the skin prickle on his arms and the back of his neck. He was awed at the man's courage.

'Stirs the blood, sir, does it not?' MacTaggart said. He gave Drake a fevered look. 'By the Earl of Hell, it takes me back to the glens.'

Screaming Stukas shrieked down through the black clouds that were darkening the sky. The bombs whistled in to explode in thunderous, deafening detonations that blew men cartwheeling off their feet. Deadly crossfire from the closing German positions streamed in, and still the piper played on. Across the roadblocks, Drake glimpsed figures of German soldiers running forward, jackboots stuffed with grenades. Enemy troops fired from rooftops, or along the streets. Loose rifle rounds and machine gun bullets twanged and tumbled through the air. Drake felt the wind of a sniper shot flying past his face, and again had the peculiar feeling that somebody was aiming specifically for him. But he had no time to stop and think. It was obvious there were only minutes left before the city finally fell.

The smoke blew ragged for a moment, and Drake saw the cathedral clearly for the first time. The building was cross-shaped, and rose to a tall tower and spire at its centre. Its roofs were holed and smoking, windows smashed, but somehow it was still standing, almost alone among the burning ruins of the city streets. The roads and alleyways around it were mayhem. Gunfire clattered, shells detonated, men screamed in a sickening din. British two-pounders thumped out shells through the barricades. Every road that led to the cathedral had been blocked. This was where the battered and bloody remnants of the Allied troops were making their final, desperate stand. Another German mortar barrage fizzed in, and the crash of the ragged explosions heaved up mountains of cobbles. Drake summoned the last of his strength and launched himself up again, running with the briefcase tucked under his arm. Tracer streaked through eddying billows of smoke as he pounded across the square, and he finally threw himself in through the cathedral door.

Chapter 81

DRAKE SKIDDED TO A stop on the tiles. The interior of the cathedral was dark, lit only by a sepulchral, fiery glow of red and orange that loomed in strangely from the tall, shattered, stained-glass windows high above. Smoke was curling around the vaultings and escaping through ragged holes in the roof. A pair of British army stretcher-bearers staggered towards him, on their way out to collect more wounded. They were middle-aged men, on their last legs, and the expressions on their faces spoke of horrors untold.

Drake looked past them. The *Église Notre-Dame de Calais* was an ancient, medieval edifice built of massive blocks of stone. The thickness of the walls offered some protection to the crowd of people who were huddling inside. Scores of French women and children were taking shelter there. MacTaggart, Leighton and Butcher pounded in through the doors, then, like Drake, stared around. The cathedral was teeming with badly-wounded soldiers and civilians who had sought a final refuge inside.

Drake looked through the dust and fumes that were drifting across the aisles. A British padre was leading a group of wounded men who were trying to sing hymns – hymns which were being overwhelmed by the terrible din from outside. Drake ignored him. He needed a French Catholic clergyman, somebody who understood continental affairs. He saw a hidden doorway in one of the chevet chapels at the back of the church, and grabbed the arm of an old French verger who was lighting candles there and handing them out.

'Where's the priest?' he said.

The old man pointed, and spoke with a tremulous voice. '*Le chanoine*, *Père* Thomas, is seeing to the wounded men.'

Drake could hear the crashing of explosions as the battle raged on outside. Chunks of plaster and flakes of burning paint fell from the ceiling as shells struck the cathedral's thick walls. Civilians, in huddles, were lighting candles or kneeling in frightened prayer. Scores of wounded soldiers were laid out on benches and the floor. A British surgeon was operating on a candlelit altar, and he was standing in a pool of blood. And – *there* – a white-robed priest was crouched over in the transept, giving water to a heavily-bandaged man.

Drake ran up the aisle. He clutched the priest's soft arm beneath his robes and pulled him upright. Père Thomas was a thin, old man, with close-cut white hair, and he blinked rapidly with surprise. A violet-coloured stole hung from his shoulders. At his feet, the wounded man coughed up water mixed with blood, and Drake saw the marks on his forehead that had been made with the holy oils.

The canon protested. '*Monsieur!* I am giving extreme unction. I must not be disturbed!'

Drake held onto his arm. 'The dead can wait. This concerns the living. The fate of nations is at stake here.' He thrust the monsignor's signet ring towards the canon's face. 'I need to know what this means.'

The canon squinted at the ring, then recoiled. His pale hand made a hasty sign of the cross. 'I cannot talk of this. It is forbidden.'

Drake gripped him tighter. 'What's forbidden?'

The canon shook his head and tried to push the ring away. 'I will not allow such things in my church. It is a sinister ideology, Monsieur. A danger to the true church and to the nation.'

The priest tried to back away, but Drake grabbed his robes and held him firm. 'What bloody ideology?'

Père Thomas glanced up at the church roof, which was sheathed in smoke. He made the sign of the crucifix. 'The cross symbolises Christ in heaven. The crown, the monarch on Earth.'

The words chimed with what Axelle had said. 'But what does it *mean?*'

The canon flinched as a heavy shell slammed into the cathedral's outer walls with a shuddering detonation, but the heavy stones held firm. 'They are proto-fascists. They are, of course, reviled by the true Catholic faith. Now will you leave me to do my work?'

Drake rubbed at his face as another shell slammed into the thick stone walls of the church. Fire belched in through a shattered window. He had to shout to be heard above the crashing din.

'There's a man with brown hair, *un pic de veuve* – a widow's peak. He calls himself the King of Burgundy. He's here in Calais.'

The priest scowled. 'He is the very devil, Monsieur. One of the most dangerous men in Europe, and that is saying quite something at this present time. Now will you leave me to my work? I will speak no more of it in this house of God.'

He tried to shrug Drake's hand off and turned away.

'Wait!' Drake spun the thin old man back round to face him once again. 'He calls himself the man of the hour, the man of destiny. Who is he? What is he trying to do?'

Instead of meeting Drake's gaze, the old canon looked oddly over his shoulder as though distracted. 'Say nothing further,' he said in a strange, sonorous tone. 'Kneel, my child, and kiss my ring.' The old priest held out his hand by his side for Drake to accept. 'Kneel! Do it. Now!' He pressed Drake forcefully down.

Drake, puzzled, crouched to a kneeling position, and a shot cracked from the other side of the church. The sound was almost lost in the thundering maelstrom of the battle outside. Père Thomas lurched as if jerked by unseen strings. He dropped the Monsignor's signet ring and fell to the floor.

Drake spun and saw a shadow fleeing along the aisles, behind the congregation. *The sniper.* He jumped to his feet, pulled the automatic from his pocket. A woman screamed. A child cried. Drake fired, but the assailant ducked back into the crowd and was gone.

'Get him!' Drake yelled to MacTaggart. The old sergeant tugged at Butcher and Leighton, and the three men ran through the crowded church.

Drake squatted down to where the canon lay writhing with his hands at his throat. He pressed his fingers to the wound, but it couldn't stop the blood that was pouring out in a great red flow.

'Father, I need a name!' Drake hissed.

The old man struggled to speak. '*Le –*'

Drake bent his ear to the old canon's lips.

His lungs rattled. '*Le – le Lion*,' he said.

It was no good. Drake couldn't stop the bleeding. The man's pale, old hands closed over Drake's, but there was no help for him. Blood pulsed in small, red, rhythmic fountains from his jugular vein, then the pulsing stopped. Drake stared at the spreading stain on the paving of the old church floor. The canon was dead.

Chapter 82

MacTaggart, Leighton and Butcher split up, combing their way through the crowded church. German mortar bombs detonated in hard, bright flashes against the dark sky outside, but in the dim stalls and all around the gloomy, smoke-filled nave and aisles, the refugees and wounded soldiers were lighting candles. Matches struck, smoking tapers were borne around the room. Faces, hidden before by the gloom, now began to emerge. The interior of the great church was slowly illuminated, candle by candle, flame by flame, from within.

Outside, sharp thumps of detonations clashed glass down from the high clerestory windows and it fell in sheets to the pews below. Civilians cried out in terrified voices. Mothers wept. Children screamed.

Drake gazed around the church as the chaos of the attack closed in. Spirals of smoke drifted up towards the grand, high ceilings. The cathedral flickered as dozens of candles shimmered soft light onto the faces of the terrified civilians and the wounded. Children clutched thin tapers in their hands. Pillar candles burned in sconces around the walls. Vigil candles flickered on pews and benches. Wounded men clutched votive tapers. There were candles on the floor, candles began to glow around every part of the congregation. Throughout the great chamber of the church, it seemed for a moment that every candle in the world was lighting up, pushing back the terror and the gloom.

Drake racked his brains. *Le Lion*. French for a lion, of course. But what had a lion got to do with it? Drake tried to see where the shots had come from. A thought snagged at the back of his mind. An image he had seen somewhere before.

Drake dragged his gaze around the cathedral's interior, searching for the shooter.

'Viens ici!' he called. 'Come out! I only want to talk!'

His answer was the crack of another shot. The round ricocheted off a massive stone pillar behind his head. Drake realised somebody *had* been sniping at him in the burning town. And now he had a good idea who it was. A shell struck the cathedral wall outside in a horrendous crash. Rafters tumbled, flaming, through the air, as the burning roof began to crumble.

Children screamed and the civilians in the congregation scattered as the timbers fell towards the nave of the church. The burning beams hit the stone floor in a series of catastrophic crashes, filling the nave with smoke and ash and burning embers. A few wounded men groaned and cried out, trapped by falling debris, unable to move. Others came to help them. Then, at the far end of the aisle, Drake caught a glimpse of a running man.

'There!' he bellowed to his men, pointing. 'Catch him!' He was on his feet and chasing the shadow through the ash and flames.

The man ran the length of the aisle. The church was too crowded, making it impossible for Drake to get another shot away without killing somebody else if he missed. He chased through the clouds of ash, through the benches filled with civilians and refugees, ignoring the cries and moans of the wounded. Pale faces glanced up at him, then away, eyes blank and dead with fear. Drake saw a torso sticking out from beneath a huge, smouldering, fallen timber, but he blanked the image out. *Dämmerung* was the only thing on his mind.

'Come out!' he shouted again, but his voice was lost amid thundering explosions and gunfire that cracked in from all around. On the floor, nearby, Drake's eye was caught by French uniforms. Twenty or thirty unarmed French soldiers were being pressed into service by a pair of British servicemen, to load ammunition into magazines for the machine guns outside. They seemed oblivious to the shots inside the church. The sound of it was lost amidst the chaos of the battle, the constant clash and roar of shells. Drake scanned the Frenchmen's faces, then disregarded them, racing past. They barely gave him a glance.

Drake climbed the apse, the curved stone steps behind the choir stalls, and slipped in a pool of blood. The British medical officer was still operating on the altar. Drake went past him and ran down to the aisles. A shadow moved, and one of the injured men jumped up, carbine in his hands. The muzzle cracked, and a bullet fizzed across the church. It ricocheted off the walls with a *twang-twang-twang*.

Drake dropped to one knee and peered over the lip of the wooden pew in front of him. His ribcage ached like hell, and his kit was drenched in sweat. His heart was thudding too fast, pounding in his head. Outside, the din of battle was building to a tremendous fury.

'Come out!' he shouted.

Another shot fired in answer, but the bullet lodged in the thick dark oak of a pew.

'Stop it, you fools!' the British medic on the altar shouted furiously as he patched and sawed at the wounded. A pair of stretcher-bearers ducked and slid away, shaking their heads, and a young girl screamed and screamed.

'I was wrong!' Drake called out again. 'You were right! I should have listened!'

'Traître!' a French voice called out. 'Fifth columnist! Fascist! *Capitulard!*'

Drake saw a flash of a face peering around the wooden panels of the cathedral gallery. A face he recognised. He signalled to MacTaggart. The sergeant and Private Butcher slipped around the back.

'It was a mistake!' Drake shouted. 'I should have let you shoot him!'

Despite the shudder of the raging battle that shook the cathedral, there was a quiet moment inside. Then a clash of shattering glass as a stray bullet from the fighting took out a window pane. The glass tinkled to the cathedral's stone floor.

Drake put his hands to his mouth and called out again, 'I just need to talk!'

'Va te faire foutre!' the voice shouted, cracking in its fury. 'Fuck off!'

There was a shout, and the sound of a scuffle. Moments later, Butcher dragged an angry, and disarmed, French officer by his collar down the aisle. Leighton followed, carrying the carbine.

Butcher hurled the officer onto a pew. Drake looked down at the man. His beady eyes stared back up with a look of sheer hatred.

'It seems you were right, all along,' Drake said. 'Commandant La-Pointe.'

Chapter 83

LaPointe's pinched face was twisted by loathing. His eyes darted around the church, then fixed on Drake's with a penetrating stare. He spat, and the phlegm landed on Drake's cheek. It had a vile stink of harsh French cigarettes. Drake wiped it slowly off with the back of his sleeve.

'Why did you kill Père Thomas?'

'Bah!' came LaPointe's reply. 'I was aiming for you.'

'He's lost his marbles, sir,' MacTaggart grunted. 'It's the pressure. What d'ye want me to do with him?'

Drake saw the Frenchman's red-rimmed eyes. He held out the monsignor's signet ring in the palm of his hand. 'Tell me about the King of Burgundy.'

LaPointe spat again, this time onto the ground. 'Ha! That's what he calls himself. I should have cut his throat, sliced out his lying tongue. But you!' He lunged for Drake, and was restrained by Private Butcher. 'You should have let me shoot him when I had the chance!'

The Frenchman's eyes darted away again across the nave as a great, cracking detonation shook the church. Heavy munitions exploded outside. LaPointe tried to get up and run, but Butcher dragged him back into place.

Drake leaned in close. 'The monarch on Earth, and Christ the King in heaven. Explain.'

The French intelligence officer's eyes narrowed. 'That man uses religion for his own twisted ends. *Christ the King?* He is closer to Satan. I had him in the palm of my hand, and you let him go. And now, because of you, they will win.'

Drake observed the shifting eyes of the French commandant. 'Win how?'

Small arms fire crackled from outside the cathedral. Drake saw the British padre trying to get the wounded soldiers to sing another hymn.

LaPointe let out a long, deflated sigh. He looked sadly at Drake, as though he'd suddenly given up. 'I *had* him. And you set him free.'

Drake crouched down, eyes level with the Frenchman, who was gradually growing calmer. 'I can still stop him, even now, if you just tell me what he's going to do.'

A shell screeched in, to slam into the cathedral wall. The entire building shuddered. A great painted plaster cross slid down from high up above the altar and shattered to the floor. A child wailed. Wounded men cried out in pain.

LaPointe gazed at the shattered crucifix. 'It's too late. The whole of Europe falls at Hitler's feet. And for thirty pieces of silver, that devil gives Hitler the sweetest kiss.'

Another section of the ceiling caved in, sending people scurrying away below. Drake stared around at the carnage, and his eye was caught by a statue of the Virgin Mary on top of the world, her foot crushing a snake. A serpent. *A viper.*

'Agent Viper was the doctor, Édouard Lambert. I killed him. So who is the other man? What's his name?'

LaPointe said nothing. His face was calm, but tears began to stream freely down his cheeks. Drake heard the rumble of tanks from the streets nearby. Machine-gun fire was almost constant now, and the noise of the battle was rising to a climax. The end was coming fast.

Eventually the Frenchman spoke again. *'La Belle France!'* he said, voice cracking as the realisation dawned, and he began to openly weep. 'France is lost.' He looked up through his tears. 'And now you will turn away, and stab her in the back. *Perfide Albion*. Yes, you too. Don't bother to deny it.'

Perfidious Albion? The old rivalry with France had reared its ugly head.

'England and France are Allies,' Drake said with a sigh.

LaPointe looked dismally up at him. 'Friends turn to enemies. Alliances crumble.'

Drake suddenly ran out of patience. He took the Enfield service revolver that he'd taken from the dead British officer and aimed it slowly at the French commandant's temple. 'So help me God, I'll shoot you right now if you don't tell me what you know.'

LaPointe just shrugged. Tears kept streaming down his thin face, but he carried on as if he was unaware. He laughed then, shaking his head. 'You arrogant English. You know nothing of affairs on the continent.'

He snatched the ring and held it up in the fiery light coming in through the shattered church windows.

Something turned at the back of Drake's mind. 'Stop talking in bloody riddles!' he snapped. 'Who's *le Lion*?'

LaPointe shook his head in surprise. '*Le lion*?' he laughed. 'Isn't it obvious? The rule of the monarch on earth, and Christ the King in heaven. He wants power when Hitler wins. He'll get no change from those atheists, though. They will put him in his place. A puppet, no more, with only the trappings of power.' Then LaPointe's laugh broke into a hysterical, choking cry. Tears rolled down his face and he made no move to wipe them away. A drool of spittle hung from the corner of his lower lip.

Drake pressed the revolver hard into the Frenchman's left temple, and pulled back the hammer with a loud, ominous click. 'But there's no monarch in France, is there? The monarchy went out with the revolution. The rabble cut off King Louis' head. There is no King of France. There is no King of Burgundy. So what the bloody hell does it mean?'

LaPointe spat on the ground once more. He reached up his hand and clasped it over Drake's, the one that was holding the revolver to his head. He patted Drake's hand in an almost comforting way. 'Go on, shoot me. I don't care anymore. Everything I have fought for is dead.'

He glanced away at the cathedral ceiling as another salvo of German shells slammed in. Flashes of bright white light shot through the window arches. Ugly cracks appeared in the vaulted ceilings above their heads. Great lumps of plaster and stone began to fall. Fire raged all around outside, and the din of the battle was growing to a hideous crescendo. The Virgin Mary crashed down from her plinth and a group of civilians screamed.

Drake shoved the muzzle harder against the Frenchman's temple. 'Tell me,' he growled. 'Just tell me his bloody name.'

LaPointe looked up, very calmly now, into Drake's eyes. 'You must clean up your own mess. I will not do it for you. But I will die a patriot of France. The man you are searching for – His name, of course, is Degrelle.'

At that moment, LaPointe's index finger slid down and pressed on Drake's own finger. There was no way for Drake to stop it. The trigger clicked. The revolver fired with a muffled thump, and the right side of LaPointe's head burst open. Half a second later, his lifeless body slumped limply to the floor.

Chapter 84

DRAKE LOOKED DOWN AT the ruin of a man that had once been Commandant LaPointe. He set down the pistol on the pew, and held his hands to his mouth. He felt like he was going to be sick. A child, who had been watching them, started a shrill screaming.

'Well, that's that,' said MacTaggart, interrupting Drake's thoughts. 'What in the Earl of Hell's trousers do we do now?'

Drake shook his head. Scratched at his face, his eyes, his hairline. He was trying to think. They had no time. Calais was falling. The Allied defence of Europe was collapsing around their ears, but now he had a name at least. *Degrelle.*

Outside, the brutal din of the firing had intensified. Cannons thudded, machine guns drilled in constant streams, and mortar bombs went off in clashing detonations. Flames leapt high into the air, all through the burning streets. Shouting, screaming came from the square outside. The roar of panzer engines, the *thud-thud-thud-thud* of German autocannons. The sound of men dying, the crushing of the final defences by the Wehrmacht's overwhelming force.

From the choir loft, the organ struck up, and in front of the altar, the British army padre raised his hand. Drake heard the stirrings of a song that pulled strangely, yearningly at his insides, as two dozen badly wounded British soldiers softly began to sing.

And did those feet in ancient time
walk upon England's mountains green?

Drake tried to shut the music out. He jumped up. Began to pace up and down, hands to his face. It would be only moments before the last remaining British forces were finally overcome.

MacTaggart ran to the cathedral door. Drake ignored him. *The passing of kings. The rabble. I will die a patriot of France.* He gazed around at the cathedral, not seeing anything. His mind was searching, far away, trying to make sense of what he'd learned. *Degrelle. Degrelle. Degrelle.*

Through the walls of the cathedral, he heard the roar of panzer engines and the clatter of tracks. Cannons thumped, rifles cracked, machine guns buzzed and rattled out streams of fire. Through it all, softly now, the melody of the hymn was spreading amongst the injured men.

And was the holy Lamb of God
on England's pleasant pastures seen?

'Come on, sir!' MacTaggart said, returning from the narthex, clutching his Tommy gun close. 'Let's get out of here. The whole place is about to be overrun.'

Drake's gaze roved blankly around the church. He was lost in his thoughts. He started pulling papers from the briefcase and spreading them on the pew in front of him. He stared at the typewritten sheets, the dense German orders in blackletter script.

'We've no time!' MacTaggart groaned. 'We've got to get out. Now!'

Drake hushed him with a wave of his hand. He looked down at the papers again, ignoring the sergeant's entreaties. He tugged his hands through his matted, filthy, blood-encrusted hair, as though the stimulation could make his brain work harder. He slapped his hand against the side of his face, hoping that the sting of it would wake him from his daze.

Dämmerung. Agent Viper. He wants power when Hitler wins. Then something changed position – an idea, a thought, just floating at the back of his mind. It kept slipping away, like a dream that makes no sense in the morning light. It was lurking in the recesses of his memory, just maddeningly out of reach. Shells crashed into the cathedral walls, and half a dozen wounded British soldiers, all bleeding badly, but still heavily armed, staggered in. One of them started firing from the doorway. The harsh crack of his rifle slammed loudly around the interior of the church.

Drake stared from one page to another, shaking his head. He flipped through a stack of sheets, and held one up. 'Look, Sergeant. There's something odd about this. It uses the verb *vorrücken*, to advance, not *angreifen*, to attack. Something's off. It doesn't make sense.'

A clash and flicker of gunfire lit the windows. Bullets thwacked into the walls. The rumble of heavy German armour was everywhere, a growing thunder outside. But he had to shut it all out and focus. *Something's rotten in the Third Republic*, the major had said, *and we think it goes all the way to the top.*

But what if the major had been wrong?

Drake heard a panzer engine outside, coming from the cathedral square. The drilling buzz of Spandau machine guns. But the sounds were distant and strange to him now. Everything went still for a moment inside his head.

'Mosely,' he said aloud. 'Oswald Mosely!'

MacTaggart gave Drake an odd look. 'What in Satan's dark domain has Mosely got to do with it, sir?'

'They locked him up. But Moseley was a friend of the old king.'

A burst of German gunfire stung in through the cathedral doors. A British soldier, caught in the stream, collapsed, shuddering, to the tiles. Children began shrieking madly. But the choir of wounded men sang resolutely on, and the soft tones of the hymn flowed through the smoke-filled church.

And did the countenance divine
shine forth upon our clouded hills?
And was Jerusalem builded here
among those dark Satanic Mills?

MacTaggart grabbed Drake's sleeve. 'You've lost me, sir. Come on, it's now or never. We've got to ruddy well go!'

Drake shook the old Scotsman off, and scanned the sheets of paper again. He had to do it. He had to figure it out. Something in the music was speaking to him, urging him on. The dream that was Britain, the freedom of thought and spirit and heart – they could not let it go, they could not let it be crushed by hatred, by fanatical Nazi ideals.

He laid the papers out in piles on the bench, but the old fashioned German typeface was difficult to read. He was almost there, but it still made no sense. It was a dead end. Mosely had no connection to France, had he? A series of shells burst on the street just outside the door, and the women and children inside the cathedral all screamed. Drake blanked it out. And it came to him at last. The familiar face. The man in the Homburg hat. The man with the widow's peak. The King of Burgundy.

What was it Bill Lucas had said? *The Valois Dukes of Burgundy ruled significant swathes of Eastern France and the Low Countries way back in the fifteenth century.*

And suddenly he had it.

'Got you!' he shouted out loud. Pére Thomas hadn't been saying *le Lion* at all. It was a name. Drake had never met him before, but he *had* seen him. Seen a picture of him, at least. A smudged photograph. In the newspaper in the major's car. That's why his face had seemed so familiar. He spoke it out loud. 'Of course! It's Léon bloody Degrelle!'

They'd locked Mosely up in England. And in France they'd locked up Degrelle too, but *that was Degrelle* – and no wonder LaPointe had been hopping mad. Drake had accidentally set him free. He blanked out the sound of firing and the desperate shouts of the men outside. The screams of the children, the crying women, the groaning wounded. The final British defensive line was crumbling all around them. *Léon Degrelle.*

Drake ignored the crash and shudder of the guns, and flicked briskly through the German order sheets again. There *was* something there, but it wasn't at all what he had expected. These were just logistical order sheets. Directions for the dispersal of fuel and ammunition. The order of battle of German units. He pulled out a few more pages, and studied them. Movement orders. Luftwaffe flight plans, deployment, missions and strengths. It was all there in staggering detail. The manoeuvre of an entire army. Drake tipped the whole set of papers out, and spread them all along the pew, moving aside the body of a dead French sailor to do so. There were hundreds of sheets. *Hundreds.* Why did the Germans have to be so bloody meticulous? He'd never be able to read through it all in time. The secrets of *Dämmerung* were hidden by a mass of distracting detail. But what was clear was that it was the logistical planning for a grand manoeuvre, the pivot of an entire army group.

Drake could hear the German tanks outside now. Men were shouting, British and German voices screaming desperate commands. The cathedral shuddered in violent spasms as a volley of shells slammed into the walls. Wounded men moaned on the benches and from the floor. A child was screaming, others were uncontrollably weeping. Outside, the rattle of machine guns was relentless.

Drake examined the pages on the bench in front of him as he went up and down the pew. He looked at his sergeant, then snapped his gaze back to a photostat of a large-scale map. The diagram showed that Army Group B in the north was to advance past the British flank all the way to

Nieuport to the east of the BEF's position. And that was it. That was the key to it all. But that was exactly where the problem lay. The orders were simply impossible. It wasn't even an order to attack. Just an advance. A mad, headlong dash to the coast.

The maps showed, in worrying detail, the full plight of the northern Allied armies. The bulk of the key British, French and Belgian divisions were now compressed into a small pocket, up near the Belgian border. They were being pushed right back towards the coast, squeezed into a thin sliver of land between the towns of Nieuport and Dunkirk. And there were orders for the German Sixth Army to pivot left, to take up new positions to the eastern flank of the BEF. But that area was manned by twenty Allied divisions of fighting troops. It was illogical, un-German. It didn't add up. *The destruction of enemy forces.* This was the final, killing squeeze. British, French and Belgian Allies compressed into a shrinking pocket, hemmed in on three sides, trapped like rats, entirely surrounded, with nowhere to go but into the sea.

And that set an alarm bell ringing at the back of his crowded mind.

He leapt to his feet. 'Entirely surrounded!' he shouted out loud.

He looked up. From outside the windows came the massed throb of tank engines. Machine gun fire clattered across the square.

'It's the end!' MacTaggart bellowed. 'We have to get out, sir! Now! The tanks have broken through!'

Drake stared across the cathedral. He saw Butcher and Leighton, alongside a half-dozen riflemen, firing desperate last rounds through the cathedral doorway. It had taken the German divisions three days to break into Calais, against only a lightly-armed brigade. Taking out twenty divisions in short order – two- or three-hundred thousand fighting men – was simply impossible, even for the Wehrmacht. Drake rubbed at his face as he tried to clear his hazed, exhausted mind. It would require the German armies to simply march through the enemy lines as though—

As though what? As though the twenty divisions, two hundred thousand fighting men, were simply not there.

The sound of the battle outside receded as though Drake were in a bubble, cloaked in his own, half-crazed thoughts. *The passing of kings.*

The organ stirred once more, bellows being pumped desperately by hand, and in the choir, the wounded men, sitting or standing, wrapped in bloodstained bandages, raised their voices, despite their terrible injuries, finding a second wind, and all of the wounded soldiers who still had breath enough began to join in.

Bring me my bow of burning gold!
Bring me my arrows of desire!
Bring me my spear! O clouds, unfold!
Bring me my chariot of fire!

Drake froze, staring into space. The hairs stood up on the back of his arms. A shudder ran down his spine. Because he saw then what he had been missing. *As though the twenty divisions, two hundred thousand fighting men, were simply not there.*

It was a masterstroke. A vanishing act of catastrophic proportions. Drake saw it all play out before him. One after another, unstoppably, like dominoes, the Allied armies would fall. The whole of Europe would collapse at Hitler's feet. The complete and utter destruction of the enemy forces. Total victory for the Nazi war machine.

Drake fixed his gaze at the map, oblivious to the cathedral, the flames, the great chunks of masonry that were crashing to the floor. A shell blasted into the cathedral wall, and the building quaked with the detonation. But Drake didn't hear it. All he could hear was the cogs, the gears, the ratchets clanking into place as the information rearranged itself into a new pattern in his mind.

Major Lyle-Smith had guessed well, but not well enough. Something was rotten alright. But Agent Viper was not the real enemy. He was just a cutout, an expendable middleman. Drake grabbed hold of the back of the pew as a sudden sinking sensation almost overwhelmed him. LaPointe had been right, more right than anybody, though even he hadn't really known why. And Drake finally understood just what he'd done.

The singing of the choir had faltered, the organ had faded to a wheeze. But the padre spurred them on. 'Come on! Sing, men! Sing!'

The organ picked up again. Suddenly all the British soldiers in the church were singing. As the melody flew towards its conclusion, all the fear and pain and despair was pushed back for just a moment by the power of the anthem.

I will not cease from mental fight,
nor shall my sword sleep in my hand,
till we have built Jerusalem
In England's green and pleasant Land.

And as the hymn crashed to its conclusion, Drake felt with a terrible certainty that he held the destiny of Britain and her Allies, the whole of Europe, in his hands.

He saw MacTaggart organising the men by the doorway. A few badly wounded soldiers were crawling in now under a hail of bullets, as the men at the door gave their last desperate efforts. Then Drake heard an order shouted from outside, 'Cease fire!'

As the crackling din of the rifles began to dwindle, a British army captain ran into the cathedral. 'Every man for himself!' he yelled. 'Cease fire!'

A moment later, the noise outside the cathedral stopped. No guns. No bombs. No shelling. For as long as anybody could remember, there had been a constant din of endless crash and thunder. But now, even the music died away. It seemed the world was spinning in the sudden, shocking emptiness of the silence.

A wounded French soldier jumped up, and hobbled towards the cathedral door, taking up the cry. *'Sauve qui peut! Chacun pour soi!'*

MacTaggart hurried back. 'It's no good now, sir! There's no way out. They've got us in the net.'

Drake quietly gathered up the papers and stuffed them back into the briefcase as a squad of heavily armed German troops started streaming in through the cathedral doors, shouting, *'Legt eure Waffen nieder!* Put down your weapons!'

The cathedral was bathed in silence, now, broken only by the crackling of fires outside and the ominous sound of jackboots on the stones.

From nearby came the quiet sobbing of a child.

'I'm sorry, sir,' MacTaggart said. He raised his hands. 'Calais's fallen. It's over.'

Drake picked up the briefcase. 'Over?' he hissed. 'No it's bloody not.' He started backing quietly away towards the rear of the cathedral. 'Softly, now. Come on. We've got to get out of here.'

And as he edged towards the hidden chapel door, he felt no pain. The drugs had worn off, but had been replaced by a desperate urgency. His brain was on fire, because now, at last, he understood what *Dämmerung* really meant. Like Saul on the road from Damascus, the scales had finally fallen from his eyes. And all he could see was the blinding, terrifying light.

Chapter 85

IN THE UNCANNY SILENCE of the ceasefire, they backed out through the small arched doorway, unnoticed by the Wehrmacht troops who were pouring in the main entrance. There was a short, low corridor then another thick, old wooden door, studded with iron. Drake swung it slowly open. The door led onto an ancient, raised cemetery. Outside, Drake stopped, blinking in the strange aftermath, in the red and orange light of the burning city. The quiet was only broken by calls from swarming German soldiers and the crackle of the fires.

In the old French style, the cemetery wall was raised ten or fifteen feet above ground level, which meant they couldn't be seen by the German soldiers on the surrounding cobbled streets. Groups of exhausted British and French troops sat sullenly behind the stone walls of the graveyard, silent, exhausted, eyes cast down, many with their weapons discarded now. Their faces were blackened and most of them were wounded. They looked utterly depleted, but Drake was surprised by just how many men were still left alive.

He dropped down to a crouch behind the graveyard walls, then peered over. It was an eerie scene. As far as he could see, everything was either on fire or in ruins. Flames leapt up through tiled rooftops, buildings crumbled, walls crashed down into piles of rubble. Those houses and apartment blocks that still stood were shattered, riddled by shell holes and bullet marks, blackened husks burned dry by the fires. Many had no roofs, and those that did had great ragged holes in them. No buildings remained undamaged. The Wehrmacht had demolished the entire city in order to defeat the small, lightly armed British brigade.

Behind them, the cathedral somehow stood like an island in the smoking ruins, still largely intact. The streets around the church were full of smoke. There were hundreds of British soldiers congregating silently in the grounds. They were still coming out of the rubble and from cellars and bomb craters. Some had hands in the air, or held their arms behind their heads, others had faces sunken into their hands. Drake saw a handful of men trying to make a break for it. The *snap-snap* of pistol shots was loud in the quiet streets as a German officer shot two of the running men, and the others quickly stopped and surrendered. Everywhere, on the barricades, on the streets, or strewn around outside the cathedral walls, lay piles of the dead. Fires still burned out of control all across the old city, even though the fighting had ceased.

Drake felt strangely empty and flat inside as the effects of the drugs were wearing off. He swallowed the last of the Benzedrine pills. 'Make sure you've got plenty of ammunition, Sergeant,' he hissed. 'We're going to need it.'

MacTaggart nodded and signalled quietly to the men. They started scavenging for bullets, automatic weapons, anything they could carry. There was no shortage of guns. Butcher picked up a Bren, still hot. Bullets and full magazines were harder to find. Drake loaded his Enfield revolver from a paper packet of rounds, and he checked the semi-automatic pistol. It had a few shots left. He put both sidearms in his pockets.

His attention was caught by a pair of heavy German tanks which were bulldozing their way through one of the barricades. They rolled into the cathedral square, engines loudly thrumming. Their grey, squat shapes were covered in bricks and dust and they were blackened by fire. It only made them appear more menacing. In the strange, still, smoking quiet, their turrets whined and slowly traversed, searching for trouble. German soldiers, almost as dusty and soot-blackened as the British, began pouring in great numbers from the surrounding streets. They held their weapons levelled at the surrendering British riflemen. They shouted out harsh commands.

'On the ground!' a German officer called out in heavily-accented English. 'Lie on the ground! Lie on your stomach! Put your face on the ground! Put your hands behind your head! If you stand up, you will be shot! Lie on the ground!'

Drake saw the men, grudgingly, comply. But not the men up in the cemetery. It seemed the Germans were still unaware of them, as they were hidden behind the wall. An eight-wheeled armoured car came into the square, its great wheels scrabbling over piles of bricks and upturned paving cobbles. It followed through the path bulldozed by the panzers. It had a bedframe-style wireless antenna above the open superstructure. A small German officer jumped off the back. He stared around, his left eye scanning the fleeing British soldiers. His right eye was covered with a white cotton patch. He wore his *pince-nez* spectacles over it. *Obenauer.*

Drake ducked his head down and grimaced. He stuffed the briefcase inside his shirt, and buttoned it up. He couldn't run the risk of being easily spotted with it. He took the overcoat from a dead British territorial, and slipped it on. It was a poor fit, and it was hot, bloody, and he was sweating already in the heated air of the flaming city. He felt the pressure of the heavy case against his aching ribs.

A section of SS men jogged into the square.

'Find Drake!' Obenauer barked. 'He has red hair. Bring him to me!'

Drake ducked down behind the cemetery wall and watched as the SS men worked their way into the square. They began to search the British soldiers who had surrendered. Obenauer paced restlessly behind them.

'Come out!' the Standartenführer called out in English. 'There is no escape! It will go better for you if you turn yourself in!'

Drake's three men looked at him.

MacTaggart shook his head.

One of the SS troopers on the square dragged a red-haired British infantryman up towards Obenauer.

Obenauer shook his head. '*Nein*,' he said. The SS man threw the British soldier to the ground.

Obenauer shouted towards the British captives. 'Turn all your red-haired men in to me at once, or you will answer for it.'

'Piss off, Popeye!' somebody shouted. Others jeered the German officer, until a burst of machine gun fire clattered over their heads.

Nobody seemed to look at Drake. He wondered why. Then MacTaggart leaned over. 'You've so much ash and dust in your hair, sir, you're grey as a ghost.' He winked.

There was a commotion to Drake's left as a pair of young British riflemen made a dash for freedom, dodging into a burning alley. The German soldiers didn't seem to notice. A few others, heartened by their countrymen's escape, began to run. That got the enemy's attention. SS troops swarmed across the streets and opened fire, and many of the men fell before they'd got a dozen yards. The others threw up their hands in defeat, and were brutally kicked into line, then forced to the ground.

'Come on!' Drake hissed, and he leapt off the cemetery wall to the cobbles below, out of sight from the main body of the German soldiers. He landed heavily, but rolled back to his feet an instant later. MacTaggart, Butcher and Leighton thumped down next to him. Drake tried to merge with a crowd of men who were standing up, hands in the air or behind their heads, but the SS were combing through them, obviously looking for him. He picked up a British helmet – there were dozens lying on the ground – and slipped it on, tilting it down over his face. He glanced around. He spotted a terraced house, front wall ripped open by a shell blast. It was still on fire.

Drake kicked MacTaggart's ankle, then nodded towards the building. He suddenly started running across the square.

'*Halt!*' yelled a German soldier, but Drake shot him with his pistol at close range.

Chaos erupted. The SS troops opened fire, but the streets were crowded with British soldiers, their own men, and troops of the Wehrmacht, who seemed less willing to shoot at prisoners. Drake and his men returned fire towards the SS as they ran.

Rounds whipped through the crowded streets. Other British riflemen and French sailors, seeing the disorder, picked up their weapons again, started firing, and tried to make a break for it. A grenade went off with a sharp crack, killing a cluster of German soldiers. The machine guns started. It was carnage. For a few seconds the streets turned into a pitched battle as German officers screamed commands, trying to restore order. But a few seconds was enough. Drake dived into the ruined house through the hole in the blasted wall. He hammered up what was left of the smouldering staircase inside the house, his three men thudding at his heels.

Out on the street, an *SS-Schütze* pointed, shouting, '*Sie sind da reingegangen!* They went in there!' He fired his rifle.

'*Holt ihn euch!*' Obenauer screamed from across the square. 'Stop that man! Catch him! Bring him back alive!'

Chapter 86

MacTaggart fired back with the Tommy gun as the SS men pursued them into the burning house. Outside, some of the British soldiers on the square erupted into a cheer. The house was tall, four storeys high, and Drake's ribcage sent daggers of pain through him as he hauled himself up the steps to the top.

'Come on!' he yelled. 'This way!'

Half the building was on fire, and he leapt across a flaming hallway, shielding his face with his arms. He kicked his way through a bedroom window, out onto a Mansard roof, then started running and sliding along the back of the burning building behind a low parapet wall. Great holes gaped through the tiles, and flames seethed through them, spreading all along through the houses. In the middle of the terrace, Drake stopped, facing a fiery chasm where an entire house had been destroyed by a bombstrike. The hellish pit was spanned only by a single, blackened, smouldering beam. Drake looked back at his men.

He was not especially scared of heights, but the flaming pit below was something else. He tried to imagine it was simply a plank on the ground – an easy task to walk along without falling off. He fixed his eyes on the far end and trod carefully as he went across above the seething abyss below. The heat rose in a searing wind from the fires.

'Hurry up, sir!' MacTaggart called out from behind him, as he came following over the furnace, a pained expression on his face. 'I'm the first to admit that there may be rare times when trousers are preferable to a kilt.'

A rattle of submachine-gun fire came from behind them, then a pair of German soldiers poked their heads out of the window and brought up their rifles. Drake shot at them with his revolver. Butcher turned and fired back, half emptying the magazine of his Bren. MacTaggart gave the

Germans a burst from the Tommy gun, and their heads ducked quickly back inside.

Drake scrambled up onto the next roof. MacTaggart, then Leighton and Butcher followed. They ran along the shattered, blazing roofline, Drake clutching the precious briefcase to his chest. His ribs seared with pain as he gasped every breath, but he just had to block it out and go on. His boot skidded on a broken tile and he missed his footing. He plunged down a slope of blackened tiles towards an inferno that raged below. As his legs slipped off the edge he felt the rush of heat surging up towards him. Moments later, a big hand grasped him by the scruff of the neck, and Private Butcher hauled him back up. Drake slapped him on the back by way of thanks, and ran on.

They kept going, slipping and stumbling on the broken and burning rooftops. At the end of the terrace, the roof was completely destroyed. Drake sidled along the broken parapet of the back gable wall. There was a chasm on either side. Blasted brickwork crumbled and fell away beneath his feet. A fizz of air touched his cheek and he turned around. Somebody was firing at him, but he had nowhere to take cover. He just had to go on, creeping along the parapet. When he got to the front of the terrace, he peered down over the gutter. The ground was strewn with rubble and the air was filled with smoke, and as the Wehrmacht took full possession of the captured city, a handful of German tracked vehicles rumbled to a halt in the street below.

Butcher came thumping along the roof, stopping to fire the heavy Bren behind him as he ran. A half-dozen SS soldiers were crawling along the rooftops in pursuit. A surge of flames billowed out through a hole in the tiles right in front of Drake's face. He had to lean out far over the edge to save himself from getting badly burned. He looked down. German soldiers were gathering on the street. An armoured car and a large, heavy half-track with a covered load on the back stopped in the ruins directly beneath them on the rubble-strewn road. German soldiers jumped down from the machines to smash open the doors of the houses. A man ran towards their building with a snail-like contraption on his back. A great jet of flame shot from a pipe he held in his hands.

'Flamethrower!' Drake called back. 'They're going to bloody burn us out!'

'Don't much fancy getting roasted, sir,' MacTaggart said. 'I'd rather fall to my death, if it's all the same to you.'

'Agreed,' Drake said. 'Anybody got a grenade?'

'Me!' Leighton cackled. 'Just found them lying about, sir!' He emptied his pockets. He had four.

Drake pulled the pins on the grenades and dropped them over the edge of the gutter and watched them fall into the street below. They hit the roadway in a series of metallic clangs. Four harsh, flat detonations followed. There was a piercing scream. Drake peered over. Most of the German soldiers were out of action now.

'See you at the bottom,' Drake said.

He swung himself over the side of the gutter and clasped his legs around a cast iron drainpipe. The metal was hot, but he held on with his hands inside his sleeves and slid down so fast that the material of his battledress trousers burnt through to his skin. His feet thumped harshly onto piles of debris as he eventually crashed to a halt on the ground. MacTaggart hit the street a split second later. Then Leighton. Butcher came down last, taking half the drainpipe with him. Drake saw that the grenades had landed right in amongst the German soldiers, dismembering those closest to the explosions. The street was a bath of blood. There was a movement, as the driver of the enormous half-track was fumbling to bring his Mauser rifle to bear in the confines of the cab.

Drake spun around and shot the driver with the last bullet in his semi-automatic. He noted that the dead man was wearing a Luftwaffe uniform, then dismissed the thought and shoved him out as he climbed up into the canvas-roofed cab.

The half-track was huge, nine or ten feet high, twenty-five or thirty feet long. It had an odd-shaped, canvas-covered cargo load on the flat back. The driver's cab had a glass windshield but no doors. It was open at the sides. The whole vehicle was vibrating. The engine was still running. Drake stared for a second at the unfamiliar controls.

It had a steering wheel, clutch, brake and throttle pedal – *thank God*. It was not dissimilar to the set-up of a British lorry, only everything was on the wrong side.

'Get in!' he shouted, and his three men clambered hurriedly aboard.

He stepped on the clutch, shoved the half-track into gear, and smashed his foot down on the accelerator pedal. The engine roared and the heavy machine jerked, clattering, forwards.

Chapter 87

Drake pressed his boot to the accelerator pedal. He heard the unmistakable sound of a V12 petrol engine beneath the bonnet as the great machine surged on. An SS soldier ran out in front of the vehicle, firing a submachine gun from the hip. Drake ducked his face down as the windscreen glass shattered, and shoved his foot down harder. The V12 engine roared.

The soldier's eyes widened as the vehicle lurched towards him. His scream was cut short as he went down under the bonnet. The man with the flamethrower came running out of the building and a jet of fire screeched towards the open cab. Drake reached out with his revolver and fired. MacTaggart gave him half a magazine from the Tommy gun and the flamethrower's fuel tank exploded. The man went up in a hideous inferno. The canvas roof of the half-track cab caught fire, quickly burning above their heads. Hunched over to avoid the flames and the bullets that were now whipping up and down, Drake revved the engine, crunching through the gears as they raced towards the end of the rubble-strewn road.

As they came to a junction, amid the burning buildings, Drake tore the steering wheel round to the right, the direction of the canal. He quickly realised that although the half-track had the same controls as a lorry, it didn't handle like one. Its drive came from the huge tracks, but it was noisy, slow and ponderous, and the front wheels seemed to be more for general guidance than actual steering. Slowly, the heavy machine came round. The tracks skidded on the cobblestones, going easily over fallen bricks and debris and abandoned military equipment. Now, straight ahead, Drake could see an open square – and the canal beyond. The whole island of Calais Nord seemed so small, now that the fighting was over. The bridges that the riflemen had fought so bitterly over were still half-blocked by barricades. And here, a line of German soldiers was filing in through the gap.

Smoke billowed across Drake's view. He accelerated and sounded the klaxon. The columns of German soldiers scattered, diving out of the way as the half-track rattled across the bridge at full speed. The big machine sent the remains of the barricade spinning away, then sped on. Drake drove them straight towards the wide boulevards of St Pierre and the suburbs of Calais. They almost ran down a Wehrmacht military policeman on traffic duty, who shouted furiously after them. MacTaggart glanced behind them, then gave Drake a manic grin.

They clattered past a column of Allied prisoners of war, who were being marched at gunpoint out of the city, helmets off, hands behind their necks. Looks of relief or utter dejection marked their faces. Then some of the men looked up, and a ripple of excitement went through the crowd.

MacTaggart snatched off his tam o'shanter. 'Take your ruddy helmets off. They're a dead giveaway,' MacTaggart said. Drake, Leighton and Butcher all obliged.

Drake kept driving, slowing now to avoid arousing suspicion. He felt a violent sense of alarm every time any German soldiers shot a look their way. The canvas cab roof had burned off, but they were so covered in soot and ash to be virtually unrecognisable as British. As far as anybody on the outside could tell, they were just another battle-scarred German vehicle driving through the town.

Drake kept going straight for half a mile, swerving through oncoming German armoured traffic that was pouring into the city. His jaw was clenched, teeth grinding, but their luck was holding, for now. He swung the vehicle left onto a wide boulevard, heading east, and in minutes the outer suburbs began to open up into a flat, scrub-covered countryside that stretched all around as far as they could see.

MacTaggart slapped the steelwork of the half-track's dashboard. 'By the Earl of Hell's ruddy trousers, I think we've done it, sir. We're out!'

They were out of Calais. The men exchanged a look and they all laughed.

'Take the wheel, Leighton,' Drake said, moving along the bench seat to let the scrawny private take over the controls. He pointed. 'Keep heading east.'

Drake was somewhat familiar with the area, having been in and around Calais during the Phoney War. They saw a marching column of

German infantrymen, and kept their eyes fixed firmly on the road ahead as they went past.

When they were in the clear, Drake opened the briefcase, flicking through the pages until he came again to the maps and charts. He studied them for a moment. The charts were a few days old now, but he doubted the basics would have changed very much. It wasn't far. Probably only twenty miles as the crow flies. The roads were getting busy again. There were lines of lorries and other vehicles, all heading northeast along the coast. The main strength of the panzer divisions would be focusing their attentions elsewhere, now that Calais had fallen.

Drake came to a swift decision. 'Left. Left here!'

Leighton swung the heavy half-track onto an unmade lane, heading due north, towards the Channel coast. It wasn't long before the farm track petered out into grass, and the ground banked up ahead. The track turned into a path, and then disappeared into a line of sand dunes.

'Straight on, Leighton. Don't bloody stop.'

The dunes were wide, but relatively shallow here. The half-track clattered as it bumped up the bank and onto the marram grass. The wide tracks had no trouble with the soft sand underneath, but the heavy machine came to a halt as they crested the highest dune.

'Now what, sir?' said Leighton.

Ahead of them, smaller dunes ran steeply down to the beach. There, the flat, hard sands seemed to stretch out endlessly in each direction. The sea was to their north, and the sands ran west to east. The tide was very low, and the beach stretched far out, perhaps a mile wide here. In the distance, the sea looked calm and shallow.

On their left, to the west, were the dark clouds that hung over the still-burning city of Calais. Drake scanned the long, flat, wide, sandy beach. To his right, on the eastern horizon, an even taller column of black smoke filled the air. It rose up, slowly roiling in on itself, high and heavy, thicker, darker and more threatening than any thunderstorm.

Drake's attention was caught by a movement at the corner of his eye. He spun around. A German motorcycle-sidecar combination had followed them down the track. They were watching. More motorcycles began to stream onto the lane, racing closer towards them, towards the dunes. A muzzle flickered in the distance, and a loud jangle sounded as bullets skittered off the back of the half-track's loadbay.

Drake returned the chart to the briefcase. He ran his fingers absent-mindedly over the swastika, *SS* symbol and the *Reichsadler* on the clasp.

'Well, sir?' MacTaggart said.

Drake nodded. 'Alright. Listen up. Come hell or high water, Lord Gort has to see what's in here. We don't stop for anyone or anything, got it? We *must* get through. The BEF – hell, Britain's very survival is in the balance.' He pointed to his right, eastwards, over towards the tower of smoke. 'See that? That's where we're going.'

Leighton shoved the machine into gear and stomped on the accelerator pedal. The heavy half-track shot forward and tipped over the crest of the dune. As they shot down the steep face of the sand towards the beach, Drake looked back over his shoulder. The motorcycles were following.

Drake patted the black leather briefcase. 'Drive like hell, Leighton. Drive like bloody hell. We've got to get this to Dunkirk if it's the last thing we ever do.'

Chapter 88

PLAGE DES HEMMES DE MARCK, NEAR CALAIS, FRANCE - 19:00HRS

THE HALF-TRACK ENGINE THUNDERED beneath the bonnet, gaining speed as it rumbled across the flat, wide sands, heading east. The lowering sun was behind them, and it cast a strange, eerie light on the colossal tower of smoke that rose above Dunkirk in the distance. Drake peered back over his shoulder. One, two – *bloody hell* – half a dozen motorcycles and sidecars were now working their way down from the dunes and onto the beach.

'Ammunition?' Drake said, looking into the empty chambers of his Enfield revolver.

MacTaggart checked his Thompson submachine gun. 'Bugger all, sir. I put the last load into that flamethrower chappie.'

'Not much,' Butcher said. He slapped the curved magazine that protruded from the top of the Bren. 'Just a few rounds in here.'

'I always keep my magazine full,' Leighton rasped. 'King's Regulations, see.'

'Good for you, laddie,' MacTaggart said. He looked around. 'Where *is* your rifle, Private Leighton?'

Leighton frowned, then his face fell. 'I put it down on the roof sir, when I was slinging hold of the gutter.' He gave a nervous cackle. 'Must have left it there.'

MacTaggart gave him a ruinous look. Drake spun around in the cab, and peered behind.

The motorcycle-sidecar combinations were speeding across the sand now, easily gaining. A hideous clashing racked the chassis of the half-track as a sidecar-mounted Spandau fired.

'Try to pick them off with what you've got,' Drake said. 'If they figure out we've got no ammunition, we're screwed.'

Butcher got his Bren into position. He flicked the selector switch on the left of the pistol grip to single shot fire. He squeezed the trigger and the wind whipped away the flat crack of the report. A rider fell a split second later, the front wheel of his motorbike snapping round to the side. The sidecar somersaulted over.

'Keep at it,' Drake said. 'Slowly. Enough to make them nervous.'

He saw that another group of motorcycles was coming down across the dunes. He had to ignore them for now. Butcher would take care of them. Instead, Drake opened the briefcase. He tried to block all the external distractions out. He thought back to the photograph the major had shown him. Obenauer. Heydrich. Jost. The *Ausland* Department of the Reich Security Main Office: Foreign Policy. It all added up. And Drake now knew why Obenauer had been so concerned about the plot being compromised – *Dämmerung* could only work with complete operational surprise.

He flicked through the papers, being careful not to let any fly off in the wind generated by the speeding half-track's progress. He ran his eyes across lines of close-typed text. Studied the diagrams, maps and charts. After a few moments, he reached the same conclusion as he had the first time round. He closed his eyes, and pinched the bridge of his nose, trying to dispel his near-constant headache. He had to be sure. Then he remembered something Axelle had said. Lambert had been a private physician in all the best circles before the war. And he'd attended the military academy – graduating in 1922. Agent Viper was the cutout, the middleman. There was no other possible explanation. And he'd done his job and thrown them off the scent.

Drake opened his eyes again. He'd been keenly aware of the sound of Butcher's shots.

'Last round,' the big man grunted.

'Save it.'

Behind the half-track were twenty, thirty, forty motorcycle and sidecar combinations. Now that the firing had stopped, they were beginning to close up.

Another clatter of machine gun bullets smacked into the rear of the half-track, fired from the mountings on the sidecars. The odd-shaped load on the half-track's flatbed deflected most of the bullets. Drake frowned as the rounds skittered off it in a series of metallic twangs.

'Here, sir,' Leighton rasped from the driver's position. He lobbed Drake a German stick grenade.

Drake caught it. 'Good man. Where did you find it?'

Leighton reached down to a box beneath the driver's seat. He dug out two more, and tossed them over.

Drake examined the grenades. They had a cylindrical canister, with a wooden handle below, and in the last war, the British soldiers had nicknamed them potato mashers. It seemed the design hadn't changed since then. At the base of the wooden handle was a screwcap. Drake unscrewed it. A ceramic ball dangled out on a string. Drake tugged at the ball, and it came away, with the string attached. Drake held it up and examined it.

MacTaggart stared, wild eyed. 'In Beelzebub's name, that's primed now! Will ye not throw it, sir?'

Drake looked at it for half a second, then tossed it back towards the German motorcyclists that were following. The grenade bounced along the sand, slowing with every jolt, then, as the motorcycles came past it, it detonated with a bright, hard crack. One of the motorbikes went over, three or four others lost control as their riders were hit by fragments or stunned by the blast. But still the rest of them kept coming, swerving around the crashed machines. There was a large officer in one of the sidecars, giving orders to the other riders, and he signalled left and right.

The foremost riders drew closer, then split up. To the right side of the half-track, a speeding motorcycle drew level. The sidecar rider dismounted his machine gun, ready to fire straight in through the half-track's doorless cab.

'Here!' Drake shouted. He lobbed another grenade. '*Fang!* Catch!'

The man's eyes widened and he released his machine gun, then fumbled as the grenade plunged into the sidecar through his fingers. He scrabbled frantically round his feet in the well, then leapt from the speeding machine. The grenade detonated and the sidecar went up in a flash of bright light, killing the rider instantly.

'That's the trouble with the Germans,' Drake said. 'They never learned cricket.'

After that, the rest of the riders hung back. They kept their distance, firing their machine guns at the half-track in short, raking bursts. The four men ducked down inside the cab, and the peculiarly solid load on the flatbed seemed to shield them from the worst of it. Each time one of the motorcyclists drew closer, Butcher threatened them with the Bren and they backed away.

Drake examined the German charts in the briefcase once more, then peered ahead into the distance. The tower of smoke was much closer now. He reckoned it was only a few miles to the Allied positions at Gravelines. He was certain they could hold on for a matter of minutes against the motorcycles.

'Satan's blood,' MacTaggart growled. 'Would you take a wee keek at that? Can ye not get this damned machine to go any faster!'

Drake looked up to where the old Scotsman was pointing. A series of dark grey shapes were appearing one by one, cresting over the ridge of dunes to their right, threatening to cut them off. They were panzers.

Chapter 89

LEIGHTON CRASHED THE ENGINE into a lower gear and stomped on the throttle until the revolutions screamed. The half-track raced over the sand appreciably faster. Ahead of them, six light and medium German tanks came churning down off the dunes and onto the beach. Leighton drove at a diagonal, towards the water and away from their trajectory.

'Come on,' Drake said, pointing to the strangely-shaped, canvas-covered cargo on the loadbay. 'We've got to get that load off the back! It's weighing us down.'

A machine gun from one of the panzer turrets jabbed fire towards them. Rounds speckled into the sand and clashed off the half-track's heavy steel wheels. Drake clambered out of the back of the cab but he stopped dead as he looked up to the dunes. Observing, from the top of the ridge was an officer in an eight-wheeled command car. He was wearing an eyepatch. *Obenauer.*

A piercing staccato sounded as a panzer fired an autocannon. The shells hit the beach nearby in a series of thudding detonations, throwing up spouts of smoke, but the damp sand muffled the blasts. Drake knew they'd need direct hits to do any damage. The panzers were almost all off the dunes now, tracing obliquely across the beach and trying to cut them off. Drake willed the half-track on. It was going to be tight. Very tight. If only they could get rid of the cargo.

The foremost tank surged down a dune to their right, and flattened out onto the beach. It was in front of them, but it had no momentum. The half-track, already going flat out, shot past it before the tank crew could react. A few of the heavier medium tanks stopped to take careful aim, while others – the lighter Mark IIs – went immediately into the chase.

'Swerve!' Drake yelled. 'Zig-zag! Evasive action, Leighton! And keep your bloody foot down.'

'Aye, Skip!' Leighton called out. 'Hang on! We're going hard-a-port!'

He swung the wheel and the half-track slewed to the left. Five seconds later, he swerved right. Drake struggled to keep his feet as he stood on the flatbed loadbay, now clinging onto the canvas-wrapped cargo. He kept an eye on the tanks. They were falling behind, for now. It would take them a minute or two to reach full speed. He shoved with force at the covered load. It didn't even budge.

He tried again, now with Butcher and MacTaggart helping. 'Come on! All together! Push!'

The three men heaved and shoved at it, using their full bodyweight. The material ripped in places, but whatever mysterious cargo was underneath, it didn't move an inch.

'It's no good, sir,' MacTaggart said after twenty seconds of trying. 'Damned thing must weigh a ton!'

Machine guns from the light panzers fired jabbing bursts, rounds drilling holes in the canvas. But the bullets ricocheted off the covered load in a series of loud metallic clangs.

'Christ,' Drake cursed. He rapped his knuckles onto the material, then looked at it oddly. He had a suspicion. 'Whatever the hell is in there, it feels like solid steel.'

A panzer cannon flashed and the shell streaked past them. It exploded directly ahead, throwing up sand and fire. The light panzers were firing on the move now, at a rapidly jinking target – an almost impossible feat. The half-track rumbled on through the smoke from the shellstrike. Gobs of damp sand cascaded down. The machine guns from the leading panzers fired again. Bullets skittered off the steelwork of the half-track's load.

Drake saw there were an axe and shovel strapped to the half-track's cab. He wrested the axe from its straps and used the blade to slit the canvas open. Inside, he saw grey metal. 'Quick, get the rest of the cover off!'

MacTaggart drew his dagger, and between them, they sliced at the heavy cloth, which ripped away in long strips, to reveal four long tubes set in a square pattern, all pointing backwards. Across almost the whole width of the loadbay was an armoured steel plate.

Behind them, on the beach, the light German tanks were quickly gaining. Drake ducked behind the shield as a panzer's autocannon crashed with an ominous *thud-thud-thud-thud-thud*. The shells screeched past. It seemed the gunner was aiming too high, unwilling to decapitate the motorcycle riders who were now weaving in between the tanks, and were getting in the way. But Drake saw the canon depress, following their path. The tanks were directly behind them now.

'Hard a'starboard!' Drake bellowed.

'Aye, Skip!' Leighton swung the wheel right, and the men in the back almost lost their footing as the machine lurched over.

Behind them, a tank fired again, but the shells went wide. Drake's half-track straightened up. They were now running parallel with, and close to, the shoreline. Small waves were lapping at the beach, and the tracks dipped as they threw up a sheet of water from the edge of a shallow wave.

On the loadbay, Drake stripped away the last of the canvas, exposing what was beneath.

He read the words on a brass plate on the breech of one of the long metal tubes, and a surge of hope welled up inside. *'Flakvierling!'* he exclaimed.

MacTaggart gave out a long, low whistle, examining the apparatus carefully. 'Satan's blood!' he said. 'Looks like we're in luck!'

Drake studied the contraption. It was a quad-mounted, high-velocity Ack-Ack cannon. Two-centimetre calibre by the look of it.

'Fire drill cannae be too different from the Bofors, sir,' MacTaggart went on. 'Only there's four tubes instead of one.' The old sergeant glanced quickly at the tanks that were following them. 'I'll look for the magazines.'

Drake slid into the metal seat that was on the right of the elevation mechanism, behind the gunshield. He found a handwheel for the elevation screw, and spun the brass handle one way then the other to elevate then depress the barrels. They slid smoothly up and down in an arc on a semi-circular trace until Drake had them facing horizontally back through the sloping steel armoured plate.

Drake found the traverse and spun the wheel, bringing the four parallel guns to the left, then right. He peered through the binocular sights, which appeared complicated to calibrate and were completely out of focus. *Sod it.* He had no time to play around. He looked over the top at the wires instead. He'd be firing over open sights.

A machine gun on one of the motorcycles flickered, jabbing a hail of rounds towards them. The startling clatter of bullets hit the gunshield and it sounded like gravel on glass. MacTaggart opened a series of steel boxes, set around the mounting on the footplate. He pulled out a curved metal magazine, about fourteen inches across. He peered at the markings. There were small windows in the steel case to show if it was loaded. 'Twenty rounds in each magazine, sir!'

There was no time to adjust the fuses. He hurriedly passed two magazines to Butcher. 'Look here, they go in like this, laddie. See?'

He locked one in with a loud clack. Then another. Butcher followed suit on the other side.

MacTaggart slapped the nearest of the four barrels. 'The gun is yours, sir,' he said.

Drake stared over the sight wires, spinning the elevation screw to depress the barrels further. The foremost of the panzers came bobbling into his sights.

Drake searched for the firing arm. He couldn't find it. He looked frantically around.

'How do I shoot the bloody thing!' he shouted.

MacTaggart shouted back, 'If it's anything like the Bofors, try using your feet!'

Drake looked down. There was a wide pedal beneath each of his boots. He stamped down hard on both. All hell broke loose as the four barrels started thumping in a cacophonic, crashing, din, too fast for the eye to follow. Flame flickered from diagonally opposed pairs of autocannons in rapidly recoiling thunder. Four streams of high-velocity Flak shells streaked out at the German panzers. Tracer from each shell guided Drake's aim to correct with the elevation and the traverse handwheels, and he played the spread of fire across the tanks. The recoil shook the heavy half-track's chassis with every thump, and the beach behind them was ripped apart by a series of flashing detonations.

A moment later, the gun ceased firing. The magazines were empty. Fumes swirled off the four hot barrels. The *Flakvierling* had let loose eighty high-explosive shells in three seconds flat. Drake stared back over the sights in shocked silence. As the smoke cleared, he saw that there was nothing left of the first group of motorcycles which had been tailing them, nothing except spare parts, and odd burning bits of uniform, scattered all over the beach. A loose wheel spun slowly, rolling along the sand. As for the tanks – two of the light panzers were catastrophically on fire. Another was smouldering, throwing out black clouds, and the crew began to bale out as it rolled to a halt.

'By the Earl of Hell's trousers -' MacTaggart began, but for once the old sergeant was lost for words.

Drake gazed at the carnage that he'd unleashed on their pursuers. 'Christ.'

Chapter 90

LEIGHTON PUSHED THE HALF-TRACK to the limit and they roared along the beach. They were being chased by three medium panzers now. They were still a very dangerous enemy, but Drake began to believe that they might really make it after all. The motorcyclists who had been at the rear were still following, but were wisely keeping into cover behind the tanks. There was an ominous sound, audible even through the rush and clanking of the tracks on the sand. Drake scanned the horizon. He saw a black shape, coming in above the beach behind them. It was moving fast, and its sound was a harsh, metallic roar.

'Satan's hell,' MacTaggart said. 'Now it's the ruddy Luftwaffe, sir!'

Drake began to spin the elevation wheel to raise the four barrels. 'Reload!'

He kept his gaze firmly on the German fighter plane. He guessed by the sound that it was a Messerschmitt. The mathematical problem of hitting a fast-moving aerial target in real time was incalculable. He had no idea how to set the fuses for low-flying aircraft, or even whether they were set for contact or time. But he figured, with the Flak gun's high rate of fire, he just had to send up a stream of shells in front of the aeroplane and hope to score a direct and fatal hit.

'Ready!' MacTaggart shouted.

'Ready!' yelled Butcher.

'The gun is yours!' MacTaggart called.

A hail of machine gun bullets clashed into the rear of the half-track. The medium panzers, swerving around their burning comrades, were firing again. A single shell, fired from a moving tank, screeched by, ten yards away, in a rush of air. They heard it land some way beyond them in the sand with a muffled crump. But the spread of machine gun fire was having a greater effect.

'Get your heads down!' Drake yelled, as another stream of bullets slammed into the half-track and the gun.

He peered over the sight wires, constantly adjusting the elevation and traverse as he tried to get a bead on the low-flying Messerschmitt. The black silhouette of the fighter was growing rapidly now, coming in at no more than fifty feet. That made Drake's job a little easier, he quickly realised. He didn't have to guess the trajectory. He would be firing almost flat. He could see the circle of the Messerschmitt's nose cone now, the slight uptick to the span of its wings. A bright glint as the sun glanced off the cockpit glass. The roar grew, overlaid with the high-pitched metallic whine of its powerful supercharger. The plane banked slightly, lining up with the half-track, and the cannon flickered in its nosecone.

'Hard-a-port!' Drake bellowed, and the half-track slewed around to the left, running close to the edge of the water. Cannon shells from the Messerschmitt thwacked wetly into the sand. The plane banked again, trying to realign, the thunder of its engine growing. Drake waited a fraction of a second more, elevating the barrels a trace, and traversing. Machine gun muzzles lit up along the Messerschmitt's wings.

Drake kicked down on the gun pedals, and the *Flakvierling* exploded into action. The quadruple breeches crashed rapidly back and forwards, and fire barked from the muzzles in an almost constant roar. The shells, spewing tracer, shot into the sky. They went up in front of the fast-moving fighter and kept going. Drake tried to correct, but he was too slow with the wheel. Flak burst a thousand feet away, far behind the plane. MacTaggart and Butcher dived behind the gunshield as machine gun rounds clattered into the half-track. Half a second later, the Messerschmitt was overhead.

Drake spun the elevation screw and fired the last rounds up at its underbelly as the Messerschmitt thundered over, impossibly loud and fast and low. Oil streaks showed on the undercarriage. He saw the white and black markings of the *Balkenkreuse* beneath the wings. The pitch of the engine dropped as it roared over, and he heard the burbling exhaust note as the fighter streaked off down the beach away from them at more than three hundred miles per hour. It was so low Drake felt he could have tossed a helmet in the air and touched it. He could taste the sharp tang of the aviation fuel. But it was already gone, and somehow, even at point blank range, he'd bloody well missed.

The tanks had dropped back now, perhaps wary of being shot up by the Luftwaffe too. One of them stopped, and Drake knew it was going to fire.

'Zig-zag, Leighton!' he shouted. 'Speed up and slow down! It'll confuse his range projection.'

The half-track lurched right, then left, then right again. It slowed then accelerated as Leighton worked the gears, and started a sweeping curve away from the sea. The ponderous machine jagged left once more. Machine gun fire from the pursuing tank went wide. Drake saw a shell hit the sand twenty yards off. Their staggered trajectory was working, but it was slowing them down, and the other tanks were closing in. Drake's jaw was rigid with tension. His brain was working overtime now. How the hell could they shake them off?

'Oi, what's that sir?' Leighton shouted.

Drake spun in his seat. Leighton pointed directly ahead.

Drake stared above the broken glass of the windscreen. Half a mile away, a long, dark line stretched across the beach from the dunes to the sea. The realisation dawned with a crashing sense of deflation. They were almost there, so close, but in the chaos of the fight he'd forgotten about the breakwater of the Aa canal – a groyne that ran far out, well below the lowest level of tide. It was a barricade of giant stones and concrete blocks, designed to stop the canal from silting. But it was an impassable obstacle. *Christ.*

Drake racked his brains. He climbed into the half-track's cab and found the briefcase. Scrabbled through the thick wad of papers until he saw what he was looking for – the map. He peered up at the breakwater again, which was rapidly approaching as they raced along the sands, not much more than quarter of a mile away now. And the nearside, he could now see, was dotted with German machine gun nests and troops. They could hear the sporadic thump of artillery pieces and the rattle of automatic weapons as fire was exchanged across the waterway.

'If this chart is right,' Drake said, 'the French are still holding the other side of the canal. All we have to do is get across.'

MacTaggart peered ahead, then gave Drake a worried glance. 'And how exactly do you intend for us to do that, sir?'

Drake looked frantically at the German positions as they rapidly closed in. 'I don't know.'

The breakwater was twenty feet high, and impassable by vehicle. They could get out and scramble up it, try to swim across, but here, by the sea, the canal must have been a hundred yards wide, with a rapidly moving current. And they'd be shot at from both sides before they got twenty feet. And even if the shooting missed, they'd be drowned by the mud and the tide.

To add to their troubles, the Messerschmitt was circling back for another go. Butcher and MacTaggart began reloading the four-barrelled Flak gun again. They were trapped between the tanks, the fighter plane, and the German assault troops on the banks of the breakwater. A spatter of machine-gun fire hit the sand around them, and a few rounds dinged off the chassis, tracks and gunshield. The motorcycles were closing in once more.

'The canal's narrower inland,' Drake said, thinking out loud. He closed his eyes for a moment, frantically calculating the odds. 'Go flat out for the village, Leighton.'

'Yes, Skip!' Leighton replied. 'Full steam ahead!'

MacTaggart frowned and peered ahead into the wind. 'You do realise that the village is swarming with the Hun, sir?'

'Precisely,' Drake said. 'They can't fire on their own positions, can they, Sergeant?'

Butcher frowned, but Leighton grinned, showing his dirty, snaggled teeth.

Drake slapped him on the shoulder. 'Whatever you do, don't bloody well stop. We're going hell for leather straight through the German lines.'

Chapter 91

DRAKE CLIMBED ONCE MORE onto the back of the heavy half-track. He took up a strip of canvas that was still loosely wrapped around the base of the Flak cannon. He wrapped the briefcase in the stiff, heavy cloth, and then used the ends to make a sling around his shoulder and waist. With the case secured, he went back and strapped himself into the gunseat again.

'The gun is yours, sir,' MacTaggart growled.

A chatter of machine-gun fire from the tanks skipped off the steel gunshield. Drake gazed coolly over the sightwires. The Messerschmitt was coming in low and fast with the glow of the sky behind it. The hard, metallic roar from the engine grew and grew, rising in pitch as the silhouette got larger. It blinked in and out of sight, half-hidden in the glare of the lowering evening sun.

Drake kept his eye on the incoming machine. It streaked in, diving, even faster than before. Drake saw the telltale banking of the wings as the pilot adjusted and straightened up his sights.

'Hard-a-starboard!' he shouted. 'Now!'

The cannon on the nose cone of the Messerschmitt flashed as the ponderous half-track slewed away to the right. Half a second later, shells flayed into the sand, sending a chain of small explosions towards them, skimming closer as the pilot tried to readjust to the machine's new line. Drake watched, his entire body locked tight with strain, as the shells ripped closer, closer, and one of them hit the side of the loadbay in a blinding flash. A deafening detonation cracked, splinters flew up, but the men were protected by the quad-gun's shield and the bulk of the breeches. Machine gun rounds followed as the Messerschmitt continued its rapid approach.

'Left!' Drake yelled, and the half-track began to turn the other way. Drake waited.

'Sir!' MacTaggart said.

'Not now, Sergeant!'

Drake watched the final moments as the aeroplane thundered closer. He spun the elevation screw until the barrels were aiming almost directly overhead. He waited until the aircraft was nearly above him, then he stamped on the pedals. The Flak guns crashed out a two second burst.

Drake spun in his seat, and watched the plane streak away. He'd missed again. How could he have missed? But then a streak of fumes came from the Messerschmitt's engine. The smoke quickly became a seething jet of flame that engulfed the cockpit and trailed out behind.

Drake watched as the Messerschmitt tipped towards the sea. There was no time for the pilot to bale out.

'Sir!' MacTaggart called out again.

Drake's gaze snapped back down to the ground. The cannon barrels were giving off smoke. But in the moments he'd been distracted by the plane, the motorcycles had swarmed in much closer, led by a big man in one of the sidecars. Drake could see his helmet and goggles gleaming in the sun. The motorbikes were trailing the half-track by only a few yards now. Spandau machine guns fired, and bullets clattered dangerously off the loadbay and the armoured gunshield. Drake spun the elevation screw and lowered the barrels of the Flak gun.

'Sir!' MacTaggart cried out again. 'We're running out of shells!'

Drake took aim at the mass of motorcycles, and had just enough time to see the looks of horror as he fired. Flash after cracking flash, and detonations erupted in a seething spew of white light and black fumes. The motorcycle troops disintegrated as the shells hit them from point blank range. Wheels and bodyparts flew into the air, before thudding back down to the sand in a gruesome radius around the impacts. Drake glanced over his shoulder, now looking forwards towards Gravelines, towards the distant smoke of Dunkirk. He saw that one of the motorbike riders had escaped the onslaught, and had shot forward to ride alongside the half-track. The big man in the sidecar was trying to jump aboard.

'Right turn, Private Leighton!' Drake bellowed.

The heavy machine swung suddenly over, knocking the German motorcycle rider and his big gunner from their contraption. The rider went under the side of the half-track with a scream. The tracks thudded over the motorcycle, crushing it into the sand, and the petrol tank went up with a whoosh of flame as it was broken open by the heavy steel links.

Drake got down from the gun seat. He stared ahead at the fast-approaching village of Gravelines. The rear echelons of the German assault force were dug into the sand on the nearside of the Aa canal. Drake felt a great surge of elation sweep through him. They were almost there.

'Keep going, Leighton!' Drake shouted. 'Don't stop for anything! We've got to get through!'

Drake felt something grab his leg, and he looked down in shock. A big hand had come up over the half-track's side and got hold of his ankle. He fell, dragged roughly down to the loadbay floor. He landed hard, winded by the blow to the wounds in his chest. Somehow the big German from the motorcycle sidecar had clung on to the mesh siderails of the flatbed, and had avoided going under the tracks. The man heaved himself up onto the vehicle. He was enormous, and had a row of wooden-handled grenades stuffed into his belt. The big man picked up the axe that was lying on the loadbay floor, then stood up straight. He must have been seven feet tall. Drake gasped, holding his aching ribs, and felt a sudden injection of fear, as the German pulled off his helmet.

The man smiled, lips splitting and blood running over a line of small grey teeth in a badly-burnt mouth. His giant, golem's face grinned down.

Drake watched in horror as Sergeant Gunther raised the axe above his head and it glinted in the lowering sun.

Chapter 92

Gunther swung the axe down. It flashed and hissed towards Drake's face. Drake rolled to his side just in time. The blade hit the wooden floorboards of the loadbay with a heavy chunking sound close to his left ear. Gunther grunted, pulling the haft back up, jerking the blade free from where it had jammed itself into the wood.

Drake rolled away, quickly regaining his feet. He pulled the automatic from his pocket, and jerked his finger on the trigger. It clicked, and he cursed, remembering they'd run out of ammunition.

He stepped back. 'MacTaggart!' he hissed. 'Knife!'

The old sergeant, on the other side of the Flak gun with Butcher, was quick to react. He flipped him his *sgian-dubh* dagger from his sock. Drake caught it in his left hand.

Private Butcher came forward, working around the Flak gun. He held his Bren gun by its barrel, and swung it towards the big German. Gunther blocked the blow with the handle of the axe. Butcher let the gun go and punched the German hard in the face. The giant man barely flinched. He slammed the knob of the axe haft into Butcher's throat.

Another motorcycle came up on the far side, and an SS *Schtütze* leapt onto the wing of the halftrack. He fired his Schmeisser submachine gun towards MacTaggart, but Leighton stood on the brakes and everybody staggered forwards, losing their balance. The SS trooper tumbled off the bonnet. Leighton accelerated again, and the heavy half-track went over him. But the surviving German motorcyclists were swarming in now. One of them grappled with Butcher. MacTaggart wrestled another off the side of the machine, and the man fell under the tracks.

Somebody fired a Spandau machine gun, and the rounds twanged off the Flak gun's steel breech, scattering through the mêlée.

'Hört auf damit!' Gunther roared. *'Nicht schießen!* Hold your fire!' The shooting stopped. Gunther pointed a big finger at Drake. *'Er gehört mir!'*

The enormous German sergeant stepped towards Drake once more, pulling the axe back for another blow. He swung it with his huge, heavy arms in a wide, horizontal arc. Drake skipped back behind the Flak gun and the blade clashed into the metal of the cannon, only inches from his face. The impact threw up a shower of sparks.

Drake looked quickly around. He saw they were racing into the rear areas of the German lines now. The Wehrmacht soldiers stationed there looked on in astonishment as the half-track, followed by SS motorcycles, raced straight past their position, covered in men wrestling on the back.

'Keep driving, Leighton!' Drake yelled. 'Don't bloody stop!'

Leighton swerved the big machine past a dug-in gun emplacement. From the corner of his eye, Drake saw field guns, mortars, machine gun pits. Sporadic artillery fire was coming in from the French forces who were out of sight on the other side of the canal. Drake noted another vehicle, haring across the sands on a course to intercept them. It was the eight-wheeled command car. Standartenführer Obenauer, eye patch bright, was leaning forward from the top of the superstructure, screaming into his radio microphone, his one good eye glaring back at Drake.

Drake turned back just in time to see Gunther heave the axe back again. Drake backed away, then tripped on an empty ammunition magazine. He sat down heavily. Gunther grinned, stretching the scabbed and dry skin of his face. Blood dripped from his mouth, but he seemed not to notice. He raised the axe high and brought it whipping down towards Drake's torso. Drake kicked his legs and shoved himself backwards. The bright steel edge of the axeblade slammed into the wooden floor of the loadbay right between his legs.

As Gunther tried to rip the axehead free, Drake grabbed the haft to stop him. At the edge of his vision he saw Butcher and MacTaggart going at it with the other German soldiers. Gunther finally tugged the axe free, and swung it again. Drake skipped back, bootheels skidding on the loadbay floor. The blade hissed past his stomach and he scrabbled to his feet. He lunged in fast with the small, sharp Highland dagger. Gunther parried with the haft of the axe, the wooden handle slamming into Drake's arm hard enough to send it numb.

Drake dropped the dagger, and Gunther laughed. He stepped forwards and smacked Drake in the face with the end of the axe shaft, sending him reeling. Drake's eyes swung round at the horizon, head spinning like he was on a fairground ride. The half-track was lurching across an area of saltmarsh between the beach and the village, pursued now by Obenauer's eight-wheeler. German soldiers, dug into foxholes, saw the cavalcade coming and scattered out of the way.

'Here, sir!' MacTaggart yelled, and threw Drake a pointed shovel which had been strapped to the half-track's side. Drake caught it just in time to block a mighty swing from Gunther's axe. Then he spun the shovel in his hands and jabbed the metal end into the big German sergeant's guts.

The colossal SS man bent over, winded by the blow. Drake hit him again with the blade, sweeping it up to the side of the man's giant head. The blade cut through the exposed skin and glanced off his skull. Gunther groaned.

Drake saw they were speeding into the outskirts of the village now. There were just a couple of rows of fisherman's cottages on this side of the wall-banked canal. Antitank shells slammed in around them, as French gunners on the other side of the water fired at the speeding German vehicles. Recovering from the blow to his head, Gunther bellowed in rage. He pulled himself upright and swung the axe again, bringing it singing down in an oblique arc towards Drake's neck.

Drake frantically parried with the shovel's handle, which cracked under the force of the blow. It jarred his arms and sent a searing pain through the wounds on his chest. Now, instead of swinging again, Gunther grasped the shoulder of the axe haft and pressed down on it, using his massive weight to press it across Drake's throat. He got his other great arm behind Drake's head and squeezed. Drake began to choke. His windpipe was collapsing. The blood was cutting off from his brain, and he couldn't breathe. From the corner of his eye, he saw Butcher launch himself at the enormous German sergeant. Butcher hit him with a flying haymaker, and for a moment Gunther looked stunned. He let go, and Drake, dazed and off balance, slipped and crashed painfully onto his knees. He clung desperately onto the big man's belt, which was stuffed with grenades. He had an idea.

Gunther swung the axe shaft and sent Butcher sprawling. As Drake felt his legs go beneath him, he grasped at Gunther's waist to stop himself falling flat to the floor. The great German sergeant brought the wooden axe handle down towards the top of his head. Drake jerked back, trying to dodge away, but it hit him with a glancing blow. After a sickening moment, Drake let go and went down. The German sergeant kicked him back with a vast jackboot and stepped away to swing the axe again. Head reeling, Drake sprawled helplessly backwards onto the loadbay floor.

Drake saw Butcher get up and hit another German soldier on the other side of the half-track with the butt of his Bren gun. He saw MacTaggart pick up his dagger and begin slashing with it. He saw that the panzers were now following them into the town. He was dizzy from the crack on the skull, and the entire world seemed to be whirling around him. Gunther's pig eyes glittered with triumph as he began to swing the huge axe around, in a final, deadly sweep.

Drake weakly raised his left hand. Dangling from his grip was a small ceramic ball on a piece of string.

Gunther stopped, mid-swing. He stared at the ball in confusion, seeming to recognise it, then suddenly looked down at his belt as he realised what it meant. It was the priming string from a stick grenade. But which one?

Drake backed away. He reckoned the fuse would last four or five seconds, tops. Two or three had already gone.

Gunther dropped the axe and began flailing at his waistline, pulling out the grenades one by one and checking them.

Drake bellowed to MacTaggart and Butcher. 'Look out! Grenade. Get down!'

He dragged himself behind the Flak cannon's gunshield. Butcher, Leighton and MacTaggart threw themselves down into the footwell of the cab.

Gunther pulled out the last two grenades. They still had the caps on the bottom of the wooden shafts. He frowned. Then he looked down again. A final grenade was stuck into the top of his boot.

He reached down, eyes wide, and managed to pull it up. The cap and ceramic ball were missing. The grenade went off in a piercing, violent white crack.

Chapter 93

Drake stood up to get his bearings, head roaring from the detonation. He felt queasy. The entire loadbay of the half-track was covered in buckets of Sergeant Gunther's guts and blood.

Drake saw they were in amongst the village buildings now, racing along a narrow lane parallel to the canal, heading further inland, away from the sea. Behind the houses he caught glimpses of Obenauer's eight-wheeled command car, tearing up a parallel lane to their right. The Standartenführer was shouting orders into a headset mouthpiece.

Up ahead, Drake saw a Mark IV heavy panzer rumble across the lane. It pulled to a halt, blocking their path. The turret slowly traversed in their direction. It brought the half-track carefully into its sights. A hail of automatic fire erupted from the tank's machine gun. Rounds clashed into the front of the half-track's engine block.

'Left!' Drake yelled, but Leighton had already had the same idea. The ponderous machine swung around, crashing off a house wall in a rending din. Leighton kept his foot to the floor and forced it down an alley that was almost too narrow. The metal sides of the big machine screamed as they tore chunks from the cottage walls.

'Don't stop!' Drake shouted, and Leighton rammed it through the gears. The V12 Maybach engine roared, and then caught fire – a fuel line to one of the cylinders must have been hit. Drake saw through the shattered windscreen that the alley ran straight towards the canal. The engine was spitting flames now, and misfiring badly. Fuel jetted from one of the carburettors beneath the bonnet. A great clash of sound shook the alley as the panzer fired, and a building exploded behind them in a bright, cracking flash.

Leighton kept his foot pinned to the floor. They were heading for a marina that backed onto the canal. Fishing boats and yachts stood on the wharf, burnt, gutted or holed from the ongoing battle. Sunken craft dotted the waters. The panzer, now in pursuit, fired again, and a shell screamed down the alley to detonate against a house wall in a skull-ripping din. Cascades of bricks and rooftiles clattered down onto the half-track, missing the men by inches. The tank's machine gun fired again, but Drake was sheltered by the mass of the Flak gun and its shield.

'Reload!' he bellowed as he climbed into the gunner's seat.

The burning, dust-covered half-track roared along the narrow alley and burst onto the marina, shattering wooden boat hulls as it tore its way through. MacTaggart and Butcher hurried to reload more Flak magazines. German soldiers, who had taken up positions on the marina to fire in the opposite direction at the French, scattered or were run down screaming by the fiery half-track. Drake turned and stared ahead but it was hard to see anything through the smoke and flame that was now billowing back from the engine block. He caught glimpses of a concrete pier that jutted out into the canal, where it almost met a similar structure that projected from the other side, with only a narrow gap in between them. His heart jumped with sudden hope. It was a large canal lock, and the gap between the two concrete jetties was only about ten yards wide.

Machine guns opened fire from the French side of the canal. Drake had to hunker down behind the cab as the rounds slammed in. The heavy half-track careened, on fire, towards the pier's end, racing closer and closer in a clattering, raging din. From the opposite bank, well-hidden antitank canons and field artillery burst into life, but the shells screeched past to hit the heavy panzer that was chasing behind them. The panzer stalled, shot up and smoking. Then a wooden yacht splintered open and the massive eight-wheeled command car came crashing through. Standartenführer Obenauer was firing a machine gun at them from the superstructure at the top.

'The gun is yours, sir!' MacTaggart bawled out through the chaos, slamming the final magazine home.

Drake stomped down with both feet onto the pedals.

The Flak gun exploded into life. A storm of shells streaked across the boatyard to hit the command car in a cacophonic maelstrom. It was raked by rapid fire at point blank range, and went up in a blinding detonation.

'Hold onto your helmets!' Leighton shouted through the din. Drake looked over his shoulder as the half-track smashed through a barrier. In a blazing, roaring dash, it went straight on, full speed ahead, and flew off the edge of the pier.

'Jump!' Drake yelled, and he leapt from the seat as the heavy vehicle shot off the end of the concrete jetty. Tracks flailing, the great machine plummeted down, down towards the dark waters below. It plunged into the canal and the flaming engine extinguished itself in a cloud of steam. Behind them, on the marina, the eight-wheeled command car exploded in a ball of flame.

As Drake fell, stomach lifting inside him, he heard a cry from MacTaggart.

'I can't ruddy swim!'

He hit the water with a hard, shocking splash.

For a moment, everything was cold and dark underwater. Then Drake resurfaced, and above his head deafening gunfire erupted from both sides of the canal. The panzer, hit by French artillery again, was sheathed in a sheet of flame.

Drake struck out through the brackish water for the French side of the lock, and thrashed his way around the central pillar, away from the German side and out of sight. He saw Butcher grab MacTaggart by the scruff of the neck and haul him across the gap. For a moment it seemed they were forgotten in the confusion of a sudden battle raging above their heads. Drake gasped for breath as his men caught up, and clung to the walls in the lee of the concrete pillar.

After a moment, they swam on, and eventually found a rusted iron ladder. They began to climb. From above, on top of the wharf, machine guns bristled and faces peered over.

'*Halte-là*,' a French officer shouted down. 'Stop! Don't move!'

'We're British!' Drake gasped. He clung to the rusted rungs and gulped in a big, painful breath. He spoke in French. 'My name is Drake. I work for Major Lyle-Smith of the British Secret Intelligence Service.' He drew in another breath and tapped his chest, where the briefcase was still strapped and wrapped up tight with the canvas strips. 'I've got to get this to Lord Gort, and half the German army's trying to stop me. So let me climb up the *merde*-ing ladder before it's all too bloody late!'

PART V

DUNKIRK

MONDAY 27 MAY 1940

Chapter 94

BRITISH GHQ, KING LEOPOLD'S VILLA, LA PANNE, BELGIUM – 10:00HRS

CAPTAIN SIR PETER HIGHAM-DAVIES sat staring at the telephone, at a desk set up in the foyer of King Leopold's Villa, which stood grandly on the beachfront of the upmarket Belgian resort of La Panne. He flinched every time a shell shrieked down and crashed into the seafront. King Leopold, staunch ally of the British, had lent Lord Gort the villa to use as his GHQ now that the armies had been forced back to the coast. In better times, it would have had a wonderful view of the beach and the Channel, but for now it had heavy blankets hung over the sandbagged windows, and was full of trails of cables, telephone exchanges, and harassed-looking staff officers.

The captain twisted a pencil stub round and round in his hand. Any minute now, he was going to get a rocket from CIGS. The Chief of the Imperial General Staff, General Tiny Ironside, didn't have the picture of quite how bad it was here on the ground. And it was the captain's job to tell him. Communications were terse, to say the least. London didn't appreciate the severity of the situation. And the French, *my God, the French.* General Fagalde was asking the impossible. And as for Admiral Abrial – *well.*

The telephone rang.

Captain Higham-Davies jumped.

He reached out to answer it, but another hand descended onto the phone, preventing him from picking up the receiver.

He glanced quickly up.

A bloodstained young officer was looking down at him. His chest was bandaged beneath his tattered battledress jacket. Liquid seeped through the dressings in a vivid, shocking red. He was bedraggled, damp, covered in estuary mud, and reeking. He looked utterly exhausted. A large red welt ran down his forehead, and his hair was a striking dark, auburn red. His skin was burnt brown from the sun, and three days' worth of beard stubble covered his face. He held a damp, canvas-wrapped bundle in his arms. The telephone rang on and on beneath his hand.

Higham-Davies bristled. 'What the devil do you think you're doing?'

Drake didn't bother with the niceties. After having marched all night, 20 miles along beaches that were filling fast with stragglers from the BEF, he had precisely zero time left to waste. 'Where's Gort?'

'That's none of your business.' The captain glared up at him. 'Get your ruddy great mitt off the phone. I'm expecting a call from CIGS!'

'Sod CIGS,' Drake said. 'This is urgent.'

He released the phone and marched right past the adjutant's desk and into the villa's foyer, looking for the way to the war room.

Captain Higham-Davies stood up behind his desk. 'Stop! You can't go in there! You're for the bloody high jump! Provosts! Sentries! Stop that man! Place him under arrest!'

A pair of lance corporals of the military police appeared.

'Halt!' one of them barked, holding out a restraining arm. 'Stop right there, sir!'

Drake brushed the arm away. 'I have an urgent message for Lord Gort. Don't stand in my way.'

'Oh no you don't,' said a thin, reedy voice. Lieutenant-Colonel Cecil Hawker stepped from a side room into the hallway. 'I heard you were back. And I had a hunch that sooner or later you'd be coming right here.'

Behind Hawker came Sergeant Cronin, Captain Esmonde, and another sour-looking military policeman. They were all armed with service revolvers.

The colonel's eyes bulged behind his thick glasses. 'You're under arrest for desertion, Drake. You stole my ruddy scout car! The battalion's been in the thick of it, while you've been dodging action once again.'

Drake ignored him. The captain at the desk was now standing, but listening on the telephone and writing vigorously with a pencil on a pad. Drake whistled, and, moments later, MacTaggart, Butcher and Leighton tramped in through the front door, all armed to the teeth.

Shells moaned overhead and slammed into the buildings along the seafront. The floor of Leopold's Villa shuddered with the impacts. Plaster dust trickled down from cracks in the ceiling.

The provost at Colonel Hawker's side turned nervously to his comrades. 'Why don't we all act sensible now, and take this matter outside?'

At that moment, a car screeched to a halt at the steps of the villa. A voice carried in. A rough voice that Drake didn't recognise. 'Drake! Tennyson Drake!'

Hawker stared at the door.

Drake called out, 'In here!'

Two tough-looking sergeants that Drake had never seen before stepped in to the villa. They had Tommy guns at their sides and had no-nonsense faces, and itchy looking fingers on their triggers. One of them aimed to cover Butcher and MacTaggart. The other threatened the provost and Colonel Hawker with his gun.

'Who's Drake?' the shorter of the two men snapped. He had close-cropped hair and pockmarked skin.

'I am.'

'You're with us then,' the pockmarked sergeant said. 'Come here.'

Drake tried to move towards them, but he was held back by the provosts.

Behind the two tough-looking sergeants, a slim officer with a boyish face walked slowly in. He took a moment to take in the scene. He nodded to Drake. It was Major Lyle-Smith.

'Got your message. Had the devil of a job getting through the traffic. Now, Colonel,' he said, turning to Hawker. 'I'm afraid I'll have to require you to let him go.'

Hawker slowly shook his head. 'No chance. He's mine.'

For a moment, the three groups of men stood in an awkward standoff.

'Release him,' the sergeant with the pockmarked face said, pointing the Tommy gun at the nearest provost.

'Now look here, Sergeant—' Captain Esmonde began.

'I said let him go,' the tough-looking sergeant repeated.

The provosts reluctantly released Drake's arms. He stepped towards the major.

Hawker's eyes bulged behind his glasses as his glare shifted from Drake to the two men with machine guns, then to the major, then to Butcher, Leighton and MacTaggart. 'What the hell is this?' he spat. 'It's bloody mutiny, that's what! In GHQ, too!'

Major Lyle-Smith pointedly ignored him. The sergeants with the Tommy guns stood at his sides. He turned to Drake. 'Well?'

'Agent Viper's dead. I killed him,' Drake said. He began to unwrap the briefcase. '*Operationsbefehl Dämmerung*. It's all in here. Lord Gort needs to see it right away.'

'*Dämmerung*?' Lyle-Smith stopped dead. 'My God. You've cracked it?'

Drake nodded. He held up the tiepin. 'Agent Viper – also known as Édouard Lambert, a medical officer. He was just the middleman. But there's something I haven't figured out yet.' He held up the damp-looking oval playing card. The medieval fool with a gargoyle's face.

Lyle-Smith examined it. 'The knave of nooses. It's from a famous Flemish hunting deck. Where on Earth did you get it?'

Drake shook his head. It fitted. 'At first I thought it was Spain. But I was wrong. *Operationsbefehl Dämmerung* is all about Léon Degrelle.'

Lyle-Smith frowned for a moment. 'But the French have Degrelle.'

'Not anymore,' Drake said.

Lyle-Smith gazed levelly at him for a moment, then the penny dropped. His boyish face went pale. 'Excuse us, Colonel,' the major quietly said. 'We must see Lord Gort right away.'

Hawker spoke angrily. 'God damn you! *I'm* the ranking officer here.'

Lyle-Smith gave him a cold stare. 'You don't know me, Hawker. But I know you. This is GHQ. You're on my turf. I win.'

The two sergeants pointed their Tommy guns at Colonel Hawker.

Hawker gazed at Drake's men, and the two tough sergeants. 'But – but...' he spluttered. A note of petulance crept into his voice. 'The man's a menace! He stole my ruddy scout car! Who the hell d'you think you are?'

The boyish major gave Hawker a chilling smile. 'Lyle-Smith. You can look me up. Now, if you'll excuse us, we're going in to see Lord Gort, and we shan't take up any more of your time.'

Chapter 95

DRAKE FOLLOWED THE MAJOR towards the rear of the grand old house and down a flight of steps. Bundles of cables and telephone wires spilled down the staircase towards the basement. The building shook with a distant *crump-crump-crump* as, outside, German bombs detonated up and down the coast.

The basement was large, dimly lit, and had four deep rooms running off a central corridor, where staff officers and telephone operators were working frantically to keep control of an entire army that was in full, chaotic retreat. They found Lord Gort leaning over a mapstand, in a war room stuffed full of telephone operators, staff officers and adjutants. A small, sharp-faced French admiral was talking up to him in a bitter tone.

'Sir!' said Lyle-Smith.

Gort ignored him, instead turning to his interpreter. 'Why don't you tell the ruddy admiral in language he can understand that the answer's no! I simply cannot spare the men.'

Drake overheard muttered conversations from signals operators. It sounded bad. Front line units were coming under increasing pressure. One by one, the communications were dropping out as the positions were overrun.

A tall, slim, middle-aged general intercepted Drake and the major. He had slicked-back hair which was greying at the temples, and his service dress was immaculate and striped with red.

'Sir Henry,' Lyle-Smith began. 'We must speak with Lord Gort at once.'

Chief of Staff Lieutenant General Sir Henry Royds Pownall, DSO & Bar, MC, raised an eyebrow at the sight of Drake's bedraggled appearance. 'I see,' he said in a laconic tone. 'And who's your... guest?'

The major glanced at Drake, and a quick smile passed over his lips. 'Right now, he's the best man we've got.'

Pownall held up his hands, and tried to usher them back through the door. 'All in good time, Major. Lord Gort is rather busy, as you can see.'

But Lyle-Smith pushed past him, to looks of amazement from the senior staff in the room. Gort was still arguing with the French admiral.

'John!' Lyle-Smith called out. 'Would you bloody well shut up and listen for a moment?'

Gort slowly turned as the room fell silent. All the staff officers and typists looked up.

Lord Gort raised himself to his full height. 'I do hope you have good reason for addressing me in that impertinent manner, Major.'

Lyle-Smith stepped forward. 'Hear us out, sir. Then you can throw us out on our ears if you think we're wrong.'

Gort glowered at him, then turned to face Drake. He stared in bewilderment for a moment. Then, slowly, recognition dawned. 'Ha! You again?' He looked Drake up and down. 'But not dressed up as a provost this time.' He shot a look at the major, with small, hard eyes. 'What in God's name are you two playing at? You can't just barge in here and demand an audience. There are proper channels!'

Drake stiffened under Lord Gort's gaze, but said nothing. He heard the distant concussion of shells hitting the coastal resort outside.

Gort grunted. 'Well I'll say something for you, Drake, you don't give up easily, do you?' He turned to the admiral. 'I do beg your pardon. Would you excuse us for a moment?'

His eyes flicked down to the bloodstained parcel in Drake's hands.

Drake peeled the damp canvas from the black calfskin briefcase, then held it out. '*Operationsbefehl Dämmerung*, sir.'

Gort studied the black leather, the embossed eagle and the swastika. The three bullet holes that were burnt through the centre of it. '*Dämmerung*?'

'We've finally broken it,' said the major.

Gort took the briefcase. He opened it and peered at the papers inside. He extracted a couple of pages, and his brow creased as he struggled to read the blackletter script.

'German order of battle, eh? Where the devil did you get this, man?'

'It's a long story, sir.'

Gort examined the papers in the dim light of the electric bulbs that hung from the ceiling. 'Henry, get this translated right away, would you? There may be some useful information.' He turned to Drake. 'But there's a damned protocol, Drake. You can't just come barging in like you own the place. Next time—'

Drake put his hand on the briefcase to stop Pownall in his tracks. 'There won't be a next time, sir. It's urgent.'

Pownall looked pointedly at Gort. 'Admiral Abrial, John.'

Gort grunted. 'I must say I don't like your methods, Drake. But there was something in what you said last time round, if I recall.' He shook his head. 'Hard military intelligence is what we're after. No more rumours and lies and chasing bloody phantoms. It's too late for that, by far.'

Drake gestured to the case. 'This *is* the hard military intelligence you've been looking for, sir. The fate of the entire BEF is hanging on what's inside.'

Gort considered for a moment, rubbed at his face, then glanced at Pownall. Pownall tapped his watch.

'Alright,' Gort said. 'You've got thirty seconds, Drake. The floor is yours. And for your sake, this better be good.'

Drake looked at the great general. 'It's not good sir. It's bad. Very bad.' A shell crashed into the buildings nearby and shook the room.

Chapter 96

Major Lyle-Smith gave Drake the nod. Drake took two steps over to Gort's mapstand and picked up a chinagraph pencil. He circled Gravelines, the coastal fishing village on the western side of Dunkirk, where they'd crossed the canal, in France.

'The French are here,' he said. 'They're holding the Aa canal. A very strong defensive position.'

Gort nodded.

'The Germans know that the BEF is trapped,' Drake continued. 'We're here.' He rapped the pointer on the coast at La Panne, just across the Belgian border.

Pownall sniffed. 'We are not unfamiliar with our own location.'

Drake ignored him and drew a loop around from Dunkirk in the south west, up the coast stretching eastwards as far as the town of Nieuport, twenty-five kilometres to the east, well over the Belgian border. The loop stretched twenty-odd miles inland. He drew a rectangle east of the coastal town of Nieuport. 'The Belgian army is up here, past the frontier. That leaves the BEF here, falling back towards the coast, all along this sector from Dunkirk to Nieuport. Am I right?'

'I know where my own army is,' Gort said. 'What's your point?'

Drake lifted a map from the briefcase. He presented it to Gort. 'So do the Germans, sir.'

Gort looked at the map.

'How the hell—'

Drake drew a huge crescent all around the Allied lines. 'Just hang on a minute. German Army Group A, is here. Army Group B, with the majority of the panzer divisions, down here.'

Drake drew arrows, pressing in on the Allied pocket. He pulled some further papers from the case and presented them to Sir Henry Pownall.

Pownall stared.

Drake continued. 'If you'll take a look, sir, the German orders are very detailed. They specify a rapid advance towards Nieuport, and then a full-scale attack on the British sector's flank.'

Gort snorted. 'Just where exactly did you come across these plans?'

'Standartenführer Hermann Obenauer of the Sicherheitsdienst des Reichsführers - SS.'

Lyle-Smith spoke up. '*Ausland* Department of the Reich Security Main Office: Foreign Policy, sir.'

'Fakes!' sighed Pownall. 'How do you know they're not fakes?'

Drake opened up his shirt to show the bloody bandages. 'If they were fakes they might have made it easier for me to take them. Instead they sent half the Wehrmacht after me to bring them back. And why would they need to create false plans? They're beating hell out of us anyway.'

Gort's brow darkened. A murmur ran through the room. 'So what was the *Ausland* Department doing with Wehrmacht army orders?'

Major Lyle-Smith nodded, encouraging Drake to go on.

'That's where it gets interesting, sir,' he continued. 'Operation *Dämmerung* is a political matter. But I'll come to that in a minute.'

He turned back to the map and drew a great scything arrow across the territory to the north of the BEF. 'According to these orders, the German Sixth Army is about to outflank us. They're planning to sweep around between the BEF and the coast, and roll up our lines with a surprise attack from the direction of Nieuport, to the east.'

Pownall snorted out a laugh. 'Surprise attack, my foot! Talk sense, man! As you yourself have just said, there are twenty fighting divisions of our allies to the east of Nieuport. The entire Belgian army is there! It would take the Germans days to break through. If they tried something like that, we'd be able to hear the guns from here!'

Lord Gort's gaze went from Drake to Lyle-Smith. 'Well, Drake? We're all terribly busy -'

Drake waited. He tried to clear his mind. He needed to be very precise. When he spoke, it was as calmly as he could manage. 'These orders come from the very top, sir.' He brandished the briefcase. 'The whole of German Army Group B is being ordered to do something unexpected. A complete re-routing of supply lines. A sudden pivot of strategy. Why?'

The two men looked at him.

Drake rapped the map with the pointer. 'Don't you see, sir? The Germans know something we don't.'

Lord Gort examined the map. His brows knitted as he tried to make sense of it. 'And what exactly is it that we don't know?'

Drake lay a dozen pages of the German movement orders out on a planning table as Lord Gort and General Pownall looked silently on. He emphasised the lines of advance on the map with thick, bold strokes of the chinagraph pencil. 'The German orders are very specific. If you will refer to the documents, you will see they do not use the verb *angreifen,* which means to attack. They use the verb *vorrücken*, to advance. Nieuport is not referred to as *Kampfziel,* the field objective. It's marked as the *Ausgangslinie*: the starting position, the jump-off line. When I saw that, I knew something was wrong. Terribly wrong.'

'That's exactly my point,' Pownall scoffed. 'It's ludicrous. Nieuport can't possibly be the starting position. It's ten miles behind the Belgian front lines.'

Drake swung around and pointed the chinagraph pencil at the general. 'Precisely.'

Lord Gort's eyes narrowed. He paused for a moment before speaking. 'I think you'd better explain yourself.'

'These orders can only mean one thing, sir,' Drake said. He suddenly realised that the whole room had stopped its bustle. Everybody now was listening in: stenographers, wireless and telephone operators, staff officers and runners. Every officer and naval attaché. Drake saw that Colonel Hawker was at the door, watching. Even the French admiral, Abrial, squinting towards them, was listening intently to what he had to say.

Drake took a deep breath. He was taking a hell of a risk. He had no real evidence to support the great allegation he was going to make. It was just inference, guesswork and supposition. Phantoms. *Hugger mugger stuff.* If he was wrong it would ruin him. There would be no way back. There was really no evidence at all, except – *except that it had to be true.*

Drake clenched and unclenched his fists. His palms were drenched with sweat. He slowly exhaled, and the silence deepened. 'Major Lyle-Smith told me there was something rotten in the Third Republic of France. And he said it goes right the way to the top.' Drake paused, summoning the courage to say it aloud. 'One of our allies is a turncoat, sir.'

Everybody turned towards the French Admiral Abrial.

The little man bristled. 'How dare you! No Frenchman will betray the Alliance. *Jamais!* Never!'

Drake directed his attention towards the major himself. 'You were half right, sir. The admiral is correct. There *is* something rotten, but it's not the French at all. We were barking up the wrong tree.' He turned back to the generals. 'Are you familiar with the name Léon Degrelle?'

Pownall nodded and furrowed his brow. A silence ensued.

Lyle-Smith spoke up. 'Degrelle, for those of you who are unfamiliar with the political state of our Allies, is leader of the Catholic Rexist Party. *The rule of the monarch on earth and Christ the King in heaven* is his line. He's a fascist, a *confidant* of Mussolini and Hitler, and a pal of Mosely's back home. Like Mosely, he's also a monarchist. Closer to the Italian model than the German one, but still, very palatable to Hitler and a thorough-going ally to the Nazi cause. In all likelihood, he's on his way to the Provincial Governor's Palace at this moment, if he's not already there.'

Drake picked up the thread. 'Operation *Dämmerung*,' he said. '*Dämmerung* means twilight. The end of an era. The passing of kings. *Dämmerung* starts with Léon Degrelle, but that's not where it ends. Degrelle escaped French custody three days ago and has been plotting with Obenauer of the *Ausland* Department of the Reich Security Main Office. Agent Viper was the go-between. Agent Viper's real name was Édouard Lambert, a medical officer. He graduated from the *École royale militaire* in 1922.' Drake gestured around at the room they were in. The generals hadn't picked up the connection yet. He remembered Axelle's words. *He was a distinguished private physician in all the best circles.*

Lyle-Smith spoke up. 'Lambert was classmates with the Duke of Brabant and was his personal physician before the war. And he worked for VSSE. That's how we know of him.'

Lord Gort's piercing eyes bored into his. 'The Duke of Brabant? Where's all this leading?'

Drake turned to the major. 'The Duke of Brabant, sir, is the heir to the throne, much like the Prince of Wales back home. That was his title at the time.' There was a deadly silence in the room. All eyes were on Drake. 'Don't you see?'

Gort spoke again. He looked as though he was about to explode. 'I'm not a ruddy mind reader, Drake! Spit it out!'

Drake felt a shudder of anxiety run through him. It was a terrible, shocking accusation to make. It was unthinkable. It was treason. If he was wrong, they'd crucify him. But if he was right—

Dear God. He had to be right.

Drake tapped the order sheets that he held in his hands. 'Look sir. He's going to let the Germans march right through unopposed.'

'Who, Drake?' Gort demanded, fists clenched. 'Who?'

Drake swallowed, his throat suddenly dry. 'The traitor is King Leopold of the Belgians, sir. He's made a secret deal with Hitler behind our backs.'

Chapter 97

A HUSH FELL ON the room. Just the background thud of distant shelling. Nobody moved. A phone rang but it was quickly silenced.

Lord Gort gave Drake a thunderous look. 'Why would Leopold do such a thing?'

Drake felt the pressure of his gaze, the weight of all the eyes from around the room. 'You will have seen in the papers that Queen Wilhemina of the Netherlands arrived a few days ago in London as a refugee, with two cardboard suitcases to her name. By treating with the Germans, King Leopold could hang onto his throne.'

Lord Gort clamped his jaw shut and Drake could see the muscles of his face working beneath the skin. 'I don't believe it,' the old general said. 'Pierlot, the Belgian premier, has sworn to fight to the end. And Belgium is a democracy, is it not? It's Pierlot's decision, and his alone. He would never give in while there's still any hope of fighting on.'

Major Lyle-Smith coughed before speaking. 'Who's the Belgian commander-in-chief?'

'General Van Overstratten,' said Gort. 'That pompous fool.'

Sir Henry Pownall shook his head. 'Actually, sir, Van Overstratten's not technically the C-in-C. In Belgian law, the king is the Commander-in-Chief.'

Drake spoke up. 'And King Leopold is about to stage a *coup*.'

'A *coup*?' Gort swivelled round. 'Think carefully before you make accusations of such magnitude.'

Drake suddenly felt the pressure. Was it him, or was the room getting smaller? The heavy walls of Leopold's Villa were pressing in. 'Léon Degrelle is working directly for the Nazis. I believe he and Lambert – Agent Viper, as he was known to us – have convinced the king to seize power, against the will of the Belgian parliament. Degrelle will serve up Belgium to the Nazis on a plate, with the entire BEF and the French northern armies for dessert. And for his service, Degrelle will want to rule a puppet Belgian parliament on Hitler's behalf.'

Drake saw that his words were having an effect at last. His audience were stunned into silence.

Drake pushed on. 'If Leopold lets the Wehrmacht through the Belgian lines... well, it will mean the end of the Allied fight. The Germans will outflank the BEF at Nieuport, and I don't need to tell you what would happen if the panzer divisions get in amongst our unarmed men on the beaches. Destruction of the Allied armies. A complete capitulation, or a bloodbath of biblical proportions. There'll be nothing left to stop Hitler reaching British shores, nothing but the Royal Navy, and even they can't do it on their own. We're talking about total victory for the Nazis.'

Lord Gort narrowed his eyes. After a moment's consideration, he spoke. 'What you say has merit, if – and I say *if* – it's true. But where's the evidence?'

Drake felt lightheaded and unsteady on his feet as he spoke. It was strange to think that the fate of nations was riding on his words. He held up the briefcase once more. 'It's all in here, sir. See for yourself. The entire German order of battle, and the Wehrmacht's detailed plans. Get it translated if you must, but hurry. Please hurry. If Leopold goes over, the Belgian army will surely go with him.' Gort seemed unconvinced. Drake went on. 'Who would you serve, sir, if you had to choose? Your elected parliament, or your king?'

Lord Gort gave him a glowering look.

'You go too far, Drake,' Sir Henry Pownall said in an ominous tone.

Drake suddenly felt the weight of the accusations he was making. The General Staff were aristocrats and royalists to a man, and he was asking if they would commit treason – hypothetically at least. He faltered for a moment. But he might as well get hanged for a pig as a sheep. He pushed on further.

'If Leopold succeeds... well, the late queen of Belgium was a Swedish princess. Sweden, Norway, Netherlands, the royal houses are all closely related. Even Britain. Leopold is cousin to King George VI. And if the house of Saxe-Coburg and Gotha could be turned...'

Major Lyle-Smith stepped quickly in. 'I believe what Mr Drake is trying to say is that such an act could have significant political ramifications all across Europe.'

All eyes fell on Lord Gort, who stood in hunched tension, deep in thought.

Eventually, he straightened up. 'King Leopold would not do such a dirty deed! Betray us to the Germans? Never! Fairweather! Where the hell is Fairweather?'

A junior naval officer emerged from behind the more senior men.

'You're supposed to be on the mission to the Belgian king, Fairweather! What have you got to say for yourself?'

Fairweather rubbed his hands together nervously. 'Well, sir, I have been making my reports, but I don't know if you have had the time to read them?'

'Stop dithering, man!' Gort bellowed. 'Out with it!'

'Yes sir. Sorry sir. I've spoken with Admiral Keyes. King Leopold has been sending some rather mixed messages. *The time will come when we can no longer hold out* and suchlike. But we would expect him to give us at least twenty-four hours' notice if he intended to capitulate. Otherwise—'

Fairweather left the sentence hanging.

Gort spoke through tightly clenched teeth. 'Otherwise, what?'

'Well,' said Fairweather, 'Otherwise he'd be rather dropping us in it, wouldn't he, sir?'

'Ha!' Gort exclaimed. He slammed his hand down onto a table, making the telephone jump. 'Dropping us in it! Ha! The understatement of the bloody century! What of Pierlot?'

Fairweather twitched. 'He's still vowing to fight on...' he looked rather shamefaced. 'From Paris.'

Sir Henry Pownall spoke quietly. 'I hate to say it, John, but I do believe young Drake here may be onto something. I don't believe for a moment that our own monarch would be swayed, but I have never trusted those foreign cousins an inch.'

Gort straightened up and paced back and forth for a few seconds. 'Politics is for the politicians. What concerns me are the military consequences. If this is true, Leopold would be letting the German Sixth Army in at the back door. They'd roll us up like a doormat. It would be the end of the BEF, that's a racing certainty, and we shan't let that happen.' He turned on Fairweather. 'Get Belgian GQG on the phone!'

Fairweather quailed before he spoke. 'King Leopold's at the Provincial Governor's Palace in Bruges.'

Gort's eyes seemed to pierce the young man's skin. 'Well, get hold of the King himself, if you must! Do it man!'

Fairweather scrambled to get a line from the telephone operators.

Gort shook his head. 'God damn it! He's supposed to be our bloody ally!'

At his side, Sir Henry Pownall rubbed his chin. 'Although Leopold never really *has* been our ally, has he, John? Think of his declaration of neutrality in '38. At one stroke that rendered the Maginot line ineffectual, and ripped up the entire French defensive strategy. Then there was his refusal to let us in before the invasion began. He's followed Belgium's interests, to be sure, but they have never been quite the same interests as our own.'

Gort clenched his jaw and spoke through gritted teeth. 'No. It cannot be. It just cannot be!'

Fairweather stood up. He looked as though he wanted to cry. 'They hung up on me, sir.'

Gort just shook his head, unable to comprehend. 'But if he was surrendering, why wouldn't he *tell* us?'

Drake coughed. 'King Leopold would get much better terms if he gave the Germans the element of surprise, rather than just surrendering when he could no longer hold out.'

Gort paused before he spoke again. He screwed up his face as he tried to swallow the distasteful information, but the logic was inescapable. 'Leopold sees he's beaten, and it's his only card left to play,' he exclaimed at last. 'He's going to trade us in to keep his throne! The rat! The bloody rat!'

Major Lyle-Smith spoke quietly. 'There's nothing we can do to stop it, John. It's an internal Belgian matter. We've nobody there. All we can do is try to mitigate the consequences for Great Britain.'

The room was suddenly abuzz with discussion, arguments springing up everywhere.

'Silence!' Gort snapped around and turned back to the map. 'Drake – I pray your information is wrong, but we can't run the risk that you might be right. We must take steps to defend ourselves against this – this *eventuality*. When is all this supposed to happen? How much time do we have?'

Drake rifled through the papers in the briefcase. He pulled out a typewritten sheet.

The room fell silent once more. All the faces were watching. Gort. Pownall. Lyle-Smith. Even Hawker had come down to the basement room. All the adjutants and staff officers, stenographers and telephonists, all were hanging on Drake's words.

He took a deep breath. His palms were greased with sweat. 'I'm sorry, sir, but I've rather lost track of the days of the week.' He held up the papers and examined them. 'Zero hour on the twenty-eighth of May,' he said, looking up. 'To our way of thinking, that's double-oh, double-oh on the night of the twenty seventh.' He stared around at the looks of alarm that were spreading through the room. He shot a look at his wristwatch. It was already almost noon. 'Am I right in thinking that that would be midnight tonight?'

Chapter 98

BRITISH GHQ, KING LEOPOLD'S VILLA, LA PANNE, BELGIUM – 15:00HRS

Lord Gort had gathered his generals, summoned from their Corps HQs along the coast. It was a *Who's Who* of the general staff of the BEF. There were miles of red stripe everywhere, and acres of gleaming brass. Drake recognised some of the faces. General Alan Brooke, commander of II Corps, had a prominent hooked nose, a wide black moustache and round glasses, and a surprisingly mild voice with a lisp. He saw the beak-like face and grey moustache of his own Corps commander, Lieutenant-General Michael Barker. General Fagalde, commander of the French land forces, had white hair and a pale face beneath a kepi adorned with half a pound of gold braid. There were other generals that Drake did not recognise, and whose names he didn't catch. He'd never seen so many high-ups together in one small room. Their looks of disapproval at Drake's shabby get-up changed to nods and handshakes when Pownall began to explain the value of the documents he'd brought. All the officers began talking at once.

Gort stood in front of the mapboard, and drew a great sweeping arrow round behind the retreating British army.

'If this intelligence is correct,' he boomed, 'The Belgian king has done a deal with Hitler. The entire BEF is about to be outmanoeuvred and outflanked.'

The room fell silent.

'Alan,' Gort continued, nodding to the dark-haired General Brooke, 'this is your bag.' He drew a line on the mapboard overlay with a chinagraph pencil, from the coast, following the line of rivers and canals. 'We're faced with an almost impossible situation. There's very little we can do. If the panzers get across at Nieuport – well, I don't need to tell you the consequences. Somehow we've to magic up a new defensive line from the coast at Nieuport-les-Bains, to Nieuport town, and all the way inland to Furnes – a distance of eight or nine miles. We must slam the door shut.' He slapped his hand onto the map, causing the board to shudder. 'Jerry wants to flank us. By God, we refuse him the flank!'

General Brooke raised his eyebrows behind his round glasses. He took a second to absorb the information before replying. 'The men in the rear echelons are in complete disarray, sir. Some still have their rifles, but they've lost all of their heavy equipment and none are in coherent units. That means we'd need to withdraw at least fifteen thousand fighting men from the defensive lines – men who are already in contact with the enemy, under severe pressure, and in retreat. And then we must conduct a ten-mile wheel under the noses of the German artillery. The troops will have to move just behind, if not through, the front lines of a fierce fight that is already underway all along the perimeter. And we could only do it under cover of darkness, otherwise we'll be cut to pieces.'

Gort nodded. 'Correct.'

Brooke studied the map. 'It'll be damned near impossible, and liable to turn into a fiasco. A withdrawal under pressure is the hardest damned thing in the book. If Jerry guesses what we're up to, a whole division could be wiped out to a man. The line will be breached, and – well, need I say more? It would be risking our entire defensive perimeter. And what's more, it would be a footrace. But if this –' and he waved a limp hand in Drake's direction, '—if this is true, if we don't get to the Nieuport bridges before Jerry does, we might as well hang up our hats right now.'

'I am aware it will be difficult, Alan, but can it be done?' A heavy weariness underscored Gort's words.

Brooke rubbed his forehead. He hesitated.

A narrow-faced major general piped up from the back of the room. 'The Third Division will do it, sir!'

All eyes swivelled to stare at the lean, sharp-faced general. He shot a look back at Gort, with a piercing, bright stare.

'Damned good job we spent the winter practicing night manoeuvres, eh?' The man's sharp voice cut through the room. 'While Barker's lot were catching VD in the *estaminets*, my men were on exercise, under fire conditions, night after night.'

Across the room, General Barker looked horrified.

Gort gazed at Brooke, then at the other general. 'Well? Can you do it?'

Brooke opened his mouth to reply but the whippet-faced general talked over him. 'My men will do anything I bloody well tell them to do. There are no weak links in *my* chain of command.

General Fagalde, the French land commander, scoffed. 'Withdrawing men from the front line and marching them under the German noses? You will need a miracle not to be overrun.'

The outspoken major general turned his small, bright eyes pointedly at the Frenchman. 'I'll leave miracles to the Royal Navy,' he said. 'All we need is damned good discipline and a pair of cast iron balls.'

The room fell silent for a moment. Nobody knew quite where to look.

General Brooke politely coughed. 'If this intelligence is wrong, sir, we'd be handing the BEF to the Germans with a needless, panicked manoeuvre.'

Gort rubbed his hand across his face, then pivoted his large frame to glare at Major Lyle-Smith. 'What are the chances that this intelligence *is* wrong?'

The major ran a hand over his thinning hair. 'It's our best appreciation of the situation, sir.' His boyish face seemed suddenly old as he turned to Drake. 'Is it wrong? You do understand what's riding on this.'

Drake saw that they were laying the entire responsibility at his door. 'I understand the gravity of the situation, sir.'

All eyes in the room were fixed on him.

'Well, Drake?' Gort snapped, breaking the moment's silence. 'Is there any shadow of doubt in your mind? I do not intend to preside over the worst defeat in British military history on a whim. So, I ask again, is there any chance the intelligence is wrong? The fate of nations is riding on your words.'

The fate of nations. The hairs prickled on Drake's arms. He took a breath, and his heart thudded madly in his chest. 'There is no doubt in my mind, sir.'

Gort nodded, then smacked his hands together. 'Get to it, then, gentlemen. The British Empire, nay, the entire civilised world is depending on our actions this day.'

Across the room, the lean-looking major general gave a sudden, dry smile. He nodded to the assembled brass hats. 'The Third Division won't let you down. You can put your last shilling on that.'

'I already have,' said Gort. There was a moment's quiet. Then he spoke again. 'Come on then, snap to it, everyone!'

The general staff jumped, finding a higher gear that they didn't know was possible. Before they had been frantic, but now they worked with a focused, deathly precision, up against the clock. Orders were written. Maps charted and copies made. Layback positions. Thinning of troops from the front line. Artillery SOS fire coordinates. Air cover – *what bloody air cover*? Transport for fifteen thousand men, organised with zero notice, amid the chaos of an entire continent's bloody rout.

Gort looked around the room, then addressed the French general, Bertrand Fagalde. 'My compliments to General Weygand. With the Belgians out of it, we'll have no more talk of any counterattack. We simply cannot spare the men. We'd be overrun in an instant. There's only one thing for it now.' He turned to a blonde-haired naval captain who was standing alertly nearby. 'How long do we need?'

'As long as we can possibly get, sir. Might I hope for forty-eight hours?'

Gort grunted. 'Forty-eight hours? That'll be a stretch. But forty-eight hours it is. Get me a line to London. We press on at full speed. The useless mouths have already embarked. It's the fighting men now. *Dynamo*'s the word.'

Staff in the HQ stopped what they were doing.

They took in a collective breath.

Dynamo.

General Fagalde put his head to one side. 'May I ask what exactly is *Dynamo*?'

Gort drew himself up. 'I suggest you speak with your commander-in-chief. My orders, now, come directly from London.'

The French general stared up at the tall figure of Lord Gort. 'You are leaving.' He snorted with derision. 'First Belgium, and now perfidious Albion. France has been your true ally, and you stab her in the back. You abandon us in our hour of need. Have you British no shame?'

Gort's eyes blazed with fury. 'What, may I ask, would you have us do?'

Fagalde's mouth turned downwards at the edges, and his head jerked back, as he strived to look down his nose at the taller Lord Gort. 'Fight on, to save your British honour.'

Gort's hands clenched into fists. They turned white at the knuckles. 'Honour? You don't win wars with ruddy honour!'

The Frenchman spun on his heel and strode angrily out of the room.

Gort shook his head. 'Honour! Damn that man! Wars are won by any means necessary. Even if that means swimming home, roundly whipped, with our tails between our legs. *Dynamo!'* he bellowed, and he stalked out of the room after General Fagalde.

Drake looked around. Everybody except him seemed to know what Lord Gort was talking about. Telephone operators sprang into action.

Officers gathered around maps, instantly in deep discussion. The naval captain collected his staff around him. One of them raced for the door. In this new emergency, Drake was completely forgotten.

He leaned over and hissed to the nearest telephonist: 'What the hell is *Dynamo*?'

But before he could get an answer, he felt the rap of a cane on his shoulder.

'You! Drake, is it?'

Drake jumped to attention, and saluted. 'Second Lieutenant Tennyson Drake, sir! First Battalion, South Devonshire Regiment.'

The lean, hawkish major general took him in with sharp, narrow eyes. His voice was as thin and pinched as his face. 'You're to come with me,' he snapped. 'We'll see if you were right.'

Drake followed the general out of the villa and onto the promenade, where his staff car, a six-cylinder Humber, was waiting. The driver smartly opened the rear door, and the general got in. Drake hesitated. Did he mean for him to follow, or go with him in his car? Then from the corner of his eye, he saw Colonel Hawker stalking towards him. He hurried around to the other side of the car and hopped in.

The general contemplated him coldly for a moment, then frowned. 'You're bleeding on my upholstery.'

Drake looked down. 'So I am, sir.' The canal water had played havoc with the dressings on his chest. He'd be lucky if he didn't get a fatal infection.

The general snorted. 'I suppose we'd better get you patched up. And might I suggest a wash? You're pungent, Drake. Bloody pungent.' He rapped his cane on the glass partition that divided them from the driver. 'Divisional HQ.'

As the driver started the engine, Colonel Hawker strode up to the car and knocked on the general's window. The general wound it down.

'Sir –' Hawker began. 'That man there, Drake. He's one of my officers, you know –'

The sharp-faced major general shot a look sharply up at him. 'Bugger off.'

Chapter 99

FURNES, NEAR DUNKIRK, BELGIUM – 22:00HRS

TWENTY-FIVE POUNDER FIELD GUNS thumped, throwing shells overhead in the darkening sky. Their impacts flashed in the distance. Dozens of lorries lined up, one behind another. Drake saw that the transports had no headlights. Just a small red taillight, hidden beneath the rear of the vehicle. The general had obviously done his homework. They could drive in convoy at night, each following the one in front like a line of Indian elephants, without giving the game away to the prowling spotter planes of the Luftwaffe. The Third Division was finally on the move.

Men ran back in echelons from the front lines, lining up to clamber into the lorries. On the front, the last men to disengage would keep up a constant stream of fire to disguise their departure. The field guns kept thumping over their heads to keep up the deception. If the Germans got a whiff of what was going on, they'd be slaughtered.

Drake found the major general where his staff was decamping into a command truck. He came to attention and saluted. He'd been seen by the general's medical officer, who had stuffed him with salves and sulfonamides and tablets for the pain. He'd acquired new kit from a staff batman, which was clean and pressed. He'd even managed to have the luxury of a cold bath and a quick shave.

The general glowered. 'Better, Drake. Much better. You almost look fit to be an officer of His Majesty's Armed Forces. Ride with me. We'll soon find out whether your hunch is fact or fiction.'

The Royal Artillery kept up a constant, thumping barrage of fire overhead, and the German guns responded in kind, with counter-battery fire. As night fell, it created the most fantastical scene. The entire fighting force of the Third Division, close to fifteen thousand men, drove through the thickening darkness between the opposing lines of guns. The shells flew from both sides in glowing parabolas, which arced high overhead. To the men in the trucks, it was as though they were driving through a long tunnel made of fireworks and fairy lights. If they were discovered, the German artillery would rain down hell on the slow-moving column of vehicles, but the major general seemed supremely confident.

'Training, Drake. Preparation in operational conditions. That's what those other fools don't understand. The Germans do it. They were ready for war. We were not. *Training*. Remember it. A man will do almost anything you tell him to, if he knows and is practiced in exactly what is required.'

Drake nodded. He stared up at the lights and gritted his teeth, expecting any minute for the shells to start exploding among the lorries. All this was happening because of him. It was agonising to watch. What if he was wrong? He began to wonder if somehow he'd just dreamed the whole thing up. Coils of anxiety slid through his guts. He shoved that terrifying thought aside. Instead, he tried to cross-reference everything in his mind to be doubly certain.

The French had been holding Degrelle, in Calais – why? It was one of the closest French ports to the Belgian border. The strange medieval playing card, the knave of nooses, was Flemish – the culture of the Low Countries that included Holland and much of Belgium. And something else clicked. He pulled MacTaggart's lucky tiepin from his pocket. The Saltire. *Crux decussata, raguly*, Bill Lucas had said. *The Valois Dukes of Burgundy ruled significant swathes of Eastern France and the Low Countries way back in the fifteenth century*. It had been resurrected as a symbol not only for Franco's fascists. It was being used by Degrelle's Belgian Rexist Party as well. It all added up, apart from just one thing.

Axelle. What was her part in all this? She worked for VSSE, and she had clearly been against the fascist plot, but why had she been so unhelpful to her allies, and in particular to him? Why had she not simply explained what was going on? It didn't make any sense, and he felt a dark, uncomfortable malaise swirling around his insides. It was a last, incongruous piece of information that simply didn't fit.

Big guns thumped in the distance, and shells crashed down on either side of the convoy in the darkness. The lorries kept stopping, then jerking back into motion. Drake slipped in and out of a stupor. He was tired. *God*, but he was so bloody tired. His chest wounds ached like hell. Every time he drifted towards real sleep, he jerked awake as rumours came down the line. *The enemy were onto them. False alarm – it was just a burst tyre*. And each time, the procession started up again, waking him with another discomforting jolt. The thoughts started racing round, keeping him from rest. It was a long, slow, fearful, enervating drive, and despite the tension that was palpable in the air, the strain of the last few days was telling. Drake's eyes kept closing of their own accord, then he'd wake not knowing where he was, veering between panic, terror, and the urge to suddenly fall into an exhausted coma.

At one point in the night, after a particularly long, nervous wait, the general's voice came through the gloom.

'Speak now, before it's too late. There'll be no repercussions. We can still get back before the Germans find out we're gone.' Drake could feel the man's eyes boring into him in the darkness. 'There are a third of a million British soldiers caught here between Jerry and the sea. On your word, and your word alone, we're jeopardising the entire defence of the BEF's perimeter. You'd better be bloody sure, Drake. *Are* you sure?'

'Quite certain,' Drake said. But it was far from the truth. He had only to imagine the panzers in amongst the crowds of retreating men of the BEF, and a thousand small doubts went off like a belt of ammunition in a bonfire. What was it that was bothering him? Was he missing anything? There was only one thing he hadn't been able to figure out. He stared out as the vehicles moved slowly through the dark. *Axelle.*

He glanced at his watch, his father's trench watch. It was two minutes to midnight. Two minutes to zero hour. Out there, somewhere, it was all happening right now. If he was right, King Leopold was signing a treaty with the Germans, and as soon as pen was set to paper, the German Sixth Army would begin to advance. The Third Division was still creeping slowly across the Belgian countryside. Drake feared they'd be too late. He rubbed at his face again, pulled knots in his hair. It was one guess on top of another, piled up like a mountain of cards. A small gust of wind, one wrong assumption, and the whole stack would fall down.

As though sensing his thoughts, the general watched, eyes piercing through the darkness.

'If you're right, we must get there in time, we must stop them from seizing the bridges, or we're facing annihilation. If you're wrong, our weakened perimeter will collapse and we'll be overrun.'

The general paused for a second, before slamming his hand down hard onto the arm of his chair. 'If you're wrong, Drake, I'll throw you to the baying bloody wolves.'

TUESDAY 28 MAY 1940

Chapter 100

NIEUPORT, BELGIUM – 04:00HRS

The sky was beginning to lighten as the lorries came to a halt. Drake snapped awake. It was four in the morning. He knew that even if the Germans had begun to cross the Belgian front lines at midnight, it would still take them hours to make it the ten miles through to the coast in force, here where the key bridges of Nieuport lay. The Belgian army had to be informed and disarmed, defences dismantled. Drake prayed to God that the Third Division had arrived in time.

The general jumped to his feet as the vehicle stopped. 'So. Now we'll see.'

Outside, in the chill coastal air, they squinted through a pre-dawn grey. Drake followed the general and two of his staff officers as they were led forwards by a heavily-camouflaged man to reconnoitre the position from a small, grassy knoll. There was a light sea mist lingering in the air, obscuring the view. Through borrowed field glasses, Drake could just make out the shapes of the Nieuport bridges. When the mist cleared a little, they could see figures on the nearest structure. Drake stared through the lenses as the light began to strengthen, straining his eyes.

'Belgians,' the general declared in his piercing voice. 'Not a German in sight. Are we chasing phantoms, Drake?'

'No, sir,' Drake murmured with more conviction than he felt.

A helmeted major of the Royal Engineers crept towards them across the grass. 'The men are in position, sir,' he reported in a stiff whisper. 'What are your orders?'

'We wait.' The hawkish major general continued staring at the bridge through his field glasses. Eventually he turned to Drake. 'I don't like it. I don't like it one jot. We can't show our faces. We can't just go charging in to seize the bridges, you understand. If this whole thing is a folly, it may create a fatal ruction with our allies. It could cause the Belgians to turn against us, and bring about the whole damned thing that it's supposed to prevent.'

'Yes, sir.' Drake observed the Belgian sentries on the bridge. 'They'll come.'

The general gave him a piercing look. 'They'd better.'

Drake clamped his jaw shut. Sweat trickled coldly down his back, even though the morning air was chilly. Slowly, by inches, the sun rose higher. They watched the men on the bridge.

Nothing happened. Nothing changed. Drake's stomach was tied in knots.

After what seemed an age, the little general lowered his field glasses and glared at him. 'So much for your theory. The Belgians are still here, and the BEF is badly exposed. I'm giving it half an hour. Then we'll have to withdraw.'

Drake shook his head. 'They'll come, sir. They have to come.'

He moved along to the other side of the knoll. He gazed at the bridge. There was no change, no sign of activity aside from the small movements of the Belgian sentries. He set down his field glasses, and rubbed at his face. There was still that one piece of missing information. Like a stone in his shoe, it chafed at him, leaving him uneasy and horribly vexed.

He couldn't understand it. The enemy movement orders were absolutely clear. *Degrelle, Dämmerung. Agent Viper. Obenauer.* Unless – and for a terrible moment he stopped and choked on an intake of breath. Were the orders *too* clear? But how? It couldn't be a fake. Could it? It was impossible. But there *was* one person who could have betrayed him to Obenauer. There *was* one person who could have led him up the garden path. She'd never really been on his side. *Axelle.*

Drake's heart seemed to stop in his chest. What was it Lambert had said? *If you were not so blind you would see that she is the traitor to her country, not I.* So, what if the briefcase Axelle had given him was a plant? What if she'd been working for the enemy all this time? The coded messages, the radio mast, the trap that had destroyed the British tanks – was it possible that it had all been set up, right from the start? And then he suddenly saw that it had been. Axelle was only half-Belgian after all.

He scrubbed at his face, pushed his helmet back and ran his fingers through his hair. It all made a dreadful kind of sense. *The traitor's kiss.* His stomach twisted into a hideous, vicious coil. And he was suddenly certain that he'd personally brought about the thing he'd been trying to prevent – the destruction of the BEF. There was a reason the Germans were not here. They were elsewhere. The attack would come at the weak point that the Third Division had left behind. The BEF would be annihilated. Had he been duped? Drake was suddenly convinced that he had. He felt like he was tumbling into a bottomless pit. *Christ.* What had he done?

He, in fact, would be the one who was instrumental in bringing *Dämmerung* to pass. It wasn't a double-cross, it was a triple-cross. A self-fulfilling prophecy. *There was no Dämmerung.* He was now convinced that he'd been the stooge all along.

They had to turn around. They had to hurry back now. Before it was too late. They might still just have time.

'General!' he shouted.

He got to his feet and ran.

Chapter 101

THE LEAN MAJOR GENERAL was still standing behind the grassy knoll, staring through field glasses at the bridge.

'Sir!' Drake called out.

The general ignored him.

'Sir!' Drake repeated. 'It's vitally important!'

'I know,' the general said. He held up a hand. 'I see them.'

Drake drew up his lenses and stared back through the cold dawn grey. A car was driving along the bridge. It stopped, near the sentries, and a Belgian officer got out. Then a man in a civilian suit. He placed a short-brimmed Homburg hat on his head.

Drake could barely believe it. 'That's Léon Degrelle!'

A few moments later, another car drove onto the bridge. Drake saw it was a matt grey Mercedes Benz. The car stopped, and two German field officers stepped out. And then another man. A man in a drab, grey uniform of the Sicherheitsdienst des Reichsführers - SS. He had a black eye patch over one eye, and one arm was bandaged.

'Standartenführer Obenauer,' Drake said. So he'd survived the eight-wheeler's fiery crash.

Drake watched as the Germans walked forward and raised their right arms in the Hitler salute. Degrelle returned the Nazi greeting, and the Belgian officer gave a more traditional gesture. A dull sound grew through the warming air, a distant rumble as a section of German Krad-schutzen motorcycle troops pulled onto the bridge. They dismounted and began to set up machine gun emplacements, securing both bridge-heads.

Drake lowered his field glasses.

The lean major general kept his lenses focused. He gave no orders.

'Sir?' Drake said.

The general ignored him. He might as well not have been there.

A rumble of engines grew, louder and louder in the pale morning mist. The clatter and squeal of tracks. From the haze on the other bank a squat grey shape of a panzer emerged. Then another. And another. An armoured column grunted slowly onto the bridge.

'Panzers, sir.'

'I see them.'

Drake looked at the general. 'Aren't you going to attack?'

The major general lowered his binoculars. His cheek twitched in what might have been a smile. Drake watched in horrid fascination as the armoured column advanced along the bridge, moving at speed towards the British flank.

Drake watched the distant figure of Léon Degrelle. He searched around, hoping to find a rifle he could use. If nothing else, he could shoot the Belgian traitor. And still the lean-faced general did nothing. He merely observed. The bridge was full of rumbling German panzers. Eventually, as the first tank was about to come off the bridgehead on the nearside riverbank, the general spoke up in a piercing tone. 'Alright. Let the RE do their stuff.'

A shout went from man to man, and moments later, a series of blinding flashes shot along the crossing. A quarter of a second later, a sequence of terrific booming shockwaves shook the air. The men on the bridge disappeared into the smoke as great chunks of masonry shot out in all directions. Pillars of fire rose up towards the sky. One by one, sections of the bridge began to collapse, and the Panzers toppled into the river below. All along the canal, the hidden British guns thundered in a stunning barrage.

Chapter 102

Back in the general's command truck, Drake slumped, utterly shattered, onto a seat. The major general sat down at the table opposite him and nodded. 'We've still got a hard fight on our hands, but you can leave that to the Third Division. We might have just saved the BEF from extinction. And that means Britain, too.'

Drake was too shaken to reply. He'd been kept awake for days by the terrible strain of it all. He thought for a moment of his little brother Alfie, back home. He wondered what Alfie would be doing. He couldn't remember what day of the week it was. *Christ.*

'You do know that you'll never get any credit for it,' the general said, jolting Drake from his reverie. 'What you have done will all get swept under the carpet. Covered up. No official record of this escapade will ever surface. Every ghastly chapter of this campaign will be buried as deeply as it can go. It'll be written out of the history books, I can promise you, and Whitehall won't let the truth of what really happened surface for at least a hundred years.'

Drake rubbed at his face. 'There's something that's bothering me, sir. Something about the Belgian king.'

The general nodded. 'Speak your mind.'

Drake hesitated. 'I can see why Degrelle would do what he did. He was after power. But I understood King Leopold to be an honourable man. Why would he hang his allies out to dry?'

The little general pulled an odd, strained face. 'This is not Britain's finest hour, let me tell you. Oh, history will write it in a different light, if we somehow wriggle out of this mess. But King Leopold has been begging for help from the BEF for weeks now. We didn't give it him. The Belgians bore the worst of the fighting in the north, and the French took it hard in the south. I'm not proud to say we refused to hear their cries. It was *us* that hung the Belgians out to dry, so that the BEF could withdraw in one piece. I don't doubt King Leopold was in fact treating with the Germans behind our backs. But I don't blame him, we left him little choice. It's deeply painful for me to tell you that Britain has cut out on her friends, and we're running for home.'

Drake was stunned. He'd grown up to believe an Englishman was straight and true.

The general sat back. 'Nobody in this entire bloody fiasco is blameless, Drake. Not us, not the Belgians, nor the French. But to our eternal shame, King Leopold will be the scapegoat, mark my words. History will not be kind to him. The Allies will turn on each other now. We'll be damned lucky if we don't end up fighting against the French.'

Drake put his head in his hands. 'So this is it? Hitler's won anyway? Divide and conquer? We're beaten, even after all we've done?'

The general scoffed. 'Beaten? Not on your Nelly. It's a defeat. Nay, a ruddy disaster. A catastrophe of epic proportions. Britain is in grave danger, there's no doubt of that, but we're not beaten yet, not by a long chalk. Calais was sacrificed to give Gort time to arrange the BEF's withdrawal. The entire campaign has been an absolute disgrace, and it would never have happened if I were in charge. And now we're leaving our allies in the lurch to take the blame.'

'We *are* leaving then?' said Drake.

'Dynamo,' the general said. He glanced up as an orderly entered the lorry, balancing two loaded plates. 'Evacuation. We've been soundly whipped, and, tails between our legs, we're dashing for home.'

The orderly set one plate down in front of the general and the other in front of Drake. The plates were loaded to the brim with fresh bacon, bangers, eggs and toast, baked beans and fried bully beef, with even a pile of black pudding on the side.

'The full Monty,' the orderly whispered with a wink, before disappearing back out of the lorry's door.

'Well, there's nothing we can do about it now, so you might as well tuck in,' the general said.

Drake couldn't remember the last time he'd eaten a decent meal. His stomach growled. He cut into a sausage, and dipped it into the yolk of a perfectly-fried egg. He took a bite. *God.* It was the first proper food he'd had in weeks, and it tasted like nectar. As he ate, Drake noticed that the hawk-faced general was still talking to him, but he couldn't concentrate, and despite the thunder of the British guns nearby, his eyes began to lose focus.

The major general stopped talking, and stared at the young second lieutenant, whose head suddenly dropped. He saw that Drake was now fast asleep. The general wiped his moustache with a clean linen napkin. He watched with mild amusement as Drake, out cold, nodded forwards towards his plate. He slumped down further and further until his face came to rest on his bacon and eggs. Second Lieutenant Tennyson Drake, of the First Battalion, South Devonshire Regiment, muttered *Dämmerung* to himself, then quietly began to snore.

Major General Bernard Law Montgomery laid his napkin on the table and smoothed it out. He shook his head. *Give me a division of men like Drake*, he thought, *and Britain will never fall.*

WEDNESDAY 29 MAY 1940

Epilogue

KING LEOPOLD'S VILLA, LA PANNE, BELGIUM – 10:00HRS

DRAKE RETURNED THE NEXT day to King Leopold's Villa, to debrief with Major Lyle-Smith. As he waited in the corridor, he saw Lord Gort and Sir Henry Pownall walking together along the basement corridor towards him.

Drake couldn't help but overhear. 'You'll forgive me for saying so, John,' Pownall said, 'but I did tell you this was going to happen.'

Gort barked out something that was more a derisive snort than a laugh. 'Last Christmas, I believe! You said the Belgians would never hold up. Well, they've done better than you expected, even if they've thrown it in now.'

Gort's eyes suddenly fell on Drake. 'You again?

Drake jumped to his feet and snapped to attention. 'Yes, sir.'

Gort pursed his lips for a moment. 'It appears you were right,' he said. 'Not once but twice.' He walked on.

Sir Henry Pownall gave Drake a slight nod as he walked past. That was it. That was all the thanks he'd got. After all he'd done.

Soon afterwards, Major Lyle-Smith took Drake's arm and they walked out of the villa, stepping carefully over the communications cables that were bundled along the floors.

They stopped in the doorway. Drake told him about his encounter in the corridor.

'I did tell you old Gort's not big on compliments, Drake. That's about as good as you'll get from him. But you've done well. Very well. I knew you'd come good in the end.'

Drake eyed the major. *No you bloody didn't.* 'It was touch and go for a while back there, sir.'

Lyle-Smith laughed. 'Come and see me in London, when we all get home. Broadway Buildings in Victoria. Now off you go and hop on a boat. You'll be home in time for tea.'

The major held out his hand and Drake shook it.

'Thank you. I will.' He started going down the stairs.

'You've got it, you know,' the major said. 'The spell.'

Drake stopped. Turned back. 'The what?'

Lyle-Smith's boyish face broke into a one-sided smile. 'A good nose. A sharp eye. An ear for something that others might miss. That's what we call it in the trade. *The spell.*'

Drake nodded to the major and walked quietly down the steps to the promenade. He rolled the three crushed bullets from one hand to another, the three bullets from his ribs that the Viper had given him. When he had a moment, he'd string them onto his dogtag chain. To remember. *Trust nobody.*

Butcher, MacTaggart and Leighton were waiting expectantly at the foot of the steps. A hundred yards away, a shell streaked down to crash into the apartment buildings that lined the Belgian promenade. A flash of light, a sheet of flame. Rubble cascaded down onto the pavement below. Somebody started yelling. Men ran in every direction. It wasn't over yet, but to Drake it all seemed like a dream now. He looked out across the calm grey-green waters of the Channel. Somewhere out there, just out of sight, was England. He ignored the scenes of chaos around the shellstrike.

He walked down to the beach, and picked up a handful of sand. He let it trickle slowly out between his fingers, then turned to his men, who were following close behind.

'Evacuation. Dynamo.' He let out an exhausted sigh. 'We're going home. They say we'll be back in dear old Blighty in time for tea.'

The three men stared at him. *Home.* After everything they had been through, it was hard to fathom.

The beach was growing crowded now. Against the odds, the defensive perimeter was holding. British, French, even Belgian soldiers were pouring through the streets of La Panne and out onto the sands. It was a strange sight. The upmarket Belgian resort was becoming overrun with unkempt, ragged troops. It was not an organised retreat. The men seemed adrift, with no semblance of military order about them. There were thousands, tens of thousands all along the stretch of sand, some bandaged, some with rifles, most without. More were streaming through the streets with every passing minute. Some, like Drake, gazed out to sea in fascination. It was another hot day, and many of the soldiers slumped down in café chairs, exhausted, while others helped themselves to the bar, and yet others flung off their kit and plunged into the water to bathe, with loud, joyful whoops. But it was no bank holiday. A mile out to sea stood the British destroyers. The *thump-thump* of naval great guns came as shells soared over their heads and on towards the German front lines, which were less than five miles inland. As though in riposte, German shells screeched in from the south, adding another salvo to the din.

MacTaggart nudged Drake with his elbow.

'Of course, Sergeant,' Drake said. He held something out on his palm. It glinted in the sun. It was the tiepin. The old Scottish sergeant took it and winked. 'I was right all along, was I not, sir? It's a lucky charm.'

Drake smiled and shook his head. 'Well, we're still alive,' he said. 'So I suppose there is that.'

MacTaggart chortled and fixed the pin to his kilt. 'I think I'll keep it as a wee souvenir. Not that I'm superstitious, mind.'

Drake heard the words, but his thoughts were far away now. In the distance, he could see the huge tower of smoke that was still rising from the port of Dunkirk. It billowed ever more ominously up into the sky. The city of Dunkirk was ten miles away, ten miles along the great, unbroken beach that curved away to their west. On that beach were smudges, long black lines of men, as more and more soldiers poured from the dunes and onto the sand. The cream of the British Army was floundering down towards the sea, hoping for salvation. There seemed little salvation to be had.

'All that hugger-mugger stuff,' MacTaggart said, interrupting Drake's thoughts once more. 'Half of it goes right over my head. But one thing's been troubling me, sir. The wee lassie. She hated the Nazis alright. But was she on our side or not?'

Drake fixed his gaze onto the horizon, far out to sea. *Axelle.* He felt a strange pang. There was still a raw, hollow place when he thought of what might have been. He sighed. *Dämmerung* had been foiled. That meant that Axelle had passed him true information, at the cost of her life. She'd been trying to help, but – and here was the puzzle – only in an indirect way. Why?

And suddenly he saw it. She was half-Belgian, half-German, but had a visceral hatred of the Nazis and everything they had done.

'Ha!' he said. It was so obvious now. 'The enemy of my enemy is my friend.'

MacTaggart frowned. 'Eh?'

'Axelle was a double agent, Sergeant. She believed there was a higher ideal – a better way. And she gave her life for that idea.' Drake shook his head, gave the sergeant a rueful smile. 'Axelle Brochard was a Belgian agent, but her heart lay elsewhere. I don't know why I didn't see it sooner.'

Drake fixed his gaze out over the water for a moment longer, as he contemplated what it meant. She hadn't actually lied to him, but she hadn't told him the whole truth either. He wondered if her feelings for him had been real, or were they part of her role? He would choose to believe they were real.

'*The Godless east*,' Drake said, repeating Degrelle's words. He turned towards MacTaggart. 'Axelle was dancing to a different tune. She was taking her orders from Moscow.'

'She was a Red?' The old Scotsman looked up at Drake in amazement, then exhaled and blew out his cheeks. 'But the Russians and the Germans are on the same side, aren't they? Or are they? Satan's hell! I'd be no damned use at this game. I like to know who in buggeration I'm supposed to be shooting at.'

Drake shrugged. 'Just keep aiming at the Germans, Sergeant, and I think you'll do just fine.'

As they watched the ocean, Drake pondered the great questions, the questions that divided nations, that turned brother against sister in the street. Who or what was *he* really fighting for? King? Country? Government? Or just the people and the freedoms that he cared about back home? It was no longer really clear. But all he knew – and he knew it now with a powerful certainty – was what he was fighting *against*. Men like Degrelle and Obenauer, and everything they stood for. He took his helmet off, and ran a hand through his tangled hair.

His scalp was itching where the old wound was healing. He wondered how England would seem to him now. He felt as though something deep inside him had shifted, changed, and grown.

Out on the water, a few hardy seamen were rowing whalers in from the destroyers and beginning to pick up a dozen soldiers at a time from beyond the surf. He watched them struggling to pull in the waterlogged men from the sea. It looked like backbreaking work.

All along the coast to the west of La Panne, the remnants of the BEF were still pouring from the dunes and onto the beach. Long, straggling columns of soldiers were gathering on the shore, and more were arriving every minute. The entire army had been routed, knocked about, kicked off the continent – but when they finally saw the English Channel and the Royal Navy standing out to sea, they smiled. Drake realised that the general had been right. The British Army was hungry, ragged, exhausted, battered, bruised, and bleeding – but not yet beaten.

Drake stared out over the Channel. Somewhere over the horizon was the Kentish coast. But there was still one minor problem. He placed a hand on MacTaggart's shoulder. He saw the old Scotsman turn and look up at him in surprise.

Drake gestured towards the beaches of Dunkirk, where the men were gathering, bemused by the lack of transport home.

'You were right about one thing, Sergeant. Whenever the British Army organises anything, if it's not a ruddy shambles, it's a total balls-up. *Home in time for tea*, my arse. How the hell do they plan to get a third of a million men off this bloody beach?'

AUTHOR'S NOTE

Hello, I'm the author, Gideon Saint.

If you enjoyed Drake's Battle, please help make sure there will be more books in the series, and keep me in business as a new writer by reviewing the book on **Amazon** and **Goodreads**!

If you would like a **free eBook or PDF** including two short stories and a more detailed historical background to *Drake's Battle*, please visit my website **drakeswar.com/drake-s-battle** where you can download a free eBook entitled ***The Making of Drake's Battle***.

Please feel free to be in touch via my contact page on my website if you have any questions or comments about the book.

Thank you for your support!

ALSO AVAILABLE:

DRAKE'S WAR

DRAKE'S ENEMY

(coming soon...)

HISTORICAL NOTE

DRAKE'S BATTLE IS, OF course, a work of fiction, but I have tried to stay as close to the recorded history as possible while attempting to create an entertaining story of intrigue and adventure. Tennyson 'Ted' Drake is a fictional character, but almost all the things that happen around him really did happen, including King Leopold's surprise *coup d'état*. The idea for the briefcase containing the German order of battle was also inspired by real events.

When dealing with the tank battle near Arras, I have tried to be as accurate as possible, but it required some significant compression, simplification, excision, and a little make-believe. Of Calais, likewise I have tried to keep Drake's actions entirely within timelines of the battle as it really happened there. I believe it was one of Churchill's few regrets about his conduct of the war that he had consigned so many men to be killed or captured in a lost cause.

It should be noted that the *Église Notre-Dame de Calais* is not, in fact, a cathedral, but I have referred to it as one because this is how many of the war diaries referenced it, and it was known as such during the battle by the British soldiers who were fighting there.

If you would like a **free eBook or PDF** with a more detailed historical background to *Drake's Battle*, including a bibliography of some of the most pertinent historical accounts of the campaign, please visit my website **drakeswar.com/drake-s-battle** where you can download ***The Making of Drake's Battle***, which also includes two short stories.

Meanwhile, Tennyson "Ted" Drake and the trusty Sergeant MacTaggart live on to fight another day. The next book in the *Drake's War* series will be out in the not-too distant future!

Gideon Saint

ACKNOWLEDGEMENTS

I would like to thank: Stuart Wheeler of the Tank Museum for his invaluable information on the militaria of the time; Guy Porter of the Royal Sussex Independent Company for his knowledge of vintage firearms in particular; Tim Lauris Pfeiffer for his help with the German Language; Barry Kirwan with the French; and Mark Hooper for his copy editing help.

I would also like to thank my agent Jamie Cowen of the Ampersand Agency for believing in the project, and Eve Seymour for her sage editorial advice. And of course a shout to Harry Bingham of Jericho Writers, without whose organisation many of us would never have got this far.

Although *Drake's War* is, of course, fiction, most of all I would like to thank my late grandfather, Colonel James Leonard Martin, who was both my inspiration to take this project on, and my way "in" to the character of Tennyson Drake.

JL Martin was a sergeant-instructor – an army barracks "schoolie" – at the start of the war in 1939; he ended it in Berlin in 1945 as a colonel. I sincerely hope that he – and all his valiant comrades – would have enjoyed Drake's Battle, and I wish he were here to read it and tell me everything I got hopelessly wrong. They kept stout hearts in troubled times.

If you would like to find out more about the background for the book, please visit my website **drakeswar.com/drake-s-battle** for a **free eBook** on the subject.

Printed in Dunstable, United Kingdom

71805815R00245